The Hollow

ANNMARIE MARTIN

The Hollow
A Black Bed Sheet/Diverse Media Book
July 2014

Edited by Shawna Platt

ISBN-10: 0-69225829-9
ISBN-13: 978-0-69225829-3

The Hollow

A Black Bed Sheet/Diverse Media Book
Antelope, CA

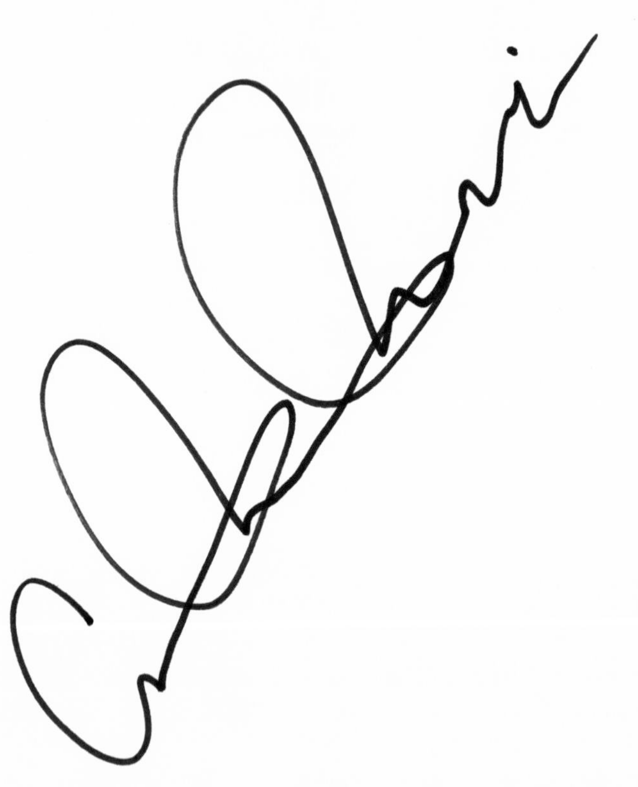

To my husband.
"…you make me braver."

Chapter 1

She couldn't stop staring at it. She stood a couple feet back, her hands deep in the pockets of her brown, tweed coat, but she could still read the inscription clearly:

Cecily Reynolds
Beloved Baby Girl
1990–1996

Just six years old, she thought to herself. A shudder went through her body as the wind started to pick up. She watched as leaves of red, brown, and golden orange swept across the green grass over the grave that was starting to have touches of brown throughout. Fall was here and Halloween was quickly closing in.

She started to creep a little closer when a family of four walked by, looking at her quizzically. She gave them a shy smile and quickly pulled back; she walked down the path away from Cecily's grave so as not to draw attention to herself. This was the third time in two weeks she had been overcome by an insatiable urge to get to the cemetery, to this little girl's final resting spot. The first time it happened she had no idea where she was going, but walked with such drive and direction through the twists and turns of the hilly cemetery, it was as if she had done it a million times before. When she found herself standing in front of it, she knew this was what she was being drawn to, but she didn't know why.

She had never known Cecily, her family, or anyone with the last name Reynolds for that matter. More importantly, she didn't know what happened to cut this little girl's life so tragically short.

Maryanne Rosa sighed as she continued to follow the paved road that wound through the expansive Sleepy Hollow cemetery, which spread out over a sweeping hill on the side of Route 9 for about half a mile. A large, wrought iron gate and a small church protected the graves and mausoleums, some of which dated all the way back to the 1700s, from the highway. The rush of the cars driving past was unsuccessful in its attempts to interrupt her thoughts. She also took no notice of the rapidly setting sun.

First the dreams and now this, she thought. For the past few months, she'd been plagued by strange visions in the night. They varied from time to time. Sometimes, she would be startled by a strange presence she would feel in her bedroom, or she would wake up to what she thought was her doorknob being rattled and shaken, with a small sliver of light coming in from the crack at the bottom of the door flickering on and off. Occasionally, she would hear strange clicking noises coming from inside her bedroom walls, right by her head, as she lie. Sometimes, they were followed by shouts from the other side of the wall, all of which she simply attributed to the odd behaviors of her strange next door neighbor, and therefore, those didn't faze her. What she did fear were the spider dreams.

The first time, she woke up in the middle of the night and saw it, right next to her head, dangling from a strand of web. It wasn't a particularly threatening spider. It didn't resemble a tarantula, more like a humongous daddy longlegs. She gasped and flew out of bed.

“What the hell just happened?” her boyfriend Rob asked. It took him a few seconds to realize she had flown out of bed and was crouched in the corner in her underwear, one hand over her eyes, the other arm wrapped around her hunched body.

He turned her nightstand lamp on. “Maryanne?”

She remained and didn’t answer. He could see her stomach heaving in and out and her shoulders moving up and down as she breathed heavily. He got out of bed, walked over to her, and crouched down in front of her. He put his hand on one of her biceps and pulled her hand down and into his own, away from her eyes, which looked hazy and confused. Eventually, she was able to focus on his face.

“Babe, what the hell just happened?”

She peeked over his shoulder at the corner of the bed where she had seen it. There was nothing there. She started to breathe easier and her body released the tension it was holding onto. Rob was still staring at her, his brown eyes filled with concern, strands of dark hair flopping down over his forehead. He tucked a strand of her hair behind her ear.

“I don’t know,” she answered. “I . . . I . . . had a nightmare.”

“Yeah, obviously,” he said with a little laugh, “You went flying out of bed and almost knocked your stereo over.”

“I’m sorry, I was um...being chased,” she stammered; and lied.

“By what?” He put both hands on her head and held them there.

She stood up and so did he. “I don’t remember,” she answered, still dazed.

She wondered why she had gotten so scared and

why she hadn't just told him the truth. She started to feel foolish.

"Come on, let's get back to bed," he said, as he put one arm around her shoulder and walked her back over to the bed.

She giggled, but frowned. "I'm sorry."

"It's okay," he said, slightly exasperated.

She cuddled up next to him and put her arm around him. "Are you mad at me?"

"No, I'm not mad at you. Just go back to sleep."

The second time it happened, she was alone, asleep on her stomach, and woke up to see a spider directly in front of her face. She gasped, threw the covers over her head, and feared she had taken it with her underneath her makeshift tent. After a few seconds of pounding at the covers in attempts to kill it, she stopped and peeked out from under them. She turned on the light. Again, there was nothing there.

They would continue to appear, once or twice a week, but more vividly and with a frightening voracity. Eventually, she started waking up to one crawling up her leg. Then, to add to her paranoia, they started to multiply. There was no denying she was fully awake and alert whenever she saw one. They would then disappear into thin air, right before her eyes.

All this she kept to herself. Maryanne held it as a point of pride that she always kept calm and in control. She didn't want Rob to think his smart, successful, disciplined girlfriend was losing her mind. No, she wouldn't, and couldn't tell him. She didn't care what anyone else thought of her, but she had to know that he trusted and respected her. How could he do that if he knew she was having these hallucinations?

So lost in her thoughts, she hadn't even realized that she had circled back around and found herself in front of Cecily's grave once again. Her spider dreams had ceased for a couple of weeks, and she had started to get excited that she was possibly rid of them. There was never a dull moment; as soon as they stopped, she started to be drawn to the cemetery.

What's next? she thought. She looked up at the night sky. When had the sunset? She didn't even realize that night had fallen. She was amazed at how oblivious she could be at times and nothing made her more disappointed in herself. "Better get home," she said, quietly. As she began to walk toward the exit, she stopped and turned to look toward the grave as a pseudo goodbye. As she did this, she could have sworn she noticed dark figures and night shadows emerge from behind trees and graves, some coming out from the mausoleums and others from the woods just behind the cemetery. She rubbed her eyes and tried to focus. After she took her hand away, she could still make them out slightly, though there were now fewer of them. All of them seemed to be headed away from her toward the northern part of the cemetery. This was too much.

She turned and broke into a light run. When she reached the exit gate, she was relieved to see that the traffic light was indeed red and she could cross the street in a hurry. She turned left and made her way over the bridge and up Pocantico Street toward the Darren Hayes apartment buildings. As she made a quick right onto Elm Street and entered the complex through the large archway entrance to the courtyard, she finally felt safe. Locals warned her and her friends to be wary because the neighborhood had gone quickly downhill. But once they entered the courtyard, all agreed that it was as if nothing could touch them.

The twenty-five buildings of the Darren Hayes apartments lined the entire block like a fortress, creating an uncovered atrium of sorts within, filled with weeping willows and charming, old-fashioned gas lamps. Each building was named by a letter of the alphabet, except for the letter I. There was no Building I, and nobody seemed to know why it had been left out.

Maryanne quickly padded up the stairs of the entrance to her home—Building J.

She checked her mailbox and took the few bills and coupon booklets upstairs to the third floor apartment she shared with her friend and co-worker, Lily Deckmeyer. As she let herself in, she heard a light thud as her black and white cat Ronald jumped off her bed. She watched him turn the corner of her bedroom into the hallway to greet her. "Hi, Ronnie," she said as she walked past the kitchen and living room. He was fast on her heels as she turned into her bedroom and hung up her coat. She sat on her bed to take off her boots. She frowned as she realized the track of mud she'd brought in with her.

After she cleaned up and fed Ronald, she sat down on the couch, sinking into its big fluffy cushions. She felt her back relax and the tension around her eyes eased as she laid her head against the armrest and closed them. *You can't fall asleep yet*, she thought to herself as she cracked one eyelid to catch the time. Only 7:30 p.m.. If she fell asleep now, she'd only find herself awake at 1 a.m., not able to get back to bed. She turned on the television and felt satisfied that it was Thursday evening and tomorrow would be an easy day at work, followed by a much-needed relaxing weekend. Lily would return from a week long business trip to Vegas, and there would be some catching up to do.

Maryanne found a movie she liked after flipping through the channels for a few minutes. After a while, her eyelids started to droop and she allowed herself to doze off. Another dream took over, but this one was different from the others.

She was still lying on the couch and only a dull hum could be heard from the television. The glare of the hallway light shined brightly behind him as he approached. A middle-aged man, medium build, probably in his 30s or early 40s, walked up to her and leaned over to peer at her face. As he did, she caught a solid glimpse of him. He had very short, very fine, almost invisible, slightly receding ash blond hair. His face was round and his skin was tanned. He wore a red and black flannel shirt and he seemed to be dirtied and grainy.

As the vision of him faded, she awoke, but not with a start. She looked around, brushed the wisps of her short, dark brown hair off her forehead and sat up. *A new twist*, she thought. *Now I 'm seeing strange men?* Her heart started to beat a little faster. Her dreams had developed from simply feeling a strange presence from time to time, to bugs, to humans. She wondered what could possibly be going on inside her head. She felt confused and anxious and continued to stare at the planks of the hardwood floor in the living room as she tried to process everything. She tried desperately to fight the idea that something could be seriously wrong.

She gave up and decided to go upstairs to see what Rob was up to. Rob lived with two roommates on the floor directly above her, which was how they met. Topping off the building on the fifth floor were Kayla and M.J. Kayla was a roommate of Maryanne's in college and their relationship had grown closer since they graduated. It was Kayla who had convinced Maryanne to quit the hour-long commute to her office from her parents' house in New Jersey that she was dealing with each day, and to take advantage of the cheap rent the Darren Hayes offered, as well as the proximity to her job.

She threw on a pair of sweatpants and some socks, and brushed her teeth; she figured she would just sleep upstairs as she didn't want to be alone in the apartment for the rest of the evening. She gave Ronald a kiss on his nose and walked out the door. She wrapped her sweater around herself and folded her arms as she went quietly up the two flights of stairs to Rob's. She rang his doorbell.

She heard him quickly shuffle to the door. He looked surprised as he opened the door. "Hi," he said.

"Hey," she said, smiling at him and kissing him lightly on the lips as she walked into the apartment. He shut the door behind her.

"I thought you said you had work to do tonight?" he asked.

"I couldn't concentrate," she lied.

"Oh." He walked up to her and kissed her forehead. She wrapped her arms around his waist and he rested his cheek on her head as he hugged her back. "You tired?" he asked.

"Yeah, I just fell asleep on the couch for a little while."

"Well, at least tomorrow is Friday," he said, as he walked over to the door and looked back at her once he reached it. "You sleeping here tonight?"

"Yes," she said, throwing him a sly smile over her shoulder as she walked through the living room, into his bedroom.

Chapter 2

Like a lot of his dreams lately, he knew he was dreaming in this one, but that did nothing to alleviate his fear. The usual wave of anxiety had taken over his body. He didn't want to go into the white room. His heart raced when he even neared the entrance. The red room had the same effect.

Others were walking into them with ease. He noticed they were all wearing rings on their left hand middle fingers. He looked down at his own hand and saw that he was not wearing one. He walked up to one of the others.

"Are you all right?" he asked an older gentleman before he entered the red room. He looked at him, slightly taken aback.

"I'm fine. Why?" he answered, obviously confused.

"I want to come in," Rob told him, "but I can't," he said, his voice cracking and shaking with fear.

"You need a ring," the old man told him and he held out his hand to show him. He looked down and the ring glowed on the man's hand. The anxiety was suddenly too much. He backed away, shielded his eyes, and turned to run into the black abyss.

"Where are you going?" the old man screamed. "We need you!"

The panic in the man's last sentence was undeniable.

Rob woke up in a cold sweat. Maryanne turned over at his sudden start.

"What's wrong, Chilly?"

"I guess I was dreaming," he answered. "God, I'm sweating." He tossed the covers off of him.

"I tend to have that affect on men," she said with a smile in her voice. She had a smirk on her face, but her eyes remained shut.

He scoffed.

"You okay, though?" she asked. She pulled in close to him and buried her face in his chest.

"Scratch me until I fall asleep?" he asked.

He turned over and she began to gently run the tips of her nails up and down his back.

Chapter 3

4:00 p.m.

Yes! Maryanne thought to herself. The best part of every week: the end of the day on Friday. Nothing feels better. She smiled and turned away from her computer, basking in the feeling of butterflies the weekend's anticipation brought. Maryanne, senior editor at Prerogative magazine, walked out of the office she shared with Lily, the editor-in-chief, and toward the kitchen in the back of the railcar-style offices that housed the publishing company. A large mug hung from her right hand that pictured a smiling sun with the words "You Mean the World to Me" circling around it. The word "Me" had been crossed out with a red sharpie and the word "Us" replaced it underneath.

She walked past Josie's desk at reception and made her way into the kitchen. As she brewed a fresh pot of coffee, she heard the light sounds of their editorial assistant Sarah's typing coming from the back of the office (or the front depending on which way you looked at it). While it brewed, Maryanne wandered over to the bookshelf that held dozens of back issues of the magazine. She picked up a particularly thick issue and flipped it open. The first page she came upon was a Letter from the Publisher page, which featured a picture of Prerogative publisher, Joseph Goldberg, raising a glass with a group of members and political advisors to the Saudi Arabian throne. *I doubt he'd be able to do the same today*, she thought.

All of the men, including Joseph, were wearing traditional Saudi Arabian garb, including a white cotton robe called a thob and a colorful kerchief worn over their heads, known as a ghoutra. Maryanne giggled and shook her head at how ridiculous he looked.

In the two years Maryanne had worked for Prerogative, Joseph had had the ability to have the girls laughing so hard over his antics and ignorance that their stomach muscles ached in pain, and in the next five minutes had them fuming with anger. But no matter how ridiculous the task was that he requested of them, or how stupid and offensive the statement made, one thing the girls couldn't argue with was the man's undying passion for politics. He was a well-known philanthropist in the area and was well respected for his contributions to a number of worthy causes. Yet, there always seemed to be something a little unnerving about the man. None of them could quite put their finger on it, but every employee who passed through his doors could cite an example of how he had made them feel uncomfortable or creeped out. Every once in a while, something would come out of his mouth that would make you think you were dealing with more than just a hot shot idea man, that there was something a little more sinister behind his motives. Prerogative magazine was Lily's brainchild though, born and raised on the dollar of Joseph's RWB Publishing Company. Prior to hiring Lily, RWB had made do on a variety of trade newspapers and magazines, all dedicated to covering the local, regional, and national political machines in a myriad of ways. After a year on staff, Joseph had come to Lily with a mock cover of Prerogative, mumbling about how he, his son, and co-owner David, thought the next best move for the company was one into the world of the constituents and citizens these politicians served. *No easy task for a publishing company with the means and the staff,* she had thought; let alone a small one with a staff of, well, essentially two staff writers (she and Joseph) and a few loyal freelancers.

"See what you can do with it," he'd said. He tossed the mock onto her desk and sauntered out of the room.

Lily's eyes had gone wide and stared at the fake cover for a good ten minutes or so as she let a panicked stream of consciousness run through her brain. When she was finished, she had come to the following conclusion: It wouldn't be easy, but the chance to create a publication from scratch and make it her own was one too good to pass up. One of the first orders of business would have to be to hire at the least one additional editor. Joseph gave her clearance for one, and one only, for the time being. She decided to take what she could get. But before that she would need to develop a concept and a look for Prerogative. It didn't take her long to know what she wanted this magazine to be; the focus would have to be on politics, and it would have to have an international scope. But the work, essentially, would not be her own. Lily had so many people around her that she admired for different reasons. They were all talented in their own unique, individual ways. She decided to translate that in such a way to make Prerogative successful. She would look to the world to bring their unique, individual voices, all talented and articulate in their own ways, with their own messages about issues that are close to their hearts. She would dedicate this magazine to them: the brightest, young, unheard-of political writers that were hiding out in the farthest corners of the world. She would find them and give them a chance to speak and be published. So Prerogative would turn into exactly that, one that exemplified their right to tell it like it is. It would be about the important issues of today's youth, told (or written rather) from their very own mouths.

Lily did well on her own for about a year. She developed the concept and direction for each issue of Prerogative, traveled the world on wobbly leads and flimsy hunches to find the writers she was searching for, while at the same time managed and produced the company's other publications. She finally decided to buckle down and find the perfect right hand man (or woman) to add to this operation.

Lily met with Maryanne at a local Panera Bread over a weekend; an unconventional interview, but not unlike Lily. She had brought her then boyfriend, who sat a few tables away while the two talked.

"So was this your idea?" Maryanne had asked as she sat down after coming back from the bathroom. She tapped the copy of Prerogative that Lily had brought along to show her.

"Sort of," Lily said. "We had traditionally just published some trade newspapers, but the owner eventually came to me with a mock-up and essentially just said see what you can do with this and walked out the door."

Maryanne smiled. "Wow," she said. "That's pretty impressive."

Lily liked her already. They chatted about Maryanne's current position as a local city beat reporter deep in the wilds of upstate New York. Maryanne was sick of the culture shock she'd experienced moving up there and was ready to come home. She'd gotten the experience she'd needed, and it was her dream to work on a monthly magazine. She loved covering crime and thought a position with Prerogative would get her one step closer to covering the courts on the national and even international level she was craving. There would be some of that type of coverage anyway, so she'd take what she could get, even if it only came in drips and drabs for now.

To Maryanne, Lily had seemed to be on a higher wavelength of intelligence. Her poise and her words were slightly intimidating. Maryanne thought she must have been one of those undercover geniuses who got a 1600 on her SATs. She would eventually come to see just how similar the two of them were.

After another two meetings with Joseph, they offered Maryanne the job.

Lily had been looking for someone to take over most of her traveling schedule so that she could focus on concept and layout. Having never traveled much before, Maryanne took it on with gusto. In just a few months, she'd been to every major city on the map and every continent except Antarctica. She'd met some of the most interesting and some of the most complex writers in the world, introduced them to the magazine, and developed their stories with them for publication. They addressed every economic, political, and societal issue that anyone could think of, and gave Prerogative a broader spectrum of world topics and views than any other magazine of its genre to date, not to mention a circulation number working its way into the millions. And the entire thing was being run by a couple of twenty-five-year-old kids out of a hole in the wall in Westchester, New York.

Maryanne snapped out of her daydream when her phone rang. She looked back at her office, then regretfully toward the kitchen and the steaming pot of fresh coffee. She quickly put down the back issue she was looking at and ran to catch the call.

She scooped up the receiver and slid into her desk chair, forcing it to roll across the floor and hit the wall underneath her window.

"This is Maryanne," she said. "Ow," she whispered quietly as she rubbed her hip after the roll into the wall.

"You're such an ass," said the voice on the other line.

Maryanne laughed. It was Kayla.

"What, you don't like it?" she asked.

Kayla giggled. "No, I think it's hilarious. How did you do that?"

"Photo Booth." It was a slow day. Maryanne had gotten into Photo Booth on her Mac and had started taking ridiculous pictures of herself. She took one in the Dent effect and sent it to Kayla. The photo showed her face pinched in at the ears, making her chin and forehead enlarged. Underneath the photo she had written: "It's aaaaaaalmost quittin' time!"

"You think that was good, check out this one." Maryanne quickly attached another photo to an e-mail and sent it to Kayla. "I just sent you another one. Let me know when it comes through."

"Ok. So, what's up?"

"Nothin'. It's really slow here. I just came in to finish up some production stuff. Lily's been gone all week."

"Oh, really? Where'd she . . ." Kayla trailed off as she started to laugh. Maryanne assumed she had received her second e-mail.

"This one is even better than the first!" Kayla exclaimed through her hysterics. Maryanne started laughing, too. The second picture had blown up the center of her face and gave her a bulbous nose that almost hit the viewer in the face.

"Anyway, as I was saying," Kayla started once she had calmed down. "Where'd she go?"

"Vegas. There was a writer's convention down there and she was one of the presenters."

"Oh, that's cool."

"Yeah. She's coming back tonight, so I figured we could get a drink across the street or whatever."

"We should go to the Setback. M.J.'s working."

"Oh, okay. Sure, that's cool. I wasn't sure if he'd switched to Friday nights yet, so that's why I had suggested Denver's."

"Yeah, last week he started. We should definitely go. Better to get drunk for free than actually pay for it."

"This is true. Well, I should definitely be home by 6 p.m., so let me know when you get out of there. Lily should be back around 8 or 9, and I'm sure Rob is practically on his way home at this point, so."

"Okay, sounds good. Yeah, I might be here a while because I'm doing everyone else's job besides my own. So, after I finish doing the work I shouldn't have to be worrying about, I'll finish up my own."

"Oh, god. It's still that bad, huh?"

"Are you kidding? Yesterday I was creating ads! Like actually laying them out in InDesign, because I was a friggin' graphic design major."

"Oh, my god!" Maryanne exclaimed. "That's ridiculous!"

Everyone dealt with work that was probably outside of their scope in publishing, but actually having a market research analyst designing ads was crossing the line. Maryanne was sure Kayla probably never had any experience with that program.

"Tell me about it. So what's the next issue going to be like? I mean you've got to have some really amazing stuff coming in considering everything that's going on."

Kayla was referring to the stormy political climate of the moment. A young, vibrant senator from South Dakota, in his first term, was starting to garner a lot of attention, not just within his own Democratic party, but nation-wide. He seemed to have a humility and common sense that was rare, if not non-existent, in a politician. He was starting to develop such a following that people were starting to talk that he might win the party nomination–for an election that was still two and a half years out.

His youth and earnestness weren't the only reason he was getting such attention. If he were to grab the Democratic party nomination next year, Donald Speedman would be the first African American presidential nominee in history.

Although his policies were earnest and his intentions genuine, at least as far as the eye could see, unfortunately racism was still alive and thriving. As intense as the movement in favor of him was, the movement against him was growing with just as much force, making for some exciting and groundbreaking issues of Prerogative with commentary from all over the world.

"Yeah, I mean this upcoming issue isn't too exciting, but let me tell you the next two are going to seriously shock some people. I expect the fan mail to come pouring in."

"Oh, boy. That's awesome, though."

"I know, it's fun. It's pretty exciting. Lily has been getting a lot of requests for commentary by the media, to make appearances, like with this thing in Vegas. So it's really starting to get a lot of attention, not just with the insiders, but with the general public now, which was always our dream."

"That's great. Seriously, that is incredible."

"Thanks!"

"Okay, let me run so I can finish this stuff up and blow this popsicle stand!"

"Ha. All right, see ya later."

"Okay. Bye."

Maryanne hung up the phone. She pictured Kayla getting up from her desk, bustling about for five minutes, and then getting into some long-winded conversation with an unwilling participant who was wishing they had realized it was too late before it was too late. An hour would pass, Kayla would realize all the time she wasted, look at the clock, and inevitably say, "What the fuck? It's 7 p.m.! Oh, fuck this, I'm getting outta here," throw her purse over her shoulder and bounce out the door.

Maryanne giggled to herself over the picture she had just envisioned of her good friend.

Kayla Jared, and Maryanne had been roommates in college and bonded immediately over their similar origins. They were both proud natives of the armpit state. They attended Ivy College & Institute, a liberal arts school in New Rochelle, NY, with professors that preached a slightly right-wing slant on life in America. This, of course, inevitably pushed most attendees sharply to the left, in the grand tradition of student rebellion.

After graduation, Kayla got a paid internship with Westchester Today, a daily tabloid that focused on the wheelings and dealings of the big-time moguls and socialites who lived and hopped around the county, but who worked in Manhattan. Once she got the job, she and her fiancé Michael James (M .J. for short) were the first to move into the Darren Hayes apartments in the village of Sleepy Hollow.

It was hard to describe the Darren Hayes apartments. Halfway to dilapidated was probably the best way to put it, but no one could complain thanks to the cheap rent and lots of space. Somehow though, the place possessed a certain character that left you oddly charmed. During the summer months, the courtyard always sported a Dora the Explorer tent used by the children who lived there, and benches under the gas lamps seated older tenants who would come to gossip about the day's happenings. A small gazebo was in the center, which was supposed to be occupied by a guard twenty-four hours a day, but usually just stayed empty and unattended. On the Elm Street end lived Isabelle, an elderly woman who sat at her window in Building L all day, and whose biggest thrill was to wave at any passers-by. On the other end was Marty, who sat outside of Building B with his dog Scoot. Similar to Isabelle, Marty's only joy was interacting with tenants rushing by him on the way to the train in the morning, the station being just down the road. Maryanne, just as many others before her had probably done, had made a mental note to herself to one day introduce these two. It might be a match made in heaven.

A makeshift playground, with brightly colored plastic pieces also graced the center of the courtyard, with a mini jungle gym and sandbox that were strewn messily across the grass right next to the gazebo. The place was usually filled with sounds of children laughing and screaming, except of course, during the darkest of the winter months. Kayla had grown accustomed to using the bells signaling the start of the day of the elementary school directly across the street from their bedroom windows as an alarm clock.

Once settled into Building J, M.J. had no trouble finding work in the area. A bartending gig at the Setback Inn on Main Street in Tarrytown most nights, and a stock room position at the hardware store down the street from there three days a week, kept him pretty busy. It paid for some of his schooling, rent, and utilities, and he usually had a little left over to save for their upcoming wedding each month. M.J.'s dream though, was to become a graphic designer for one of the big-name animation companies. His associate's degree wasn't going to cut it, so he worked on his bachelor's through online schooling between his many shifts. This didn't leave Kayla and M.J. much time for each other, but they knew if they continued to work hard for the next few years, it would pay off.

Their relationship had always been a rocky one, filled with screaming matches, complete with a thrown object or two at times; but it seemed the two had bunkered down just long enough to realize what it takes to love and be there for one another.

After Maryanne had accepted the job with Prerogative, whose offices weren't too far away from Westchester Today, Kayla finally convinced her that it would be worth it to move into the Darren Hayes. At the time, Lily was also looking to get out of her parents' house and reduce her equally horrendous commute, so the situation just made sense. Kayla suggested they get an apartment together and maybe even try to find a third roommate to help reduce the rent even further. Darren Hayes was one of the last decent places you could find for cheap rent, and it would be only a ten-minute drive now to work for Lily and Maryanne. So they both made the move and scored an apartment just two floors below Kayla and M.J. in Building J. Maryanne recalled her days of battling traffic every morning to get to RWB and shuddered. Moving to Darren Hayes had been one of the best moves of her life in more ways than one.

Maryanne went to finally pour herself a cup of the coffee she had made and went back to her desk. She checked a few recent e-mails that had come in and gave Jenny, the art director, a call to see if the proofs she was waiting for were done.

"No, not yet, but I should have them for you in the next…Vik!" Maryanne pulled the receiver away from her ear and winced as Jenny screamed at her Russian assistant. "I don't fucking care where you have to go! Just get it done!"

Vik, who had once been a paginator for a Russian newspaper in the 1970s, took a daily beating at the hands of Jenny Tranfaglia, a five-foot-nothing, ninety-pound woman who seemed to think her word was from a divine intervention as far as Prerogative magazine went.

"Sorry," she said as she turned back to her conversation with Maryanne. "I'll have them to you in the next twenty minutes."

"Okay."

"Thanks!" Click.

Maryanne sighed. "Hey, Sarah!" she called out. "You can go, it's practically 5 p.m.."

"I know," she replied. "I'm just wrapping up, and then I'll get outta here."

"All right."

Maryanne turned toward Lily's desk just as Lily's phone started to ring. Maryanne got up to look at the face of the phone at the caller ID. It read Lily's cell phone number. The boss was most likely calling in to retrieve her messages.

Maryanne smiled mischievously and picked up the phone. "I thought you would have been shoving the head Pussycat Doll off the stage by now. Or at least gotten married by Elvis to David Sedaris."

For all Lily's travels, this was her first time to Las Vegas.

"Oh, my God, I met him!" she said.

"Shut up! Really? What was he like?" David Sedaris was one of Lily's favorite writers and comedians, who was also a presenter at the writers' conference.

"He signed my book!"

"That's awesome! Oh, Red, that is so cool!"

"I know. So anyway, I'm at my layover in Chicago, and I take off in about twenty minutes, so let me call back and get my messages. I need to see if Joseph left me the number for that guy in France's manager."

"A manager?" Maryanne asked. She didn't think Prerogative had ever published a writer with a manager before.

"Yeah, I know," Lily said with a sarcastic tone, "but he's really pushing this guy on me, so I've got to go through the motions for now. Worst comes to worse, I'll just tell him I didn't think he was right for us."

"All right, well, when will you be home? M.J.'s at the Setback tonight, so I just talked to Kayla and we thought we could go celebrate your return."

"That sounds good. I should be back by 10 p.m. I'm gonna be pretty tired though."

"Yeah, it's alright. I'm not going to want to stay out late either. I just figured we all haven't been out together in so long."

"Okay. Well, I'll call when I'm in the car on my way

home."

"Okay." Sarah walked past the door and waved. Maryanne pulled the receiver away from her mouth. "Night!"

"Goodnight!" she heard her reply before the door closed behind her.

"Sarah?" Lily asked.

"Yup."

"She's leaving already?"

"Yeah, well, it's almost 5 p.m. here."

"Oh, right. Okay, I'll see ya soon."

"Okay. Bye."

Maryanne got up to shut off the coffee machine. As she left the kitchen and passed by the entrance to the staircase leading downstairs, the door swung open. It was Vik.

"Here you go," he said in his thick Russian accent, handing her a pile of proofs. "So, vat is dat?" he asked, pointing to the top one.

"Vat is vat?" Maryanne asked, subconsciously mimicking his accent.

"No better pictcher?" he asked.

"No, that's all we've got," she said as she started to walk away. Vik and Jenny tended to take editorial license whenever they could. Often, the actual editors were forced to keep them in line, which could make for some uncomfortable situations.

"Ooook. Vell, goodnight." With that, he swung the door open and headed back downstairs.

Maryanne sat down in front of her computer. She looked at the proofs that now lie next to her phone and then out the window longingly. She pushed her guilt out of her mind and started to shut down her computer. These could wait until Monday. She ran to the back to turn all the lights and the heat off. There was an extra skip in her step as she went back to her office to grab her bag and keys.

When she got to the door, she turned the knob to make sure it would lock behind her. Her head disappeared through the small view window on the door as she barreled down the stairs toward the freedom of the weekend.

Chapter 4

Rob sighed. It was past 4:30 p.m., almost 5 even, and he was still nowhere close to finishing up. He looked longingly at the exit, which he could see directly from his desk. It often taunted him. He knew Maryanne would probably be on her way out soon. He longed to get out of the hellhole he was stuck in and see her smiling face. He knew once he saw her, all the frustration of the day would melt away.

The spreadsheet he was working on was such a large file that it had crashed his computer three times already. He had just started up again after the third and was getting back into it when his boss, Geffin, called out to him.

"Rob!" His pitch went up in the middle of the word and back down again as he finished it. He looked toward the door to his office, then back at his computer. He frowned, got up, and walked out from behind his desk toward the main office. When he got there, Chief Operating Officer Geffin Marcus and Chief Executive Officer Norman Racketts were standing outside Geff's office, poring over some document.

Geff looked up as Rob approached them. "What's going on?" Rob asked.

"This doesn't make any sense," Geff said as he looked up at Rob. Rob took the reports from them and flipped through about three pages worth of expenditures.

"What doesn't?"

"Well, you didn't include any of the additions we

made onto the residence at 77th Street, but you included the renovations we did last year on the drop-in center."

Rob looked down at the report as the two men stared at him. He quickly glanced to the top right corner of the first page and realized the year read 2007, not 2008. Randall, his associate, had printed out last year's report for him.

Rob looked up at two very puzzled faces. For the heads of the company, they certainly didn't act like it sometimes. The two were out of touch with many of the day-to-day operations, and Rob tended to feel resentment toward them as he knew how vital he was to the company. Without him to keep everything together, he felt like the place would fall apart.

"Sorry, this is last year's report." He walked over to Randall's desk and lowered his voice. "Man, you printed out the wrong report, this is 2007," he said through gritted teeth. "Please, print out the right one and hand it to Geff and Norm."

"Uugh," grunted Randall. Rob turned from him and rolled his eyes. If you want something done right, you've got to do it yourself. That was the mantra Rob had adopted when it came to Randall.

Rob worked at Shelters for Hope (SfH), a non-profit for the homeless that provided job placement, financial advisement, medical attention, and of course, shelters and residences for their clients. They serviced thousands of homeless people in Manhattan each year. CEO Norman Racketts was a former, upstate defense attorney, where he would often defend those who couldn't help themselves, including minorities and the mentally and physically disabled. When he and his wife made the move back to the city five years ago, the position at SfH seemed to be a natural step in continuing his fight for those in need. He had proven to be one of the most aggressive and affective heads the organization had ever seen; he argued for more funding, more housing units, and better care in general for their clients.

By the time Rob turned around, Geff and Norman had already scrambled back to their offices and were typing furiously at their keyboards. Rob wondered what could be so important at 4:30 p.m. on a Friday afternoon to hold their attention so tightly. As he walked back to his office, he heard his cell phone ringing. He picked up the pace to catch it in time.

As he approached the phone he saw the blue face of it light up. He picked it up and held it close to his failing eyes to see who it was, but he had already known when he first heard it ringing. It was Maryanne.

"Hello."

"Hi, babe!" she said.

He smiled. "What's the dilly, Chilly Willy?"

"Nothin'. I'm just on my way home. Are you on the train?"

He scoffed at her assumption. "I wish."

"What? Well, are you on your way out, it's after 5 p.m."

"It is?" he asked, surprised. The clock on his computer must have slowed even more than he had originally thought.

"Yeah. Get out of there."

"I can't. I have to finish this thing up and then I'll leave."

"All right, well, let me know when you're on your way. I'll come get you."

"That'd be nice," he said, teasing her.

"Yeah, I'm nice like that," she answered. "Oh, mind going out for a drink tonight? Lily will be back and

Kayla said M.J.'s working."

"Well I'm not going to turn down free drinks tonight, that's for sure."

"Yay!" Maryanne hadn't been sure if Rob would be up to it after the week he'd had. "Great, I'll tell them you'll come. I'm going to stop at the supermarket, you want me to get anything specific?"

"Cherries."

"Chilly, cherries are out of season."

"I know," he said with a smile. Rob was staring at the calendar he had hanging next to his desk while he talked to his girlfriend. His eyes narrowed in on today's date. With all the craziness at work he hadn't realized it was the special one he'd been waiting for. He wasn't sure if Maryanne had realized it either. He glanced under his desk at the small brown box that had been delivered to him a couple weeks ago in preparation for it.

"All right," she said, moving quickly, "I'll get some stuff for later and tomorrow. Just let me know what train you're on."

"Okay. Bye."

"Bye, babe."

As he hung up, he sat back down at his computer, determined to get down to work and out of there by 6:30 p.m..

Only ten minutes had passed when he was summoned by Geffin once again. He walked back into the main office.

"Ughhh, Geffin, what? I'm trying to get out of here!"

"I know, I know," Geffin said. "Here, just sign these rent approvals for me."

As Rob signed them, Norman walked out of his

office. “Speedman was just on television. He’s pushing for a pull-out of troops in three months.”

Geffin whipped around to face him. “Really? That’s great!”

“Yup,” was all Norman had to say in return. He stopped at the front desk to sign some papers.

Rob looked up. “Wow, you know I’m really starting to like that guy. Everything he says just makes sense.”

Geffin was obviously excited. “Yeah, and he advocates full and open communication with any and all enemies, no preconditions. I mean, it might sound crazy, but it’s really the smartest thing. If there isn’t an honest and open dialogue happening then no good can come of any situation.”

Rob nodded. “I’m telling you,” Geffin said as he walked back over to the front desk to put the rent approvals in the outgoing mailbox, “come election time, things are going to get really interesting.”

“Isn’t he for abolishing income tax, too?” Rob asked as he walked back to his office. He looked over his shoulder and smiled at them.

“Yeah, I wouldn’t hold your breath on that one, Rob,” Norman said.

“Ha!”

Chapter 5

Norman Racketts looked out the glass facade of his office into the main office of SfH. He wouldn't have to keep up his daily charade for much longer. He would be leaving soon anyway. He hoped once he made his way through the filthy streets of the city that his wife wouldn't be home upon his return. With any luck, she would still be out doing whatever it was she did all day. He turned back to his computer and continued writing the letter he was composing to one of the government agencies that provided them with a funding contract.

A half hour passed before he was able to shut down and pack up. As he shut the lights off in his office, he realized a light was still on in one of the cubicles. Thinking one of the idiots had forgotten to shut it off in order to raise the utility bills, and cause yet another asshole board member to be on his case, he cursed to himself as he walked over to the cube. “Oh!” He jumped back in surprise as he came around the corner to its opening and found Randall Hardgrove still typing at his computer. Randall turned around to look at Norman, barely phased by the interruption.

“What are you still doing here?” Norman asked him.

Randall didn’t answer. A man like Norman Racketts didn’t deserve his respect or his attention.

“Look at me when I’m talking to you, nigger. I asked you what you are still doing here,” Norman hissed, the hatred seeping from his words as he walked up behind Randall and stood there, as menacingly as possible.

The fury raged within Randall. He refused to turn around. His eyes glanced over the items on his desk. He considered grabbing the letter opener sitting next to his keyboard and spinning around to catch Norman off guard, plunging it deep into his stomach. He thought better of it. Norman let a few moments pass. He reached up from behind Randall to turn off the desk lamp that started the confrontation. He brought his mouth close to Randall's ear and lowered his voice. "Whatever it is you're staying late and working so diligently on, don't bother. You're worthless either way."

With that he turned on his heels and walked away. Randall heard the door click behind Norman as he left. As the moments passed, Randall's breathing intensified and the anger in his eyes flashed behind the frames of his glasses where the reflection of what he was typing could be seen:

Dear Mr. Oliver,

I am writing this letter to make you and the rest of the board of directors aware of the despicable acts I have seen . . .

Chapter 6

Maryanne couldn't have been happier as she drove home. It was Friday, and she was about to hang out with all of her favorite people. She refused to let her recent dreams and strange occurrences worry her tonight.

Her cell phone beeped, and she picked it up out of the holder next to the driver's seat. It was a text message from Kayla saying she had just left work and should be home in a half an hour if she wanted to grab some dinner. As Maryanne waited at a light she texted her back saying that she just picked up some food from the supermarket and would be cooking that up. She extended an invitation to join her.

The light turned green and she eased the gas pedal. She passed a set of trees on her left just before the cemetery emerged. It was beautiful and scary, all at the same time. Her mind went back to a night when she was driving past it with Rob. They were on their way to Pleasantville, meeting up with some friends who had gone to dinner and were now going to Lucy's, a local martini bar, for a drink.

As they made their way up Route 9, she'd kept Rob entertained with stories about Joseph, who went a little more senile with each passing day.

"The best was when he came up to me and told me that the headline I wrote for his story didn't make any sense. Meanwhile, he was the one who wrote it."

Rob eyes squinted and his smile was broad as he laughed. When they came upon the cemetery, he suddenly looked to his right to stare at it.

"Did you see that?"

"See what? I'm driving."

He kept his eyes fixed on it. Then she saw it, too, a red beam of light that flashed like a sort of beacon in the night. It had come from amongst a cluster of tombstones on the arch of one of the many hills.

Neither of them could tell from which one exactly it was coming from.

"There it is again!" He pointed and turned quickly to look at Maryanne. "Did you see it?"

"Yeah. It's probably just some sort of reflection of light."

"Probably."

Even after they had driven past the large expanse of land that the cemetery covered, Rob was still looking back at it, searching.

She arrived home and parked the car in the lot down the street. As she lifted the three bags of groceries out of the passenger side, she heard her phone sound off that another text message had come in. She sighed, and balanced two bags on one hip and the other in her left hand, while she dug for her phone through the black hole that was her purse. When she had finally fished it out, she saw it was from Rob, letting her know he would be getting on a 7:23 p.m. train. *That will put him in around 8 p.m.*, she thought to herself. So she decided to go upstairs, start dinner, then leave it with Kayla while she went to pick him up.

She eventually made it to the J building and began climbing the stairs to her apartment. When she got to her door she heard one open and shut on a floor above her and footsteps lightly padding down the stairs. As she reached her door on the third floor, she looked to her left and saw Kayla coming down the staircase leading up to the fourth and fifth floors.

"Hey!" Kayla said, her face beaming with excitement to get the weekend started. "Let me help you." She reached out and took one of the bags from Maryanne.

"Thanks," Maryanne said, out of breath. She put down one of the other bags and once again dove into her purse to dig out her keys.

"Oh, my God, are you ever going to clean that thing out?" Kayla asked.

"You sound like Rob," Maryanne said, not taking her attention away from the task at hand.

"Well, now I know why he's always complaining about it."

Maryanne shot her a look. Finally, she pulled out the keys and opened the door. The girls walked in and went immediately into the kitchen where they chatted and put the groceries away. While Kayla finished that up, Maryanne started on dinner.

"Yeah, so I just got up and walked the fuck out of there at 6 p.m. I had been there since 8 a.m., for Christ's sake. There was no way I was staying there past then when I'm not even getting overtime," Kayla told Maryanne as she husked three pieces of corn and dropped them into a pot of boiling water.

"Seriously," Maryanne said. "What that place expects of you is just ridiculous." She looked at her watch and jumped, her eyes going wide. "Oh, crap, Rob's train will be here in two minutes." She wiped her hands on a dishtowel she had resting over her shoulder.

"Okay, so what needs to be done?" Kayla asked.

"Nothing. Just keep an eye on that chicken in the

oven. Oh, you could make the mashed potatoes if you want. It's just the kind in the packet. Milk is in the refrigerator."

"Sure, I can do that," Kayla said. She opened the refrigerator to make sure there was enough milk.

Maryanne ran into the living room to slip on her flats and grabbed her keys and bag from the makeshift dining table in the living room. "I'll be right back!" she said to Kayla as she opened the door. She took the stairs as fast as she could, walking swiftly down the block and back to her car. She got in and drove along the Hudson River to the train station. She glanced at the lights of the bridge that were twinkling in the night and smiled. When she pulled up to the station, the train was just pulling away. Rob had spotted her already and was walking toward the car.

"Hi," she said as he got in the car, and gave him a peck on the cheek.

"Hi," he answered. He had his large backpack with him, rather than the smaller messenger bag he usually took, a detail that Maryanne took no notice of at first. She pulled away from the station and headed back toward the Darren Hayes apartments.

Rob put his hand on the back of her head and stroked her hair. "So what's goin' on?" he asked.

"Nothin'," she said. "I started on some dinner. Kayla's back there now, keeping an eye on it. I'll just need a couple more minutes once we get back."

"Good. I'll just go upstairs and change, throw some water on my face and come down. Is she eating with us?"

"Kayla? Yeah."

"Good. So do they wanna go out later?"

"Yeah, I mean I don't think anybody's looking for a

long night out, just a quick drink. I know I'm tired, so I don't want to be out late."

"Yeah, me, too. All right, so we'll eat and just head over once Lily gets back and has a few minutes to settle herself?"

"Yeah. She should be back by 10 p.m.," Maryanne answered. She paused for a few minutes just for emphasis. "So, what's in the bag?" she asked as she smirked and looked at him sideways. They were almost back to the parking lot.

He smiled slyly. He didn't think she'd noticed that he had his backpack with him when he got in the car.

He didn't say anything for a few minutes. "What's today's date?" he asked nonchalantly, as if he couldn't remember.

"The 28th," she answered, amused. She found it funny that Rob thought she wasn't aware of the significance of the day.

"The 28th! Geez, the month flew by," he said.

"Yup," she answered. "Before you know it, it'll be Halloween."

They parked the car and got out and started to walk back to the apartments, Rob straggling behind. They were almost at the end of the parking lot at the sidewalk, when Rob stopped in his tracks. "Oh, babe," he said feeling his pockets. "I think my keys fell out of my pocket in your car. Can we go check?"

"Sure," she said and walked quickly back over to her silver Subaru Forester. Not exactly the coolest ride on the block, but it had served her well for almost ten years.

When she got back to the car, what she saw sitting in the driver's seat first surprised her, then confused her, then melted her heart. She turned to look at Rob who was now walking toward her smiling. She opened the door to pull out the Chilly Willy stuffed animal that was sitting there, buckled in and everything, waiting to drive.

She turned around to give Rob, who was at her now, a three-way hug with the doll. “Happy Anniversary,” he whispered in her ear as he hugged her.

Rob and Maryanne met on a lazy Sunday night one year ago when she was feeling particularly down. She was struggling to open a bottle of wine with a broken corkscrew that she had gotten in a tiny shop in London as a souvenir. It had a small ornament of a London tour bus attached to it. She knew a group of guys that were around her age lived on one of the two upper floors, but she couldn’t remember which. She considered trying to find them to ask if they had a bottle opener she could borrow, but didn’t have the guts to ring doorbells until she’d hit jackpot. As she struggled with the bottle, she heard footsteps coming up the stairs. She ran to the door and flung it open. She looked up the staircase and saw a man’s reflection in the window at the top of the first flight. He was standing at his door trying to get in.

“Hello?” she called up to him. “I need some help.”

“Oh, you need help?” asked a sympathetic and intoxicated Steve, one of Rob’s roommates. He came bounding down the stairs and into her apartment. She was a little taken aback, but thankful for the assistance.

“I just baked some cookies. Can I give you some to pay you back?”

“Oh, thanks!” he said. As Steve struggled with the wine bottle, Rob and his other roommate, Scott, came up the stairs and developed some very confused looks on their faces when they found Steve standing in Maryanne’s doorway.

“Uh, Steve,” Rob started. “What are you doing?” he

asked. The entire group laughed nervously at what was quickly becoming kind of an awkward situation.

"I needed some help with this bottle," Maryanne explained, as Scott and Rob stood eagerly in the doorway. As she said that, Steve popped the cork out.

"Hallelujah!" Maryanne said.

"Why don't you drink your wine upstairs?" Rob asked. He had a warm smile that seemed so genuine and simple.

"Um, uh, okay," she stammered. "Give me a couple minutes and I'll come up. What number are you guys?"

"420," Rob said, holding her gaze.

"Okay."

The boys all shuffled out and Maryanne closed the door, butterflies in her stomach.

When Maryanne went upstairs, the three of them were waiting for her, but the other two quickly faded away as the connection between her and Rob became obvious. The two of them took their glasses of wine and retreated to the privacy of Rob's room, where she teased him over his extensive collection of audio tapes and archaic computer.

"Wow, so you were born about a decade too late, huh?"

"What do you mean?" Rob asked with a smile.

"Alice in Chains, Guns & Roses, The Cure," Maryanne read off the titles as she fingered through the rows of tapes he had in a case on the floor of his room.

For their first official date, they'd decided to take advantage of the Indian summer and have some ice cream at a local parlor, then watch one of Rob's old 80s horror movies, on VHS of course, back at his apartment.

"I can't believe you actually own a VCR," she said to him as she sat down on his bed.

"Don't be silly, Chilly Willy," he said. "Lots of people still own VCRs."

"Did you just call me Chilly Willy?"

He looked at her a little embarrassed. "Yeah."

She laughed, but secretly had no idea who the character was. The next day, she looked the name up online.

She swiveled her office chair around to face Lily. "Do I walk like a penguin?"

Lily turned around with a perplexed look on her face. "Huh?"

"Or do I look like one?"

"What? No, what are you talking about?"

She didn't answer. Instead, she copied and pasted a picture she had found into an e-mail and sent it to Rob.

She wrote in the subject line: A penguin?

When Rob read it, he smiled broadly and knew this was the start of something special. The rest is history.

"I love it!" she gushed over the stuffed animal she'd just found in her front seat. "Where did you find it?"

"Don't worry about that," he said, grabbing her hand and leading her back to the apartments.

She buried her face in the toy and tried to keep herself from skipping. Rob made her happier than she ever thought possible, which was why she couldn't risk him losing his faith in her by telling him about her dreams and her recent unexpected trips to the cemetery.

They got back to the apartment and Kayla had everything finished and plated.

"Wow!" Maryanne said as she walked into the living room and saw the table set and ready to go.

"I know! I'm awesome, right?" Kayla said with a giggle as she folded up some napkins and placed them next to the four plates, one for her, Rob, Maryanne, and Lily.

"Oh, I'm not sure if Lily will be back to eat."

"Oh, okay," Kayla said. "I'll just put a cover on it and keep it on the stove to keep it warm for her in case she gets back anytime soon."

The three sat down to eat and after about an hour of food and conversation, they heard the rattle of a suitcase being wheeled up the pathway to the building.

"Is that Lily already?" Maryanne asked, as she turned to look at the window.

After a couple minutes, they heard her keys jingling in the lock. The door swung open and Lily appeared in the hallway.

"Hey, showgirl," Maryanne said.

"Hey." Lily looked a little flustered as she walked in, dragging her suitcase behind her. She looked up when she got to the living room, brushed her hair out of her face, and gave them all a big smile.

"So, where'd they put you up? The Golden Nugget?" Rob asked her. They all laughed. RWB was notorious for sending the girls to some of the remotest places on earth, on the cheapest dollar possible.

"No, no. Not quite," she said as she put her bags down and plopped down onto the couch with her laptop. "The trip was actually funded by the convention, not RWB."

"Aaah," Rob said, shaking his head that he understood. "Nice."

"Actually, Maryanne, I think I'm going to send you out there sometime within the next couple weeks. I met some pretty bizarre writers who said they are very interested in writing for us."

Maryanne let out a small laugh. "Bizarre?"

Lily laughed, too.

"Yeah, I mean, I'm not sure if I really like their ideas or if they're too particularly off the wall to even make sense."

"Oh. Okay. Yeah, I'll go check them out."

"I already set up a few appointments for you, so I'll give you all the contact info. Then, you can book all of your arrangements."

"Cool."

As Lily settled in, she entertained the other three with a story about the night she spent at a drag queen burlesque show at The Flamingo, with one of the conference organizers named Toni, a tiny Asian man who barely cleared Lily's shoulders. Once that show let out, a man in a golden sequined cowboy hat and blazer was scalping Cher tickets.

Toni got so excited Lily thought he was going to pass out in the street. He insisted they buy a pair. They ended up in the nosebleed section of the theater at Caesar's Palace, where she watched Toni dance and sing his heart out to every song.

She had them rolling on the floor with the details. Before long, it was 10:30 p.m.

Kayla looked at the clock. "Wow, it's already after 10 p.m., so I'm going to go upstairs and get ready to go out, and then I'll come back down."

"Me, too," Rob said.

"All right, so meet back down here by 11 p.m.? You guys want to walk over there?" Maryanne asked.

"Sure," said Kayla.

Rob shook his head yes.

"All right." Maryanne kissed Rob on the cheek and he and Kayla shuffled upstairs to prepare for the night.

He watched as the four of them left the building. The guy put his arm around the dark-haired one and pulled her head in toward his chest. She gave his waist a squeeze in return. The other two paired off behind them and started a conversation of their own. He made mental photographs of all of them in his mind: short and very curvy, with curly brown hair, tall and very thin, red head, etc.

The small group headed down the pathway to the south exit of the complex.

It seemed the couple would be difficult to drive a wedge between, but no task was too great for them. He knew what needed to be done, and it would be done sooner rather than later. In fact, the initiation had already begun.

Chapter 7

They had gotten home a few hours ago and Maryanne and Rob had both passed out practically before their heads hit their pillows. A long week, mixed with a couple of drinks and some laughs provided by M.J. once they'd all arrived at the Setback, had done them in.

Maryanne awoke slowly in the middle of the night and lifted her head. She saw the neon glistening on the wall. It was a bright green writing, in script, on a diagonal, directly on the wall in front of her. The night was still deep and dark in her room and her sleep was still pretty thick. She tried to shake some of it off. The fan was making its comforting whir. She was forced to use it year round thanks to the sweltering heat they were subjected to during the winters in the Darren Hayes, an element they had no control over. This time, she wasn't scared; a timid curiosity was taking over her.

Her eyes couldn't focus enough to read it, so she turned on her bedside lamp. The light revealed a clean white wall.

Chapter 8

"It said, *Slimer was here*," M.J. said, cracking himself up in the process. Maryanne gave him an unamused glare. She saw Kayla swallow a giggle, give him a stare that could have frozen the waters of the Caribbean, and then turn to face her. It was Saturday morning and the three were taking advantage of an unseasonably warm fall day. There would not be much time left for them to relax on the deck they shared with four other fifth-floor apartments, before the colder temperatures arrived.

"So, you couldn't read it at all?" she asked.

"No, I couldn't focus on it, and then, like I said, when I turned on the light it was gone."

"So strange."

"There's more," Maryanne said quickly.

They both stopped what they were doing to look at her.

"The day before, I was taking a nap on the couch."

"Uh huh," Kayla said, listening intently.

"This time I was definitely asleep, but in my dream, I was still lying on the couch, asleep. I opened my eyes and saw a man walk up to the couch and look over at me."

Kayla's eyes went wide. "What did he look like?"

"Well, his skin looked dirtied and his hair was blondish, but looked like there was dirt or soot in it, too. He looked like he was covered in a layer of dust or something. He was in his 30s or 40s, I'd say. He had on a red flannel shirt."

"Creepy," M.J. said and went back to futzing around with his grill.

Kayla rolled her eyes and put her head down on her forearms. "Who do you think it could have been?"

"I don't know, Kayla," Maryanne said, obviously frustrated.

Kayla wasn't aware of the other experiences she had had over the past couple of months, but when she'd gone upstairs to hang out with her and M.J., Kayla saw right through Maryanne's feigned happiness and knew something was bothering her friend. Kayla didn't back down, and Maryanne was tired of hiding things.

"All right, I'm just asking. Jesus, there's no reason to get snippy."

"I know, I know. I'm sorry. I'm just aggravated right now, that's all. And please, do me a favor, both of you," she said, emphasizing the last part by raising her voice so M.J. could hear. "Just don't say anything to Rob about this."

"Okay, we won't. What's the big deal though, it's just a couple of strange dreams. I'm sure it's just all the stress from work that's getting to you."

"I know," Maryanne said, trying desperately to think of a good reason. "He's just really stressed thanks to his job and I don't want to give him anything else to be bothered with."

"Okay."

Maryanne got up to leave. "Thanks for the talk. I'm gonna go back downstairs and relax for a while."

"Good idea."

"Yeah, why don't you take a nap or something," M.J. shouted from across the deck, bending over and holding himself from laughter. He'd managed to crack himself up once again.

"Ignore him," Kayla said as she hugged Maryanne goodbye.

"Ouch!" she heard M.J. say as Kayla punched him in the arm while she was leaving.

"Why do you have to be such a god-damned ball buster?" she shouted at him.

Maryanne pulled her sweater on as she made her way to the door back into their apartment. All she could think of was something Kayla had said just before she got up.

I'm sure it's just all the stress from work that's getting to you.

She found it odd that Kayla related her dreams to her job, but she didn't have time to linger over that thought because another quickly pushed it aside. It washed over her like a wave. She was feeling it again. She needed to get to Cecily's grave. Immediately.

Kayla watched Maryanne from her bedroom window as she saw her leave and heard the creak of the J building's front door as it closed shut behind her. Her eyes followed Maryanne as she broke into a light jog along the path toward the archway that would lead her out of the Darren Hayes courtyard.

Chapter 9

Maryanne groaned as she sat up in bed Monday morning. She had hit snooze about six times and figured the seventh time was the charm. She shuffled over to retrieve her towels from behind the bedroom door. Ronald followed too closely, almost tripping her twice. "Jesus, Ronald!" Her yelps jolted the sleep right out of her. Ronald bolted into the next room and hid amongst the piles of Lily's boyfriend John's junk.

7:33 a.m. Fuck! Still plenty of time to make it down the block for the 7:50 a.m. train, but not enough time to stop for a coffee. She needed to take some meetings in the city today.

Occasionally, Maryanne and Lily would publish some general news pieces throughout the essays in Prerogative and she was working on one for the next issue.

She sprinted in and out of the bathroom and her bedroom, tossing clothes and makeup every which way, shoving a variety of notebooks either into her bag or back out of it. "Okay, need this one, not that one, need this one. Let's go."

She was down the hallway and almost out the door. She turned on her heels and ran back into the bedroom one last time, opened the bright blue-green Tiffany's box on her desk, and put on the necklace that Rob had gotten her for Christmas last year. It was a delicate silver chain that looped through a heart, topped off with a small pearl left to dangle at the end. She loved it, and loved even more that he had come to know her so completely in such a short amount of time, that he was able to pick out something that suited her so well.

When the door finally slammed shut, five rejected outfits lay sadly all over her mattress. When she got down the first flight of stairs the dizziness started. The hunger pangs made her regret not having left enough time to have a small bowl of cereal or something before she left. *I hate going into the city*, she thought to herself. *Maybe I can meet Rob for lunch if he can get away from the office*. Her head was down and intent on getting to the ground floor when she ran into their second floor neighbor Beth, leaving her apartment to take her dog Fritz on his morning walk.

"Oh, hi, honey."

"Hi! Sorry you scared me. I'm in such a rush, I was trying to catch the 7:50 a.m. train," Maryanne said. Her shoulders slumped in defeat, realizing there was no way she would be making the 7:50 now.

Beth watched all the gusto seep right out of the girl's body and down into the concrete floor.

"How are ya, hun? Taking care of yourself?"

Beth had lived in the Darren Hayes apartments for nearly forty years. She and her husband, who had passed away too soon at fifty years old, had raised five kids in these teeny quarters that Maryanne and crew complained about on a regular basis. While none of their children ever had a bedroom of their own, that apartment was probably filled with more love than any of the greatest mansions of the world could ever hold.

"I'm trying, but it hasn't been easy."

"Is everything all right?"

"I haven't been sleeping," she said bluntly, and a little too quickly.

"Oh, honey, you're preaching to the choir. I've never been able to sleep well in this place. With all the yelling and sirens and chatter that goes on incessantly around this block, it's a wonder anyone can. I'm grateful when the summer months come and I can block it all out again by putting my air conditioner in the window! I remember when Greg was ten and he had such trouble sleeping, that we . . . "

Maryanne interrupted. "No, it's not that. I've been having these dreams."

"Dreams? Mmm." Beth shook her head a little too knowingly, looking Maryanne up and down with a furrowed brow, making the girl a bit uncomfortable.

"I mean, I've really gotta run, I can't go into detail right now, but," she answered, drifting off awkwardly. "I saw this man in a flannel shirt," she said with a nervous laugh, not knowing quite why she'd blurted that out.

Beth continued to look at her intently, waiting for more information.

"Well, this was the most recent one. I was trying to nap on the couch and in the dream I was still lying down, opened my eyes and saw a man come up and look over at me. He had on a red flannel shirt, and had short, kind of spiky blond hair, but it was fine, not long and course, " she rambled. "He had a round face and looked dirtied, like he was covered in a dust or something," she said, shrugging.

Beth's intense, almost scolding look, began to take an obvious turn to one of worry and anxiety. They stood staring at each other for a good ten seconds. Beth snapped out of it first.

"Well, come see me for dinner soon, honey, and just try to take it easy, relax, and don't stress over things too much. Stress is killer. Try to pray and have faith and everything will be fine."

Maryanne gave her a polite 'yes,' but couldn't help but wonder why the woman was telling her to have faith and pray when all she had revealed was that she was overtired and having odd dreams.

"Have a good day, hon," Beth brushed hurriedly past her as Fritz frantically led her down the stairs, obviously annoyed by the delay. Maryanne thought her exit was a bit strange, but didn't have time to think about it as she was now going to have to run to make the 8:20 a.m. train. She followed Beth down the staircase. As the two exited, Beth made a right under the archway to Elm and Maryanne sprinted left toward Beekman.

"Bye!"

"Bye, hon," Beth said, barely glancing back as she threw a hand quickly into the air and brought it back down to her side. She walked intently toward the street, the whole time led by Fritz, who had such strength for such a tiny creature.

Chapter 10

The next day, Maryanne was back in the office and RWB Publishing was abuzz with life and chatter. Papers were flying, phones were ringing, and plans were being made.

"All right, I'd like you to fly in on the 5th and stay until the 10th. One of these guys is giving a talk I'd really like you to attend, incognito, on the 9th. Adam told me about it, so he won't know anyone from the company will be in attendance," Lily told Maryanne. The two were discussing Maryanne's upcoming trip to Las Vegas.

"Okay. When is my actual meeting with him?"

"The 10th. If you go to this talk and don't like what you hear, then just cancel with him. I'm on the fence about this guy as it is, so I figured if you go see him speak, and he doesn't know you're in the crowd, then he'll truly be himself."

Maryanne narrowed her eyes at her. "What's the talk about?"

"Speedman," Lily said, giving her a devilish smile.

"Aaah, you little sneak you."

Lily laughed just as Joseph shuffled into their office. They both looked up at him. Joseph was a tall man at about six feet, one inch, and time had not treated him well. He was only sixty years old, but looked close to seventy. Square-framed glasses sat atop his bald head, and he walked with a limp thanks to an arthritic knee that would soon need to be replaced. One might think he wouldn't be an intimidating man, but Joseph had the ability to surprise you from time to time with words that were so biting and unabashedly offensive.

"You know, I don't know if I like this," he said.

Maryanne and Lily looked at each other. Another problem was you never quite knew when he was listening in on your conversation.

"Don't like what?" Lily asked.

"You two are trying to trap people into falling in line with your own beliefs, your own personal political agendas. This is not what journalism is all about."

Maryanne rolled her eyes and turned back to her desk. Lily always handled Joseph better anyway. She'd let her do the talking. Whenever she tried to take him on, she usually got nervous and panicked, and either tripped over her words or lost them completely.

"Well, no, we're not trying to *trap* people. We're just trying to make sure people are honest. That they're…" Lily paused as she put her hand on her head, a nervous habit when she's looking for just the right words. "That they have a genuine, original message, and they're not just looking to have their name in our magazine."

Joseph turned to Maryanne as if he didn't even hear Lily's explanation. "You better have your meeting with that guy; I don't care what he has to say in his speech." He walked out of their office, and they heard him stomp down toward the library.

The girls turned to each other and rolled their eyes, thinking he was finished with the conversation. As they turned back to their computers, he stormed back into their office and threw down a stack of magazines onto Lily's desk. He took one and opened it up to the article he was looking for. He lifted his glasses up and held the magazine close to his eyes as he scanned the article for the line he was looking for. Maryanne and Lily glared at him.

He finally found it, "If the country continues to allow itself to be ruled by this dynasty, we will see unspeakable losses not unlike those we saw during the Great Depression, ones that will take years to repair." He looked up and gave Lily a disapproving look. It was a line from her editor's letter two issues ago.

He threw that issue down on the ground and picked up another one. He found what he was looking for right away this time. "Ah, this one's on you," he said pointing at Maryanne.

"As Walker put it," he read, "it's funny how Republicans are usually fighting something that's actually hiding within themselves."

He looked up and asked them, "Now what does that sound like to you?"

"It's how they feel," Maryanne started to say, "you can't just sensor…" He cut her off before she could finish.

"Exactly! I didn't start this magazine so we could be left-wing cheerleaders. I spoke with Carry Gregory last week at a luncheon for the NGA, and he told me that he would have bought a two-year ad schedule if we hadn't printed this piece," Joseph said, his voice raising.

"The magazine is called Prerogative!" she yelled back at him. "Well, you're contradicting yourself, don't you think?" Lily asked him. "We can't just print more pro-Republican pieces to please your supporters. That's not what journalism is all about either." Joseph was standing over her looking at the magazine and shook his head.

Maryanne wasn't sure if she should open her mouth

again, but decided to go for it. "Is that July?"

"Huh?" he said too loudly and looked up at her.

Maryanne swallowed and got up. "Is that July?" she asked again and looked at the issue he was holding. "Yeah, it's July. That was the issue in which we printed that essay by the writer in Athens who was fiercely pro-Bush, and that was definitely when we put in that huge feature on the workings of the Office of Faith-Based and Community Initiatives, which painted them in a highly positive light by that writer."

"Where's that?" he asked.

Maryanne flipped through the book and found both pieces. She dog-eared the pages and handed the book back to him.

"Thanks, I'll go read these," he said, and walked out of the office as if on a mission.

Maryanne and Lily turned to each other, eyes wide with frustration, Maryanne started to shake her head when they both broke into fits of laughter that they silenced by covering their mouths with their hands.

Sarah looked over at them from her desk and shook her head in agreement, giggling to herself.

"He doesn't read the friggin' issue!" Maryanne said to Lily in an exasperated whisper.

Lily took a deep breath. "I know," she said. "You have to know how to handle him, that's all. If you show him why he's wrong and explain it in a way he can understand and visually see, then he'll back off for the most part. Which you did very well, by the way."

"I guess," Maryanne said, sitting back down in her chair.

"So anyway, like I said, book for the 5th to the 10th, four meetings in total, and if you can, get some interviews in for that Supreme Court of the Future story that you're doing for December."

"Right, okay." Maryanne got down to making appointments and arrangements for her trip.

About twenty minutes passed before Joseph walked back into their office. He walked up to Maryanne. "Let me show you something," he said.

He put an issue down next to her on her desk and pointed at a headline that read, "Separation of Church and State?" His finger was next to the question mark at the end of the sentence. "Why is that there?"

"Why is what there?"

"The question mark."

"Well, we're trying to say that this new bureau might be compromising that a little, don't you think?"

"No, I don't think so. Why shouldn't the government be supporting these charities? They're doing great things, things for the good of the people."

"I'm not questioning that," Maryanne said. She stared at the paper for a moment to collect herself.

"I'm sure they do wonderful, charitable things, but government money might be better served elsewhere as these foundations have more than enough to function on private donations." Joseph didn't say anything. You could almost see the wheels turning in his head as he tried to decide how to respond to her.

"Anyway, this is a moot point because the article barely addressed that anyway. It was all but an advertisement for it if you ask me."

"Then why put the question mark?" he asked.

Maryanne took a frustrated breath. "Because I felt it was an important part of the story that needed to be addressed, even if it was as brief a statement as that."

He shook his head and turned away from her. Joseph was not known for his lengthy attention span. He turned to Lily. “I want that Turner piece pulled from the next issue.”

“But we already paid him,” she answered.

“I don’t care. Pull it, and save it.”

“The layout is almost done!” Lily was pulling out all the stops. If Joseph hated anything, it was wasting money and having two fees paid for nothing would usually be enough to push him over the edge.

“Just save it for another issue,” he threw over his shoulder as he walked out.

Lily growled under her breath when she was sure he was out of earshot. “He just did that out of spite.”

“Is that the one you spent forever putting together?” Maryanne asked.

“Yeah, that’s pretty much three weeks of work gone down the drain.”

“You can’t use it again?”

“No, it’s all related to that big event he’s holding in California next month. It’s going to be totally irrelevant by then. He’s pulling it because I used that huge interview with Barbara Boxer, and she pretty much damns the war to Hell.”

Maryanne shook her head. Joseph seemed to have no concept of how much went into putting this magazine together. In his guised attempts to make the magazine more objective, he was really just doing what he was accusing them of doing—keeping the publication in line with his own political ideals and beliefs.

Pulling that story was going to cost them weeks of unneeded scrambling to fill its spot. She decided to do something about it.

“Joseph?”

“Yeah?”

She got up and walked out of their office and into

his. When she got to the doorway he was just putting on his jacket, obviously on his way out.

"Is that really necessary? Lily spent weeks perfecting that Turner piece. It's pretty much ready to go. I mean, it might just need one more round of layouts, but that's it."

Joseph put his hat on and picked up his briefcase and walked up to her. "Let's get something straight. This is my magazine and this is my company. I've been doing this for much longer than you have, young lady, and I know what is best for this place." Lily appeared at the doorway. "I'm telling you both," he said as he pushed by them, "that story better not be in the final proofs, and if you know what's good for you, you both better start understanding your roles here." He slammed the door shut as he left.

Maryanne felt a chill run down her spine. She made sure to settle herself before she turned around to face Lily. When she did her friend's eyes were wide and the corners of her lips were turned up ever so slightly.

"I don't know what shocked me more. What he just said or the fact that you stood up to him."

Maryanne frowned at her. "I stand up to him," she said, walking past Lily and back into their office.

Lily followed. "I know," she said, "but never this clearly."

Maryanne frowned, disappointed that her friend had confirmed her self-proclaimed status as a wuss. She looked to her right over at Sarah who had kept quiet as a mouse during this entire altercation. Her eyes were bugged out of her head so much that Maryanne was afraid they might drop out of their sockets. "I love how he referred to it as *my* magazine," she said as she got up and sat down on the floor of their office.

"I know, right," Lily said, laughing. Lily had built that magazine from the ground up. Joseph had simply given her the venue, which she of course, appreciated, but if he was going to attempt to take creative license on Prerogative, it was nothing less than offensive.

At least she's taking this in stride, Maryanne thought to herself. Joseph was most likely on his way to the semi-annual Westchester Hometown Society dinner, where the plates cost approximately $5,000 a head. Joseph was a very rich man and contributed to a number of organizations on a monthly basis. The Westchester Hometown Society was one of his favorites, as its mission was to maintain the "integrity" of the county he grew up in. What exactly that meant or how they went about accomplishing that was a mystery to outsiders.

Within the Westchester Hometown Society were smaller sects of sorts for each municipality that consisted of city councilmen, wealthy socialites, and businessmen who lived and worked in that specific locale. Many of its members frequented the cover of Westchester Today, the newspaper where Kayla worked. That fact combined with a little backstage information Kayla would often get from her friends in editorial, made one question how genuine their humanitarian efforts to keep up these cities and towns were. According to Kayla and her sources though, Joseph had somehow managed to keep his dealings, whatever his motives, very private.

"Well, I'm sure he's on his way to that dinner, so he won't be back, thank God," Lily said.

"So, what do you want me to do with the Turner story?" Sarah asked from her spot on the floor.

Lily paused for a moment. "Just leave it in for now. He won't even remember this conversation by tomorrow."

"All right," Sarah said. She got up and went back to her desk to finish the essay she was editing.

Chapter 11

Norman Racketts swirled his drink as he wandered around the room. He hadn't spotted Joseph yet, but that didn't mean he wasn't there. He would see him when they finally sat down for dinner anyway. He had made sure his contacts had seated them next to each other; now there'd be nowhere for him to hide.

As he waited for Joseph to find his seat, he recalled a recent run-in with his Director of Finance, Robert Martin, at the SfH office and smiled to himself at the level of stupidity he was faced with on a daily basis.

"And who is this?" he had asked Robert while in the boy's office. Of course, he'd already known the answer.

Rob turned around from the file cabinet in his office and saw Norman looking at the frame on his desk that held a picture of him and Maryanne in Atlantic City for Maryanne's birthday. A huge statue of Caesar stood behind them.

"Oh," Rob said, with a shy smile. "That's my girlfriend. We were in Atlantic City for her birthday."

"Caesar's Palace?" Norman asked, still staring at the photo.

"Yeah."

"And what is her name?" he'd asked, feigning ignorance, and interest for that matter.

"Maryanne," Rob said, standing next to Norman, hands in his pockets as he too looked at the picture of the two of them. He remembered how soaked they'd ended up when they got stuck in a rainstorm while on the boardwalk.

"You wanted to go away for your birthday," he had teased her as they ducked into a doorway for refuge. Neither of them could stop laughing.

"What does she do?" Norman asked as he finally walked toward the door of Rob's office.

"She's actually an editor at Prerogative magazine."

"Really?" he said, pretending to be impressed.

Rob looked up and laughed a little at Norman's dismay. "Yeah, trust me, it's not as glamorous as you might think," he said. Lucky for Norman, Rob had thought nothing more of their short exchange on the matter. He went to sit back down in front of his computer, eager to finish his tasks for the day.

"That's interesting though," Norman said as he walked out of his office and back toward his own. "Very interesting . . ."

Everyone was starting to take their seats at the semi-annual Westchester Hometown Society dinner. Joseph didn't even notice him as he took his seat next to Norman at the table. That night, Norman made sure he had his ring on before he left. The same ring he knew Joseph would be wearing, on the same finger—middle, left hand; the same one others in the room would be wearing as well.

As the gentlemen sat down, some introductions were made. "Joseph Go…" Joseph started to say, turning toward Norman finally, hand extended.

"Norman Racketts." Norman took Joseph's hand and shook it firmly, keeping up the charade. He could see Joseph's face harden instantly.

"Nice to see a fresh face here," Joseph said jovially, but through gritted teeth.

"Thanks! Wife and I moved back to the city a few years ago. Just recently heard about the Westchester Hometown Society though and seeing as we've been considering retiring here in a couple years, I thought I'd come see what you guys are all about. It was tough wrangling a ticket to this thing, let me tell you."

Joseph laughed. "I'll bet. You can't be a part of this if you're a penny pincher," he said, putting an emphasis on the last two words. Joseph paused and looked down at Norman's folded hands. Norman kept his eyes trained on him as he did and watched as Joseph's eyes focused in on Norman's ring, a simple, white gold band. Joseph lifted his gaze to meet Norman's. The corners of Norman's mouth turned up slightly as he fought the smile that was dying to form thanks to the joy of watching Joseph squirm. They didn't even notice when the waiter approached them and asked if they'd made their choice for their main entree yet.

"Why are you here tonight?" Joseph asked under his breath, looking around to make sure no one else was paying attention to their conversation.

"I understand you could use some help gaining back control."

Joseph hung his head in shame, pretending to be interested in the bread basket.

"I have it under control," he said. "There's been some upheaval, but I'll iron it out," he said, glancing around.

"Doesn't seem like it. We keep waiting for it to turn around with each issue, but after six months it's still the same content, and I haven't had an update on China in weeks."

"I told you . . ." Joseph started to respond.

"Joseph!" The two were interrupted by a short,

stocky man who had already started on his salad. “I didn’t even see you there, buddy. How are ya?”

Joseph tried to muster a smile. “Hi, Ralph.” He cleared his throat to regain his composure. “I’m good, yourself?”

“Good, old man. Let me tell you I’ve been reading Prerogative religiously lately, and I’ve got to give you some props for all the risks you’ve been taking.”

Norman looked at Joseph sideways.

Ralph Ramsey was a young, up-and-coming entrepreneur who owned a number of establishments in the Hollow and surrounding towns, including a country club, a restaurant on the Rockefeller estate, as well as Castle on the Hudson, an elegant hotel and banquet hall that resembled a Medieval remnant. Joseph didn’t care for him as he only added fuel to Lily and Maryanne’s fire.

“Thank you, thank you,” Joseph said, trying to look as disinterested in the conversation as possible so as to ward Ramsey off. He didn’t want him adding fuel to Norman’s fire either.

“So, what’s your personal take on Speedman?” Ramsey asked.

Although Norman was secretly on the edge of his seat, both he and Joseph became visibly uncomfortable as everyone at the table seemed to perk up at the question, eagerly awaiting his answer.

Joseph stared at his folded hands for a couple of seconds, gently shaking his arthritic knee under the table. Joseph was notorious for his public silence over his political views.

“I mean, he's a smart guy, but can he hack it as the Leader of the Free World? I don’t think so.” As Joseph finished his sentence, he held his hands out to indicate that was all he had, but Ramsey wouldn't stop.

A few other balding, grey and white heads at the table nodded in agreement, so slowly it was barely discernable. There was a clear distinction and line between the new blood and the old blood within the Westchester Hometown Society.

Ramsey looked at Joseph as if he were crazy and laughed gently. "You don't know? I mean, what more do you need?"

Joseph swore to himself he would maintain his composure. Ramsey was trying to goad him into something, and Joseph didn't intend to find out what. If he blew up, he might end up revealing too much.

"First of all, I wasn't asking if you think the man can be president. He's a long ways away from that anyway. He hasn't even completed his first senate term. That being said, I still think he's exactly what this country needs right now. I'm talking about everything he's done thus far. Isn't he a breath of fresh air?"

Joseph saw Speedman as anything but, more like a threat to everything he stood for. The rest of the table kept quiet as they observed the exchange between the two men. The main entree was about to be served, and the presentations and workshops would soon follow.

"Not exactly, Ramsey, the man's got enough corruption in his past to rival every mob faction combined."

"What! Don't tell me you are buying into all that gossip."

"It's not gossip, Ramsey, it's a fact that the man has had close ties with a number of terrorist groups who have funded his way to the top," Joseph said matter-of-factly. "Can you pass the butter, please?" he asked as he started to dig into his flounder.

Norman couldn't believe what Joseph had just said. It was practically career suicide on his part. As the publisher of a political magazine that was also used as a valuable tool for them, a lot rode on Joseph remaining neutral publicly. Nevertheless, the man was acting as if he had simply just commented on the weather. The pressures of what he was dealing with were obviously starting to affect his day to day life.

Ramsey looked around the table to see if anyone else was as dumbfounded by that statement as he was. They seemed shocked, but Ramsey knew it was only because Joseph had revealed his true feelings about the politician; a rare slip that was almost unheard of for the publisher. They themselves probably couldn't be more thrilled with the accusations that many right-wing conservatives were slinging about Speedman.

"Well, it's disappointing to hear that a man in your position, at the helm of one of the youngest, most influential and freshly political magazines today, is viewing this man's historic rise from such a skewed vantage point."

"You don't know what my vantage point is, Ramsey," Joseph said in between bites.

"Oh, I think you just made it pretty clear."

"That's enough, Ramsey!" Joseph said, slamming his palm down on the table.

This time half the room looked up from their plates. It became abundantly clear to Norman that Joseph Goldberg had just snapped. *All the better to take advantage of,* he thought.

"I did not come here to discuss politics. I am here to discuss how we can get our towns and villages back to the level they were at when we grew up here!" he said, pointing around the room.

Norman rolled his eyes. Who is he trying to kid with that one? he wondered.

"Politics has everything to do with maintaining quality of life," Ramsey said.

Joseph stood up. "Well, I'm not leaving my future up to one of them." He threw his napkin down and walked out of the room just as the keynote speaker was taking the stage, leaving the table and those adjacent to them, breathless at the insinuation of what he had just uttered.

"Excuse me," Norman said, getting up and walking briskly after Joseph.

Although Norman knew exactly what Joseph meant by that last line, he was hoping the others who had been present or had overheard didn't make the connection. *Fat chance of that*, he thought.

"You better get it together, Sir," he hissed at Joseph once he caught up with him. Joseph finally hobbled his way out into the lobby of the banquet hall, Norman fast on his heels. "Another outburst like that and you are finished, if you haven't dug your own grave already."

"Huh?" Joseph flung around to face him, angered by Norman's sudden and unexplained intrusion that evening. "I think it's about time you let me know exactly what you're doing here."

"I came to help."

"How?" Joseph asked quickly.

Norman moved in closer and dropped his voice down to almost a whisper. "We will get to her through him."

Joseph didn't make eye contact with Norman. He paced slowly, hands on his hips, as he looked down at the floor, defeated. Norman watched him for a few seconds. When Joseph stopped, sighed, and took off his glasses to rub his eyes, Norman came up next to him and put a hand firmly on his shoulder.

"Come on, old friend. My driver is outside. Let's go talk." With that, the two walked out, leaving their jackets behind. The whoosh of the revolving door softened as its aimless spinning began to slow, and the banquet hall erupted in an unheard applause.

Chapter 12

Maryanne was tossing and turning more than usual that night, wrestling with her comforter, trying to sleep for more than an hour or two at a time without waking up. After cleaning the apartment top to bottom, she had expected to pass out immediately, but she didn't. The light whir of the fan was comforting, yet not enough. She listened to the sound of the occasional car passing by on the street underneath her window.

Suddenly, the hardwood floors glistened and she looked up to see that her laptop screensaver had gone off and the screen had lit up as if someone had touched the mouse pad. From her position in bed, she could see the arrow was starting to move around. She stumbled out of bed and sat in her desk chair, staring at the screen in amazement as a Microsoft Word document opened, as if the computer had a mind of its own. She touched the mouse pad and tried to gain control of it, but to no avail. Her jaw dropped as she watched the keys begin to be pressed by invisible fingers that were delivering a haunting message:

Your dreams will soon become even more real.

She ran out the door without thinking. Thankfully, the door didn't shut behind her completely. She took the stairs two at a time and started frantically pounding on Rob's door and ringing the doorbell. As a few seconds passed, her common decency kicked in and the thought occurred to her that maybe she should have checked what time it was before she started waking the dead. The door swung open and the anger in Rob's eyes was undeniable, even though they were only half open as he squinted, blinded from the harsh light of the hallway. The anger quickly turned to concern as he saw how upset she was.

"What happened?" he asked hurriedly, grabbing her forearms.

"Come downstairs," she said.

He grabbed his keys, followed her down the stairs and through the door, into her room. She stood in front of her laptop, stunned. It was off.

"Um, babe? What the fuck is going on?" he asked.

She put her hands to her head and pulled at her hair. She tried to rub the sleep out of her eyes. She sat down at the desk to catch her breath, staring at the blank computer screen. Rob was still staring at her, waiting for a response. Ronald circled both sets of legs.

"I was lying in bed and all of a sudden the computer screen lit up."

"Right."

"And I could see the pointer on the screen moving around, so I got up to see what was going on." She took a second. Rob waited for what had better be the clincher of his life.

"So it looked like someone had somehow logged in to my computer from another location or something and was using it because they opened up Word and a new document. And then the keys started to press down as if someone was using them and typed into the document…" She trailed off.

"And? What did they write?"

“They wrote that soon my dreams will get more real.”

“What dreams?”

“I’ve been having strange dreams.” She tried to choke back a few tears that were threatening.

“Dreams about what?” he asked, trying to hide the frustration in his voice at this scene that had jerked him out of a deep sleep. He didn’t want to say anything, but he’d been having a dream of his own, one that certainly would not have sat very well with her.

She shrugged, looking down in her lap. "I see different things. Sometimes spiders, sometimes people." She felt beyond mortified and couldn't even look up at him.

This seemed strange to Rob, and he admitted to himself that it did give him a slight chill, but it was all too much to process at 2:30 a.m., with a 6:30 a.m. alarm looming. He decided to put it to rest until they could properly discuss it tomorrow.

“Babe, it was another dream. That’s all this was.”

“No, it wasn’t.”

“Yes, it was, babe. Look, your computer is not even on.”

“I’m telling you it was real. I saw this!” she exclaimed with frustration.

“Well, hopefully they saved their work and we can check it out in the morning,” he said with a laugh.

“Very funny,” she said, still staring at the screen.

Rob sat down on her bed. Ronald jumped up next to him and head-butted his arm for attention. “Come here,” he said. She got up and went to sit next to him. He pulled her legs up onto his lap and wrapped his arms around her. She fit perfectly and he kissed her forehead, resting his chin on the top of her head.

"Listen, you've been so exhausted and stressed with all the traveling you've been doing that it wouldn't be unusual to have a strange episode like this, right? I really think it was just a figment of your imagination."

She sighed. *He thinks I'm nuts*, she thought to herself. What she had dreaded was coming true: Rob knows, and although she wanted to believe their love could outlast anything, the insecurity in her feared it was only a matter of time before this started to pull them apart if she didn't make it stop, fast.

She knew what had happened was real. No dream. No figment of her imagination.

"Come on, let's just go to sleep. We can talk about this tomorrow if you want. I need sleep, I have a thousand meetings scheduled for tomorrow."

She felt awful, but something was happening. Something was brewing within her and she knew she couldn't take it anymore. She was determined to find out exactly what this was that was plaguing her, and who, or what for that matter, was trying to tell her something.

Chapter 13

"He thinks I'm nuts."

"Oh, stop it," Casey said to Maryanne, her voice crackling over the long distance phone line. Casey was thankful for the static so Maryanne couldn't hear the real fear in her voice.

It was 9 a.m. in Shanghai, 9 p.m. in New York. Casey, Maryanne's cousin, had just woken up and was staring out her window of the Millennium Hotel at the haze sitting over the city—a haze she had grown accustomed to over the past eight weeks since she'd been there on assignment for Prerogative. Casey had just graduated from Marist College in Poughkeepsie, New York, and after a few weeks of not hearing anything from the forty some odd application packages she'd sent out to newspapers all over the country, had started to panic. Maryanne had swooped in like the guardian angel she had traditionally been for her growing up and sat Joseph down to talk to him about her brilliant cousin who just couldn't seem to catch a break. Joseph agreed to offer her a significant amount of freelance work at a raised rate, as well as the opportunity to travel. Of course, it didn't hurt that Casey was nearly engaged to her Jewish boyfriend of five years, which Maryanne made sure to slip into the conversation. Joseph kept most of his preferences and opinions hidden, or at least he tried to, but what was all too obvious were his Semitic preferences.

Casey met with Joseph to sign a contract, and she

was packed and on a plane to Shanghai one week later.

"I'm sure he's right and it was just a dream," Casey said as she flopped down on the couch in the makeshift den of her hotel room and rubbed her temples. She tried to process the maze of details of cemeteries, computers, and spiders that Maryanne was throwing at her right now. She had just managed to fall asleep a few hours ago and was not happy that it had been interrupted by Maryanne's phone call. Sleep was becoming a rare luxury for her lately.

"I don't think so, Casey," Maryanne said.

Casey gathered herself and knew she had to keep Maryanne calm and within her bubble of illusion Joseph had created for her. "Rob loves you and respects you, no matter what you might think. That was obvious from the first minute I saw you guys together." She hesitated for a moment, hoping Maryanne was taking the bait. "Did you guys get a chance to really talk about this yet?"

Maryanne frowned as she folded a few dresses and put them into her suitcase. She was packing for her trip to Vegas. She was scheduled to take off tomorrow, mid-afternoon from JFK Airport.

"Well, not really. I leave for Vegas tomorrow, so I'm trying to pack, and as it is I only got home about an hour ago." She picked up a pair of strappy black spiked heels and threw them into her suitcase, too, praying she wouldn't have to wear them.

"How come?"

"There was this event in the city that was pretty necessary, so Lily said she'd spare me the last night of production if I would go to it for her. Rob picked me up from the train station when I got back and he started asking me about my visits to the cemetery. He seemed mostly concerned with that."

"Well, I don't blame him."

"Yeah, I know," Maryanne said, slightly embarrassed. "Anyway, we got back and he said he'd give me a couple hours to pack, then come down and we'd talk about everything. Honestly, I think this is all either going to have to be flushed out in a phone conversation from Vegas or when I get back. I'm already exhausted, and I'm sure he is too, so I'm not sure how long we're going to last before we both fall asleep."

"Yeah. Well, at least he's not ignoring the problem and wants to talk about it." Rob was Casey's last hope to protect Maryanne. She was pretty sure he was still in the dark, and therefore, the safest of all of them.

"Yeah, that's true," Maryanne said. She was starting to feel a little more at ease about the situation, but was still afraid that she'd really pushed it with that scene last night.

"I don't know though, Casey, I feel like I'm losing it. It's scary." Casey could hear a deep worry in her cousin's voice.

"I know," Casey said. "I'm sure this is all just stress related."

"Well, I hope you're right."

"Are you okay?" Casey asked.

Maryanne smiled. Although she was four years older than Casey, she had always felt that her younger cousin was the older relative trapped in the younger one's body.

"Don't be worried about me, little girl, just look after yourself over there on the other side of the world. I probably shouldn't have told you, you don't need anything more to be dealing with over there. I just really needed someone with an objective opinion to talk to. You know, someone who can't possibly get any further away from the situation."

Casey giggled. "That I am. It's all right. I know you can handle yourself, but I'm afraid you might be dealing with forces that are beyond you."

"Yeah."

"Go finish packing so you can talk to Rob. I've got to get ready for a few interviews I have today anyway."

It was a bit of an abrupt sign-off, but Maryanne admitted she did have a lot to attend to and it was already closing in on 10 p.m. "All right, I'll talk to you soon. I love you. Hey, what do you have on deck for today, by the way? You know, in case Joseph asks me."

"Well, I had an 11 a.m. phone interview that had to be postponed. He said he'd call me back shortly to reschedule. I told him I'm on a tight deadline and really need to get this done today. So, I'm just hoping he follows through." Her voice trailed off slightly.

Casey sounded a little discouraged. Maryanne could tell her cousin was having a more difficult time than she was letting on. *I guess that makes two of us*, she thought to herself.

"Everything okay on your end, buddy?"

Casey paused. "Yeah, of course. I'm in China for Christ's sake!" she said, forcing a laugh.

"You'll be home soon at any rate," Maryanne reassured her.

Here's hoping, Casey thought to herself and hung up the phone.

Chapter 14

When Maryanne's alarm went off the next morning, Rob groaned, but rolled over and wrapped his free arm around her waist and pulled her in close to him. She stroked his head and they took each other in for a few minutes in the fuzzy early morning light of her room. Maryanne would be in Vegas for the next five days, and they wouldn't get a chance to hold each other for almost a week. The fan whirred steadily as Rob got up and got dressed to leave. Maryanne rolled over and turned the lamp on next to her bed to give him some light. She rested her head back on the pillow, her left hand resting under her cheek as she watched him. Once he had his keys, she walked him to the door. When they reached it, he turned to her, took her face in his hand and kissed her swollen lips.

"I'll see you in a few days," he said.

She smiled lovingly at him, his hair sticking out every which way. She shook her head in agreement. "I'll call you when I land," she said.

She sighed as she watched him walk out the door and it shut behind him. The whole building was silent, but she knew tenants were in their apartments engaging in their own personal morning routines—papers being read, coffee brewing, and outfits being laid out for post-shower review.

When Rob had come back downstairs last night, they got ready for bed and snuggled in under the covers. As they did, they began to talk about what had been happening to her these past few months. She decided that if she was going to come clean, she was going to do it right and tell him everything. He was supportive and attentive throughout the conversation, looking right in her eyes and stroking her hair, pushing it behind her ears. When she got to the part about the man in flannel, he pulled his head back slightly, eyes wide, half -smiling and let out a nervous laugh. He looked away from her.

"Um, are you trying to freak me out right now?" he asked, running a hand through his hair. He shook his head, rubbed his eyes, and turned back to her. "Anyway, go on." The look of horror on her face at his reaction made him back track.

"I'm sorry, babe," he said. "Really, I'm sorry, I'm just worried about you that's all. I can't believe you haven't told me any of this!"

"Well, I was afraid of the exact reaction you just gave me!" she said, her eyes welling up.

"Come here," he said, pulling her toward him.

She started to cry. "What the hell is wrong with me?" she asked.

"Nothing." Rob said, kissing the top of her head. "Nothing is wrong with you. Listen, I'm sure most of it can all be attributed to stress and this overactive brain of yours," he said, tapping a finger on her forehead. "They're just dreams."

She took a deep breath and started to resign herself to the fact that maybe, in fact, that's all this was; but that still didn't explain these trips to the cemetery.

"But that still doesn't explain your cemetery visits," Rob said, reading her mind.

"I know."

"So, when you have the urge to go there, to this grave, what happens to you?"

She thought for a moment while she wiped the tears away from her eyes. Both of them were now sitting cross-legged on her bed, facing each other.

She shrugged her shoulders. "I don't know. It's just this sense of extreme urgency that comes over me. Like I have to get there, because if I don't, something awful is going to happen. Something awful," she repeated, "and to someone I love, too. It's the feeling you would get if you knew something bad was about to happen to someone really important in your life and you only have a short amount of time to stop it."

"Huh," he said, intrigued. He tapped his finger on his lips and looked away for a minute. He looked back at her, and the worry in her eyes as she stared back was so heavy, it was practically sinking them. He hugged her again. "I love you so much," he said into her ear, and as if again reading her thoughts, he said, "and I still think you're an amazing girl. Okay?" She shook her head yes, but couldn't shake the feeling he was hiding what he really thought. She shrugged it off as her own paranoid insecurities and again shook her head.

"Okay. I love you, too, Chilly Willy."

He smiled in a way that made his eyes narrower, but his face immensely softer and gentler. All the love in him came out through that closed-lip smile.

"Now, let's go to sleep," he said. "You've got a long day and a busy trip ahead of you. We can talk about this more when you get back next week. I want to take a walk over to that grave once you do."

"Okay," she said, pleased that he was taking an interest, rather than shying away from the situation.

"What's the name again?"

"What name?" she asked.

"On the grave."

"Oh. It's a little girl. Only six years old. Cecily Reynolds."

"Strange name."

"I think it's pretty."

They shut the lights and kissed each other goodnight.

"Cecily Reynolds," Rob mumbled as he fell asleep. "Name doesn't sound familiar."

"Yeah, for me either."

"Of course, not for you, you didn't grow up around here," he said teasingly.

"Goodnight," she sing-songed over her shoulder to him, indicating she was done with the conversation for now.

He giggled. "Goodnight." He rubbed her back while they nodded off to sleep.

Maryanne was fairly satisfied with last night's talk, but it bothered her that he, along with everyone else, didn't seem to be phased by what she was going through. No one was taking it seriously. Since there were so many naysayers, she had fallen asleep almost convinced that they were right: these were all just dreams, and that was that, but once awake, she approached the situation again with a new found vengeance. What happened with her laptop the other night was certainly not a dream, of that she was sure; but she had no way of proving it, and more importantly, no way to figure out how it might have occurred.

Wait a minute, she thought. "That's it!" she said in an excited whisper, so as not to wake Lily. She slapped the coffee table and got up. She shut off the early morning episode of "Saved by the Bell" and walked swiftly into her bedroom and shut the door.

She went to her laptop and turned it on for the first time since Tuesday night. It was possible that since the program was probably turned off unexpectedly, it would have recovered the unsaved document that had popped up that night, showing the time and date it was shut down. “Come on,” she mumbled to herself as the computer took forever to load up. She watched as her desktop icons popped up slowly, painfully.

She moved the cursor to the Start menu, and her heart skipped a beat as she clicked on Microsoft Word.

She sucked in a gasp of air as Word started, and on the left the recovery menu popped up with just one document in the box. Underneath it read: (10/2/07; 2:18:42 AM).

Oh . . . my . . . God. I was right, she thought. She had expected it, but felt no sense of retribution whatsoever. She turned away from the computer for a moment, staring at her room behind her. She let a few seconds pass before she turned back to her computer. The document sat there, taunting her, daring her to open it, and save it even. She frowned and clicked on it. When it opened, she felt all the wind blow out of her sails. The document read:

Your dre ly;<

Shit! Whoever (or whatever) it was who performed this little magic trick, had tried to delete the sentence before shutting down the computer but got, sidetracked? “This is absurd!” she said under her breath as she ran her fingers through her disheveled hair. She grabbed her towels, frustrated, and stomped into the bathroom. She turned the shower on full blast and got in. As she lathered up, she tried to make sense of everything.

Could she have done it herself? she wondered. Was she sleepwalking and translated it into a dream when she awoke? Had she truly been just dreaming the whole thing? The questions continued to flow. She considered the absurd. Could someone have hacked into her computer remotely? Was that even possible? And if so, how would they know she would be awake to see it? Could there have been someone or something else in the room? A presence that did this?

The water was hot, but she felt a chill run down her spine at that thought. She reached behind her to turn the knob that controlled the hot water and turned it up slightly, sighing as she did so. If she hadn't done this herself, why would whoever did try to erase what was in the document letter by letter like that, or at all for that matter?

She finished up in the shower. As she got out and blow-dried her hair, she knew she could spend forever analyzing this strange happening and not get anywhere. There was no way to know how it happened, so the best she could do was file it away. Forgive, but not forget, so to speak. She decided it wasn't worth even bringing it up again to Rob until she returned. What would it prove anyway?

She finished packing up a few last minute items. She poured herself a bowl of cereal and started channel surfing. Her mind was blissfully blank until she noticed the time on the cable box.

10 a.m. already. Her flight was at 4 p.m., so the car would be coming for her at 1:30 p.m. She had some work to finish up and e-mail back over to Lily before she left. She reluctantly peeled herself up off the couch and went back into her room to sit in front of her laptop.

Around 1 p.m., she finished up, shutdown her

laptop, and tucked it away in its travel bag. As she was getting dressed, her cell phone rang. She looked at it, confused at the unknown number.

"Hello?" she answered. A foreign accent replied, but she could understand that it was her driver calling to say he was already downstairs. She dragged her luggage down to the main entrance of the Darren Hayes, where he cheerfully greeted her, and with that, they were off.

She flew through check-in and security and made it to her gate with an hour to spare before take-off. She picked up a sandwich from a nearby food booth and sat down, resting her purse and her laptop case next to her. She took out her cell phone and saw that Lily had tried to call her.

"This is Lily."

"Hey, you called?"

"Yeah. Are you there? At the airport I mean?"

"Yeah, I'm here. Just got to my gate, actually."

"Are you sitting down?"

Maryanne's forehead wrinkled as confusion took over again. "Yeah?" she said, with a question in her voice.

"I have yesterday's copy of Westchester Today in front of me."

"Okay?" She was curious to find out what Lily was getting at.

"Front page. A Rare Slip."

"What the hell are you talking about?"

"Our boss really outdid himself this time."

"All right, are you going to explain or what?" Lily was starting to annoy her.

"It seems there was a bit of a scene the other night at the Westchester Hometown Society dinner."

"Oh, God, what did he do?" Maryanne asked,

exasperated. That was all she needed. If anyone she was about to meet with in Vegas had gotten wind of something, it might make for a really frustrating trip.

Writers are a finicky bunch, and it wouldn't surprise her if people would start to not want their name associated with a publisher whose actions are unpredictable and offensive. Because whether they liked it or not, his actions and words would unwittingly become the words and actions of the magazine.

"Well, I won't bore you with the gory details, but apparently, there was some sort of confrontation between him and Ramsey when Ramsey asked him about Speedman. It doesn't seem like Ramsey was even being that antagonistic, but it says Joseph stormed away from the table after saying, 'Well I'm not leaving my future up to one of them.'"

"Referring to Speedman? Please tell me he meant a Democrat."

"Well, that's what the rest of the article is speculating about. It's Westchester Today, so they're of course, insinuating he meant a black person."

"Well, what does it say, exactly?"

She heard Lily rattling the pages of the paper as she looked for the relative parts. "With that, the usually politically tight-lipped Goldberg left the table, leaving those still seated flabbergasted at the seemingly unnecessary scene."

Lily continued. "They made speculations as to what he could have meant, quoting Ramsey and a few others: 'I mean, 'one of them?' What exactly was he referring to with that statement? Race? Political party?'"

"Oh, no," Maryanne groaned. She hoped the story stayed confined to the small town tabloid, otherwise, they would have a lot of explaining to do for Joseph.

"It gets better: 'I for one am quite shocked by his insinuation. His archaic preoccupations with race and ridiculous partialities to the current gossip of the hour is something I want nothing to do with.'"

"Oh, God!" Maryanne exclaimed. "Who said that?"

"Eric Lowe."

"Oh, please! That guy is the most racist bigot going in the county. He's just using this as an opportunity to move the spotlight off of his own blatantly prejudiced activities."

"Seriously."

"God, how did they find out about this? Who wrote it? They usually never let press into those things! We never were."

"Stacy Rockaport. I think she was there, sitting at a nearby table. She definitely wasn't at his."

"How did we miss this yesterday? I'm going to kill Kayla, how could she not have called me? It's on the front page?"

"Yup."

"Is he there?" Maryanne asked, lowering her voice as if Joseph might be able to hear her.

Lily scoffed. "No. He wasn't here all day yesterday either and we were sitting here like idiots wondering why. He only called in about an hour ago to see how everything was going, and then he mumbled something about having a doctor's appointment. I don't expect him to show his face until Monday."

"You know we're going to somehow get blamed for this."

"Exactly. He's probably going to say we got him into such a tizzy that he couldn't even talk to people."

Maryanne couldn't help but laugh. "All right, well, I'm going to be boarding in a few minutes. Did you see the stories I sent you?"

"Yeah, thanks for editing them for me. It really helped me out. They were good, right?"

"Yes, I was just about to say that. The one by that guy Janice? Edward Janice? About immigration? Really sharp. To the point, just like I like it."

"Me, too. We can use him again I think. All right, well, safe flight. I'll talk to you tomorrow sometime. Who are you meeting with first by the way?"

"The guy who lives in Henderson. The one who's pushing nationalized legal prostitution." Maryanne giggled, nervously.

"Geez. I hope you're meeting him in a public place."

"Yeah, don't worry about it."

Lily laughed. "Okay. Bye."

"Bye."

As soon as she hung up, Maryanne immediately called Kayla to ream her out for not telling her about the embarrassing front-pager on Joseph and to see if she could get any more details. Kayla's voicemail picked up.

"Um, yeah, we just got the copy of yesterday's rag, and I'd like to know why you didn't call me immediately to let me know it was running! What's the deal? Are you okay? I can't imagine you not warning me about this. Call me back. I'll be in Vegas by tonight."

Maryanne was wondering if Kayla had called in sick yesterday and didn't even know about the story. It was strange for her friend to not have notified her about what was going on. She was about to call Kayla's desk number when she heard the announcement that her row was boarding. Ugh! It would have to wait. She shut down her phone and finished up her sandwich. She tossed the foil wrapper in the garbage and heaved her carry-ons over her shoulder. She unwillingly trudged her way over to the gate entrance and gave the attendant her boarding pass.

Chapter 15

She could see the bright pink lights of The Flamingo flashing in the distance as the taxi driver sped through the streets toward the Las Vegas strip. She rolled her eyes. *Just once, would it kill them to let us book a decent hotel for ourselves?* she thought to herself. Once she landed, she had called Rob to tell him so and he was acting strangely aloof and disinterested. Despite numerous exclamations from him that he, and everything else for that matter, was all right, she didn't believe him, and the conversation was weighing heavy on her mind. After checking in, she rolled her suitcase through the flashing lights of the ringing casino and made her way up to her room. She text messaged Lily and her mother to let them know she had gotten there safe and sound. After using the bathroom and splashing some cold water on her face, she flopped down on the bed and turned on the television. She glanced at the alarm clock on the bedside table and saw it was almost 7 p.m. *Time for dinner*, she thought. As she was in no mood to go back out, she opened up the large black binder that included every bit of information you could think of about the hotel, including the room service menu. She forced herself to skip over the burger she really wanted, and went for the grilled Caesar salad instead, knowing that the week probably would not fair well for eating healthy. The salad wasn't too much of an improvement over the burger, but it was a little better for her, she convinced herself.

She hung up the phone after ordering and pulled out the itinerary she had printed out before she left. It was pretty full except for the next day when she would have to take a cab out to meet with the Henderson writer at 11 a.m., a couple hours there, then a dinner meeting at the Wynn, which she was looking forward to. There would be a lot of time to kill in between, and she planned on using it to get some sun by the pool.

The salad came quickly and she shoveled it into her mouth, starving after the nearly five-hour flight and half hour wait at baggage claim. After she ate, she took a shower and was out like a light by 9 p.m. She slept better than she had in months.

She was back at the hotel by 2:30 p.m. the next day. She squinted in the glaring sun as she made her way down to the pool and frowned once she saw how crowded it was. It seemed like every lounge chair was taken, so she made her way through the maze of people, taking care not to step on any oil-slicked body parts. A makeshift cave lined the left side of the pool, and there was about an inch or two of dry space next to it, right by the pool steps. It even provided a bit of shade. *What a find*, she thought to herself. She laid her towel and her bag down and took out the latest issue of Prerogative. She hadn't gotten a chance to look it over since the copies arrived at the office.

As she sat down on her towel, she put some suntan lotion on, bunched up her bathing suit cover-up into a pillow, and put it under her head. She laid down and brought the magazine up to her face, but the sun glare was too strong and she could barely see. She groaned and lifted herself up onto one elbow so she could scrounge around in her bag for her sunglasses.

“Is that the latest?” asked a male voice. She turned her head toward it too quickly, and was again blinded by the intense desert sun.

“Ouch,” she said under her breath and turned away, covering her eyes with her hand.

“Sorry,” the voice said.

“Oh, that’s okay,” she answered. She rubbed her eyes and looked back up toward the sky. He had positioned himself in such a way that he was blocking the sun. It helped, but she still couldn't get a good look at him. Now he was a black silhouette of a man with a bright light outlining him.

“I’m sorry, I’m really blinding you.” With that, he stepped out of the sun and sat down next to her on the edge of the pool, putting his feet in. He was an older man, probably in his 60s, she figured. He gave her a warm, closed-lip smile and held out his hand.

“I’m Andy.”

“Maryanne,” she answered, shaking his hand. She tried not to let the disappointment that was growing in her show, as she had been looking forward to a few solid hours of solitude before evening rolled around.

She hoped “Andy” wouldn’t overstay his welcome poolside.

“I didn’t quite catch what you asked me just now,” she said politely.

“Oh. I asked you if that was the latest,” he said, pointing at Prerogative. “The latest issue, I meant.”

“Oh! Well, yes, this is October, but November should be out in a few days.”

“Ah,” he said. He let his head drop and began to lightly kick his legs back and forth in the water. “I used to know the publisher of that magazine.”

“Really?” Maryanne said, unable to hide her

surprise.

He looked up at her and shook his head yes, again with a closed-lip smile. She tried to get a better look at him to see if she recognized him. He was short, probably not much taller than her five feet two inches. He had a horrible orange tan and his salt and pepper curls peeked out from a maroon baseball cap the color of which only emphasized the awful shade of his skin. She had to refrain from offering him some suntan lotion right then and there. No, she definitely did not know this man, nor had she ever met him.

"How did you know November would be out soon?" He looked at her with almost knowing eyes, which she could tell behind them he was starting to make the connection.

"I'm actually an editor there," she said, giving him a shy smile.

"Ahh," he answered, giving her the first sights of his too-white teeth, which again, did nothing to downplay his skin. He looked back out at the pool, still kicking his feet in the water. "Mariiaa . . ." he said slowly as he turned back to her with a question in his voice.

"Maryanne," she corrected him.

"Right. Sorry."

"That's okay!"

"So how long have you worked for Joseph?"

"About two years."

He shook his head knowingly. "So you've seen some things." He said it as a dreamy statement, rather than a question.

"Oh, yes. I mean, I've been everywhere I'd never thought I'd be able to get to even in my lifetime," she said, flashing him a wide grin, assuming that was what he was referring to. Her smile faded as she realized it was not.

"No, I mean, you've seen how he operates."

"How he operates?" she asked.

He turned back to her, seeming almost offended by her confusion. "Yeah, how he operates."

She sensed the attitude in his voice and it pissed her off. *Who does this guy think he is?* she thought to herself. *Did I even ask him to sit down next to me? I'm just trying to enjoy the sun here!*

He interrupted her thoughts.

"I'm sorry," he said, putting a hand on her forearm. "Let's start over." He threw both his hands in the air in mock surrender.

She narrowed her eyes and cocked her head to the side like a curious puppy. "Okay."

"You must have…a lot of…" he searched for the word, "respect for him."

"You're patronizing me," she said.

"Not at all," he answered, shaking his head back and forth.

"The only thing I have respect for in that man is his love for what he does. Other than that, I think he's arrogant, greedy, and biased. Oh, and not to mention shady, because his employees are the only ones he unleashes his true self onto. Everyone else thinks of him as this unbelievably giving, caring, religious philanthropist."

"Not everybody."

She looked at him quizzically, waiting.

"Joseph and I were on village council together in a past life."

"So you used to live in New York? Westchester?"

"Yes, ma'am."

"Wow. How'd you end up here?"

"Eh," he said, waving his hand at her. "Long, stupid story."

"I've got the time," she said, her interest now peeked.

He scoffed. "You'll be disappointed."

"Try me," she said, giving him a sweet smile.

"I grew up in the Hollow, born and raised there. My dad was always active in local politics, particularly passionate about the school system, as he was a retired professor. I loved the area myself, so I followed in his footsteps. Even ran for mayor when I was around your age, but never made it into office. So I settled for councilman positions for about ten years. Until I left the area when I was forty."

"Why'd you leave?"

He looked out at the pool for a second, then turned back to look at her. "I didn't like what I saw behind the scenes in town."

"What do you mean?" She was starting to get frustrated by his evasions.

He paused again, so long in fact, that she almost picked up the magazine again and started reading, thinking he might be indicating that the conversation was over.

"There was a reason I wasn't elected mayor, and it's pretty obvious why not."

She looked at the shimmering waters of the pool as she tried to figure out what he was getting at. She only knew the names of the past two mayors, each of which had served two terms, but that wouldn't even put her close to the time frame he was referring to. She looked up at him and shrugged her shoulders.

"Every mayor since 1975 has been related to each other; all part of the same family. Kind of like a more localized version of the Kennedys, but they keep it under wraps pretty well. Nobody really knows that. I'm surprised you didn't though," he said, smirking at her sideways.

"Well, I know the names of the current and previous mayor, but the last names don't match. They're not closely related then."

"Exactly. Second and third cousins, distant aunts, uncles, very close friends, etc. They keep it quiet, but definitely within this one circle of people."

"Huh! I didn't know that. I wonder if Lily…" she trailed off. Lily had grown up closer to the area than she did, but she still doubted her friend would know anything about this—if this were even true.

"I had a very successful campaign. My proposals would really have bettered the community as a whole, not just a select few." He made air quotes around the words *select few*.

"I had a great plan to clean up Beckett Street, which at the time was the name of the road that led down to the train station and the surrounding areas, by giving the unemployed people who were living there the very jobs that would rebuild their own neighborhoods."

"Yup, that's still the name of it."

"Anyway, people really embraced it, and I had a really strong following, but on election day…" he trailed off.

"What?"

"I saw that there was no such thing as a democracy in that town."

"What do you mean?" she asked, intrigued, leaning forward slightly.

"Well, voters proved themselves and showed up in droves. I made the rounds to the various polling spots and most of the people there were very encouraging, so I was pretty confident as the night came to a close. The stations were reporting that I was way ahead."

"So, what happened?"

"Well, I noticed by the time I got to the last few polling stations, I was being followed."

Maryanne raised her eyebrows. *Was this guy for real?* she wondered.

"Every time I went into a place, three men and one woman followed me in. They tried to be discreet about it, but I could tell what was going on. I had been warned."

Maryanne narrowed her eyes at him, as he continued.

"Anyway, I watched at the last couple of locations as they would come in and one of the poll workers would slide out from behind the table they were manning to meet one of the men outside where they exchanged folders. The others would distract the people left inside, talk to voters, mingle about." He stopped, glanced at her, and shrugged his shoulders.

"What do you mean you'd been warned?"

"Joseph," he said, and turned to look at her again, this time more directly.

"What about him?"

"He told me I would never get elected."

"He told you that?"

"Yes."

"Directly? Like, point blank, that's what he said?"

He scoffed and started shaking his head.

"What?" she asked, annoyed.

"You obviously don't know this man in the way you say you do."

Maryanne kept looking at him, making sure not to

waver in her gaze. She wanted to get to the root of this conversation.

He sighed. “Joseph was serving on the council when I ran. One day, after a meeting I had spoken at, he took me aside and asked if we could walk to our cars together. He told me he thought I was dead on with what I said during the meeting, whatever it was, and that he thought the town could really use someone like me in office, but I would never get elected, and that it was something that was out of my hands so I needed to give it up now.”

“What does that mean?”

“He wouldn’t explain. He just said that was all I needed to know. It wasn’t even an issue of how much fight I would need to have in me in order to gain control, because no amount would even make a dent. ‘The power was not on my wavelength,’ I think were the words he used. ‘It was about things I would never be able to understand,’ he said.”

“Again, what does that mean?” she repeated, throwing the hand she wasn’t resting on in the air.

“Money. I assume he was referring to money. That the office of mayor was not one that was up for grabs. It was more like a stock that was traded and sold, and no matter what any one candidate did to pursue it, the group who held it was so powerful and wealthy they would never allow it to be taken away. So they would always have the money and the willpower to hold onto it. Those like me who came along and tried to take it were just ants to be squashed. Nothing more.”

Maryanne kept staring at him. She hadn’t even known that Joseph had ever held any sort of public office. “So what do you think these three who were following you around to the polling stations were doing?"

"Who knows for sure, but whatever it was they did was securing the position of my competitor, Tyler Meuris. His father had served prior to him, so he, of course, was within the circle."

"So, why would Joseph try to discourage you from even running against them if it was so guaranteed?"

He gave her a very demeaning look that was unappreciated. "Again. Money."

"Joseph has plenty of money."

"Well, it's not just about money, young lady, it's everything that goes along with that money. Kind of an 'I scratch your back, you scratch mine' type of situation."

She shook her head to indicate that she understood. "So why did you stay on the council for so long then?"

"I foolishly, and stubbornly, thought I really could change things; that I could prove him wrong. Finally, I gave up. I saw just how tight a grip they had on that town. My wife is a doctor, and after our kids all left for college, we decided it was time for a change. We moved out here and she opened her own practice in Henderson that has been very successful. So successful, in fact, I really don't need to be working."

"Are you? Working, I mean?"

"You're looking at it," he said and opened his arms out in front of him in presentation. He started to laugh.

"You work here? At the hotel?" She couldn't help but allow the corners of her mouth to start to curl up into a smile, especially since the man was so openly unashamed that he was working at one of the tackiest hotels on the Las Vegas strip.

He nodded his head. "I'm a maître d' in one of the kitchens. I've always been a foodie. I spent a good forty years of my life as a pro bono lawyer, so a few years ago I decided it was time to start doing what I loved, rather than what I felt obligated to do. Something for me before I retired for good. You know I was surprised when I heard he was starting this magazine. It seems like such a convenient…front. A little too convenient and a little too obvious." He shook his head and looked down at his hands. He mumbled something.

"A front for what?" Maryanne asked.

"Nothing," he said and got up quickly. So quickly that it surprised her, and she had to lean back on both arms to let him get up and pass. "I was just on a break, and I like to come sit by the pool sometimes. I'm sorry I bothered you," he said, and bent down to shake her hand.

She studied him, puzzled, and slowly reached out her hand to shake his. "Not a bother at all," she said. "Nice to meet you, Andy," but he was already walking away.

"You, too," he threw over his shoulder.

She looked down at the gravely concrete and reviewed in her mind what just happened. Maybe she and Lily had been so preoccupied with politics and issues on a national level that they'd been ignoring what was going on right under their noses. Was it possible that their boss was one of the ringleaders of it all? What a great article it would make to examine how deeply corruption runs, even in the smallest of villages… *SNAP OUT OF IT!* she scolded herself. Stop thinking about how to turn this into an article and start thinking about what this could potentially mean. She had to tell Lily right away about what she'd just learned about their boss' past behaviors, but she had one other phone call to make before that.

“Ugh!” she grunted in frustration and checked her cell phone to see what time it was. She picked up her bag and her towel and threw them both over her shoulder. She walked fast through the maze of lounge chairs and beach towels, her phone still in hand. She lifted it up and searched through her contacts list until she found who she was looking for. She put the phone to her ear and waited for the line to connect as she dialed Ralph Ramsey’s cell.

“This is Ralph,” he answered.

“Hi, Ramsey,” she said. Nobody ever called him by his first name so she didn’t understand why he bothered to use it.

“Maryanne? How are you?” he asked jovially. She assumed he knew why she was calling.

“So what happened the other night?” she asked in a mock scolding tone.

“Ha! Your boss has developed quite the short fuse.”

“So it seems.”

“Seriously though, it was strange, Maryanne. I really wasn’t trying to provoke him, which I thought was pretty obvious, but I don’t know, I mean, is something else going on? It’s very unlike him…at least publicly.”

She ignored him and was walking so fast that all the palm trees, lounge chairs, and bikinis she was passing were beginning to blur together.

"Listen, Ramsey, do you know anything about this sort of, um, I don’t know, kind of mayoral dynasty in town?”

“Where’d you hear that from?”

“Some guy I met by the pool at the Flamingo.”

He laughed. “The Flamingo? Where are you? Vegas?” he asked.

“No, Ramsey, I’m in midtown. What do you think?”

"All right, all right, take it easy. What is going on with you guys? You're all usually so even-tempered."

"Whatever. Look, when I get back can we talk about it?"

"Talk about what?"

"The mayoral seat in town and how it is bought, not voted upon."

He paused for a minute. "Just call me when you get back," he said, in a more subdued tone.

"I'll do that." She had made it back to her room and hung up just as she walked through the door. She closed her cell phone and as the door shut behind her she noticed a white envelope on the floor with the Flamingo logo in the upper left hand corner. She'd been moving so quickly that seeing it was like hitting a brick wall.

Someone must have slipped it under her door while she was gone. She started to feel a little lightheaded from the heat. She picked it up, threw it on the bed, and then went to splash some cold water on her face. She walked back into the bedroom and sat down on the bed, making sure to take a few deep breaths. She picked up the envelope, opened it, and took out a folded piece of paper, also on hotel stationary. When she opened it up, she read a single line:

They meet in the cemetery.

Her eyes went wide. Who left this? An image of Andy popped into her brain. She walked over to the phone on the bedside table and dialed the front desk.

"Concierge."

"Oh, sorry, I tried to dial reception. Um, I'm staying in Room 425, and there was a note left under my door. I was wondering if anyone knew whom it was from. It wasn't signed or anything."

"Let me check, m'am." She heard him typing quickly, checking to see if her room had any messages attached to it, she assumed.

"Hmm, there doesn't seem to be any messages waiting for you, either voice or written. Perhaps the note is from a friend, m'am? Are you staying here with anyone?"

"Um, yeah, you're probably right. Thanks," she said, and hung up, feeling thoroughly annoyed at this point. She knew the note had to be from Andy. He worked fast, considering he had found out what room she was in and got the note delivered within the ten minutes or less it had taken her to get back. More importantly, what in the world did this mean? Who meets in the cemetery? What the hell was he talking about?

She got up and took a quick, cold shower. As she stepped out and her toes hit the cool tiles of the bathroom floor, none of the information swimming around in her head had managed to find any sort of order as she'd hoped it would. The cold water was supposed to have shocked it into making some sense. She walked back into the bedroom, drying her hair with a small towel as she did. She walked over to the note still lying on her bed.

They meet in the cemetery.

She felt her nerves start to take affect. She flashed back to one of her most recent visits, when as she was leaving, she thought she saw dark shadows heading toward the looming oak trees of the woods behind it. A chill went through her, and even though she was well aware that she was thousands of miles away from the place that was haunting her, she turned and examined the room behind her, making sure she was indeed alone.

She threw the note down on the bed and went back into the bathroom. She didn't have time for this nonsense and needed to get ready for her dinner meeting.

Chapter 16

Rob shuffled quickly down the stairs and into the subway station at 86th Street. The sun was starting to set as it was just about 5:30 p.m., but unfortunately, he wasn't heading home. He was on his way to a finance committee meeting downtown, close to the Brooklyn Bridge; a meeting that he should have been mentally preparing for, but Rob's mind was elsewhere. Maryanne had been in Vegas for just a couple of days now and he missed her terribly. He felt awful that she had had to travel in such a distressed state and that they hadn't been able to truly come up with a game plan for dealing with what was happening to her before she left.

Rob's own bizarre dreams had also begun a few months ago. He didn't reveal any of them to Maryanne, not yet. He didn't want to upset her further before she left for almost a week-long business trip, and he wanted to have some time to process what was happening to his girlfriend, and how and if it related to what he was going through. Rob had been hoping this was some sort of phase or something, and that it would all eventually fade away; but time had begun to prove him wrong, and somehow what was happening to Maryanne only made his own strange nightmares all the more real.

Rob's dreams involved more people. Usually groups in different settings, sometimes involving people he knew and were close to. Many of them had him questioning his trust in his loved ones and the others surrounding him at the time, wondering if they were part of some secret organization—an organization that was always after Rob in some way or another. He recalled his most recent dream, which had revealed more than he cared to know about this group that haunted his subconscious. His cousin, Alex, also his best friend, was with him in the lobby of a hotel, where they were having a couple of drinks to calm their nerves. They knew they were being chased and didn't know whom inside the hotel they could trust. The scene reminded him of that described so many times over and over again on a variety of news programs, documentaries, and tributes, of the Ritz Hotel; just as Princess Diana and Dodi Al-Fayed tried to figure out the best way to exit the building and escape the waiting throngs of paparazzi. They eventually ran into his cousin's girlfriend, who they couldn't tell if she was part of this group or cult that was chasing Rob or not. He never knew or understood why they were chasing him or why they wanted him. What he did find out during this dream was what happened to the "agents" if they weren't able to catch him. They were forced to slit their own throats.

He shuddered in his seat and squeezed his eyes shut at the vision as the 6 p.m. train he'd gotten on hit a curve and the rails screeched furiously against the rims of the train's wheels. He remembered the vision of the young man's blood spraying out of his neck and onto the fresh, white carpet of the hotel room he was sharing with Alex and Desiree, Alex's girlfriend. The young man had broken in during the dream, but Alex was armed, and as he held the shotgun to the man's head, he whipped out the knife. The other three were only able to see the glint of light hit it before he brought it to his throat and dragged it across his pale, white skin.

After the man killed himself and slumped to the

floor, there was a sudden pounding at the door. As the three turned their heads toward it, Rob woke up, realizing there really was someone pounding on his door. It was the night Maryanne's computer had come to life on its own to send her a message. Or so she says . . .

When Rob opened his eyes, he shook his head like a wet dog would, trying to rid himself of the visual. He rubbed his eyes with his hand to wake himself up. He wanted to be going to this meeting like he wanted a hole in his head. As he opened his eyes once more, as wide as he could, he happened to glance to his left. At the far end of the car, standing with his back toward the door that lead to the next car, was a frighteningly haggard man. His gray, wavy hair seemed almost wet, yet it hadn't been raining when Rob made his way into the subway. His eyes were blood shot and absolutely hooked on Rob, and Rob alone. They were filled with a wild desperation and determination that froze Rob with fear.

Rob locked eyes with the man for a few seconds. It wasn't very cold out yet, but he noticed the man's oversized, red parka that he was wearing. He broke his gaze away and looked around to see if anyone else was taking notice of this person, who certainly stuck out amongst the group of bored riders who weren't interested in anything else besides getting where they needed to go and getting off and out of the underground. No one else seemed to be paying him any heed. The train was slowing, and as it did, he turned to look back at the man who was still frozen and staring at him. Rob sensed that behind the man's eyes, he seemed almost panicked now, and his whole body seemed to lean slightly forward, as if ready to pounce, flee, or chase at any moment. As the train came to a stop at Grand

Central (42nd Street), the man pushed himself off the door he was leaning on and started to move toward Rob.

Rob's eyes went wide, and although he was a few stops north of where he needed to be, he was suddenly gripped by the need to get away from this man as quickly as he could. Rob stood as the doors opened, and just before he ducked out, he caught a glimpse of the man temporarily entangled in the fresh crowd of passengers that filed on. He weaved through the rush-hour crowd, trying to find the nearest staircase that would lead upstairs to the main concourse. Blond, curly hair, a large, brown and black messenger bag, man with glasses—his mind was registering certain details around him as he passed one weary New Yorker after another, trying not to seem too rushed or panicked, so as not to draw attention to himself. He glanced quickly behind him and he felt dizzy with fear as he saw the man was following him, also zigging and zagging through the throngs of people, weeding through with his arms as if those around him were piles of junk. He seemed to tower over everyone else, standing a full head and shoulders above the others, which wasn't lost on those around him. At first, those passing were simply annoyed and inconvenienced by the man who was rudely pushing his way through, but as they started to take notice of his size, they began to make it easier, parting to make way for him. He passed turned head after turned head of bugged-out eyes. Shit! He realized the man was gaining on him. He didn't know what the man wanted, but he did know that now was not the time to stop and think about why he was after him.

"Where the fuck are the stairs?" he muttered under his breath. He still hadn't made his way to a staircase that would lead him to the next level. He came upon a descending staircase that led down to a 7 train, but quickly looked up as a 4 express train came flying through the tunnel.

He crossed the platform and figured this was his best bet. If he was able to lose him, he would still be heading downtown and might even be on time for his meeting. As the train slowed, the crowd seemed to thin out a little, and Rob was able to walk further down the platform more easily, trying to put more distance between him and the stranger. He turned once again to see if the man was still behind him.

He wasn't.

Rob did a complete three-hundred-and-sixty degree turn to make sure he hadn't somehow circled around him. As he turned to his right, he saw the man coming toward him more quickly than before and still with the same desperate, locked stare. Rob gasped, but thankfully looked to his left just as the doors were about to close, shutting him off from his convenient escape. With one big step, he made it onto the train, the automatic doors brushing lightly against the sleeve of his jacket as he passed through by the skin of his teeth. A wave of relief washed over him that he wasn't willing to trust just yet. He wasn't sure if the man had been able to hop on before the doors closed. Although it was crowded, he didn't see him in the subway car. He decided not to take any chances and put some distance between them, hoping he was going in the right direction and that he'd evaded the man once again. He turned and passed between a few cars, looking behind him intermittently. When he didn't see the man continuing pursuit, he began to feel foolish. He took his hat off and wiped the sweat from his forehead, tucking his hair behind his ears. Could he be so stressed that he had imagined this?

He took a deep breath and closed his eyes for a moment, returned his hat to his head, and tried to let the tension leave his body. He put one hand on the metal pole in front of him and shrugged his shoulders, turning his head from side to side to crack his neck. He looked to his left and to his right, giving the two women flanking him polite smiles. A few more moments passed, and as the train flew by 23rd Street, he knew they would be at Union Square shortly. He looked around once more for good measure, and his breath caught in his throat as he saw the man standing at the other side of the car, towering above the other heads. Rob couldn't believe his eyes. The man must have caught up to him within the last few seconds, but he hadn't noticed him. This time the man wasn't staring at him. His right side was toward Rob, as he leaned both hands up against the metal pole that ran above the seats. A bit of a stretch for most, but the man's elbows hung very bent and loose. His head was in between his hands and his damp, graying waves of hair slightly covered the right side of his face. Rob could tell the man was looking at him sideways, finally understanding that his intense gaze had given him away to say the least. Rob turned away from him, his jaw set. He knew what to do. He got off quickly once the train stopped at Union Square, understanding the game that was being played; the man would not give himself up to the crowd, he knew that now. He relaxed to a degree, adrenaline replacing some of the fear he felt. He made a beeline for the police bag check table that he had always seen sitting outside the staircase leading up to the northeast exit of the square. He started to breath a sigh of relief when he passed through the turnstile. He would stand near the two or three policemen that would be manning it, pretending to look through his bag for something until the man got lost. If he lingered, he would simply alert the police to what was going on. Except, today, there was no checkpoint table. No policemen.

What the fuck! The one freaking day I need them! he thought.

He flew up the stairs past the spot where the checkpoint typically stood, mumbling to himself about mind control, conspiracies, and the facade of free will, more frustrated than anything at this point. He didn't bother to look behind him. *I can lose this asshole. It's fucking New York City for Christ's sake. If I can't get lost in the crowd then I deserve to get caught.*

He checked his watch, a few minutes past 6 p.m. He was late for the meeting already. He expected his cell phone to start ringing furiously soon, with Geffin calling to see where the hell he was, as Rob had told him he'd be right behind him as he left for the meeting. *Well, I was right behind him*, he thought. Rob didn't look behind him as he exited the station, walked over to cross Broadway, and headed to the northwest entrance of the subway. He went right back down, the whole time willing this to just not be happening anymore. As he went back down yet another flight of stairs to head back downtown again, he hesitantly turned his head as he went through the turnstile again. There he was. Rob caught a glimpse of the red parka as he turned back around to head for the trains. For a split second, Rob considered just confronting him. What could he possibly do?

As he turned, ready to put an end to this charade, he looked directly into the man's eyes, which bored straight through him. He shuddered, a new wave of fear taking over, and all but ran deeper into the station, desperate to get away. He heard the roar of a train pulling in and realized it was coming from the L train entrance below him, which he knew would take him across town. He didn't care where he was going at this point, as long as it would get him as far away as possible from this man, who seemed crazed to catch up with him. In his panic, he ridiculously felt relief over the fact that he didn't take a bag with him today, which would have weighed him down.

Thank God for small favors.

He flew down the stairs and into the train. The man was fast on his heels as the doors closed behind them. Rob's heart almost thudded right out of his chest, as they were so close to each other at this point, a physical attack was possible; but the man just stood there, and Rob held his ground. The two or three passengers in the car looked up, watching them with confused stares. Rob and the man held each other's gaze and sat directly across from each other, lowering their heads at the exact same time, as if they were trying to mirror each other.

Rob was mesmerized by the man's eyes, and all that lay behind them. He couldn't look away and couldn't speak either. He sensed the man felt the same way. Rob knew the man was trying to get him alone and that he could not let that happen if he valued his life.

Once the train came to a stop, he would only have a half a second, maybe less. As it started to slow down, he tensed the muscles in his knees, getting ready to sprint, the whole time not taking his eyes off the man. He thought he might have an advantage as the man seemed almost in a trance as he stared back. The other passengers in the car stared at him, trying not to let their fear become too obvious. The second the doors began to part, Rob made a break for it, which made the man snap out of it. Rob was sitting directly across from the doors while the man sat right next to them, and as Rob ran passed him, the man reached out to grab Rob's coat sleeve. Rob jerked it away and ran blindly through the station across the platform, hell bent on reaching the staircase that was marked as the path to the F train. He had no idea where that would take him, but he was willing to risk that in order to try to reach a train that the man wouldn't catch as well.

He saw those around him looking at him with wide eyes, frightened for him, but he was sure more so for themselves as they wondered what he was running from. They ran out of Rob's way, dropping things and tripping as they did. He slammed right into a short, balding man in a suit, who was so immersed in the documents he was reading, he hadn't even realized Rob was coming at him. As he knocked the man out of the way, the papers flew into the air, and Rob ran through them as they swayed lazily back and forth to the floor.

"You fucking asshole!" the guy screamed after him. The man in the parka raced by him and he followed that up with, "What the fuck is the matter with you two?"

"Help!" Rob screamed. "I don't know why he's chasing me!"

"Maybe he's in love with you," said one of two men who were walking together as Rob ran passed them. They both doubled over with laughter at that.

"How sweet," choked out the other one. "Look at the lovebirds chasing each other." With that he was overwhelmed with another spasm of laughter.

Only in New York can someone be chased and everyone around thinks it's fucking funny! he thought.

He could still hear the two men laughing, and the anger he felt toward them was giving him a fresh rush of adrenaline. He turned his head and saw that he was quite far ahead of the man now, who he could see even from a distance, was sweating profusely and whose eyes seemed to glow almost red, becoming even more bloodshot than before thanks to the chase. Rob panted as he ran, trying to maintain his lead. He finally reached the F train platform and saw there was a train sitting there with the doors about to shut.

"NO!" he screamed and ignored the last four steps of the staircase, jumped over the railing, and threw his arm into the crack of air that was still left between the closing doors. They slammed onto his arm, which stung immensely, and he felt the blood stop where they smashed against his veins. He screamed in pain, but the move had served its purpose. The doors popped back open for Rob to squeeze through. As he did, he heard the man's footsteps behind him on the staircase. He turned to see the doors close again and the man flying down the stairs. Just as he reached the doors, the train started to pull away. The man scowled and slammed a fist into the side of the train, but even more gratifying was the officer he saw sauntering toward the man. As the train disappeared into the tunnel, the last thing he saw was the man pointing toward the train, saying something to the officer whose back was now turned to it.

"Yes!" Rob said, pulling in a fist. He leaned his neck back and stared at the ceiling, breathing hard. "Thank God!" He took his hat off once again and wiped the sweat off his face with his sleeve.

As he sat down, he looked around and realized most of the car was staring at him. He pursed his lips. "Sorry," he said, sheepishly, with an embarrassed laugh. Most lost interest quickly, some shaking their heads as they looked away.

Now where the Hell am I going? he wondered. He looked around the train, but there was no digital marquee or a sign with the lineup of stops. They quickly pulled into West 4th. He checked his watch as he got off and saw that it was past 6:30 p.m. By the time he found his way back to the meeting, it would be past 7 p.m. and it would be practically over. *Not worth trying to make it,* he thought to himself. He climbed the stairway out of the subway station and made a deliberate and final step onto the sidewalk. As the cool breeze of the night air hit his face, the enormity of what just happened hit him like a ton of bricks.

He looked down and let out a quiet sob. When he looked up a couple of tears had begun to stream down his face. He wiped them away and took out his cell phone. He sniffed and tried to compose himself as he opened it, dialed, and waited for Geffin to pick up.

"Hello?"

"Geffin, it's Rob."

"What happened? Where are you? We're just wrapping up." There was a panicked edge to his voice.

Rob let loose a few sobs.

"Rob, what happened? Talk to me."

"I was just chased."

"Chased? What do you mean? By who?"

Rob leaned against the railing to the subway. "I don't know." His breathing was unsteady.

Geffin paused for a moment before speaking again. "Look, are you okay? Do you need us to come to you?"

"No," Rob said, quickly straightening up and pushing his chin out, shaking his head. Wiping the last of his tears away, he said, "No, I'm fine." The last thing he wanted was to have Geffin and Norman fawning all over him.

"Listen, where are you right now?"

"West 4th."

"All right, you have to go file a police report. You understand me? You go straight there. Are you hurt?"

"No, I'm fine, just really shaken."

"Okay. I'm serious. Find the nearest station. Now. If we don't see you tomorrow, I'll give you a call. If you want to stay home feel free."

Rob didn't answer, he was trying to catch the breath that had gotten away from him.

"Rob?"

"Okay! Yes, Geffin. Thanks."

"All right. Be careful, please."

"Okay."

He hung up the phone and looked around. He was completely unfamiliar with the area. He wouldn't even know where to start in his search for a police station. At that point, exhaustion took over. He had absolutely no energy to even attempt to find one, or even just a lone cop. If he could, he would have lied down right in the street and slept this off. He knew he should've listened to Geffin, but he was too tired and out of it. He would get himself back to Grand Central and try to find a policeman to talk to there. He couldn't think of anything else at the moment other than getting himself home.

He'd barely taken one step back into the station when his phone rang. He looked down at it and saw that it was Maryanne. He stared at it for a few moments, trying to decipher before the call reached his voicemail if picking up was a good idea right now. No, he decided. He knew if he answered her now he wouldn't be able to hold it together and would be forced to tell her what happened. His breakdown would only make her panicked and worried herself, enough so that she would probably fly back home immediately to be with him. He told himself to wait until he was home, safe and sound, before calling her back. Even then it would be difficult not to tell her what happened tonight.

He got back underground and checked his watch again. 6:45 p.m. He knew there was a 7:23 p.m. train coming out of Grand Central. He might not be able to make that, but he knew the blue ACE line would go up to 125th Street, where the train would also stop, probably around 7:33 p.m. That he could make. He got on the A train heading uptown and slumped into the closest seat. He leaned his head back against the wall, a move that would typically skeeve him (and anyone else for that matter) out, but he was too tired to care. His mind was blank for the better part of ten minutes until he started to replay the recent events in his head.

He pictured the man who had been chasing him again, flipping through a running catalog in his brain of people he knew, people he barely knew, people he may have recently met, or people he noticed. Nothing was even vaguely familiar or ringing a bell. Then he crossed over into the realm of ridiculous and started to rack his brain to see if there would be any reason why someone would be after him, and then his thoughts crossed over into the horrifying. He asked himself why and if someone would want him hurt, or worse, dead. Could it be a wronged SfH client?

No one wants you dead, asshole, he thought to himself. He didn't run his fingers through his hair or drop his face into his hands. Rob's anxieties, no matter how weighty, were always strictly internal, except for his facial expressions and the depth his eyes took on. If Maryanne were here, she would have had a field day.

"What's wrong?" she'd asked him once on a night

when he'd been particularly quiet, brooding as usual about a grueling workday.

He turned to her, surprised and almost offended, his arms crossed stiffly across his chest, his shoulders hunched. "Nothing!"

She'd frowned and turned back to the TV. "Doesn't seem like nothing."

"What do you mean? I'm fine!"

"This is your face right now," she'd said, and as she turned back to him, she pursed her lips out like a duck and creased her forehead, giving him a goofily confused and frustrated look. He'd laughed heartily in spite of himself. She always saw right through him.

"Look, I've told you a million times. You can't go by the look on my face. It means nothing." He smiled slyly as he knew that couldn't have been any farther from the truth.

"Yeah, right."

He smiled, remembering that scene. Suddenly, all of his feelings for her piled up into a huge lump in his throat that was making it almost hard to swallow, only deepening the growing crease between his eyes. What he wouldn't give to just be laughing with her right now somewhere, anywhere, but here.

He saw they had just passed 103rd Street, which helped him snap out of it. Shortly, they'd be at 125th. He was on schedule and should make the Metro North train he was targeting with quite a few minutes to spare. When they reached 125th, he knew he was in trouble the second he stepped off the subway. He looked to his left and saw a prostitute making her way down the platform. He looked to his right, and as he made his way toward the exit, he saw her target customer: a very handsome, very well dressed businessman, who couldn't look any more annoyed by where he was at the moment. He barely avoided her by sidestepping quickly onto the train that Rob had rode in on. Rob quickened his pace, hoping she wouldn't decide to go after him next. As he made his way out of the station, a man with a thick, woven, beige ski cap pulled down over only the left side of his forehead, covering a white do-rag, and wearing a large green canvas jacket walked by him, smoking a large blunt, the embers ablaze. Rob slowed, staring at it as he passed, amazed at how unabashedly brazen the man was being.

When he finally exited the station, Rob looked around confused. "Fuck!" he said loudly, throwing his hands up in frustration as he realized what he had done. It caused a couple people to turn and take notice of him, but certainly caused no one any alarm, not in this neighborhood. He'd been so out of it, he didn't realize he was riding up to the wrong side of 125th. He was at St. Nicholas Avenue, when he needed to be at Lexington Avenue in East Harlem. He looked around for the downtown entrance, and as he did, he was thankful he was getting back underground. Once he spotted it, he started to walk toward it, but something stopped him in his tracks. He knew who it was the second he was grabbed from behind. The man with the red parka grabbed him in a headlock and dragged him backward. He was headed for an alley between two red brick buildings. Rob choked and scratched at the man's arms, but it was no use, seeing as they were covered by the parka. Rob's legs went out from under him as he tripped over garbage bags that were in the alleyway. As he was dragged, he saw a couple of people pass by the opening and glance in. They saw what was happening, but didn't even attempt to stop and help him.

How the hell did he find me, or catch up to me for that matter? he thought to himself. He looked around for some sort of weapon, anything he could use against the man, but there was nothing but a few empty and crinkled paper cups lying at his feet he had managed to pull from the garbage.

For the first time the man spoke, interrupting his thoughts. "Did you think you got away from me? Huh?" His voice was gritty and hoarse, matching perfectly with his appearance, and then something very strange happened. The man let him go.

He stood Rob up, directly across from him on the other side of the alley, even going as far as to dust him off and smooth his hair with his hands, all the while remaining at arms length. Rob just stared at him, breathing heavily and taking in the precious air, his head tilted back, but his shoulders slumped in defeat.

"Listen, I came as a messenger. You can't escape it." The man paused for effect before saying, "They need you." As he said that, he took his left hand and placed it over his heart. Rob saw that he was wearing a ring on his middle finger. *Just like my dream…*Rob thought, his mind fading as panic set in for the hundredth time that night.

That was it. He decided he was putting an end to this charade once and for all. The man opened his mouth to speak again, but Rob didn't let him. With all the force and strength he had left, he punched the man in the stomach. He let out a yowl that caught in his throat, and as he dropped to his knees, Rob took his head and slammed his face as hard as he could into the metal fence that was, for some reason, separating them from the other side of the alley. Rob climbed over the six-foot fence, figuring the more obstacles he could put in the man's way, the better. As he got over the top and jumped to the ground, he turned to run, and this time, he didn't look back; but apparently, Rob's defenses weren't enough to put the man completely out of commission. As Rob ran down the alley, his focus hell bent on breaking through to the safety of the street at the end, he had one final message for him.

"If you value your life," he shouted, before pausing to cough, "and hers!" he shouted down the alley even louder to make sure Rob heard him, "you'll keep your mouth shut!" He began to cough and sputter.

As Rob hit the street, he could barely make out the sounds of the man vomiting where he lie behind him.

Chapter 17

In spite of recent events, Maryanne couldn't help but be in a good mood. She was in the middle of an unbelievably delicious dinner with writer Taylor Kiptch at the Wynn, one of the newer hotels in Vegas that represented part of the town's reinvention and displayed the type of luxury they now wanted to be known for, rather than the hokey, side-show venues whose days had come and gone.

The interiors of the Wynn could be likened to an adult version of Alice in Wonderland, with luscious greenery and oversized butterfly and flower sculptures everywhere. The movie "Eyes Wide Shut" also came to mind for Maryanne, as the nightclubs and restaurants Taylor had shown her unveiled a sense of pageantry that made them seem like sexy costume parties in remote hideaways.

She took a sip from her glass of Chardonnay and looked around the restaurant they were in. The stonewalls and their integrated water features were calming, yet she was still worried that Rob hadn't answered his phone earlier. She shook it off quickly, convincing herself everything was fine, and that he had just gotten stuck late at work. She was sure he would give her a call as soon as he got home. She turned her attention back to Taylor.

"So, let's discuss the piece you wanted to write," she said, taking out a notebook and pen. He raised his eyebrows and smiled devilishly in response. She lifted her glass again, hoping it would shield the rolling of her own eyes. He was nice enough. He'd gone out of his way to drive from Henderson to pick her up from the Flamingo and then drive them to the Wynn, but he was very young and entirely too cocky.

There was some hope behind his eyes, and even some of his words, that suggested he would grow out of it though. She had read some of his previous articles and liked what she saw, as did Lily, so they thought they'd give him a chance. He put his elbows on the table and folded his hands in front of him.

"Well, as you know, prostitution is legal in Nevada."

"Yes," she answered, dryly.

"It's an extremely lucrative business for the state, bringing in about thirty-four billion dollars a year; because of that it is treated as a *business*," he said, emphasizing the word.

"I'm sure every low-life pimp, madam, and hooker out there will tell you the same thing, that they are professionals and what they are a part of, or run, is a streamlined, efficient business, that helps society run smoother," she said, shrugging her shoulders. It was her turn to play devil's advocate. She wanted to break down his argument as much as she could to make sure it was valid and that he could stand behind it and craft it into a truly engaging and fresh article, with a viewpoint that others hadn't heard before.

"Yes, but any other establishment out there is a 'prostitution ring,'" he said, using air quotes around the word, "simply because of the nature of what it is. By that, I mean, illegal. The resources that are available to us here in Nevada are just not possible for those in other states. Let me clarify that by professional, I don't mean just any seedy escort service run by some fifty-year-old, can't get laid, pot-bellied loser out of his mom's basement. What I'm pushing are quite upscale, classy organizations that only provide the best, cleanest, talent out there."

Maryanne narrowed her eyes at him. "Excuse me?" That could possibly have been the most disgusting language he could have used.

"Well, you know what I mean," he said, gesturing at her and smiling another dazzling smile. He took a big gulp of his beer.

"No, I don't actually. Enlighten me." She was beginning to fear this meeting was going to turn out to be a huge waste of time. If he had been arguing that legal prostitution brought in more money to the state to help other programs that truly needed it, such as those that addressed poverty or education programs, she would have been willing to work with him in sending out his message. If he'd said that it would be more beneficial to work with these businesses, in order to make it a safer institution for the women involved, rather than waste the money on enforcement against it that is obviously not working, as prostitution is probably the oldest business in the history of time, she could understand his point of view. She didn't have to necessarily agree with what a writer wanted to say, but she had to be able to understand his or her side. She was starting to see she would neither understand nor empathize with his side.

"Well, statistics show that men generally prefer a certain type of…um…provider." Now, he was uncomfortable. Maryanne was not taking to his suggestions like he thought she would.

"Huh?" She was getting close to flying off the handle. "What are you talking about, Taylor? I don't have time for these word puzzles."

He sighed and answered her quickly, as if he wanted to get the words through his lips as fast as they could tumble out after each other. "Customers prefer a certain type of woman, especially when they are paying the type of prices they would at the establishments I'm suggesting that reign supreme in the industry."

She stared him down, waiting.

"They want white women!" He kept his eyes down on the table.

She swallowed and pushed her hair off her forehead. She aligned her silverware, then folded her hands in front of her and looked at him. "What kind of a publication do you think we are exactly?"

"One that lets writers say whatever they want, even when they've been turned away by all the others."

"Okay. Well, what type of article did you think you were going to get away with? One that suggests that successful, high-class escort services should be allowed to operate wherever, and whenever they want, because those are the ones that provide the type of beautiful, insanely hot, strictly white pussy that men prefer when they're cheating on their wives and girlfriends?"

He looked up quickly, eyes wide. "No! I mean…ugh, no, not exactly," he said, frustrated and stuttering. "Look, I went over this with Jos—"

"Excuse me?" She cut him off before he was able to get Joseph's full name out.

"Yes," he said, seemingly confused. "I ran all this by Joseph, and he was very open to what I was saying." He paused for a moment to gulp. "Am saying, here." He kept his eyes averted.

"Wait a minute, are you telling me you have been in contact with Joseph Goldberg, our publisher, about this article, and he agreed to it? I thought you met Lily at the writer's conference here a couple weeks ago and that's how you got connected with us."

"Well, yes, but not initially. I'd met Joseph a year ago at an event that the two new Nevada senators held, hosting various members of the media. I really don't remember how I got an invite," he said, waving his hand in the air.

"I don't care how you did either. So you are telling me that you ran this article by my boss and he was all for it? Let's be painfully blunt here, what you planned to write for us and get published in the magazine did have the general tone I just described?"

"Yes," he said quietly, his shoulders curling, sort of shrinking into himself at this point. "Sort of."

"So, then what?"

"Well, Joseph gave me his card and said to get in contact with Lily, but I got so overloaded with assignments in the months between that I never got around to it. Then I saw that she would be speaking at the conference, so I just approached her there."

Maryanne stared at the table for a few seconds, her face stone. He occasionally stole a couple of glances her way to see if she had softened at all. Unfortunately for him, she did not.

"I have to go." She got up and threw her napkin down on her chair.

He looked up at her horrified. "Oh, come on, don't go! At least finish your meal!" He caught her hand as she lowered it to swallow the last of her wine. Her eyes widened and she shot him a look that made him shocked that his own didn't simply melt right in the sockets.

"Let. Go," she said icily.

He did and sat back in his chair with a huff as she

picked up her bag, only forcing her to throw him another evil stare. "Oh, I'm sorry. Am I frustrating you?" she said, raising her voice at this point.

The fear had left him and now sheer annoyance had taken its place. He shook his head, and his mouth was set in a firm line when he looked back to meet her eyes. "Not at all," he said.

"Well, perhaps this little piece of information will push you over the edge: We won't be publishing your article!" she yelled as she leaned in even closer to his face. She grabbed the light jacket she brought off the back of her chair and stormed off. She looked back as she made it to the door and saw him staring at her, nostrils flared as his hands sat one on each tailored pant leg. He was leaning back, legs apart, in an easy position, but there was nothing easy about the expression on his face.

She left the restaurant and made her way to the entrance of the Wynn. She was irritated even further as she had to make her way past the line of excited, scantily-clad twenty-somethings waiting to enter Tryst, the hotel's nightclub. A humongous man-creature reached out his overly-muscled arm and grabbed her shoulder as she passed. His t-shirt was so tight that she was afraid it was going to cut off his circulation.

"Hey, where do you think you're goin' in such a rush?"

She jerked her arm away and moved even faster toward the sanctuary of the exit.

"Aw, come on, party with us!" he yelled after her. She could hear his friends roar with laughter. She didn't get a chance to do a dramatic burst through the doors, as one soldier in the army of doormen that lined the entrance had seen her coming from a mile away. He opened the large, golden-framed door for her with perfect timing and precision for her to ease gracefully through it. Once she was outside, she took a deep breath of the unseasonably cool night air. She dug in her purse for her cell phone. Luckily, there was no cab line, as now was the time when everyone was just arriving for dinner, drinks, and dancing—not heading away. She lifted her cell phone to her ear. Lily picked up just as another doorman opened the door to a cab, and Maryanne slid into the backseat.

"Hello?"

"The Flamingo," Maryanne told the cab driver and turned her attention back to Lily on the phone.

"We have a problem."

Chapter 18

"I'm sorry for putting you up to that. I should've known that little shit would've been a problem after meeting him."

"No, it's all right. I could handle him. It was what he told me that sent me over the edge," Maryanne said with a scoff. She'd explained the day's events to Lily on her way back to her hotel, including the note. She did not say anything to her, however, about her visits to Cecily's grave.

The elevator to her floor opened, and she took a quick glance at herself in the mirrors that surrounded her inside it before she stepped out and made her way down to her room.

"So, wait a minute, what was the other guy's name again?"

"Andy. I mean I don't know which was worse, hearing that Joseph was the main catalyst behind a manipulated political scandal or…"

Lily cut her off. "So you just so happened to meet a guy who used to live in the Hollow while you are more than halfway across the country by the pool at a hotel in Vegas?"

Maryanne paused in the middle of her room, not sure exactly what Lily was getting at. For a minute she wondered if her friend was questioning her honesty.

"Well, when you put it that way, I guess it does sound pretty crazy."

"Ah, yeah," Lily said with a little laughter in her

voice.

Maryanne dropped her purse on the floor and sat down on the bed. “So what are you saying,” she asked, trailing off. “You think he was, I don’t know, planted here or something?”

“Well, I don’t know, I’m not exactly saying that. That’s just about as ridiculous as coincidentally meeting someone in Las Vegas who was actually involved in small-town politics with Joseph.”

“Yeah, did you know that? I didn’t even know he was ever on the town council.”

“He’s mentioned it once or twice. Never really talked about it in detail though.”

“Hmmm.”

“Yeah, seriously, maybe now we know why. All right, I’ll try to bring these things up to him.”

“I don’t know about that,” Maryanne said. The last thing she wanted was for Joseph to become more irritated by them and think they were kicking up more shit.

“Why?” Lily asked.

“Well, I mean, I don’t know. Don’t you think we should keep this stuff to ourselves for right now? If he’s as evil as he’s shaping up to be, I don’t think we want him knowing we’re on to him.”

“I guess.”

“I don't know, let’s just not tell him until I get back and we can talk to Ramsey and get a little more information.”

“All right, if that’s what you want.”

“I think that’s best for right now.” Maryanne glanced at the clock, and then turned back to the phone. “Ugh, I’m going to try to go find this Andy guy, see what more I can get out of him, and see if it was really him who left the note."

"Which restaurant is he in?"

"I don't even know. I've got to try to find him though."

"They meet in the cemetery," Lily mumbled. "What does that mean? This is all kind of freaking me out," she said, suddenly. "Maybe you need to come home."

"No, I'll finish the trip. I'm fine. It's not like anyone's threatened me. You're the one who needs to be careful. Our God's gift boss might not exactly be who we thought he was." Maryanne also wasn't ready, just yet, to tell Lily about her own cemetery visits.

Lily laughed, probably at the thought of Joseph actually being dangerous to anyone but himself. Maryanne had to admit it was a laughable notion, in a way. She wished she could convey to Lily that she shouldn't be as easy going about this as she was acting.

"Okay," Lily said. "Just let me know what happens."

"I will."

"Talk to you later."

"Bye."

Maryanne sat back against the mountain of pillows on her bed to set herself for a moment. Then she swung her legs off of the bed and pushed herself up and off with a little bounce, heading for the door. She went downstairs to the concierge desk, realizing she knew nothing about Andy except his first name, his physical description, and that he worked at a restaurant in the hotel. Finding him might prove to be difficult. She approached the desk, not knowing exactly how to start. She waited for the concierge to acknowledge her. He was putting some things away underneath the counter, but when he looked up, he smiled.

"Good evening, miss, is there something I can help

you with?" he asked, folding his hands at the waist. Maryanne thought he kind of looked like a flight attendant in his crisp, blue suit, with some sort of medal medallion pinned over his heart.

"Um, yeah," she answered slowly, placing her forearms on the counter in an attempt to look extra casual. "I'm trying to locate one of your employees. I met him by the pool today, and I need to speak with him further."

He gave her a sly smile, probably assuming this was some sort of love match Maryanne guessed. "Okay," he answered, positioning himself at his keyboard. "What is his name?" he asked her, a little too eagerly.

"Well, see that's the problem. He never gave me his last name. His first name is Andy, and he said he's a maître d' at one of the restaurants here." Maryanne cringed slightly after she had explained, once she saw the puzzled look on the man's face. She was sure his theory of some sort of romantic hook-up had dissolved quickly. He obviously knew the man.

"Yes, I know Andy. Kind of short, curly, dark hair, some grey right? Very, um, tanned skin?" he asked, raising an eyebrow at her. The embarrassment was getting to be almost unbearable for Maryanne.

"Yeah, that's him!" she said, pointing at the concierge in a game-show host-esque way.

"Well," he said, finally smiling again, "you won't have to go far." He gestured over her shoulder. Maryanne turned around and saw what seemed to be a classic old Italian restaurant nestled just beyond the check-in desks and a few rows of slot machines. The name was Tremonto's. Somewhere between classy and family-friendly, it seemed like a perfect fit for Andy. Maryanne turned back to the concierge and pointed at

Tremonto's raising her eyebrows as if to ask: this is it?

"Yep. Just ask if Andy is available. I'm sure he's hard at work though, so you might have to settle for an after-hours meeting," he said, smiling mockingly at her. She gave him a wane smile of her own in response, and then turned for the entrance of the restaurant.

When she got closer, she realized just how crowded the place was. Waiters whizzed back and forth in between each other with plates held high above their heads. It looked like some sort of Broadway musical at work. The line for a table was quite extensive, and there were a lot more families than she'd realized. There was a particularly loud one at the head of the line, with a mom who was attempting to separate her daughter and son who were both screaming, crying, and pushing each other. She noticed older, white-haired couples at the tables and some middle-aged couples sprinkled throughout; a scene from the old Vegas that the new developers and promoters were desperately trying to kill off. Maryanne frowned and looked away, shaking her head. She marched up to the hostess table, pushing her way through the crowd. A very tiny girl, who was one of two manning the table, with breasts that were way too big for her body, looked up at her with a very annoyed look. She was probably wishing she was dancing on a platform in one of the more swanky nightclubs in town, telling herself that as soon as she put in a few more months at this dump she would be able to do just that, Maryanne could only assume.

"M'am, there's a line," she said, exasperated.

"I know. I don't need a table," Maryanne said, hurriedly. "I need to talk to your maître d', Andy?"

"Okay, Allison will show you to your table now," she said to quite a large party. "He's working, obviously."

"Well, can you just tell him that Maryanne with Prerogative magazine is here to see him?" Suddenly Maryanne had her attention. She turned on her immediately with a degrading and disbelieving look.

"You're the press?" she asked, putting one hand on her bony hip.

Maryanne breathed out and pressed her lips together tightly before answering. "Yes."

"Ugh, come with me," she said, and turned on her heels with a menu still in her hand. It took Maryanne a second to respond, so she had to move quickly to catch up at first. They weaved through crowded tables, waiters, and patrons who were up and about. *God, this place is packed*, she thought to herself. Once they reached the kitchen door, they barely missed slamming into a waiter coming out of it with three plates running up each arm.

"Woah!" he said. "Sorry." He sidestepped them gracefully and made his way swiftly over to his table.

The hostess caught the door just as it was coming back to hit her in the face and walked through it. Maryanne was close behind. Once entering the kitchen, it was like they literally hit a wall of hot air. Maryanne felt like she was instantly drowning in sweat, but she made sure to keep her concentration trained on the hostess who was still leading the way.

"Andy!" she yelled over to her left, as she tossed the menu she was holding to a chef standing to her right. He was caught off guard, but didn't let it drop just the same.

"Geez, Destiny," he said and buried his face in the menu.

Maryanne had to stifle a laugh. *Destiny?* she thought. Adorable. She watched Destiny disappear into the depths of the kitchen. When she was done rolling her eyes, she looked to her left and saw Andy, dressed in a suit and bowtie, staring at her with an expression that seemed like fear. He eventually broke his stare, sighing as he walked over to her, grabbed her wrist, and dragged her into a supply closet.

"Ouch!" Maryanne said once they were inside. She pulled her wrist away.

He turned to her and asked accusingly in a hushed tone, "What are you doing here?"

"What did that note mean?" she asked, stiffening up so she could meet him eye to eye, and put her hands on her hips. He paused for a barely recognizable moment, which Maryanne took as proof that he knew what she was talking about.

"What note?" he asked.

"Don't play dumb! 'They meet in the cemetery.' What did that mean?" They both stared at each other in silence.

"Please," Maryanne said, an edge of desperation to her voice now. "I have to know."

Andy gave in momentarily to the pleading in her deep brown eyes, then thought better of it. "I am working!" he said and tried to push past her out the door. She didn't let him.

"Okay, fine, then let's talk after you're off," she said, putting a hand on his chest and gently pushing him back.

He paused for a moment, but then pushed past her again, succeeding this time. "No!"

He walked out of the supply closet and back into the sweltering heat of the kitchen. Maryanne wondered how he wasn't sweating in that monkey suit. *Must be the shield of his leather skin,* she thought.

She refocused herself. "Andy! Please!" She grabbed his shoulders from behind and spun him around. "I work for this man. I need to know everything you know about Joseph. This is all I've ever wanted to do with my life, and if I'm working for a fraud, that means my friends are too, and everyone in town. Hell, everyone within walking distance of a synagogue in Westchester County is being deceived! We are only perpetuating the deception through Prerogative on a much bigger level!"

Andy stared at her, embarrassed, confused, and obviously scared. She felt bad doing this to him in his place of employment, but she had no choice. If he got away from her, it wouldn't be hard for him to lose her in a city like this one. She needed to know whom it was that met in the cemetery. Andy frowned and wiggled out of her grasp. She followed him out of the kitchen and over to a small nook that held a register, some menus, trays, and glasses. They were pretty much hidden away from the patrons. A waitress who was entering in some orders at the computer raised an eyebrow at them as they entered, but she seemed pretty disinterested. She left quickly.

"Listen," he said, pointing a hand in her face. "I said way too much this afternoon. I don't know what I was thinking. I think it's best if you just forget we ever met and we both go our separate ways." As he spoke, the crease between Maryanne's eyes grew deeper and she started to shake her head in disbelief. This got more bizarre by the second. Andy had pulled a complete one-eighty from this afternoon.

Seeming so nonchalant and forthcoming with information, he had been almost glad to be releasing it. Now the fear and anxiety that was seeping from his words was completely confusing, and scaring Maryanne as well. She got a hold of herself and tried a calmer approach.

"Andy, I don't understand this. Why? Why can't you explain anything to me?"

He stared back at her with a hard expression on his face.

"Who meets in the cemetery?" she said again, with more force and a shrillness to her voice than she had intended. This time, a waiter and a couple of diners turned to look their way and into the tiny hallway they were standing in.

"That's it!" Andy said, shaking his hand and crossing his arms in the air like an umpire declaring a slider safe. He stalked off, but he wasn't able to clear the corner completely before Maryanne asked him this one last question:

"Who is Cecily Reynolds?"

Andy stopped dead in his tracks. He let his head drop slightly, and Maryanne saw his arms slump to his sides in defeat. He turned around to look at her, breathing heavy, his eyes glassy.

"It wasn't a coincidence that we met today, was it?" she said, staring at him accusingly. "You didn't just happen to walk by the girl with the issue of Prerogative magazine, the publisher of which you just so happened to serve on city council with in a town halfway across the country? You were sent here, weren't you?"

He gave her a hurt expression, as if she'd just kicked him in the gut. He shook his head once again and took one small step forward, leaning in. "If you come near me again, I'll call security on you." He spun around and turned the corner out of the hallway. She stared after him, frozen in place. That was the last time she ever saw him.

As Maryanne stumbled back up to her room in a daze, the ka-ching of the slot machines and boisterous crowds she passed through, weren't enough to break through her stupor, but magically her cell phone ring was. She looked down and saw Kayla was finally returning her call. She quickly opened the phone and lifted it to her ear.

"Hello?"

"Hey." Kayla's voice was subdued and indifferent.

"Hey! Where have you been? You are not going to believe what has been going on!"

"Yeah?"

Maryanne stared out in front of her, confused by Kayla's attitude.

"Yeah, listen why didn't you call me to tell me about what happened with Joseph?"

Kayla sighed. "I know, I'm sorry. I was out one day, and when I got back I was literally buried in paperwork. I really didn't even get the details until just now. I caught a glimpse of the front page and couldn't believe it, but before I got a chance to let you know I got slammed. I just dug my way out a little while ago."

"Oh." Maryanne softened. She knew how tough Kayla had it at work.

"Where are you right now?" Kayla asked as the noise level began to grow.

"Vegas. I'm in the Flamingo this time."

"Oh, God."

Maryanne couldn't see it, but knew she had rolled her eyes. Then Kayla took a deep breath and started. "I was going to call Lily next if I didn't get you, just to let her know what is going on. So apparently, he made that scene, stormed away from the table and this other guy followed him out. Stacy follows them both, watched them have a short conversation in the lobby, then saw them leave together. She was able to even tail them by car and she said they ended up back at your offices and went upstairs. She said she figured she would be pushing her luck by going up after them to listen."

"Yeah, she wouldn't have made it in after them anyway with the alarm."

"Right. Plus, she hadn't been prepared for anything like this anyway. So she sits in her car for about a half hour to see if they come back down and go anywhere else, but they just stayed up there. It was getting late and she needed to get back and get her story filed for deadline, so she left."

"Interesting. I wonder who the other guy was?"

"I know. Stacy said she didn't recognize him at all. They put another reporter on Joseph for a couple days, but they saw nothing out of the ordinary."

"Even at night?"

"Yeah. It was twenty-four hours. I'm telling you they saw nothing."

"You already said that."

"I know, well, I just think you're making a mountain out of mole hill."

Maryanne took the phone away from her ear and actually looked at it perplexed, as if it was the actual being coming up with the offending words. "I'm not making a mountain out of anything." Maryanne hadn't even told her anything else that had occurred yet, and Kayla was already accusing her of freaking out, when she had barely even commented on the situation.

"All I'm saying is that when you think about it, this little scene really isn't so out of the ordinary for Joseph."

"I guess." Maryanne was now staring hard at the brightly colored carpet floor, one hand on her hip.

"So I wouldn't go thinking there's something behind it other than his usual, crazy antics."

"It's not what he did, it's what he said. He's never that public about his views."

There was a pause as Maryanne waited to see how Kayla would react to that. It seemed her friend was preparing to choose her words carefully.

"I know, but I mean, stupid things fly out of people's mouths all the time in the heat of the moment." Maryanne could see Kayla wave her hand flippantly off to the side as she made that last statement, her fingers lax and shimmering with a glittery nail polish of some sort.

"Yeah," Maryanne said with a bit of defeat. She couldn't help but feel like Kayla was being slightly leading in a way, but also knew that, unfortunately, she had a strong point.

"So what's been going on over there?" Kayla asked with more of a hint of interest in her voice. Suddenly, a wave of exhaustion came over Maryanne and a pain started to form over her left temple.

"I don't know, nothing really," she said, lying. "Listen, can I just call you tomorrow to fill you in? I'm so drained I can barely stand up right now."

"Oh, okay," Kayla said, offended, Maryanne could tell.

"I promise I'll call you tomorrow or just fill you in when I get back. I'm so exhausted I just need to go to bed."

"All right, you do that."

"Okay, love you, bye."

Kayla hung up.

Maryanne made her way up to her room. As she did

that, in New York, Kayla put her cell phone down on her desk and picked up her work landline to make another phone call.

"Hello?" answered a man's voice.

"Hi," Kayla said seductively. "So I think I threw her off."

"Good. We've been really happy with you, Kayla."

She smiled broadly and couldn't help the glee that she felt. "Thank you," she said, almost laughing with happiness at the satisfaction she felt, basking in the approval.

"Keep up the good work. Continue to talk to and nurture M.J. We are confident you will achieve your goals in time."

"I will," she said with a small, but determined nod. "I will." With that, she hung up. She grabbed her purse, turned off her computer and her desk lamp and shut off the lights in the advertising department. She locked it up as well, heading for the stairs to the parking lot. She couldn't wait to see her future husband.

Chapter 19

Maryanne sat up slightly to look down at her clothes and see if they were wet. She was lying on her stomach in the park on top of a blanket reading, and began to realize she was feeling slightly damp. She tried to remember if it had rained anytime in the past few days—not that she would know. She had just come back from Vegas yesterday.

They were now closing in on Halloween, but the Indian summer was hanging in and everyone was loving it. *At least the weather is on our side*, she thought. She had come back from her trip very weary, and she thought a few hours of relaxation in the fresh air would do her good. Rob had insisted on picking her up from the airport. When they saw each other, they sank into each other's arms, but she could feel there was something a bit more desperate and panicked behind his embrace.

While they drove home, he was quiet and stared straight ahead with a concerned frown on his face, one hand on her leg, as he listened to her stories from her trip; from Andy's tale that he'd refused to elaborate further on, the mysterious note, and the dinner conversation that had dug Joseph's grave even further.

He didn't comment much, which prompted her at one point to ask if he was even listening. He started to laugh and turned to her. "Of course!" he said. "I'm listening, I'm just trying to drive. My contacts are bothering me."

"You have your glasses on," she said.

"My glasses, I meant my glasses."

Okay, she thought in her head. Something was bothering him, and he was busy thinking about it in his own head. She had learned her lesson before that he is the type of person who needs to come to you, not the other way around. He would tell her in his own time. He didn't have anything to say about the situation until they were finally in bed. He held her to his chest and stroked her head.

"Listen, see what you can find out about everything going on with Joseph, everything you found out in Vegas. You and Lily should talk to as many people as you can, but be discreet about it, and keep your guard up around him. I'm starting to not trust the guy."

"Yeah, me, too," she said. She pulled her head back and looked him in the eyes. She decided to take a stab at it. "You okay?"

Not his favorite question.

"Yeah, I'm fine. Just a lot of crap going on at work, as usual."

"All right."

He kissed her forehead, then whispered in her ear, "I love you," but she frowned and didn't feel settled, not one bit.

The next day was more of the same. When she asked if he wanted to talk a little further about her dreams and cemetery visits, he told her he needed a nap and wanted to be able to sort things out a little further before they did. So she told him while he did that, she would take a walk to the park and do some reading.

Her clothes weren't wet, but while her head was up, she noticed an oversized man sitting on a bench by the playground. He was on his cell phone, keeping one eye on his children, a blond, curly-haired little boy and his older sister, a tiny little bit of a brunette. Both were running around in the grass, enjoying the beautiful day. He had a purple t-shirt and jeans on and his hair was wavy and graying.

Suddenly, the little boy went down with a thud and rolled over. He stood up with a little smirk on his face, which you could tell was just a front to hide the tears that would inevitably follow.

“Are you okay, Allan?” his sister asked.

“Yeah,” he said, his voice quivering slightly. He started toward his father. It looked like he wasn’t sure if he wanted to commit to the full run and cry to daddy, which would inevitably put his manhood into question, especially with the little Spanish boy whizzing around on a scooter who had fallen at least a dozen times already, each time springing back up and into action without so much as saying, “ouch.”

His father had noticed the fall and motioned to Allan to come to him. Allan finally gave in and broke off into a little run.

She got back to the book she was reading and didn’t even notice when he got up off his bench by the playground and came over to gather the kids. She heard someone start to giggle not too far from her. She looked up and saw the man looking at her, his lips turned up in a sly smile. She gave a little snicker back and said, “Hi.” *Great*, she thought, *I thought I'd filled my quota for the month of annoying random encounters with older men while I'm trying to read*.

“Did you arrive at the shocking conclusion?” he asked.

"What?" she asked.

"Your jaw just dropped in dismay."

"Did it? I didn't even realize. Yeah, it's a pretty good book, but everything's kind of all starting to come together now."

"Nice. What's the book?"

"It's a Dean Koontz novel. Not the stuff for mental giants, but it's good enough for me."

"Yeah, I think I've read a few of his books."

"Oh, yeah?" she asked, smiling politely.

"Yeah, I like to take books like that on long business trips. Ones that don't require too much thought."

"Allan slow down! Remember what just happened to you?"

Allan stopped running, turned around with a pouty look on his face, and stomped back over to his father. His sister had run off to play on the swings.

"Do you live around here?"

She looked back up at him and rolled her eyes. "Come here often?"

"I didn't mean it like that."

She laughed lightly—very lightly. "I live in Sleepy Hollow."

"Yeah?"

"Yup." *Why is he still here?* she wondered. "Why?"

"Just wondering. My nephew lives down that way, too."

"Where does he live?"

"He lives on Christopher Street. Not a very good area down there is it?"

"No, it's not." She was trying her hardest at that point to look like she really wanted to get back to her book.

He let a few minutes pass while he watched the kids.

He giggled again. "I like his picture on the back of the book."

So much for a quiet afternoon in the park.

"I like how the golden retriever is also taking credit for the novel," he said.

She looked at the back cover. Dean Koontz was smiling back at her with a horrendous comb over, his golden retriever by his side, also smiling broadly.

She laughed. "Yeah. He's probably a rental." Wavy and graying laughed, too.

"Mind if I take a seat?"

Oh, Lord, this is not ending. "Help yourself."

He took a seat on her blanket. "Yeah, my wife couldn't take the kids anymore, so she asked me if I would just take them down here for a while."

"Couldn't take them anymore?"

"Well, you know, just couldn't take all the noise and chaos. She's had a lot going on lately, just needed some time alone to lie down."

"How many kids do you have?"

"Just Allan and Amanda."

"Oh. You're making it seem like you've got a house full of screaming children."

He smiled. "No, just these two knuckleheads. You'd be surprised at the handful they can be sometimes though."

"Yeah, I'm sure."

Why is this still going on? she asked herself. *What does he want?*

"So you live down there in the Hollow, huh?"

"That's what I said the first time."

"What do you guys do down there?"

"What do you mean?"

"Well, is there anything to do?"

"You act as if it's another part of the country."

"No, I just mean, it's not a great area, like around Beekman and Broadway."

"Yeah, I live on Beekman." *Damn it.*

"Do you?"

"Yeah, there's a couple bars right on Beekman and a coffee house down toward the water, but if we go out, we'll either come down here into town, you know, go to Main Street, or go over the bridge to the mall. We hang out in Pleasantville a lot, too."

"Yeah, there's a lot going on in Pleasantville. I used to go there a lot when I was younger."

"And when was that?" she smiled slightly, still looking at the pages of her book. The conversation was sort of starting to peek her interest.

He looked over his shoulder at her and smiled. "Ha ha."

Allan came and flopped down on the blanket.

"How ya doing, buddy? You tired?"

"Yeah."

"All right, well, why don't we go get you and your sister something to eat and then head back home to see how Mommy's feeling."

"Okay," he said in a child's drawl.

"Amanda! Come on, let's go."

Amanda flung herself off the swing and fell into the sand.

"Ugh. You kids have to be more careful. You and your sister are like little maniacs today," wavy and graying said, half to his son and half to nobody.

The kids ran over to him and started chasing each other all over again. Maryanne started to get up.

"Let me help you with that," he said, as she started to fold up her blanket.

"Who's that, daddy?"

"I'm not sure," he said, smiling at her. "Why don't you ask her her name?"

The little boy started toward her, but she decided it was time to nip this in the bud for good. She didn't need some creeper knowing even her first name after she had already told him where she lived.

"I'd better go," she said, blatantly turning her back to the father and son.

Wavy and graying dropped his head, smiling shyly, but obviously embarrassed.

She saw, and in spite of herself, felt bad for the guy. "Bye-bye," she said quickly, getting into her car.

"Well, nice to meet you," he said, a pair of dark sunglasses covering his eyes now. He came around to the driver's seat and reached out to shake her hand. She was taken aback by his forwardness.

"Good to meet you, too. Bye, Allan."

"Bye," Allan said as she slammed the door shut.

Wavy and graying stood on the sidewalk looking at her, confused, and awkwardly gave her a half wave. She gave him a stern smile back, then turned her head to back up the car.

After Maryanne left, Rob tried to grab a quick nap, but gave up after tossing and turning for about twenty-five minutes. He rolled over and started to reach for his phone that sat on the small dresser next to his bed to call Maryanne, but he stopped himself, struck by a seemingly better idea. He would let his girlfriend relax and get some much-needed peace and quiet for a while, while he went to find the gravesite of the little girl that had been calling to her as of late. He got up, went into the bathroom, and threw some water on his face. He grabbed a sweatshirt and breezed past his roommate Steve who was strumming a guitar on the couch.

"Hey, man, where you going?"

"Just out for a few minutes," he mumbled over his shoulder at Steve. "I'll be back."

He pulled the door shut and bounded down the four flights of stairs to make sure no one would have the chance to catch up to him. It was a little brisk when he got outside, but nevertheless, he didn't really need his sweatshirt. He looked up toward the sky and let the sun hit his face full on. He knew there wouldn't be many warm days like this left.

He walked quickly down the hill, passed Kykuit and crossed Route 9. He had made it to the huge wrought iron gates of the cemetery entrance in just five minutes. He had no idea where to start.

Maryanne had mentioned that the grave was on the west end of the cemetery, farther from the entrance, but that didn't narrow things down much. He was having a bit of a time even remembering the name. *Ugh, come on!* he thought to himself. *Sissy? Sicily? No, Cecily, that's it. Last name starts with an R.*

He walked over hill after hill, up and down endless aisles. Suddenly, the sun glinted off something and he winced as it momentarily blinded him. When he was able to focus again, he saw a grave a few yards away, atop of one of the rolling peaks, with a small, pink-stained glass, iridescent cross on top of it. The cross was outlined in silver. The glass had an almost shell-like, shimmering quality to it. He started walking toward it immediately. As he got closer, the words engraved on the tombstone came into focus.

Cecily Reynolds
Beloved Baby Girl
1990–1996

"Oh, my God, this is it!" he said out loud to no one. The stone had a strange, coppery-gold color to it, which also helped it stand out from the others. He crouched down in front of it, so he was face to face with the tomb. "Only six," he mumbled under his breath. He absently touched the engraving with his fingertips. He frowned and stood up. He looked around and saw that, despite the beautiful day, the cemetery was pretty much deserted.

Rob took a deep breath and tried to process everything that was happening around him. Trouble had followed Maryanne even out West. It had rendered him pretty much speechless while she reported everything that had happened on the way home from the airport. He had gone to pick her up, prepared to tell her about his experience in the subway, expecting the outburst of the century that he wasn't sure how he was going to handle. He was hoping she would stay calm and collected, but it was he, in fact, who had to work to compose himself.

At first, Rob didn't know what to make of everything that had happened to Maryanne in Vegas, from this new Andy character, to the strange note that someone left in her room, which was the element that creeped him out the most. Did someone else know about her grave visits and was trying to ward her off?

He looked around once again, letting his eyes sweep over the rows and rows of gravestones, some of them almost white with age, and the mausoleums sprinkled throughout. It was a beautiful day, and in the serene sunlight it was difficult to imagine that something sinister might be going on in here once things went dark.

Once he realized she had even more to deal with now, he decided again to keep quiet, for better or for worse, until he could find out more information as well. He was hoping the whole scene had been a case of mistaken identity, that his pursuer had simply had the wrong guy. Since so many days had passed already, he felt stupid going to the police and thought it might throw suspicion on him for no reason at all because he had waited so long to come forward. If there really was someone or some group after him, as his dreams were suggesting, there was no way in hell was he going to put Maryanne in harm's way. He shuddered as he recalled the man's life-threatening warning as he ran to safety down the alley.

"You can't escape it," the man's voice rang through his head. "They need you."

Rob shivered as he pictured the man placing his left hand over his heart, remembering the glint of that ring. He took one last look at the grave, turned, and shrugged off his worries. Nothing mattered except Maryanne, and helping her through this. Everything else was just crazy talk.

He couldn't see it, but as he walked away, a sharp streak of sunlight glistened off the soft pink cross atop of Cecily's grave, making a low sweeping arc over the bright colors of the fallen leaves.

The light strums of Steve's guitar playing floated from the living room into Rob's bedroom. He breathed quietly, but steadily, as he slept next to Maryanne, his back leaning up against her left side. He hugged the pillow that his head rested on as he always did when he slept.

They'd both returned from their individual outings, Maryanne still trying to read, but unable to finish her book. Her encounter with the man in the park was, for some reason, plaguing her thoughts. Rob shifted in his sleep. She looked over at him and a pang of guilt hit her hard in the chest. He was so tired and stressed, and she was only adding to it with all of this. She kissed him lightly on the forehead.

Someone knocked on the front door and Maryanne heard Steve get up to answer it. She heard Kayla's voice and got up to see her friend standing in the doorway, an easy laidback look on her face.

"How you been?" Steve asked, smiling at her.

"I'm good, how about you? Ah, here's my girl," she said as Maryanne walked toward her. She returned Kayla's warmth with a smile of her own. "Lily said you were up here. What's everyone doing for dinner?" she asked.

"No plans yet," said Steve, hands on hips.

"Well, I just got back from the store and bought like a ton of food, so I thought I'd cook."

"Sounds great!" Steve said.

Maryanne sighed internally at Steve's eagerness. "Rob's sleeping," she said. "I'll wake him in a few minutes, tell him we're going up for dinner."

"Yeah, definitely," Kayla said. "M.J.'s going to get the grill started, and we have the furniture all set up on the deck. I finally put up those twinkle lights. It looks so pretty. I figure we should get some use out of them while the weather is still cooperating."

"Awesome." Steve beamed from ear to ear. He couldn't have been more delighted to have plans set with good people.

"Good," Kayla said as she turned to leave. "I'll go let Lily know," she tossed over her shoulder as she walked out the door. She stopped suddenly and turned around. "Hey, Maryanne, can I talk to you for a sec?"

Steve bowed his head and backed up, walking back into the living room. Maryanne stepped into the outer hallway and shut the door lightly behind her, just enough so it wouldn't lock.

"What's up?" she asked Kayla.

"I just wanted to know if you heard anything further on Joseph," Kayla pulled her chin in slightly, blinked and winced, the way she does when she is in a confrontational situation that is making her uncomfortable. As subtle as it was, it didn't get past Maryanne. She looked at her friend for a moment before answering.

"Not yet. We're kind of going to lay low on it, not really confront him about anything and just keep our eyes and ears open. I'm going to meet with Ramsey on Monday to see what he knows about what that Andy character told me in Vegas."

Kayla shook her head in understanding. "Oh, that's good. Let me know what happens."

"Okay," Maryanne said, a little warily. She watched Kayla trot back up to the fifth floor and couldn't help but feel like the two of them were slowly moving toward opposing sides. She decided to shrug it off. "Always the paranoid one, you are," she mumbled under her breath as she walked back into Rob's apartment.

As the door shut and she walked down the hallway, Steve popped his head out of the kitchen. "So should I go get anything? Like maybe some extra burgers or hot dogs or something…" He trailed off as she gave him a polite smile and breezed past him.

"No, I'm sure they've got it under control."

She went into Rob's room and shut the door. He was awake, but obviously still sleepy as he lay amongst his mound of pillows, remote in hand as he channel surfed. Maryanne climbed back into bed with him.

"Was that Kayla?"

"Yup."

"What's going on up in 520J?"

"She invited us all up for dinner on the deck."

"Oh, that's nice," Rob said, a grin spreading across his face. "What's she cooking?"

Maryanne shrugged. "I guess burgers and stuff, because she said M.J.'s got the grill going. Maybe some corn on the cob, too."

"Very nice."

His right and her left hand interlocked.

"Yeah, she just didn't sound right. I don't know. I hope she's okay over there. I'm sure Joseph is probably driving her crazy with twenty-five different dead-end leads, direction that makes no sense, and sources that hate his guts."

Maryanne was sitting across from Lily at Kayla and M.J.'s deck table, describing her most recent phone conversation with her cousin Casey. The top of Building J was sparkling in the cool October evening, decorated with tiny twinkle lights that Kayla had wrapped around the umbrella that covered the table, as well as around the doorway and the sides of the railing. It was elegantly cozy and the scene enveloped each and every guest with a warmth that was palpable.

"You guys want cheeseburgers, or plain?" yelled M.J. from across the deck, interrupting them momentarily.

Lily looked over her shoulder to answer. "Um…I'll

have plain," she said, shaking her head.

"Yes, cheese," Maryanne said. Both girls held Coronas in their hands.

Lily turned back to face Maryanne. "Yeah. Well, tell her she can always call me if she feels lost or if anything Joseph says doesn't make any sense."

"I know, I will."

"Did you guys see that lightning the other night?" Rob asked, a big smile on his face as he walked over to the table and sat down, a Corona in hand. Steve and Scott followed shortly after, each holding one handle of a monstrous cooler as they carefully stepped through the doorway onto the balcony. Maryanne glanced over her shoulder, then back at the table, rolling her eyes at Lily and Rob.

M.J. walked up to them grinning, smacking their hands in hearty shakes hello. He helped them carry the cooler over by the grill. "Glad you guys could make it," he said.

"Yeah, man. We're always up for some grillin'," Steve said beaming, his goofy laugh resounding off the balcony. A few others from an apartment in the connecting building stepped out onto the deck, joining them.

Lily turned to Rob. "Seriously, it scared the fucking shit out of me. I was driving back from the mountain and the sky was green. All you saw was the clouds and this really intense lightning behind it. I just kept gripping the steering wheel, willing myself not to look up."

Rob smiled. "Yeah, I just kept staring out the window looking up at it like, wow!" He twisted his face into a ridiculous stare with his mouth and eyes as he pretended to be looking out of an imaginary window. He pointed at Maryanne. "She was like, 'Would you come back to bed! '" he mocked her in a fake cackling hen voice.

"I couldn't sleep with the blinds up and it flashing in my face every five seconds!" Maryanne shot back.

"Yeah," he said, "then it just started pouring, like shhhhhhh," he imitated the rain smacking against the air conditioner and shook the air down with his hand in a spider-claw figure for emphasis.

"I know," Lily said. "You should have seen the cemetery the next day…yesterday."

"Why, was it a mess or something?" Maryanne asked.

"Yeah, it was crazy. The winds must have been insane. I had gotten back by then, thank God. It honestly hadn't sounded like the winds were that bad, but they had to have been because tombstones were moved in the ground. Like tilted one way or another, some knocked over, practically uprooted."

"What?" Maryanne asked, sitting up. "That's crazy. To say the winds had to have been bad is a bit of an understatement, no?" she said with a nervous laugh. "I mean to bring a tombstone out of the ground is no joke."

"I know. That's what I said. The…"

"I didn't hear any crazy wind after that though," Rob said, interrupting Lily.

"I didn't see. Did you notice that?" Maryanne turned to Rob. "Do we pass the cemetery on the way to Blockbuster?" The two had just returned some DVDs last night.

"Yeah, I don't remember seeing anything. We were both probably so damn oblivious because we were in a daze."

"Bad winds can't pull a tombstone out of the

ground," Maryanne mumbled, almost to herself. "Unless they were hurricane caliber…" she trailed off.

"Oh, that's right!" Lily turned to Rob excitedly, making for a quick change in subject. "How was the NIN concert? I forgot you guys went to that!"

It took a lot for Lily to lose her composure and it was happening slightly. It always warmed Maryanne's heart to see her friend get so excited. Kayla came out with a mound of corn on the cob on a huge plate. M.J., Scott, and Steve were talking sports and laughing loudly in the background.

"It was sick. I'll tell you, the lights were fucking amazing. There was this huge screen in front of them, and they would do stuff like," he paused as he thought of the best way to describe it, "it would look like someone smashed a glass window in front of them when they started playing guitar, like when the song started. It was really good. You should try to go. I think they have another couple of shows they're doing upstate. If you could go, you should."

"Yeah," Lily looked away, deflated. There was no way in hell she was going upstate for anything, let alone to see a favorite band perform.

Kayla had sat down with the rest of them at the table and had been staring at the plate of corn she'd placed in the middle of the table since she did. She looked pissed.

"Hey, smiley," Maryanne said, turning to her. Rob and Lily continued to talk about the show. Kayla turned to her.

"What? Oh." She seemed to have been jerked out of a trance. "I just can't take their jabbering anymore. It's driving me crazy." The words seethed out of her. Maryanne glanced over Kayla's shoulder at M.J., Steve, and Scott who seemed to be having a genuinely good time. It didn't seem like Kayla to be bothered by such a thing.

The couple on the other side of the balcony took their food they had quickly cooked up on their own grill and went inside. The woman glanced behind her, looking back at their table. She turned her gaze back to Kayla who was still staring at the table, eyes wide, breathing heavily.

"Hey, how's that food coming? I'm hungry," Rob said, interrupting Maryanne's thoughts, and seemingly Kayla's, too, as she jerked her head up at his start.

"Seriously," she mumbled to herself. Maryanne narrowed her eyes at Kayla and crinkled her brow in confusion. She wondered what was up with her typically jovial friend.

M.J. looked over at them all, smiling. Steve and Scott turned, too. "Almost!" he yelled out. M.J. turned to the grill again, spatula in hand to finish working the burgers. He started to toss a couple pieces of yellow American cheese onto some of them.

Kayla pushed her chair back and stomped back inside. Rob and Lily pretended not to notice. Scott and Steve came over to join them.

Maryanne went to follow after Kayla. When she got inside she found her friend putzing around in the kitchen with various condiments. It didn't seem like Kayla was even doing anything constructive, just moving various bottles around on the counter. She had an absent-minded look in her eyes.

"Hey, you okay?" Maryanne asked. Kayla looked up at her for a second, then back down at what she was doing.

"Yeah, I'm fine. Sorry, I really don't know what's wrong with me lately."

"What do you mean?" Maryanne asked as she walked over to the counter. Kayla turned from her and walked over to the other side of the kitchen. "I don't even know," she answered, her back toward Maryanne.

Maryanne stared at her turned back for a second, a quizzical look on her face.

"Hey, I've gotta run." Lily appeared in the hallway. John just called me, he's ready to get picked up."

Kayla spun around. "You mean you're not staying for dinner?" She lifted a plate with small piles of chopped onions, pickles, and roasted peppers off the counter and began to walk toward the hallway. I guess she'd been doing something, Maryanne thought to herself. "That's pretty fucking rude," Kayla said as she breezed past Lily into the hallway.

"Oh, well, M .J. said he'd wrap my burger up, give it to…" Lily, clearly embarrassed, was interrupted by the sound of the door having slammed behind Kayla. Lily turned back to Maryanne who shrugged her shoulders and put her hands up in defeat.

"I have no idea," she said to her roommate.

"All right, well, I really didn't mean to be rude, it's just that he's going to be waiting for me, and I could already tell he's in a mood by the tone of his voice."

Maryanne rolled her eyes. She had just about enough of John and his ridiculous mood swings, which had gotten more intense and frequent over the past few months. She was even more fed up with the fact that Lily put up with it on a regular basis.

"It's all right. Just go do what you have to do. Let us know what you guys are doing later on."

"All right." She gave Maryanne a frown and a quick wave.

As Lily was leaving, Maryanne heard her pass by

Scott and Steve on their way in to get more beer and the condiments Kayla had forgotten.

"Leaving already?"

"Yeah, gotta go pick up my child," Lily answered with a nervous laugh.

"Ha. Well, I guess we'll see you later. You going out?"

"I'm not sure. I'll keep in touch though."

"All right, cool."

"Okay, see you guys."

"Bye."

Maryanne passed by the two and went back out onto the deck where she found Rob awkwardly twiddling his thumbs, while Kayla was speaking quietly, quickly, yet furiously, at M.J. He appeared confused, but wasn't backing down.

Kayla had sensed Maryanne was back and was trying to quickly wrap up the tense conversation. Maryanne only heard a small snippet when she came upon the group.

"No . . . NO!"

M .J. mumbled something in return.

"Just fucking deal with it!" Kayla said, and turned to sit back down. Maryanne had never seen Rob look more uncomfortable. She cleared her throat to try to ease the situation and bring a more light-hearted conversation back to the table.

"Do you believe what she said about the cemetery? I mean tombstones ripped out of the ground? That's insane!"

Rob saw what she was trying to do and immediately tried to help. "I know," he said, turning back to the table with a smile. "Kayla, didn't you guys go for a walk through there last weekend?" he asked her, trying to engage her in the conversation. “Maryanne and I have yet to get over there to do that.”

“As if it’s far?” Kayla said snidely. Maryanne winced at her rudeness, feeling responsible somehow. She paused for a minute.

“We were supposed to go, but lard-ass over here couldn’t get his butt out of bed for practically the entire weekend,” Kayla explained.

M.J. spun around. “Hey, I had worked three fucking double shifts in the past three days. I was exhausted!” While there was still some fire left in him, Maryanne could tell he was losing steam, starting to be more hurt by her words than angered by them. Maryanne had never seen Kayla act like this. Okay, whom was she kidding? Kayla always acted like this, but this time was different somehow, and everyone felt it.

Kayla sat in her seat, obviously fuming. M.J., who finished preparing the burgers, turned around to look at her, shaking his head in disgust as he turned back to the food. Scott and Steve returned to the deck.

M.J. brought a plate of both burgers and cheeseburgers over to the table. His arm passed over Kayla’s head with the plate and after he set it down, he bent down to kiss her cheek. Still seemingly infuriated, she turned her head away.

Maryanne sighed. What she thought would be a really nice night was turning into an uncomfortable mess.

“Thanks, man,” Scott said as he prepared his burger.

“No problem,” M.J. said, obviously upset over Kayla’s odd behavior.

“Did you guys happen to see the cemetery?” Rob asked Scott and Steve.

“No, man,” Scott said.

"No," Steve shook his head.

"We should go take a walk there tomorrow," Rob said to Maryanne. She smiled lovingly at him, relieved that the two of them had never treated each other the way Kayla and M.J. had just displayed.

"Sure," she said, thinking it would be a nice activity for a lazy Sunday, even though she'd been there more times than she'd like to admit lately.

M.J. sat down finally. "So how was The Machine the other night?" he asked Scott.

The Machine is a Pink Floyd cover band that M.J. loved. Scott managed The Paramount Theatre; a small venue in a nearby town that hosted a variety of small bands, cover bands, and comedians. The Machine had played there last Friday.

"It was awesome, dude, too bad you couldn't make it."

"Yeah," M.J. said, glancing over at Kayla. Maryanne took that to mean that Kayla was also to blame for the fact that he missed one of his favorite bands play.

As the boys talked about the concert, Maryanne was able to draw Kayla into a conversation about wedding details. They had gone for cake tastings last week and had sat with the church's music director a few days ago to pick out the arrangement for the service. Kayla's mood softened slightly as she told Maryanne about her plans for her meeting on Monday with the florist. M.J. overheard their wedding talk and looked over with a smile, seemingly relieved that the tension looked like it had eased.

"Did you tell her our idea for the tree?" M.J. turned to Maryanne and explained. "We're going to have the florist make a tree out of flowers, and we're going to hang the ornaments, which will be the favors, from the branches, and . . ."

Kayla didn't let him finish. "You need to stop using the word *we* because there has been nothing collaborative about this," she said to him icily.

M.J. looked over at her, stunned. It was obvious he had no idea where all this was coming from. "What are you talking about? I've helped you every step of the . . ."

"You've helped with nothing!" Kayla screamed. With that, Kayla picked up her glass of Coke and threw it across the deck with such force that it smashed against the brick wall approximately thirty feet away. She stormed back into the apartment.

M.J. followed the glass, wide-eyed, as it made its flight across the deck, and then Kayla as she ran back inside. Everyone else stared down at their plates, scared to even breath too loudly, trying not to move a muscle as if they did it would only exacerbate the situation.

Maryanne turned to M.J., her expression equally as stunned as his own at Kayla's display of anger; a scene out of character, even for her. "What the hell is going on?" she asked him, a slight panic to her voice.

M .J. looked at her, then got up without saying a word to go after Kayla.

Once M.J. was back inside, Steve looked up from his plate. "What should we do?" he asked, his voice filled with concern.

"I don't know," Maryanne said.

The group could hear M.J. and Kayla arguing quietly in the kitchen. Maryanne could see half of Kayla's silhouette through the window into the kitchen. She could see her hands were on her hips and she was standing tall, all five feet of her. After a few minutes their voices began to rise.

"No!" M.J. said firmly. "I'm telling you, you better

get this out of your head, and fast!"

Kayla answered, but all they could hear was a mumble. *What the hell are they talking about?* thought Maryanne.

"You promised! …who…they asked me to do it."

"What?"

"You heard me!"

They were now screaming.

"I'm serious, Kayla," M.J. trudged by her. It looked like he was headed into their bedroom.

Maryanne stared intently at the window, as did Rob. Both were ready to get up and jump on the situation if things started to turn ugly, which it seemed they were escalating toward.

"Where are you going?" Kayla was fast on his heels. "No!" They heard her scream.

Rob got to his feet. Maryanne stood and put a hand on his shoulder.

"I can't believe you just did that!" they heard her yell.

After a few moments of silence, Kayla stomped her way past the window that was their view into the argument, and out the door, slamming it shut behind her.

Immediately after she left, Maryanne made her way into the apartment, with the rest of the crew following close behind. They found M.J. sitting on the couch, staring at the ground fuming, eyes wide, with his head in his hands.

"You all right, man?" Rob asked, putting a hand on his back. M.J. didn't answer and didn't look up. Rob looked back at Maryanne who had her sweater on and bag in hand. She gave a slight nod toward the door, implying she thought it was time they left.

"Let us know if you need anything," she said as she

went up to M.J. and kissed him on top of the head. "I'll see if I can get in touch with Kayla."

As the four of them went to leave, M.J. threw a, "Don't bother," over his shoulder, walked into his bedroom, and slammed the door.

Way too much door slamming for one night, Maryanne thought. As they left, she made a mental note to call Casey tomorrow night.

Chapter 2∅

Maryanne exhaled a big breath and tossed her bag onto the loveseat that sat along a back wall in Rob's living room. It landed with a loud thud. Steve and Scott shuffled in behind them and Steve made a beeline for the kitchen.

"Friggin' bowling bag," Rob mumbled under his breath as he walked past her into his bedroom. She frowned at him and placed her hands on her hips for a second while she tried to decide what to do next.

It didn't take long to decide. She immediately began to rummage around in her bag for her phone and went straight to Kayla's number. As she lifted the phone to her ear she was reminded of another occasion when Kayla had sped off after a fit. They were in college and she'd gotten the cotton tip of a Q-tip stuck in her ear canal, panicked, and decided to drive home to New Jersey to have her mother, a nurse, remove it. Maryanne found herself wishing that this time also possessed the humor associated with that past fiasco.

"Ugggh!" she huffed as the phone went to voicemail. She threw her phone into her bag as Rob walked back out into the living room.

"She's a fucking maniac," he said shaking his head, heading for the kitchen. Steve walked out with a turkey sandwich in his hand, stuffed with all the fixings. Rob laughed at him. "Hungry?" he asked as he opened the refrigerator.

"I didn't get to finish my burger!" Steve said,

laughing, small bits of food flying from his mouth as he did. "I had it like right here!" he exclaimed and held the edge of an imaginary burger in front of his open mouth, getting ready to take a big bite. "And then they started screaming."

Maryanne was getting frustrated by their laughing. "This isn't funny, babe. Where the fuck did she go?"

Rob looked at her wide-eyed. "I don't know. She's a big girl, babe, I'm sure she's just driving around trying to blow off some steam." He started to shake his head and opened up the refrigerator again. "I'm telling ya though, if you ever talked to me like that or embarrassed me like that…" He shook his head some more and both he and Steve started laughing again.

She whipped her head toward him. "What the hell is that supposed to mean?"

"I'm just saying!" he said. "That was awful! He didn't deserve that! What the hell is the matter with her? You don't act like that in front of company, in front of people you invited over."

"So how did that get turned on me and you giving me a warning?"

Rob laughed again. He found it so funny when she got feisty like this. "I'm not turning it on you," he said, still giggling. He walked up to her and put his arm around her shoulders, kissing her on the cheek. "I'm just saying it's no way for anyone to act. I wouldn't expect you to put up with that from me either."

"I know," she said, and put her arms around his waist in return and squeezed. She looked up at him and pecked him on the lips. Then frowned, "I'm worried about her."

"I know," he said sympathetically and ran his hand down the back of her head. "You want to go drive around and look for her?" he asked.

"No. I guess I should just leave her be for now."

"Good," he said emphatically. "Now who wants to go over to Denver's for some burgers?"

"Definitely, dude," Steve said, immediately putting down his turkey sandwich and heading for the tin foil to save the rest of it.

At the mention of Denver's, Scott emerged from his room, a smile on his face. "Let's do it."

Denver's was a bar and restaurant they frequented across the street from the Darren Hayes. Their kitchen closed pretty late, and they could probably still catch a good dinner.

"I guess," Maryanne said, deflated. She followed the three boys out the door again and picked up her phone to text Lily their new location for the night.

Maryanne sat at the Moonbean cafe, a small coffee shop right next door to RWB's old offices, and directly across the street from an Italian restaurant that Ralph Ramsey was in the process of buying. To Maryanne, it seemed like small potatoes for Ramsey, a businessman who liked to set his sights a little higher, but she didn't give it too much thought. She spoke to him Sunday night, and he said he would be there for a few hours on Monday, sorting things out with the current, but soon-to-be-former, owner. So they agreed to meet at the Moonbean to discuss Joseph's past.

Maryanne could tell by Ramsey's tone over the phone the night before that it probably wasn't going to be easy getting any information out of him. As to why he would choose to keep quiet, she wasn't sure. She was beginning to wonder if he would show up at all after waiting for him for twenty minutes, but Ramsey eventually breezed through the door to the cafe; the small bell on top of the pendulum went ding as he swung it open.

Instead of saying hello to Maryanne first, he went straight for the counter. She wasn't sure if he had seen her as she was sitting in one of the booths along the back wall that was covered with featured pieces from a local artist.

"Abbey!" he greeted the owner, smiling broadly. "Is Maryanne here? Maryanne Rosa, they used to work next…" he trailed off as Abbey leaned over the counter and pointed over at Maryanne.

"Hey, Ramsey," Maryanne said, giving him a little wave as he turned to look at her, surprised.

"Oh, hey!" he said with a smile as he started over to her. He stopped short to turn around and give Abbey his order. "Latte over here for me, Abbey?"

"Sure."

"I walked right past you." He came over to the booth and leaned over to kiss Maryanne on the cheek. She looked at him, keeping her eyes wide and focused.

"Hi," she said. Ramsey had helped Maryanne and Lily out a lot in the past, serving as a reliable source for many a local and regional story and putting them in contact with the right people at the right time, as he also knew a great deal of other business owners and politicians.

She didn't want to immediately put him on the defensive, but she had to wonder if he had kept something major from them about their boss, how many other things had he tried to conceal and how many times did he try to steer them in a certain direction while they were working on a story or a lead in order to make sure it stayed concealed.

Maybe she was getting ahead of herself, she thought.

"How'd everything go over there?" she asked, cocking her head toward the restaurant across the street Ramsey had just come from.

"It's good! Almost ready to sign off on everything, just ironing out a couple of details," he said, folding his hands in front of him on the table. They looked at each other for a long moment before either of them spoke again. Ramsey went first.

"So, what was this guy's name again that you met in Vegas?"

"Andy. I didn't get a last name, but I could probably find out."

He nodded his head in understanding. He started to feel in his pocket for something and pulled out a folded piece of old newspaper and set it on the table. "From your description of him last night, I had a hunch on who this guy was. I made a couple calls to some old friends of my father, and they said there was a guy named Andrew Dayton who ran for local office a while ago that matched your description. I went to the library and guesstimated the year this might have been in and did end up finding a picture. Is this him?"

Ramsey unfolded the newspaper and showed it to her. She was looking at a picture of six men, all in suits, with their arms around each other. Standing second from left, with the widest grin she'd ever seen, was a much younger Andy Dayton than the one she'd met a little over a week ago. His hair was curly, but raven black. His skin was dark, but more chocolatey, rather than the leathery-orange he was sporting nowadays, but it was definitely him.

"Yup, that's him," she said, shaking her head, but not taking her eyes off of the photo. She wanted to read the caption: Edward Remmy, principal of Sleepy Hollow high school, Andrew Dayton, executive editor, Westchester Today . . .

Her jaw dropped. “What?” She looked up at him and smacked the newspaper down on the table. “You’ve got to be kidding me!”

Ramsey smiled. “Read it and weep, my friend.”

“I can’t believe this. He didn’t tell me that. I’ve got to talk to Kayla.”

“That’s not the only thing he didn’t tell you,” Ramsey said, interrupting her. “Father was indeed a professor at NYU, served as town assessor for a while, but there’s a little something your buddy conveniently left out of his story.”

“And what’s that?”

“That his father wasn’t just involved in local politics with an interest in the school systems because of his teaching background.” Ramsey paused for effect.

“Oh, for Christ’s sake, Ramsey, what?” Her already worn-thin patience was becoming nonexistent.

Ramsey giggled slightly and held up his hand. “All right, all right. His father was Albert Dayton.” He waited to see if she recognized the name at all.

“Why does that sound…” she narrowed her eyes and trailed off as he watched her try to place the name.

He nodded. “Albert Dayton was a chairman of the US Senate Committee on Health, Education, Labor & Pensions.”

“So he was a senator?”

“Yes. He was very highly praised in his day, but after he was long gone out of the spotlight, and almost on his death bed really, a lot of skeletons decided they needed to remove themselves from his closet.”

“Really? Like what?”

"Well, it seems that Andy's father was moving a lot of money around while he was in office. Apparently, he took a number of large, private donations for the committee, other various organizations he was involved in, his campaign, and at times, he'd help out a 'friend in need or two.'" Ramsey used air quotes around "friend in need."

Maryanne kept her gaze locked on him and waited.

"Apparently, Joseph was one of his friends in need."

She kept staring at him, trying to read him. After a moment's pause, she asked him, "How do you know this?"

"Can't tell you that," he said, shaking his head. He tried to hide it, but there was a smugness in his face.

"All right, well, then keep going," she said, annoyed. If Maryanne didn't know every last detail, it made her uncomfortable. She hated feeling like someone had one up on her.

"Andy told you only the beginning of his conversation with Joseph. Joseph did tell him that he would never stand a chance at becoming mayor, unless he started to understand how the powers that be operated and he used his own, uh . . . assets to his advantage."

"He meant his father."

"Right."

At that she lowered her voice slightly. "What is this about the mayor's seat being passed down like some throne? Do you know anything about that?" she asked. There was a concern on her face as it came out.

Part of her didn't want Ramsey to be involved at all. The girls liked him and to have their image of him tarnished would be extremely disheartening.

He frowned, but didn't hesitate. "Look, this is off the record, and I need your word as an honest and respectable journalist that it will stay that way."

She didn't hesitate either. "You've got it."

"It's true. What Andy told you in Vegas is true."

"Are you serious? So are you telling me that people's votes really don't matter?"

"Well, to an extent. I mean they try to keep in line with the way the population swings and who they favor so it doesn't become too obvious, but when it comes down to it, no."

She ran a hand through her hair. "Ramsey how do you know all this? Who else knows? I mean, if this happens here, then it means it happens in a lot of other places and who knows to what level it rises to."

Ramsey didn't say anything. He just kept looking at her, frowning, almost apologetically.

"This is crazy!" she blurted out.

"And off the record. Remember what I told you."

"Why? You've been good to us, Ramsey, at least it's always seemed that way. I think you're a good person. If you know this is happening, why wouldn't you want it revealed?"

She almost knew the answer before the question came out of her mouth. Understanding washed over her, and she sat back in her chair with a knowing and accusatory look on her face. He was a part of all of this. She started to shake her head at him.

"It's all very intricately woven together, Maryanne," he said, leaning in. "They take care of each other and those around them very, very well. I've known two of them, and they both have helped tremendously to get me where I am today. I couldn't do that to them; rat them out. Not after all they've done."

Maryanne didn't look him in the face while he talked. She just stared down at the table. "You are the company you keep, Ramsey. I don't care what they did for you. You should be bigger than all of this." She got up and started to walk away from the table.

"Maryanne, sit back down, there's more. Not much, but there is. You should know this about Joseph."

Maryanne scoffed. She turned around and went to sit back down, still not looking directly at him.

"Anyway, Joseph told him that he could get Andy around all this and make him mayor, if Andy could get his father to help Joseph out with a purchase he was looking to make."

"What purchase?"

"I don't know that."

Maryanne narrowed her eyes at him.

"I'm serious, Maryanne. I have no idea what he was looking to buy, what he ended up buying, or if he even did ever use the money. All I know is that's what he told Andy. He needed the money and whatever it was for, it was something big."

"How much money did he ask him for?"

"I don't know that either."

"Well, you're a lot of fucking help," she mumbled. Ramsey frowned, but kept going.

"So anyway, the father went for it, of course, wanted to further his son's career and all that. Joseph got his money, but didn't follow through on his end."

At that Maryanne's eyebrows perked up. "Really?"

"Yup. Turns out he even campaigned around town alongside Andy, made himself known as a full-fledged supporter."

Maryanne shook her head. "He wanted to make it as believable as possible until the last second," she paused, "right before he pulled the rug out from under him."

"That's probably right. He made him believe like he

had secured the mayoral seat for Andy and in the end, on election day, he went right ahead with business as usual. Hence what Andy told you; that he witnessed the followers who came to each polling station, saw the exchange of folders, which I'm guessing would account for any extra votes his opponent needed at that particular station."

"Followers?" she said.

"What?"

"You said followers. He witnessed the followers?"

Ramsey shrugged. "I just meant whomever it was he saw coming in after him. They were obviously hired help."

Maryanne gave him a bit of a confused expression, but let it go. She found his choice of words odd though.

"So anyway, his opponent gets in. Andy realizes Joseph didn't come through, but can't expose him because if he does, Joseph would return the favor on him and his father."

Maryanne thought for a moment. "Do you think it was a coincidence that I met this guy?"

"Andy you mean? Yes. Everyone I've talked to does corroborate the rest of his story. He settled for councilman positions. He fought against Joseph for years, trying to change things, but couldn't go too far as he didn't want to destroy his and his father's careers in the process."

"Is the dad still alive?"

"No. He died recently, I think. Andy did retire to Vegas though before that happened, and lives in Henderson and works at the Flamingo. His wife owns her own practice." Ramsey paused for a second, then said contemplatively, "Maybe he saw an opportunity with you that he wasn't willing to follow through on."

"What do you mean?"

"Well, his father is gone, so there's no chance of him damaging his career; his legacy, maybe, but not his career. Andy himself is thousands of miles removed from it all, living a relatively happy life that Joseph probably can't touch. Or so he thinks. He happens to meet you by the pool, gets overly excited and looks at this as a way to finally vilify himself. Plant a seed in your head, so to speak." Ramsey tapped his index finger in between Maryanne's eyes—a big brother-type move that won a little smile out of her. "But then after he leaves you and has some time to think, he becomes not entirely sure of Joseph's reach, and decides not to chance anything further. Hence, why he decided to not say or do anything more when you confronted him at the restaurant. He probably figured he got a little too brazen for his own good by the pool."

"I guess that makes sense." Maryanne hadn't told Ramsey about the note that was waiting for her in her room after she had met Andy, and that that was the real reason she had gone to confront him at the restaurant he worked at. For some reason, she had felt it prudent to keep that information to herself.

They sat in silence for another few seconds. "Well, that's all I got for you, kiddo," Ramsey said as he threw his hands up in the air and then took a sip of his latte.

Maryanne looked at him and then down at her empty coffee cup, wanting to order another. She suddenly felt exhausted. "Abbey, can I have another one to go? With an extra shot, please?"

"Long night ahead of you?" he asked.

"Yes, Lily and I are headed into the city in a little while. We're going to that Green Light annual benefit tonight."

"Oh, wow! Really?" Ramsey asked, his eyes lighting up. "That's great. It's in the Pegasus Room at the top of Rockefeller Center, right? Ever been there?"

"No," Maryanne said with a polite smile. She was really feeling worn out at this point.

"It's an incredible view. Three-hundred-sixty-degree windows. You'll be impressed."

"Yeah, that's what we've heard. Speedman is supposed to be there."

"That's right, he's a huge supporter of green jobs," Ramsey said, shaking his head. "Is Joseph going?" he added, hesitantly.

"No. It's just Lily and I."

"Good. You girls go and enjoy it."

"Thanks, Ramsey," she said. She slowly rose out of her seat as she saw Abbey put her second latte out on the counter. She started to take her wallet out when Ramsey grabbed her wrist. She looked at him, eyes wide as he was now standing over her, a little too closely.

"Listen, I know you don't agree with my silence. I'm not too comfortable with it myself. This isn't easy for me, no matter how it seems."

She frowned, but nodded her head in understanding as she looked down at the table.

"Just…be careful with Joseph. Okay?"

She shook her head yes.

"I'm still on your side. I wouldn't have told you all this if I wasn't and didn't know I could trust you. Just like you can trust me."

She wanted to laugh in his face, but didn't. "Okay ," she simply said.

He squeezed her wrist and gave her a closed-mouth smile. "Thanks, Abbey!" he said, and turned to leave.

"Bye," Maryanne said to his turned back, to which

he threw a wave over his shoulder. She walked up to the counter and paid Abbey for her latte. As she walked out, she watched Ramsey's Lexus go by her out of the driveway to the Moonbean. She checked the time on her cell phone and quickened her pace to her own car as she realized she only had a couple hours to get ready and catch a train into New York City.

A few hours later, Lily and Maryanne were on the sixty-fourth floor of Rockefeller Center, each wearing various items from each other's wardrobes. Maryanne wore her own shimmery black cocktail dress, Lily's black shoes to match, as well as a pair of her earrings, her own black shrug, and a small silver evening bag, also from Lily. She topped it all off with her Tiffany's necklace from Rob. Lily went down a bit more of a colorful route, with a sparkling purple knee-length, spaghetti strap dress that she picked out at a thrift shop over the weekend. It reminded Maryanne of what a 1940s lounge singer might have worn on stage, large blood-red orchid tucked behind her ear, as she crooned into one of those old-fashioned square head microphones. Lily didn't go for the orchid, but did wear bright red lipstick and carried a pink beaded clutch that Maryanne got as a gift one year from one of Prerogative's advertising reps in India. Maryanne's silver heels and black cardigan for when Lily got cold, because Lily always got cold considering her extremely skinny frame, finished the outfit, as well as a black ring Joseph brought back from Turkey that Maryanne had gotten first dibs on.

They were both a little sluggish upon their arrival, but the incredible views of New York City spread out below immediately revived them, and Maryanne filled

Lily in on her meeting with Ramsey.

"Wait, he was a mayor?"

"No," Maryanne said, getting a little frustrated with the indifference Lily was addressing all of this with. They walked along the edge of the room, hugging the windows so as to stay as far from the crowd as possible. "Apparently, he's very close with two people within that circle who did become mayors, because he said they 'took very good care of him,' or something like that. Got him where he is today. I forget the exact verbiage he used."

"Oh, okay," Lily said in understanding. They stopped to look at the view.

"How are you being so calm about all this? I mean, I'm having like an identity crisis here and you're acting as if I was just explaining, I don't know, what I had for lunch," Maryanne said, letting out a nervous laugh.

Lily laughed, too. "Well, does this surprise you? I mean we know what he's really like. This might shock anyone else, but us? You know the most important thing in the world to him is money."

"Yeah, but this is a little different, don't you think? This is on another level. It makes me question what I'm doing."

"What do you mean?"

"What do I mean? We're putting together a magazine that promotes fair politics, meanwhile the guy in charge is screwing people and pushing ideas we've both worked really hard to abolish; hell that entire generations have worked hard to abolish!"

Lily kind of looked at her sideways. "What are you talking about?"

"What do you think he meant when he stormed out of that dinner after that fight with Ramsey?"

"Calling Speedman 'one of them'?" Maryanne asked, looking at her friend pointedly. She was now facing Lily and her hands were on her hips.

"Well," Lily said, pulling her chin in and putting her hand on her head, smoothing her hair out in the process. "That could have meant anything."

"Yeah, or it could have meant one very specific thing. If it did, we're not only dealing with a liar and a cheapskate, but we're also dealing with a racist bigot, and I can't, in good conscience, continue to work for someone like that."

"But we're not doing it for him, we're doing it for each other, and for the product we put out every month. We're doing it for the writers we publish who have nowhere else to voice their opinions, and we're wakening a whole new generation to caring about what's going on in their country."

"I . . ." Maryanne started to respond, but they were interrupted by a booming voice erupting from a microphone at the head of the room. They both turned to see who was speaking and what was going on.

"Come on," Lily said, obviously annoyed at the interruption. Maryanne followed her to the podium where the action was taking place. As she made her way through the crowd and tried to keep up with her, she managed to get her digital camera and a very small notepad and pen out of her purse. *Old school reporting shouldn't be allowed at formal events*, she thought to herself.

The girls were no stranger to Green Light! It was the company Casey was covering over in China, and she was putting together a big investigative report on their purposes and findings. It was considered the premiere organization that was leading the charge for sustainable living and initiatives, which Casey was out to find if this was really true or not. It was started thirty years ago, long before the green trend became more than just a trend, but a movement that was sweeping, and terrifying, the world. Terrifying as it was becoming quite clear what would happen to the earth if no one started taking better care of it. Green Light! had been the first out of the gate and was now trusted globally as the most comprehensive and successful not-for-profit organization dedicated to a happier and healthier earth. The event tonight was being held to announce their new offices in Shanghai, another reason Casey was stationed in the city. Speedman, although not a founder, had become a huge supporter and proponent of the group over the years. Sometimes he was harshly criticized for it, as many thought some of Green Light! Foundation's proposed alternative energy sources could be considered questionable or were just afraid they would take away from the oil industry. Whatever the reason, not everyone was on board. Green Light! was on a mission to change that.

"I'd like to welcome you all here tonight," said a short, balding man with glasses, wearing an elegant tuxedo with a bright-red tie that almost seemed inappropriate. He amazingly didn't have to hush anyone more than once. The guests listened intently, waiting to hear what he had to say.

"My name is Michael Marano, and I am the events committee chair at the Green Light! Foundation. We are honored to have each and every one of you here to celebrate and support Green Light!'s efforts in making this a better, brighter earth for us and all of those who will come after."

The gentleman paused a moment to turn a piece of

paper over on the podium. “I hope you enjoy tonight’s festivities, but more importantly, I hope you’ll be just as excited as I am about the news that I am about to share. As you probably know, Green Light! has leagues in more than fifty countries around the world and soon we will be welcoming one that has been long overdue." He took an exaggerated pause for effect; one long enough for Lily to glance at Maryanne, roll her eyes, and for Maryanne to return the act.

"China," he said, his face breaking out into a huge smile, leaving no doubt in the minds of anyone watching him of his sheer joy over the announcement. The crowd broke into an enthusiastic applause.

"Now," he said, starting up again, "we will have a grand opening ceremony of the headquarters, an introduction to the Chinese league's efforts within their own company and globally within the next couple of weeks, and we are inviting every press member here tonight for an all-expense paid trip to Shanghai to witness all of this first hand."

Maryanne looked at Lily out of the corner of her eye and saw her friend's eyes widen. She turned to her, and they both tried to speak at once. They laughed at the jinx.

"Go ahead," Maryanne said.

"No, I was just going to ask, I mean we can do it right? You don't have anything for the next couple of months do you?"

"I really don't. I was going to say this will be great. It will give me an excuse to go check on Casey, maybe help her out a little in the process, I mean, depending on what the schedule is like."

"Yeah, sure. All right, I'll make sure you get on the list."

With that, Lily turned and started pushing her way through the crowd toward the table for which they had directed all interested journalists to go and sign up for the trip. Maryanne stood there awkwardly for a few moments, camera in hand, looking around and wondering what to do next.

"Hey, Maryanne."

She turned to see whom the voice belonged to.

"Oh, hey, how are you?" Maryanne said with a smile.

Standing in front of her was Stacy Rockaport, a reporter from Westchester Today. Stacy was friendly with Kayla and the two often had lunch together during the workday. They had all hung out in a group only a couple of times, but from what Maryanne knew of her, she liked Stacy and her practical, no-nonsense attitude toward both work and life, which was typical for a reporter.

"Swanky, huh?" Stacy said, passing the hand which she held her drink with in a small arc so as to indicate the room they were standing in.

Maryanne laughed. "Yeah, pretty amazing views. Have you ever been up here?"

"No, first time. I lucked out because Brandon was supposed to cover this, but got sick last minute."

"I see. You going to go?" Maryanne asked, pointing over her shoulder toward the sign-up table.

"No, no, no. A little too heavy for our type of coverage if you know what I mean," Stacy said with a smile and a wink.

Maryanne giggled and nodded her head in understanding. Suddenly, her memory kicked in. "Hey! Weren't you the one at that Westchester Hometown Society din…"

"Yup," Stacy said, raising her glass and taking a swig as she interrupted her. "Pretty interesting scene, but I'm sure Kayla filled you in on everything."

"Yeah," Maryanne responded, nodding politely. Kayla's own little scene from the other night was still very fresh in her memory and her name still stung a bit. "Have you followed up on that at all?" she asked, leaning in a bit and lowering her voice.

In return, Stacy's face got a lot more serious. "Not exactly. I'm still trying to find out who it was who left with him, but I can't get the guy at the damn Society to send me the roster of attendees!"

"Well, what do you mean, like he says he won't give it to you period? Or he's just taking his sweet time?"

"Right, when I initially requested it he said he'd get it to me right away, no problem. Then I never received it and now he's MIA. I've left him a million voicemails and e-mails, and he hasn't responded to a single one."

Maryanne frowned. Something really strange was going on, and she was having trouble even processing it all at this point.

"What did he look like?"

"Um, I don't know, pretty generic. Brown hair, kind of receding. Regular build. Probably in his 50s, maybe 60s," Stacy said, shrugging dejectedly. "I've gotten a hold of some of the others who were sitting at the table with them, but everyone either didn't know who he was because the guy was a new member apparently, or didn't even remember him at all because they left so quickly."

"I'll have to ask Ramsey if he knew him. Or if he remembers him for that matter."

"Oh, that's right! Of course, he was sitting at the table, too."

Maryanne nodded.

"All I have to go on is this 'meeting spot' I heard them mention after they left your offices," Stacy said, nonchalantly.

Maryanne's heart dropped to the bottom of her stomach. It was a good thing Stacy looked away momentarily otherwise she undoubtedly would have seen the panic flash through Maryanne's eyes. Andy's note had popped into her head, and for a moment she was back in Vegas, opening up this strange folded piece of paper that had slipped under her door.

They meet in the cemetery.

That wasn't all. Kayla had lied to her. Her friend had told her that once Joseph and his mystery guest had gone upstairs to the office, Stacy had left before they came back down.

"You saw them leave?"

"Yeah, I thought you said Kayla filled you in . . ." Stacy answered trailing off as Maryanne began to shake her head "no."

"Kayla said you sat in your car for a while, and when they didn't come down, you decided to leave as you had to make deadline."

Stacy furrowed her brow deeply and shook her own head in confusion. "No, I didn't tell her that. I parked in the lot and sat on the street bench that's pretty close to your front door."

Maryanne just looked at her with a hurt expression on her face.

Stacy lifted her hands in exasperation. "I told her all this."

"I'm sure you did."

"What is going on with her?"

"I don't know," Maryanne said. "So what happened after you sat down on the bench?"

"Well, I'd say I sat there for close to a half an hour. I really was about to leave when they finally came down. When I heard the door open I got up quickly and ran to hide behind the fence behind the bench there. Of course, they weren't exactly talking loud enough for me to hear. As they passed by I heard the other one go, 'At the next meeting, your local spot.' That was all I got."

"That could mean anything," Maryanne said.

"I know."

"That was all? Where did they go after that?"

"They kept going up the street, toward their cars."

"You sure?"

"Well, I waited a couple minutes, peeked out, and they were gone, so unless they just walked off somewhere," Stacy said, shrugging. "Why wouldn't Kayla tell you that?" she asked again.

"Has she been acting strange at work lately?" Maryanne asked her. "Have you noticed anything?"

"Maybe she's been keeping to herself a little bit more, but other than that," Stacy looked back at her and shrugged.

"Hey, guys." Lily returned with an excited smile. "So I got you down."

"Hi, Lily," Stacy said politely.

"So how long is the trip?" Maryanne asked Lily.

"Ten days."

"Wow. Okay."

"Yeah, it's a little long, but I think it's important that we be there."

"Yeah, you're right," Maryanne said, but she couldn't help but be disheartened at the thought of being away from Rob for another ten days.

Lily smiled and took a deep breath in and let it out before turning to Stacy. "How's it going?" she asked.

“Okay,” Stacy answered.

“Are you going on the trip, too?”

“No, it’s a bit much for us to take on. We’ll definitely make a mention of it though.”

“Yeah.” Lily turned back to Maryanne. “Well, we should probably get some work done before we get out of here.”

“Sure,” Maryanne said, taking hold of her camera and pen. The two would go around taking some people shots to show on the events page of Prerogative, and then take down the names for the captions. They would also gather up any bits of information that could be potential leads and sources.

“Well, you guys have fun,” said Stacy, giving Maryanne a worried smile, which Maryanne returned.

“Thanks, you, too. What time are you heading home? Maybe we can meet for the train?”

“Oh, that’s okay, I’m actually meeting up with some friends after this. We’re not writing it up right away so I don’t have to get back immediately.”

“Okay,” Lily said with a little wave. “See ya.”

“Bye.”

As Maryanne and Lily turned, they saw a small group in front of them comprised of a few politicians, some of which they would have recognized, but only one caught their eye. It was Donald Speedman.

“I didn’t know he was going to be here!” Lily said excitedly, under her breath.

“I heard he might be,” Maryanne said, staring at him, her eyes wide.

“Let’s get a picture of them.”

“Oh, yeah,” Maryanne said, snapping out of it. She tightened her grip on her camera and approached the small group of gentlemen.

“Excuse me, would you all mind getting together for a picture for Prerogative magazine?”

They gave the typical response, looking around at each other embarrassed, holding onto their drinks, before one brave soul finally steps up as organizer. “Gentlemen? What do you say?”

“Anything for Prerogative magazine,” Speedman said. Lily and Maryanne giggled appreciatively.

“Okay,” Maryanne said as they formed a line and put their arms around each other. “Everybody ready? One, two, three.”

Maryanne checked the picture to make sure it had come out well. “Looks good!” she said with a thumbs-up sign. “Now nobody move because Lily here needs to take down your names.”

“Rafael Macabre.”

“Vincent Leugont.”

“Marc Dean.”

They said and spelled out their names for Lily as she went down the line. Finally, she came to Donald Speedman.

“I think I know who you are,” she said with a little smile.

Speedman laughed. “Well, just in case, it’s S-P-E-E-D-M-A-N. You never know,” he said, shrugging. He flashed her a huge smile. “You know, I’m a big fan of the magazine.”

Lily looked at him, her blue eyes wide. “Really? Thanks! That’s a huge compliment coming from you.” Maryanne was beaming as well beside her.

"Of course! You guys are the voice of a whole new generation and it's great! No holds barred on what you cover and what you say. Keep it up, seriously. You're making young people not afraid, or should I say, you're waking them up."

"Thank you," the girls said in unison, causing the whole group to laugh.

"No problem. You going on the press trip to Shanghai?"

"Maryanne here is."

"Good, good. Make sure you give it a good amount of coverage," he said to Maryanne, pointing at her and giving her a parental look as if to say this is what I expect from you.

"Sure will," she replied.

"All right. Enjoy girls." He walked away nonchalantly, apparently unaware of the importance of his current position. Lily and Maryanne turned to each other and smiled. Side by side they went off into the crowd to make some more connections.

He didn't have to move much in order to keep an eye on them. He basically kept himself glued to the bar most of the time and was able to always have a view from a distance. Leaving and heading back to town, however, would be a different story. He hoped he would be able to stay on them and get on the same train. If not, he was in trouble, and what he had seen up until now had already left him unsettled.

It was bad enough that the brunette had been seen with Ramsey earlier today, and once she had met up with the redhead here, the two had walked the perimeter of the room for almost a half an hour, talking heatedly about something, and he had a strong hunch as to what the topic of conversation had been. He hoped Ramsey was being taken care of as he watched them so the idiot couldn't do any more harm. The man had become too big for his britches anyway and needed to be taught a lesson.

He tried to decipher how much exactly it was that the little brunette knew. Part of him wondered what her name might be, and what she might smell like up close, but he quickly pushed those thoughts out of his head whenever they crept in. He didn't know their names for a reason, and he knew it was best it stayed that way.

Something was definitely troubling her though, and her mood only seemed to deepen after she'd spoken to that nosy little Westchester Today snot while the redhead went to sign up for the press trip. More bad news. They didn't need Green Light! getting any more positive press, especially among the youth vote, than it already had, or giving that disgusting porch-monkey Speedman any more of a boost either, for that matter. He knew the two of them would do exactly that once whoever was assigned had come back from the trip.

They had managed to start pushing the brunette and the boyfriend in different directions, but those efforts had yet to prove themselves fruitful. Hopefully, they could make a dent on these two. Their future depended on it.

His future depended on it.

Chapter 21

Rob frowned as he looked out the window of Lily and Maryanne's apartment into the courtyard of the Darren Hayes and a very dark and rainy night.

"Everyone better have on sneakers or boots because it's going be really muddy out there," he said loudly, so as to make sure he was heard over the din of the crowd that had developed in the girls' apartment. He made his way through them toward Maryanne's bedroom where she was getting ready with Sarah and a couple of the other girls. He frowned again when he saw that her attire was entirely inappropriate for what they were about to go do. "Babe, no."

She looked over at him wide-eyed. "What is the problem," she asked.

"Have you looked outside? It's gross out!"

"I know," she said with a whine, "but we're going out afterwards."

"So what!"

"All right, all right," she said, looking over at Sarah who was sitting on the floor doing her makeup in front of Maryanne's full-length mirror. "I'll put my heels in my purse and just layer up over the shirt."

"Yeah, exactly," said Sarah, shrugging.

"Yes," Rob said. "That's what I like to hear. Layer up. I don't want to hear you complaining that you're freezing."

Maryanne shot him a hurt look.

"Don't look at me like that!" he said, laughing. They

stared at each other for a good five seconds. "Get over here!" he said and came toward her, wrapping her in a bear hug. She laughed into his chest, which her face was smashed against. After a few seconds, she pushed him away and out the door.

"All right, out of here! I've got to finish getting ready."

"Well, hurry up, it's almost 8:30."

Rob turned and went back into the living room where everyone was gathered together to go to the pumpkin blaze at Kykuit Rockefeller Estate down the street. Next weekend was Halloween, and every year for the three weeks preceding the holiday, the grounds keepers would carve thousands of pumpkins and arrange them into eerie scenes that were breathtaking when the sun goes down and the jack-o-lanterns were all lit. The group had all planned to have a walk through tonight, but the weather was kind of putting a damper on that.

"Hey, maybe we should just think about going next weekend!" Rob called out from the living room.

"No!" Maryanne and Sarah replied immediately and emphatically in unison. They both started laughing.

"Come on, the rain and puddles will make it more festive and…dirty," Maryanne yelled back between giggles, trying to find her words.

"Whatever," Rob threw at them as he passed by the doorway to use the bathroom. He wasn't exactly in the mood for this with everything they were dealing with, but Maryanne really wanted to go and use the excursion as a chance to do something fun and get their minds off of things. Rob enjoyed the pumpkin blaze, too, but doubted it would do the trick for him.

"Gosh, who's here now?" Maryanne asked Sarah as the voices coming from the living room had seemed to multiply within the past few minutes.

Sarah just shrugged. "I don't know."

"Hey, you guys ready yet?" Lily asked, peeking her head around the corner.

"Yeah, I am," Maryanne said, grabbing a hat and throwing her heels in her bag. She glanced back at Sarah.

"I'll be out in a sec," she replied.

"Okay."

Maryanne followed Lily into the living room where quite a crowd had formed. There was Steve and Scott and a few friends of theirs, who probably had also gone to high school with Rob, Lily's boyfriend John and two people Maryanne recognized as friends of his from work, as well as one of Sarah's friends from her hometown in Connecticut, and a few others that Maryanne recognized from around the apartments.

Steve and Scott must have rounded these people up, she thought to herself. *No wonder Rob's annoyed.*

Emerging from the bathroom, Rob came up behind her and circled one arm around her waist. She looked up at him. "They all have tickets?" she asked under her breath.

"Yeah, apparently, Scott can get everyone in."

Scott worked for a local theater and as a perk of the job would usually get free tickets for area events, the pumpkin blaze included.

They heard the click of Maryanne's bedroom light go off and saw Sarah come out. "Okay, I'm ready," she said, grabbing her coat off the back of one of the chairs in the living room.

Maryanne watched Ronald dart out from underneath the table and into her bedroom. "Okay, let's go!" she said loudly. She stood at the door while everyone filed out. Rob was the last one and dropped a kiss on her forehead before she locked up.

Once they got outside, most people lifted their hoods over their heads and paired up under a variety of umbrellas. The rain had lightened, but it was definitely still lingering. Maryanne put her arm through Rob's and stayed close as she tried to keep up with his usual fast pace.

They were toward the back of the group so she thought it was okay to speak at a normal pitch and not whisper. "Who are all these people?" she asked him. "I mean, I know most of them, but those others…" she said, trailing off.

"I don't know. Scott probably asked them to come. He thinks he's a fucking big shot because he got all these people there. Meanwhile, he probably barely knows their names."

Maryanne looked down, swallowing a smile at Rob's frustration. She had known he wasn't keen on going to the blaze this year, but she thought it would be good for them. She knew he was only there to make her happy. She had to admit she was a little nervous about the proximity of the event to the cemetery directly across the street, but figured she should face that head on. If the urge to visit Cecily's grave came over her again though, she knew she wouldn't be able to resist it.

As they walked down the hill, Maryanne smiled up at Rob as they were able to see through the trees surrounding the estate to the twinkling sea of jack-o-lanterns in the rain. They seemed to roll in waves over the hills of the property.

The group moved down the block quickly, and Scott went through them handing out tickets as he went. Once they got through the entrance to the estate, they needed to follow a dirt path lined with tiki torches, which led them around a small part of the perimeter of the property and across the bridge over a small pond. Sarah and her friends drew the strings on their hoods super tight and took advantage of the opportunity to mimic "The Blair Witch Project." They ran to the front of the line screaming and flailing their arms above their heads and disappeared around the bend over the bridge.

"Idiots," Maryanne mumbled, shaking her head. As the rest of them got closer to the fields where the blaze was held, the hills of the cemetery began to loom closer and closer in the distance.

They meet in the cemetery.

She winced as a picture of her own hands unfolding the note in the doorway of her hotel room flashed through her head. She felt the note had most likely been left by Andy, but of course she had no way of knowing for sure, especially since he had refused to admit to anything or answer any further questions when she had confronted him in the restaurant. If it was him though, was this another reference to Joseph?

W ho are "they"? Did this have any truth to it or was Andy just looking for revenge at any cost for Joseph's lies to him? She was willing to bet there was indeed some truth to it. Especially after what Stacy told her the other day at the Green Light! event. Again though, that could have meant anything.

Rob had noticed her glance at the cemetery and wince. He sighed and decided he needed to make the best of this, for her. "So are you excited to go to Shanghai?" he asked, smiling down at her.

"What? Oh, well, sort of."

"Sort of? Come on, you're going to get to go to China!"

"I know, but I was just away for a little more than a week and now I'm going to be gone again, so soon for almost two." As she said that her grip tightened slightly on his bicep and he knew what she was thinking.

"I know," he said, as they came upon the first patch of carved pumpkins. Some were more ornate than others, but the sheer volume of them was what made it all so eye-catching. They stretched as far as the eye could see, back into the woods that lined the estate, some hanging from the trees, others arranged in sculptures.

"It'll be all right, babe. I bet it will go fast. I've got a lot going on at work so I'll have to be in bed really early during that time anyway. So it's not like I'd be that much fun. You'll get to see Casey, and I bet you guys can do some site-seeing together, you know? It's not like you'll be alone like you usually are and China's a country you really wouldn't go to on your own. You should try to take advantage of it as much as possible. Maybe go see the Great Wall."

At that point, he felt a pang of guilt that he had not yet told Maryanne about his real-life action scene through the NYC subway system, but he had been unable to find out any further information, as he had no idea where to even start. He shouldn't be trying to make light of a situation that was anything but light. She had a right to be concerned about leaving when they were both going through so much; so much that could possibly drive them apart if they let it.

A scream closing in on them from behind made them both jump out of their skin. Two seconds later, a figure jumped on Maryanne from behind.

"Oh, my God, you scared the crap out of me!" she yelled at Sarah, who was still hanging on her back like a monkey. Sarah laughed and hopped back onto solid ground. Her friend Samantha was now standing next to them as well. Maryanne could see her overly white teeth gleaming through the dark in a huge smile. None of her blonde hair was visible thanks to the hoodie pulled down far over her face, almost covering her eyes.

"Come on," Sarah told them. "They've actually got the headless horseman."

"What do you mean?" Rob asked.

"A guy dressed up like the headless horseman is riding through one of the scenes up ahead."

"All right, we'll get there."

"No, come on! Everyone's up there and they're letting people go over to the cemetery, too. Besides, all the setups are the same as last year."

She grabbed Maryanne's arm and started to practically drag her down the path that led through the glittering pumpkin scenes. Maryanne looked at Rob as she passed, and he rolled his eyes at her and followed. The four of them made their way through a herd of dinosaurs, a spider's web, and finally, a few snakes before coming upon a small clearing that was sectioned off by a large wooden fence. People were gathered up against it, and a huge man dressed in a cape was riding a horse up and down the fence, holding his jack-o-lantern head in his hand. You could tell the costume covered his head as his torso seemed abnormally large.

They came upon the rest of the group who cheered every time the headless horseman passed. Sometimes the actor would slow the horse to just a trot, other times he had him running at full speed, which really gave the crowd a thrill, even causing a few of the children to start crying in fear. Maryanne turned to Rob and smiled. He came up behind her and laughed. He put his arms around her waist and kissed her cheek. He was glad to see her smile.

“That’s awesome!” he exclaimed. “They didn’t have this last year.”

“I know. That’s weird, I wonder how he sees?”

"I have no idea. He must be a very skilled equestrian to be able to ride that horse with only one hand, while the other one holds a lit-up pumpkin, and not to mention his entire face is covered with a big black cloak."

“Yeah, right,” Maryanne said laughing. She turned to Sarah who was standing next to her. “Where’s Lily?”

“I think she and John and his friends from the restaurant went across the street to the cemetery already. At least that’s what they said they were going to do when I ran back to get you.”

“Oh.” Maryanne was working overtime to seem nonchalant. She hadn’t experienced any overwhelming urge to get over there though, and considering she was so close to it at this point, she guessed the feeling would most likely not be surfacing since it hadn’t already. *So there really is no reason to be nervous,* she told herself.

“Let’s go over there!” Sarah said.

“Yeah!” chimed in Samantha.

Crap.

“Eh, I don’t know. We haven’t seen everything yet over here,” she said, turning to Rob, grabbing his hand and squeezing it tightly to get the point across that she thought it best if they stay on the other side of the highway.

“Come on,” Rob said, taking the hint and leading her away from Sarah and Samantha. “I’m hungry I want to go get a funnel cake or something. I saw a sign before that they’re selling food over by the barns.” There was also a farm on the Rockefeller Estate.

Maryanne looked over her shoulder at the girls and shrugged, a wave of relief washing over her. She gave them a short wave.

"Party poops!" Sarah called after them.

Maryanne watched them head across the grass toward Route 9. A few of the others broke away from the group in front of the fence to follow, as well as Steve, Scott, and a couple of their friends who had come along.

"Thanks," Maryanne said as she turned back to Rob. "No problem, babe. You think I want to hang out with those clowns anyway?" He smiled down at her. "Besides, I really do want a funnel cake."

"Okay," she said with a laugh. Once they reached the barns, most of which had been cleared out to create walk-through haunted houses, they also came upon a number of food stands and bonfires with people dressed in early nineteenth-century garb, telling stories of how they used to run the barns and work the land to any child who had the attention span to listen. Maryanne turned to look at the old barns and shuddered.

Whoever had decorated them had certainly outdone themselves. The breezes and the drizzle whipped through them as a white iridescent light glowed through the windows. She could see old, tattered rags hanging within, which she assumed were meant to serve as ghosts that swung lightly back and forth.

This is like aversion shock therapy, she thought.

She turned to see that Rob was no longer standing next to her, but caught a glimpse of him walking back toward her munching on a funnel cake he had already gotten his hands on just as her phone began to ring. She fished it out of her bag and looked at the face to see that Lily was calling.

"Hey," she answered, just as Rob reached her. He took a bite of the funnel cake, getting powdered sugar all over his face. He held it out to her. She shook her head "no thanks" in response.

"Hey, are you guys still over there?"

"Yeah."

"Well, we're all over in the cemetery walking around if you guys are interested."

"Um, I don't know. Rob just got a funnel cake," He raised his eyebrows at her as if to ask what was going on.

"Oh, okay. Well, we're here if you want to come find us. I just didn't want you guys to be wondering where everybody went."

"Oh, everyone else is there, too?"

"Yeah, I'm pretty sure. Sarah and Sam just got here and I'm with John. I thought I saw Scott and Steve a couple minutes ago, too. I don't know. I could be wrong. It's pretty dark here, we could use a flashlight."

"Are there little kids over there?" Maryanne was hoping it was more of a family scene rather than just a bunch of teenagers who got bored with what was going on on the other side of the road.

"No, not really. I think I saw a couple making out behind a tree, but other than that…"

"Oh, God," Maryanne said, laughing. "We'll head over in a bit. Call you when we get there."

"Okay. Bye."

"Bye."

"Was that Lily?" Rob asked.

"Yeah," Maryanne answered quietly, looking down.

"What's going on?"

"They're all across the street," she said, pointing over his shoulder.

He kept munching on his funnel cake, and then turned to glance back there.

"So let's go," he said shrugging, trying to ease her mind about the situation. "You're okay, right?" he asked, putting an arm over her shoulders and leading her in that direction.

"Yeah, I guess. I mean I haven't felt the need to go over there or anything."

"Okay, so let's just go for a little bit," he said. Rob doubted whoever "they" were that the mysterious Vegas note had referred to would be out and about with this event going on.

They were still headed toward the exit where they would hit a crosswalk that would lead them to the cemetery entrance. Rob thought going over there would help her, and him for that matter, be able to face what was happening to Maryanne head on, together. At the very least, it might make them a little more comfortable with that space.

They crossed the street, and as they passed through the huge wrought iron gates of the entrance that were typically barred shut at this time of night, Maryanne wrapped her arms around herself. Rob tightened his grip around her shoulders and pulled her in closer.

"We're all right, babe."

"I know that," she said softly, but the crack in her voice convinced him that she didn't truly believe it. Luckily, as they made their way up the slight incline that led them into the first patch of tombstones, they started to hear voices and saw a few dark shadows dart out across the path in front of them, laughing and chasing each other. It was definitely a sense of relief to Maryanne to know they certainly were not alone within this vast field of dead souls.

"Why don't you call Lily?" Rob said.

"Oh, right." She took her phone out of her bag and dialed her.

"Hey."

"Hey, we're here."

"Oh. Well, we're toward the center, kind of near that big huge central mausoleum building."

"We'll head that way."

"Okay. See you in a minute."

"Where are they?" Rob asked.

"By that big building in the center."

"Let's go down this way then."

"Yeah."

The two had begun to head uphill again, which would have placed them on the northern perimeter of the cemetery, putting them along the edge of the woods, but giving them a full view over the entire cemetery as the whole property was on a slant. They turned down into the sea of ancient tombstones once again in order to go meet up with Lily and John.

"AHHAHAHAHAHHHAHAHHhhhahaaaaaaaaaa!"

The two of them looked at each other and smiled but rolled their eyes. Lily's boyfriend John's explosive laugh was better than having a flashlight to find them.

"We didn't even need to call her to find out where she was," Rob said.

"Yeah, seriously."

The group was standing in the middle of the road in a circle. Once you got into the real depths of the cemetery, the walking path widened enough for cars to pass through. Maryanne caught a glimpse of Lily's red hair as the moonlight caught it for just a second.

"Yeah, that's them," she said, after she and Rob had hesitated for a few moments. They headed down the hill to meet them.

As they approached, Lily broke away from the small group, seeming relieved they had arrived and she no longer had to be a part of the drivel that often was John and his work friends' conversations. The overweight chef, whose name Maryanne still did not know even though he would often show up to outings such as these, was currently seeming to mimic a Strongman Competition contestant carrying a humongous bolder across the finish line. John and their other friend could not have found this any funnier.

"Where's everybody else?" Maryanne asked.

"I'm not sure. Sarah and Samantha are in here somewhere, and Steve and Scott passed by us a couple minutes ago saying they were heading back toward the entrance because Steve wanted to have a look at the old church. I think they're having tours through there."

"Oh, really?" Rob said. "That's cool. Maybe we'll go by on our way out."

Maryanne looked at him sideways.

"Or maybe not," he said, laughing at her reaction. Before they could get any further John called Rob over.

"Rob! Hey, man, didn't you say your dad used to raise goats or something in France?"

"Um," Rob hesitated and turned to Lily and Maryanne with a confused smile on his face.

"Well, he grew up on a farm, yeah," he said laughing. "Why?" Before Maryanne could say anything he was walking toward the three guys to join what would inevitably be a pointless and ridiculous exchange.

"We were just thinking that maybe we could volunteer at the farm over there," she heard John say as Rob went over to them.

Maryanne turned to Lily and raised her hand in the

air in question. Lily just shrugged, obviously embarrassed—her usual response to John's rantings. The two of them sauntered off away from the boys.

"So, have you called Casey yet to tell her you're coming to Shanghai?"

Maryanne looked up, eyes wide and started shaking her head in disgust with herself. "No, actually, I haven't." She lifted her hands in the air, not believing it hadn't even occurred to her to let her cousin know sooner that she was on her way. Lily looked at her in her matter-of-fact way.

"Well, it's okay, I'm sure. You can even call her later tonight. It'll be morning there."

"Nah, I'm not going to call her tonight," Maryanne said, waving her off.

It was only for a split second, but Maryanne caught it out of the corner of her eye—a quick flash of red light on her right that had seemed to come from one of the tombstones. Lily noticed her eyes go wide for a moment.

"What's wrong?" she asked.

"Oh, uh, nothing. Thought I saw something."

"Lil!"

The two girls whirled around at the sound of John's voice. The four guys were all turned, looking expectantly at them.

"Yeah?" she answered.

"Could you come back here a sec? I want to ask you something."

"I'll be right back," Lily said to Maryanne. She dug her hands in her pockets and walked quickly back over to the group. The second Lily was gone, Maryanne turned to look back at where she had spotted the quick flash of light. At first there was nothing, but after a few seconds another quick beam of it ran across the ground in front of it. It was coming from a small extension sticking up off one of the tombstones. She locked her eyes on it and started toward it. Not much was running through her mind at that point. She had been looking at the back of the grave and realized a few seconds before she came upon it, when she was able to round the piece so she was facing the front of it, that this was Cecily's tombstone.

How could I not have realized I was so close to it? she thought to herself as she stood in front of it. She looked up to see where the light source was coming from. A small blood-red cross extended off the top of Cecily's grave, something she had never noticed before, even in all of her previous trips to visit it. "How could I not have seen this?" she whispered as she slowly reached out to touch the cross. Just as her fingertips were about to make contact, she saw him.

He was quite a ways away, but she knew him instantly. He was standing at the base of the woods, half of him hidden behind a tree, but she saw him clearly nonetheless, and it froze her in place.

He wore the same flannel. His facial features were unmistakable: round face, short-cropped, ash-blond hair. Even though he was far away, she could tell his face, although clear with no stubble, was dirtied, ever so slightly.

It was the man from her dream, who abruptly turned and walked off into the woods.

She gasped and started in fright. The feeling was coming over her, an overwhelming sense of urgency. This time she needed to follow this man, otherwise, something awful would happen. She began to walk uphill toward the spot where he had disappeared.

The others were so involved in their conversation they didn't even notice. Steve, Scott, and company had actually come back over to join the group, further occupying their attention as Maryanne walked further and further away.

She walked low and fast, trying to keep to the shadows. She reached the edge of the woods within a couple of minutes. She didn't know where this adrenaline and courage was coming from, but she entered the darkness of its threshold without hesitation. She needed to follow him, no matter what.

She couldn't see him anymore. She didn't even catch a glimpse of him, or anything else for that matter, but she still somehow knew where she was going. She felt her way through the woods as if she were trying to find the bathroom late at night, feeling the familiar corners and edges of her apartment until she reached the light switch. The trees grew taller and stronger as she moved in deeper.

What are you doing? she thought.

It was as if a light bulb finally went on in her head and she now understood exactly where she was and the danger surrounding that from so many angles. She was in the middle of the woods, in the dark, far enough now from her friends that they might not be able to get to her in time if something were to happen to her. Add in the possibly dangerous boss who might or might not be part of some sort of group whose dealings required them to meet in a cemetery. That was bad news, all around.

Just as she had snapped herself out of it and was about to turn back, she saw something that was hidden by a more clustered grouping of trees up ahead. "What the hell is that?" she whispered, although there was certainly no one around to hear her, no one she could see that is. She moved closer and saw that she was looking at a shed, maybe even a very small cottage of some sort. It was made of wooden slats and had a simple angled roof with shingles dotted by the few that had fallen off over time. The windows looked like they had been blacked out with spray paint. She began to walk toward it when she started to hear her name being called out.

"Maryanne!"

Rob. She turned to look over her shoulder and didn't see anyone behind her just yet. She looked back at the shed, torn. Sighing, she began to walk back toward the cemetery. The poor guy was probably having a heart attack and she knew he didn't deserve any more worry than she had already offered up in the past few weeks. As she walked, she kept looking back at the shed and all around her, trying to memorize her location.

"Mar!"

This call was audibly more panicked than the first.

"I'm here!" she yelled back. "I'm coming!" Rob's silhouette began to take shape up ahead as he weaved back and forth through the trees in search of her.

"Babe!" she yelled and raised a hand in the air to wave at him. Before she could, she tripped over a raised tree root and fell, hitting the ground with a grunt.

As she slowly started to sit up, she heard the crunch of Rob's foot falls on the twigs and leaves as he was now running toward her at full speed.

"Jesus Christ, babe!" he said, slowing himself as he came upon her. He kneeled next to her where she was now examining a very scratched and bloodied knee. She pulled it up to her chin and hugged her shin, giving Rob a pained and tired look.

"What are you doing here?" he asked, but more gently, stroking the side of her face with his hand. "I didn't even see you walk off!" He helped her to her feet. "Can you walk on it?" he asked.

"Are the others around?" she asked, looking up into his eyes and searching. Her brown eyes looked almost black as coals in the dark.

"Well, Lily and John were behind me, but who knows what happened to those two. Probably got distracted by something. Why?"

"I saw him again."

"Saw who?"

"The man in flannel."

"Who the hell is that?" As soon as he said it, his eyes went wide and he pulled back. "You mean the guy you saw in your dream?"

She shook her head "yes."

"The guy you said you saw in a dream in your apartment, you're saying you now saw here?"

"I was standing in front of Cecily's grave, and I saw him standing at the top of the hill, right in front of the woods."

She paused as Rob was still staring at her, wide-eyed. "And then what?" he asked, almost screaming.

"Shhhh!" she replied. She turned her head to see if anyone was closing in yet. No one was behind them, but she figured she needed to hurry up with the story. "He turned and walked into the trees, so I followed."

Rob still stared at her.

"Say something!" she shouted at him.

"Okay, are you fucking nuts?" he finally responded. He turned from her and ran a hand through his hair, which was gaining considerable length she noticed. When he turned back to her, his eyes were still wild. "I mean…Maryanne?" he finally settled, unable to think of any sort of viable response to what had just happened.

"Hello?" Lily was coming up behind them. They turned and saw her stick-thin figure making its way through the woods, just as Rob's had a few minutes earlier. "Guys?"

"We're here," they yelled back to her in unison.

"Don't say anything," Maryanne said fiercely, yet under her breath to Rob as he passed by her and grabbed her hand roughly.

"Oww!" she complained as she started to hobble. "My knee, remember?"

He slowed and looked down at it. "Oh, sorry," he said with the first hint of sympathy she'd heard from him since he'd found her. He looked back up at her and shook his head.

"What?" she whispered.

"You know what!" he threw back over his shoulder. They finally reached Lily.

"Hey," she said with a cheerful smile, which quickly turned into a frown at the site of Maryanne's knee. It was now bleeding. "Oh, my God, what happened?"

"I wandered in here and tripped over a tree root," Maryanne answered quickly before Rob could even open his mouth. She looked up at him and gave him a tight-lipped smile. He looked down at her and the anger behind his dark eyes told her she was in for it tonight, but there was a force inside her now. Rather than being scared or confused, she felt determined. Determined to find out what was happening around her, to use these messages and strange occurrences to her advantage. In other words, she wasn't going to let him stop her from doing anything. Not now.

Lily looked from one to the other for a few moments, trying to figure out what was going on. She knew they were covering up something, but it didn't hold her interest enough to pry. People usually came to her anyway and she could wait them out. "Okay," she drawled out with a little laugh.

"What happened to John?" Rob asked as he motioned for the three of them to walk out of the woods and back into the cemetery. He was moving fast again, pulling Maryanne along for the ride. They swiftly moved ahead of Lily who saw she was going to have to quicken her pace in order to keep up.

"Um, he and the others wanted to go back across the street, so I said I'd follow you in here and come back with you guys," she said, moving to almost a trot. "I've kind of filled my quota of their ridiculous restaurant stories for the night."

"Yeah, I don't blame you," Rob said, a little too quickly, and a little too roughly. Maryanne winced and turned to look back at her. Lily held out a hand in Rob's directly and shrugged, as if to ask, "What the hell is his problem?" All Maryanne could do was shake her head in response and shrug back.

"Why are we running exactly?" Lily asked. No one responded.

The three of them tripped down the hill through the cemetery, which now had a lot more visitors and seemed brighter somehow than when Maryanne had followed the man from her dream into the woods; a little too bright, in fact. She wondered if the event organizers had set up some sort of floodlights to ensure people could make their way through it, especially the children. They made their way through pretty quickly, and as they got closer to the entrance, Maryanne was surprised at how they kept passing more and more crowds of people headed toward the endless rows of tombstones and mausoleums.

"Wow," Lily said. "I guess the blaze is pretty boring this year."

"Ha. I guess they'd better start changing it up next year."

"You guys want to go to Denver's?" she asked them when they reached the cross walk to get back over the highway.

"Sure," Rob said immediately, but still with that edge of anger to his voice. The two girls looked at him a little shocked, especially Maryanne. She had expected him to say no as it seemed he was anxious to get home and talk this out more. "We'll meet you there." With that he was off again, Maryanne almost stumbling in tow as he held firmly onto her hand. Lily stood at the corner watching in confusion. She eventually grabbed her phone out of her bag to locate John.

"What the hell is your problem?" Maryanne asked as they trudged up Route 9 and were finally out of earshot. "And why are we going this way?"

"Because it will give us more time to talk," he said over his shoulder.

"Not much time," she said under her breath, and looked down at the sidewalk as he dragged her along. He finally slowed and turned to look back at her. The sad look on her face was enough to make him cry. For him, nothing in the world was worse than seeing her upset.

"It makes me nauseous," he had told her once.

He pulled her up so she was by his side and slipped an arm around her waist and the other over her chest and pressed his cheek against hers as they walked, pressing her against him. Maryanne looked around to see if anyone was watching. It was kind of embarrassing.

"Um, babe?"

He just kept walking and hugging. She saw out of the corner of her own eye that even his eyes were closed.

"Babe?"

After a few more seconds he sighed, stopped and took her by the shoulders and turned her toward him. "I don't want you to go to Shanghai."

She frowned and narrowed her eyes at him. "What? Why? Earlier you were the one trying to psych me up about it, and now you're saying you don't want me to go?"

Rob just stared back at her. This had certainly thrown him for a loop.

When they were back in the cemetery and he had turned around to see that Maryanne was nowhere to be found, he felt like his heart had literally stopped beating. He tried to swallow, but couldn't even manage that. The others continued talking and laughing as he took a few steps away from the group, tentatively, and looked around.

"Maryanne?" he said, his voice raised just a notch. He ventured out a little further and did a wide sweep of the area with his eyes, first right, and then left. They strained in the dark, as he tried to use the little overdraft there was of the streetlamps on the highway, as well as the moonlight, to investigate every little corner, nook, and cranny he could find. There was no one in sight at that point. What he did see, located slightly downhill from where he was standing was a slowly pulsating light, of a deep blood red that was shining onto the grave in front of it. Just as Maryanne had been, Rob was facing the back of the tombstone. He began to walk down the hill toward it. He glanced behind him to see the group was still joking and laughing light-heartedly. A flash of envy went through him at how carefree they all seemed.

He walked down to the grave, and as he came around to the front of it, he gasped when he saw whose deathbed it was. He had stood in that same spot only a few days ago. "Cecily Reynolds," he whispered. He looked up and saw what must have been the light source: a red cross on top of the stone, but it had gone dark.

Was this what I saw? I don't remember seeing this the other day, he thought.

Before he could contemplate it any further, he remembered why he had come down here in the first place. He looked around once more to make sure he wasn't just being paranoid. When he confirmed that she was indeed nowhere in sight, he called up to the group.

"Hey, guys!"

No response.

He walked back up the hill toward them. "Guys!" he yelled, much louder. This time, they all turned. "You know where Maryanne went?"

"Oh," Lily said, confused, looking around herself. "She was just here a second ago. Maybe she went to find Sarah?"

"No. I don't think so," Rob answered, putting his hand on his hips. "I'm going to walk up to the woods to see if she wandered in there."

Lily and John exchanged a look. Lily stepped forward. "All right, well, we'll come with you. Don't want you going in there by yourself."

"Yeah. Hey, maybe we can do a remake of 'The Blair Witch Project,'" John said. With that, he lifted his arms and started screaming Maryanne's name and running up and down the aisles of gravestones. His two friends doubled over with laughter.

Rob dropped his head slightly and just walked past them, unable to put up with their antics at this point. He wasn't sure when he had lost them, but the fact that Maryanne hadn't responded to John's screaming her name was making him nauseous with worry. Even if she had gone all the way across the cemetery to find Sarah, she would have heard that. When he reached the top of the hill and the woods that lined it, his stomach did a flip. *Where is she?* he screamed in his head as he pictured the face of the man who had chased him through the subways.

I should have told her, I should have warned her! What if he's gotten hold of her? "Maryanne!"

No answer.

"Oh, God," he said under his breath, then followed it up quickly with another call, this time as loud as he could. "Maryanne!"

He could barely see, but as he got deeper into the trees he realized that up ahead the moonlight had found its way through the canopy which would make it slightly easier to see once he got to that area. He also noticed a black silhouette not too far in the distance.

"I'm here!" he heard her say. It was like the huge cloak of anxiety and fear he'd felt he was wearing lifted up and off his body, disintegrating into the leaves and branches that twinkled with raindrops above him.

When he finally saw her in full view and watched as she fell, he took off at full speed, as at first it had looked a lot worse than it actually was. He finally got to her and a huge wave of anger washed over him as she proceeded to tell him so matter-of-factly how she had been dumb enough to follow a man she had seen in the distance into the woods alone, at night no less. He almost hoped that she had visually incarnated a man she had dreamed about so he could be sure the man who had chased him hadn't reared his ugly head again, because if he had, they had a major problem on their hands.

He was holding her firmly by the shoulders at arms' length. She continued to stare back at him and eventually shrugged her shoulders.

"Because," he started, "I need you as close to me as possible. I need to be there to protect you." His voice cracked on that last sentence.

"Oh, babe," she said, and brought herself to him. If they weren't a sight to see before, they certainly were now, standing on the side of a highway, embracing each other as if it was for the last time.

When they parted it was she who took him by the hand this time to lead the way. "Listen, Chilly Willy, I know there's a lot of stuff going on right now that we don't understand."

Tell me about it, he thought to himself.

"But we're going to figure this out. I'm going to figure out why all of this is happening to me." His heart started to race when he glanced at her face and saw her chin held high and her brown eyes almost black with the fire of an unbreakable resolve.

Chapter 22

Fire.

There was fire. Fire all around him.

How did this happen?

Who started all this?

Once the panic within him subsided, Rob started to realize that it was having no affect on him. He felt no heat, no burning. In fact, he lifted his hands to his biceps and rubbed them feverishly.

He felt oddly cold. Suddenly, he heard a whisper from behind him. He turned to see the shape of what seemed like a face fading back into the flames that continued to rage all around him. What did it just say?

He didn't have to wonder too long because someone else spoke, again, just behind him.

"We need you."

Rob turned abruptly, this time completing a full three hundred and sixty degrees. He saw not one now, but two shapes, which also looked like faces to him in the flames. He couldn't be sure, as they were appearing and then disappearing ever so quickly. Like bubbles.

As he stared, more and more showed themselves through the fire.

"We need you." It was barely above a whisper, but he was sure that's what was being said. His breathing accelerated, and he shuddered as the cold he was feeling, despite the flames, continued to intensify.

"We need you both."

"We need you. Both of you."

"Both?"

Rob looked around him. He saw no one else besides the faces that continued to fade in and out of existence through the flames. He squinted to try and make them out, but could not.

"We need you both." They continued to say it, almost chanting it.

Who are they talking about?

Suddenly, slicing through the intense cold he was feeling came a burning sensation on his left hand. He ignored it as he continued to try to make out the faces in the flames. After a few seconds, the burning turned into a searing pain at the base of his middle finger. He looked down and saw a gold ring begin the process of charring through his skin. Rob screamed, ripped the ring off his finger, and threw it into the fire. As the ring hit the flames, he heard horrible moans and screams. He squeezed his eyes shut and jammed the palms of his hands up against his ears. "No! Stop it!" he screamed.

When he opened his eyes, he saw the faces materializing again, but this time they weren't disappearing. They were coming toward him, emerging out of the flames. He watched in amazement. They were all shapes and sizes, young and old, male and female. As they started to close in on him, and the bodies attached to the heads became visible too, they stepped from the flames and he was spurred into action. He turned to run in the other direction. When he did, he was faced with a series of three rooms.

These weren't here before. He wasn't sure when the rooms had appeared, as he was sure he had been surrounded by flames. He didn't care, as he could feel them all, people, ghosts, whatever they were, beginning to bare down on him. He ran straight ahead for the red room, but as he drew closer, the fear he felt was almost debilitating. He cut to the right instead at the last second and entered the pink room. Relief started to take over, but not for long. It was only a couple of seconds before he heard Maryanne's screams.

"Rob!"

He skidded across what seemed to be a gravel floor as he immediately turned on his heels, intending to sprint back out of the room. He somehow knew her cries were coming from the red room, but as he neared the door (the frame of which was now shaped like a cross), it slammed right in his face.

Rob sat straight up in bed, panting and sweating just like a scene out of one of those cheesy, made-for-TV movies. His light-blue sheets were soaked with his own perspiration.

"Shit," he muttered. He peeled them off his stomach and pulled his legs out from underneath them. When the cool air of his bedroom hit his ankles and thighs, it woke him a little bit more. He sat at the edge of the bed, staring at the radiator, his whole face drawn down. He shook his head and hung it even further.

"What is going on?" he asked the darkness as he tried to rub the rest of the sleep out of his eyes. *Another dream*, he thought. *More of this "we need you" crap. I wish I knew who needed me so fucking badly. I've never been wanted so much in my entire life.*

He glanced over at his alarm clock, which read 5:30 a.m.. *Might as well just get up.*

He finally stood and opened the door to his bedroom. He saw the thin strip of light coming from the base of the bathroom door and heard the familiar buzz of the showerhead.

Steve.

He's up late.

Steve, who worked on Wall Street, was typically already out the door, down the block, and on a train into the city in order to make the closing bells of the markets overseas. Rob knew he'd have to move fast in order to get to the kitchen for a drink of water and back safely into his room without getting in Steve's way. He wouldn't have felt like talking to his roommate under normal circumstances at this hour, not even a simple "good morning." He was pouring himself a glass when he heard the shower go off.

"Shit!" he whispered. He threw the water pitcher back in the fridge, grabbed his glass off the counter, and spilled some along the way as he sprinted back to his room. He had his door shut and locked just a second before he heard the bathroom door open. He listened to Steve's squishy footsteps go back into his room just across the hall from Rob's.

"Idiot probably got water all over the place, but thank God I missed him," he said under his breath.

He took a few big gulps of water and a deep breath. He went to sit back down on his bed, but sprang quickly back up from the sticky sheets as they reminded him of why he'd awoken in the first place.

Once he turned around, staring him in the face from the opposite corner of the room was his computer.

Maryanne.

If it was 5:30 a.m. here, that meant it was 5:30 p.m. in Shanghai. He went over to it and turned it on at the slim chance that she might be done for the day and online. She had left for Shanghai just a few days ago.

"Piece of shit," he threw at it as it took forever to boot up.

"Yeah, insult it, that'll make it go faster," she would have said to him if she were here. He scoffed lightly and the corners of his mouth turned up slowly into a shy smile.

"Rob?" Steve knocked on his door. Rob spun around in his seat and threw his hands up at the locked door. He turned back to his computer shaking his head, long, dark strands of hair tickling his eyelids.

I'm not fucking answering that idiot.

He continued to shake his head in disgust as he signed into his AOL Instant Messenger account. He hated this thing, but Maryanne had insisted he get it when they first started dating so they could talk more easily when she was overseas. He had to admit it was pretty convenient. At least she wasn't trying to push him into any of that Facebook or MySpace crap. He had told her once that the day she ever asked him to start tweeting would be the day he broke up with her.

Ugh! He almost put his fist through the monitor as he lost his Internet connection. While he tried to log back on, he decided it was time to take stock of his situation.

It seemed that every time he tried to figure things out with Maryanne, she had to go off on another business trip, and he wasn't going to worry her or get her nerves twisted in knots before she had to get on a plane for these long flights. He knew how stressed that alone made her. He hadn't been able to find the right time before she left again to finally tell her about his own dreams he'd been having, and more importantly, how he was chased through the subways of New York City; and most importantly, the connections between those two.

It had been no use in trying to convince himself that night had been just a random and horrible crazy thing that happened to him. He tried to blame it on the city, tell himself that shit like that has probably happened to a lot of people. He kept picturing the man put his left hand over his heart, and saw the glint of the gold ring on his middle finger as he did so. Just like the gold ring on his left hand that had almost burned right through his own middle finger in his dream just now.

He kept hearing his words: *They need you.* Then the words of the faces in the flames: *We need you. Both of you.*

Most importantly, there was the warning from the night he was chased. That final warning he had screamed at Rob as he had run down the alley to safety: "If you value your life…and hers…you'll keep your mouth shut!"

And hers…

He knew exactly whom his pursuer had been referring to, and it was probably why he had listened to him and not gone to the police that night. He could blame it on laziness and confusion all he wanted. He knew deep down it was ice-cold fear that had stopped him. It had even stopped him from telling Maryanne. He knew he couldn't keep that up for long. At this point, keeping things from her was putting her in more danger than maintaining her safety. Suddenly, he was antsy for the computer to connect. He felt a dire urgency to tell her everything, even if it had to be through the computer.

His heart sank as the connection failed again. He looked at the clock. It was drawing close to 6:30 a.m. and he would have to start getting ready. He had to be in the office before 9 a.m. today to be on time for a meeting. He sighed and shook his head.

Just get ready, he thought to himself. *She's fine,*

probably safer over there than she is here. She'll probably give you a call later today and you can tell her everything then. Even if it's just a shortened version of it.

He had heard Steve leave a few minutes before, so he knew the coast was clear. He showered, got dressed, and as he lied on his bed watching the morning news, he decided to do something he never did: eat breakfast.

"Hell, it might do me some good," he grumbled, wiping the sleep out of his eyes and yawning as he shuffled into the kitchen. He searched the cabinets until he found what he was looking for— an old box of Fruity Pebbles he'd bought a couple months ago, but had never opened. He separated the cardboard at the top and unsealed the bag. He munched on a couple pieces and decided it was still fresh. He poured himself a bowl and realized she'd probably be making fun of him for this, too. He smiled. What a ball buster I'm with.

As he walked back to his room, he decided there was one more thing he needed to do. He sat at the computer again and saw that the connection to the Internet had started up.

"Of course," he said out loud to the monitor. "Now that I'm walking out the door." Part of him was happy though because it meant he'd be able to complete his task. He logged into his e-mail account and pulled up a new message template, addressing it to Maryanne.

It's only 7:15 a.m. and I'm having a bowl of Fruity Pebbles and thinking of you. Get home soon.

Love you and miss you lots
Rob

The combination of food in his stomach and the

feeling that he had connected with her somehow made him feel good, despite the bad sleep he'd just had. Hopefully, it would last at least until lunchtime. He sent the message and shut down his computer.

As he left the building and began the ten-minute walk down the block to the train station, he realized just how eminent winter was. He could see his breath coming out in short puffs right in front of his face, and he found himself wishing he'd brought a heavier jacket with him. Being hit with the cold reminded him that all was not well and he needed to get his act together and address it, head on this time. He refrained from using his iPod so he could concentrate.

Someone or something was after them, or at least trying to tell them something. That was obvious, but there was so much that was unexplained he didn't even know where to start processing and organizing it all. The question still remained if what was happening to him was even related to what was happening to Maryanne.

He still wasn't entirely convinced, although she had adamantly and boldly insisted over and over again that it was, that whom Maryanne saw in the cemetery on the night of the pumpkin blaze Halloween festivities was the man from her dream. Rob hadn't told anyone about the scene in the subways, but wondered if the guy had found them just to make sure and leave a little reminder somewhere on Maryanne by drawing her into the woods that night. It was a far distance from Cecily's grave to the woods line. When he was after Rob, the man had worn a red-and-gray parka. Perhaps she could have mistaken it for a flannel.

Ugh. I don't know, he thought.

Still, he felt he was pulling at straws. He knew he needed help and although long overdue, he needed to go to the police. He decided he would do it today, on his way home from work. It won't be so bad. I'll explain that I was scared and wasn't sure how serious everything was until Maryanne saw this guy again in the cemetery. I can say I thought the guy was just some kook who'd been trying to rob me.

Maryanne. He swore again, up and down, to tell her everything as soon as possible. He pictured her face in his head, her eyes wide and alive with resolve, as they sat in a corner of Denver's that night of the cemetery sighting.

"Did you see the red light, too?"

"Yes!" she said, pointing a finger at him and getting even more excited. "It's why I went over to the grave in the first place."

"Yeah, me, too," he'd replied, frowning and shaking his head. He rubbed at his eyes, and then slapped a hand on the table, making her jump.

"I mean, this is crazy, babe. Do you realize what you're saying? What are we supposed to tell people? That you saw some sort of a ghost?"

"First of all, we're not telling anyone, and second of all, who says it was a ghost?"

He leaned in closer before answering. "You saw a guy that you had never seen before in your life after having a dream about him standing in your living room. Then he virtually disappears as you follow him into the woods."

"Well, maybe I have seen him before I dreamed about him, but I just don't remember. Like blocked it out somehow or for some reason. Like around town somewhere or in a photograph." She shrugged nonchalantly and took a sip of beer, sitting back in her chair and throwing an elbow over it. She shot him a look of defiance that dared him to challenge her. He had sat back himself, stunned at her attitude.

How can she be acting like this? he remembered thinking to himself. The change in her had been so quick and it was all thanks to what had just transpired. He stared at her for a moment and then leaned in again.

“Did you see anything else while you were in the woods?”

“Yes.”

“Well, what was it?”

She looked down at the table for a moment and then brought her big, brown eyes up to meet his. “I think someone is trying to tell me something.”

“Maryanne, what else did you see?” he asked, more sternly this time. Sometimes he felt like she was his wayward daughter he needed to keep pulling back on track, rather than his girlfriend.

“It was an extremely small cabin, really. Like really small. You can barely call it a cabin. It was more like a big shed almost.”

“Did you go inside it?” he asked, almost panicked at this point.

“No, no. You came before I went any further.”

“Well, thank God for that!”

She shook her head. “Chilly, I think he wanted me to see it.”

“But why?”

“I don’t know, but I’m going back to find out.”

“No, you damn well aren’t!” A few people turned to look at their table, as Rob’s voice had managed to rise above the roar of the crowd.

He turned quickly and lifted a hand to them. “Sorry.”

“Shit,” he said quickly as he turned back to her and ran both hands through his hair.

She smiled slightly in spite of herself, and she pushed a few strands out of his troubled eyes as he met hers again.

"Babe, you are not going back there. At least not alone."

"Okay," she said, "So let's go check it out together, tomorrow."

"Fine," he said, nodding. He paused for a moment and stared at the table as he ran over everything in his head. He looked back at her with a crinkled forehead, his eyebrows almost touching. "How do you explain the light?"

"What do you mean?"

"Coming off of the tombstone?"

"Oh, right, from the cross."

He stared back at her with a knowing look. They both averted their eyes from each other and took a long drink, too spooked to actually say it out loud.

"Someone, or something, needed us both to get to that spot tonight," she said, leaning in and lowering her voice once again.

"I think we were both meant to see the location of that cabin. Do you think you'd be able to find it again?"

"Yes. Definitely."

"All right. We'll go check it out tomorrow. In the daylight!" he added quickly.

"Deal."

They never made it. Maryanne got sick the very next day, probably from wandering around all night in the rain, Rob had pointed out. In order to ensure she would be healthy by the time she had to leave for Shanghai, she had barely left her apartment.

It was just as well, because he had wanted to go check the place out by himself anyway. It couldn't be that hard to find he'd figured and besides, the farther away he could keep her from any sort of trouble, the better. So he was relieved inside, even though he felt terrible watching her try to fight it off as best she could. Somehow, for all the bravado he talked, he couldn't bring himself to go out there alone.

He winced and squeezed his eyes shut with embarrassment over his fear. He held them closed for a moment, took a deep breath, and then opened them again. He stared out of the train car window at the brown, cold, murky waters of the Hudson River, only to look away again in disgust. *Nothing but ambiguity all around me*, he thought.

Once the train finally pulled into Grand Central Station, he shrugged on his jacket and headed out. He could feel the loss of that one hour of sleep starting to weigh on him.

He realized once he'd stepped on the subway and was headed uptown that the same underlying problem with going to the cops still remained. Certain details would be very difficult to explain, or get around for that matter. He imagined how the conversation would go in his head.

"So, you say you were chased through the New York City subways by a man whom, when he finally caught up to you, told you that you are needed by someone or something. Then he put his hand over his heart and you saw that he was wearing a ring?"

"Yes, that's correct."

"And this ring was particularly frightening, why?"

"Because the people in my nightmares wear the same type of ring, on the same finger."

"Oh, right, of course. Then he threatened your life as

you ran away, and the words 'her life,' you assume was a reference to your girlfriend whom you say later saw him in the Sleepy Hollow cemetery."

"Well, see I'm not sure it was definitely the same guy. I think it might have been, but my girlfriend says it was a man that she's seen in her own dreams."

"I see. So she's having dreams as well?"

"Yes."

"So why did she decide to follow this man into the woods at night?"

"Well, officer, first she had seen a glowing red light that was streaming onto the grave that she's been drawn to over and over again for a while now, and once she got there, she looked up toward the woods and saw him standing there. So she thought he wanted her to follow him."

He frowned and shook his head as he held on to the hand pole in the subway car.

"This is ridiculous," he mumbled. A businesswoman who insisted on reading her paper, although there was barely enough elbow room in the car, shot him a nasty look.

"What?" he threw back at her.

She was obviously taken aback, shook her own head, and buried herself back in the words that were so important she had to read them before she got to where she was going.

Jesus, what's wrong with me? he thought.

As the doors opened at 59th Street, she turned to get out. "Hey, I'm sorry," he said. She turned to look back at him. "I'm sorry, seriously," he said again. "Bad morning."

She actually gave him a knowing smile and nodded. "Well, I hope you have a better day."

“Thank you.”

The doors shut again just as she stepped onto the platform. He shook his head again at himself. *You're turning into one of them*, he said to himself. Them being one of the nasty New Yorkers he despised.

The underground scenes he was so used to whizzed by in a blur as the subway flew through the belly of New York City. He waited patiently for his stop. As he did, he glanced to his left. Standing in the corner of the car was a girl wearing a dress that had very thin straps and sandals. *Is she nuts? She must be freezing!* he thought.

It was probably about forty degrees outside and this chick was having a difficult time letting go of summer. He noticed just below her right shoulder, in blue, intricate-looking script, was a tattoo.

What the hell does that say?

He squinted, but she was far away and he was near-sighted to boot. He made his way over to the other side of the car, slowly, so as not to be too obvious.

Can 't fucking make it out.

As he got closer, he could distinguish an "E." He could also make out some sort of abstract design surrounding the message that looked kind of like stars. It was difficult to read, but once he was standing just a couple of feet away, he finally saw what the girl had specifically requested to have written on her body: "Everything Changes"

He laughed quietly to himself and shook his head. "You got that right." A couple people turned to see whom he was addressing, but quickly lost interest as the train pulled into 86th Street. Rob exited the car.

By the time he’d gotten to his desk, he was feeling much more alive. As he went through his morning e-mails, he perked up even more when he saw Maryanne had responded to his e-mail from earlier this morning. He opened it immediately.

Hey, Chilly,

Sorry I wasn't online this morning. Casey was still showing me around the city, and we actually mapped out my route for tomorrow, as she won't be able to accompany me on my appointments because she has meetings of her own. Shouldn't be too bad, I think I'll be able to find my way. I might even try to take the subway, just for the story really, as I've been warned against it a number of times.

Anyway, I'm very proud of you for having breakfast! What brought that on? Listen, I know you're probably really stressed out right now, but like I said, as soon as I get back from this trip we're going to figure this all out. I want answers as to where these dreams are stemming from and who Cecily Reynolds is and how she died. That has to get us somewhere, right? I can't believe I haven't gone as far as to further research her death yet. There has to be some sort of explanation just in that itself.

They had Googled Cecily's name, and even Andy Dayton's, to see if there was some sort of connection between the two after Maryanne's meeting with Ramsey. They found nothing referring to a young Cecily Reynolds, and everything that emerged for Andy was completely kosher, just articles from the local paper detailing his political activities, including when he was beaten out for mayor and even a small story about he and his wife moving to Las Vegas.

"Well, I guess that answers our question of if he had anything to do with the little girl," Maryanne had said.

"Yeah, that or somebody did a really good clean-up job," Rob answered as he clicked aimlessly through the Google results.

"And Google is not the authority on everything, babe." She'd giggled in response.

"If you say so."

He went back to her e-mail:

All right, gotta run. It's dinnertime and I'm meeting Casey, obviously LOL. Love you so much. Let's try to schedule a phone call in a couple days. How about Sunday? I'll have plenty of time. I'll e-mail you with when I'll be calling. Miss you so much and wish you were here with me.

Xxooxoxoxxxoooxxoxoooxxxxxxxx

Maryanne

"Rob?"

Rob jumped three feet in the air at the sound of his name. He looked up to see Norman in his doorway. He'd wondered how long his boss had been standing there.

"Sorry! I was…I was just, reading this e-mail…" he mumbled.

Norman snickered. "That's okay. Everything all right? Your face was kind of um…twisted up in pain for a minute there, to put it lightly," he said, raising his eyebrows at his employee.

"Oh. Yeah, I'm fine. Everything's fine," he answered, smiling at Norm now. "What's up?"

"Just wanted to see if you're ready for this meeting."

"Oh, yeah, yeah absolutely!" Rob jumped to his feet

and grabbed the pile of folders he had set out on his desk last night in preparation for it. He came around his desk, and then realized he hadn't clicked off of Maryanne's e-mail.

"Oh, crap, just one more thing." He went back to his computer and exited his e-mail, Norman watching him the whole time. When he turned back, his boss' stare stopped him dead in his tracks. They stood facing each other for a few moments.

"Ready," Rob said.

"Okay."

Norman lead Rob out of his office and into the main workspace of SfH. They walked to the back room that served as a meeting room when necessary. Today was one of those days. Most of the office was seated around the large rectangular table in the middle of the room.

"All right, everybody," Norman said, taking his seat at the head of the table. "This meeting is to update everyone on the results of this year's audit, which was again very successful thanks to Rob and Geffin."

Everyone gave them a pitiful round of applause.

"Don't forget Randall, Norm," Rob said.

Norman didn't even look up, let alone address what Rob had just said. He was a little taken aback. Rob knew Norman didn't like Randall for whatever reason, but it was definitely a deliberately rude gesture not to acknowledge the guy's hand in this. Rob glanced at Randall as Norman went on with the meeting. He saw that his co-worker's nostrils were flaring. *As they fucking should be!* he thought.

Rob decided he owed it to Randall to speak up again. Maybe Norman really just hadn't heard him the first time.

"Excuse me, Norman," Rob said, raising his hand

this time.

Success, as almost everyone at the table looked over at him this time. Rob pointed at Randall with his pen. "Randall was a big part of this, too, he deserves recognition."

Norman stared back at Rob for a moment.

“Oh, that’s true, Norm,” Geffin looked up and chimed in. He’d been preoccupied scouring the audit report in front of him to make sure they’d dotted their Is and crossed their Ts.

Norman shot Geffin a look, who was never able to receive it because his head was buried once again in the report. Norman pushed his seat back slowly, which really caught everyone’s attention at the table. Rob noticed Randall was still staring down at the document, nostrils flared, eyes wild, breathing heavily.

“Well, Rob,” Norman said, walking over to him with his pile of notes that were presumably to help him take everyone through the report step by step, “since you obviously think you’re more fit to run this meeting than I am, be my guest.” With that he threw the pile of papers and his copy of the report on the table in front of Rob.

It was only a quick glimpse, but undeniable. Rob saw the white gold ring, placed firmly on the middle finger of Norman’s left hand.

Chapter 23

"Rob?" Geffin tried to get his attention after almost a full minute had passed.

The entire table was staring at Rob staring at the pile of papers that Norman had just thrown down in front of him.

"Rob?"

When there was still no response, Geffin got up out of his seat and circled the table until he'd reached Rob.

"Rob!" he said more firmly, putting his hand down hard on Rob's shoulder.

"Huh?" Rob snapped out of it and looked up at Geffin. "What?"

He was completely disoriented. He kept picturing Norman's hand descending over and over again, dropping the slightly curled papers and revealing the ring. Every time they landed in his mind, they hit the table with the resounding thunderous thud of a gong.

"It's all right. It's not your fault. He just, uh," Geffin frowned and turned to look behind him a second, "overreacted, that's all. I don't know why. Don't worry about it; I'm going to talk to him. Just go back to work, everybody, we'll continue this later," he said to the group.

Light moans and humphs could be heard as they all shuffled out of the room. Rob was back to staring down at the papers Norman had thrown at him. Randall had managed to steady his breathing and picked himself up, but his face showed that he was still far from calm.

"I'm sorry, Randall," Geffin said, going up to him and putting a hand on his shoulder before he could walk out of the room. "As your direct supervisor, I want you to know how important you are to the operation. We know how much you helped with the audit," he said, pointing at Rob then back to himself. "And that's what matters."

"Thank you, Geffin," Randall said, raising his chin.

Geffin nodded and moved out of Randall's way so he could exit the room. Once he was gone, Geffin turned back to Rob.

"I don't know what his problem is with that guy," he said, walking listlessly over to the window. He leaned against it, looking out at the tops of the buildings that surrounded them. "But he better get over it, whatever it is, before he gets himself, and us for that matter, into trouble." When there was no response from Rob, he turned, only to see an empty seat where the kid had been. Geffin shook his head and gathered up his stuff. "I don't know what the fuck is going on around here today."

Rob had made his way to the bathroom and splashed ice cold water on his face. He'd followed closely behind Randall when he'd left the room. Geffin had been saying something as he did, but he was only a voice in the distance. Rob could barely concentrate on it anymore than he could on putting one foot in front of the other at this point. He looked up at himself in the mirror as he leaned over the sink.

Get a hold of yourself. So he had a ring on. So what?

"God, I need a shrink," he said as he pushed himself off the sink and paced for a couple of seconds. He ran his hands through his hair to get it off his forehead and out of his eyes. Suddenly, the door swung open. He turned to see who it was and standing there was Randall.

"Oh, hey, man."

"You all right?"

"What? Oh, yeah, I'm fine."

Randall walked toward him slowly, holding his gaze the whole way. He stopped, right in front of Rob, and the two stared at each other. For a minute, Rob wasn't sure if Randall was going to try to hit him or kiss him. But eventually, he spoke.

"Thank you for sticking up for me."

Rob nodded. "You're welcome."

Randall looked down with such sad eyes that it almost broke Rob's heart. Then he walked quietly over to the sink to do what Rob had done just a few moments ago. Rob wanted to ask him if there was anything else bothering him, but the two had never really spoken about anything outside of work, and he felt awkward crossing that boundary. He decided to leave Randall be. He left the bathroom and peeked his head into the main lobby.

"Iris, I'm just going to go get some air for a minute," he told their secretary.

"All right, hon," she answered, looking up at him over the reception desk.

When he hit the street, the blast of cold air that hit him cleared his head and his lungs. He took a deep breath and headed left, just planning to circle the block until he could properly calculate what had just happened.

Norman was wearing a ring, and although simple in design (pure white gold) it was on the same finger and the same hand as the man who had chased him through the subways. Not to mention the ones he'd been seeing on the people in his dreams.

God, what does this all mean?

He wondered if this could all just be a crazy coincidence. If Norman's ring was something he'd seen in passing one day and that's why he was now dreaming about it, but he had one on too.

The man who'd chased him was wearing the same ring, on the same hand, on the same finger. That was the chilling X factor that he couldn't get past. He tried to take deep breaths of the cool, fall air and get himself to relax. He still felt like he was only going to make a fool of himself by going to the cops, but he tried to console himself with the fact that he'd be sitting down with them by the end of the day.

All right, you have work to do. Get back upstairs.

He made his way around the block and back to his building.

"You okay, Rob?" Iris asked when he walked back in.

"Yes. I'm fine," he said, pulling his seat into his desk and getting to work. Whether he liked it or not, yes, he was fine.

Chapter 24

Two offices over, Norman Racketts was glaring at his computer screen, still seething. *How dare that little shit disrespect my authority like that, and in front of the entire God damn office!* he thought.

No way in hell was Norman going to give Randall any sort of recognition. He made it a point to not even address that peon directly. As far as he was concerned, the monkey wasn't fit to even look him in the eyes, let alone speak to him, but he had to tolerate his/their existence, in order to keep his views properly concealed. Something his brother, Joseph Goldberg, had not done a very good job with as of late. He hadn't spoken to Joseph in a few days. He made a mental note to schedule a get-together with him to discuss where they stood currently.

After Joseph's outburst at the Westchester Hometown Society dinner, the two had gone back to the Prerogative offices. Joseph had explained to him how he'd originally started the publication to give rise to their group and the major players within, but he'd lost control more recently with the hire of his two senior editors, one of them being Rob's girlfriend, Maryanne Rosa, over the past few years. He had hoped to eventually bring them into their circle, as they were young, and moldable, but they quickly took the reins and led the book in the completely opposite direction of where he had hoped before he even knew what was happening really. They had tipped it so far to the left that there was no chance anymore of using the publication to the group's advantage. That is, of course, unless they fixed the problem, or better yet, removed it completely. Prerogative had the potential to be a huge resource for them, but not if those girls weren't on their side. They were making it increasingly more difficult to maintain Joseph and the group's control over the content of the magazine without becoming totally and blatantly conspicuous. If they were successful in recruiting Rob, and were able to properly utilize another key prospect, they might be able to turn the tides back in their favor.

Kayla Jared had had a difficult childhood. Her relationship with her father, an Egyptian immigrant, had always been strained, to put it lightly. She could never live up to his expectations. When she came to visit Maryanne one day at the office, Joseph jumped on the opportunity to tap into that. He listened to her as she cried to her friend about her father's latest foul up. The man had fallen asleep, or so they think, at the wheel and smashed his car into a telephone pole. When they finally found him at 3 a.m., he wouldn't speak to either her, her mother, nor M.J., and still has not explained himself as of yet.

He smiled to himself in his office. Even just by listening to her, he knew she was a perfect prospective recruit: young, female, and dumb. Plus she worked at Westchester Today, and it was always good to have another in at the local paper, if he could even call that rag a newspaper. After Kayla and Maryanne had finished their lunch, and Kayla left to get back to work, Joseph snuck out the back door to try to catch her in the parking lot.

"Kayla!" he yelled out to her, moving as quickly as he could on a bad knee.

She turned to look at him, obviously confused. Once he'd reached her, he put a hand on her shoulder, which definitely caught her off guard, he could tell.

"Listen, I couldn't help but overhear up there, and if I can do anything. Anything at all…" he told her, putting on the thickest pity party of his life.

"Thanks," she said, examining him quizzically. He held out a small piece of paper, which she took, with his name and number written on it.

"Even if you just need to talk," he told her.

She looked back up at him and shook her head again, giving him a polite smile before getting into her car. Despite her confusion, he was pretty sure he'd hit his mark. He could be very convincing when he wanted to be.

It took a few days for her to respond, but the protective, concerned father-figure act, one she would have given anything for growing up, that he'd faked that afternoon worked. As time went on and she continued to come to him for advice, attention, and sometimes more, he continued to spoon feed it to her like a daily, necessary medication. He drew her into them, slowly but surely, and now she was completely devoted. Something she proved when she covered up his tracks after his outburst at the Westchester Hometown Society dinner. He'd seen Stacy Rockaport out of the corner of his eye as it was all going down and knew what would be coming the next day.

Turning her against Maryanne hadn't been easy. He had to establish her loyalty to him before he could even begin to chip away at their friendship and the life that she'd been preparing for with her fiancé. They'd decided together to try to bring him on board as well. Norman knew Joseph would eventually show her though, that this community of people understood her and accepted her in a way that no one else ever had, ever could, or ever would. That included her filthy Muslim father, M.J., Maryanne, and anyone else she could think of.

Joseph and Norman had considered putting Kayla on the sacred suicide mission to reel in Rob. That certainly would have been amusing to watch play out, but they decided instead to assign her to her own fiancé. After all, they'd known for quite some time that Patrick was the only one for that job.

Patrick was different in that he actually sought them out, on behalf of his wife. Joseph hadn't heard from Sandra in a long time. Not that he'd minded. She hadn't remained too active, only showing up to the occasional meeting and only getting her hands dirty for the random project or two each year. He got the feeling sometimes that she was ungrateful, that she didn't appreciate how he'd turned her heartache into a source of power and determination. What she felt or thought didn't matter though. It was Patrick who mattered, and he was undeniably and unshakably obsessed with his new wife. That obsession would lead him to do absolutely anything for her. She was quite beautiful. Joseph gave him that. The problem was that she could use that beauty to lead Patrick down the wrong path, a path that led away from Joseph and his goals. The day that happened, he vowed to make her very sorry.

For now, Sandra had her head screwed on straight and she'd pushed Patrick in the right direction. Patrick had finally contacted Joseph through their rabbi, who often brought him potential recruits. He had been told it was Sandra's new husband who wanted to meet him, but that didn't excuse him from having to prove himself. He and Norman knew that Rob would be the perfect candidate to test him on.

The beliefs that they practiced could be likened to the most radical forms of any religion in its raw, unforgiving nature. In their opinion, the rewards far outweighed the extreme dangers and risks, which were a necessary evil in their quest to heal society and keep it locked within their own interests, of course.

Patrick's progress at this point was still unknown. So Norman opened up an e-mail that asked Joseph to meet and discuss Patrick later this week. As he looked down at the keyboard to start typing and placed his hands on the keys, he'd realized he'd forgotten to take his ring off last night.

"Shit," he mumbled as he pulled it off and stuffed it into his shirt pocket. As he did, he paused for a moment. Rob had frozen in place when he'd thrown the papers down in front of him, and the look of shock on his face hadn't been lost on Norman.

Could it be possible that he'd noticed the ring? Even if he did, could he have realized the significance of it at this point? He decided not to worry about anything until he'd been updated by Joseph. He exhaled a deep breath as he typed his e-mail to him. He'd have to go make nice with the kid before the day was out so he didn't suspect anything further.

Chapter 25

Despite the morning's outburst, the rest of the day had turned out to be relatively uneventful. A gentle quiet had settled over the office, and Rob had actually been able to get a good amount of work done. His nerves were calmed and his panicked mind soothed, at least for the time being. He heard a knock and looked up to see Norman standing in the doorway to his office.

"Oh, hi, Norm," he said. His heart fluttered lightly. His nerves were back, any efforts to straighten them out during the day, immediately undone.

"Hi, Rob. Listen, I'm sorry about this morning."

Rob expected a bit more of an explanation, but Norman didn't offer any. He just stood in the doorway, motionless, staring back at him.

"Um, sure. It's all right. No problem," he answered, raising a hand and giving Norm a nervous laugh.

Norm nodded then hung his head for a moment. He was holding onto the doorway with his left hand and Rob noticed the ring was now gone. Norm looked up suddenly and Rob averted his eyes as quickly as he could, but he had a sneaking suspicion that Norm had caught his glance. He took a step into Rob's office. It looked like he wanted to say something to Rob, but was still debating over whether or not this was the right time.

"It's not that I don't appreciate what he does," he began.

"Randall?" Rob asked. *He can't even give the guy the respect of saying his name?*

"Yes, Randall," Norm answered, swallowing. "It's just that, well," he started to laugh and raised his hands up, "They all have a ghetto side that's just dying to get out, right?"

Rob was sure his jaw had hit the floor with that one. He couldn't believe what Norm had just said to him, to his face.

Norm looked at him sternly, but somberly. "I'm just waiting for his to make it known."

"Rob?"

Both men jumped at Iris' interruption. She walked over to Rob's desk and placed a sealed envelope with his name on it down in front of him. "Randall said to give this to you. He had to leave early."

"Oh. Okay, thanks."

Iris stepped back and glanced at Norman, and then back to Rob, obviously confused by the tension in the room. She shook her head and then waved both her hands at the two men.

"Whatever. I'm going home. I'll see you tomorrow." With that she walked out of the office and Rob could see her gathering up her belongings at her desk in their small main lobby. He slowly reached out and took the envelope off his desk. For a moment, he thought Norman was going to try to snatch it away before he could grab it. Norman had kept his eyes trained steadily on it from the second Iris placed it on his desk. Finally, he looked up to see Rob's face. He looked like a puppy that he'd just kicked.

"I'm sorry," Norman said. "I shouldn't have said that."

Rob kept his eyes trained on the desktop, willing this encounter to just be over with already.

"Why don't you go home," Norm suggested. "It's

been a day." He turned and walked quickly out of Rob's office.

His train car swayed from side to side while it hobbled along the track and Rob pulled his messenger bag closer to him so it wouldn't slide over to the other side of the seat. He leaned his head back and looked out at the Hudson River. So much had happened today, he didn't even know where to start.

You can start by going to the police, he thought.

Even though he was exhausted, he knew that's what he needed to do.

The train lolled lazily underneath the Tappan Zee Bridge before pulling into the station. Rob looked out at the huge concrete columns, which led up to the hulking metal structure that seemed graceful almost with its arc over the river. When they came to a stop, he gathered his things and stood up to exit the train. As he stepped onto the platform, he felt that extra weight again come crashing down on his shoulders. If he didn't know any better, he'd think he gained about fifty pounds over the past few weeks. He sighed, thinking of the hill he had to walk up just to get back to civilization. Beckett Street was a mess at that. The housing development that took over most of the block, and the tenants who seemed to have nothing better to do all day than hang out on the sidewalk, could sometimes make for an intimidating atmosphere. Junkyards and the now darkened windows of establishments that had tried, but just weren't able to afford to stay open, would inevitably deepen an already depressed mood. So Rob knew this would do him no good. The sun was already setting and the wind was picking up. He shoved his hands into his coat pockets as he walked at an unusually slow pace. Usually, he charged up the hill, eager to get home and get it over with, but today he just couldn't seem to get going. He felt wary and cautious. He took his iPod out of his pocket and turned it on, thinking the music might rev him up. He put on his headphones and paused for a moment as he shuffled through the songs, trying to pick out one that suited him.

Suddenly, he felt something coming at him hard and fast from his left-hand side. He gasped and whipped his head to the left, expecting to be pushed to the ground as he did, but there was nothing. What he was staring at was the dark underbelly of the overpass that led to the other side of the train tracks (those closer to the water). All he could make out were patches of grass and garbage sprinkled around, becoming more dense toward the corners of the steel canopy that touched the ground. There weren't even any homeless seeking shelter in those corners that evening. Rob figured the temperature hadn't dropped that much for them to need the shield yet. He looked back even further to the small parking lot that sat beside it and even though he saw nothing, he still got the feeling that something or someone was lurking there, watching him. He immediately crossed the street, looking behind him at the area below the overpass a number of times, almost tripping once he got to the sidewalk.

You're losin' it, he thought.

He readjusted his bag on his shoulder. He felt himself becoming increasingly more paranoid again, almost dizzy with it. So Norm had just proven himself a bigot on top of the occasional asshole that he could be. What he'd said was a huge contradiction to what the man worked toward every single day, and it made his whole career a bold-faced lie. Rob didn't know if he could continue working for someone like that.

Not to mention the guy could possibly be associated with a certain “they” who have been trying to chase him and his girlfriend down. So whether his body liked it or not, he would make a right at the top of the block, walk passed the Darren Hayes and the bed that was calling his name, and up to the police station.

The wind whipped through him again, this time picking up a pile of leaves that crackled lightly as they skidded along the sidewalk. This side of the street somehow felt safer and more occupied. He watched a group of kids playing basketball and yearned for a time when his life was simpler. Just as he was starting to feel numb, another sense of impending attack came over him. He pulled out his earphones and whirled around, ready to face the man who’d chased him through the subways, running at him, but again, there was nothing. The two kids who’d been walking behind him actually looked startled by his reaction.

“You all right, man?” one of them asked as they passed by him.

Rob didn’t know what he was more shocked over, the fact that the kid had been concerned enough to say something or that there was nobody dangerous behind him. He was breathing heavy at this point and all he could do was shake his head “no.”

The kid shrugged and walked faster to catch up with his friend who’d gone up ahead. Rob buried his face in his hands and rubbed his eyes with the palms of them.

Almost there, almost there. Just move.

He took his hat off and turned it around so the brim was now in the back and started walking again, briskly and purposefully. He’d keep blinders on for the rest of the way and block out whatever this force was that was trying to keep him from his destination.

He had to keep his presence unseen. Felt, yet unseen, which was no easy task. Potential candidates needed to know that although they initially felt fear and confusion, they were always surrounded and looked after. Someone was always, always behind them. As he turned to face uphill again, it looked like there was more determination in his step.

There you go.

Maybe he'd finally overcome his nerves. Patrick hoped so. He stayed behind him, utilizing the shadows of dusk and the alleyways between buildings to stay hidden. When they'd reached the top of the block, Patrick expected him to cross the street and go through the archway into the courtyard of the Darren Hayes apartments, but he was puzzled when the man took a right instead and started walking toward Route 9.

Where's he going?

He got slightly careless in his confusion and was now out in full view.

Is he meeting the brunette somewhere? No, of course not, she's in Shanghai.

Damn it! He couldn't lose him again, not after he'd already failed to get through to him in New York.

Patrick continued to follow him up the street. He was getting dangerously close to the Village Hall, which meant he was getting dangerously close to the police station as well. If that's where he was heading, Patrick was in serious trouble.

He decided he needed to try to distract him. He saw a car coming and without thinking dashed in front of it. A couple people yelled out, thinking for sure he was going to get hit. The driver leaned on his horn immediately, but Patrick was able to get across in time, as he knew he would be. Once he reached the shadows again, he turned around to see if he had even noticed. It didn't seem like he had so much as batted an eyelash, and Patrick's heart dropped as he watched him turn onto the pathway that led to the station entrance. He stood there for a moment, just staring at the double doors that he had just went through, not knowing what to do next. Or who to call for that matter, Joseph or Norman?

He figured Norman would be the better option as he had the most direct access to him.

He turned and headed down the block he'd just run to and pulled out his cell phone. As it rang, he got progressively more nervous, wondering what the repercussions would be for all this. Finally, Norman answered.

"Hello?"

"Norman, we have a problem."

"Ah, Patrick. Joseph and I were just discussing you. What's the matter?"

"He's in the police station right now." There was a long pause from Norman.

"Come to the cemetery. You know where we'll be."

"On my way."

Patrick hung up, and headed straight there.

Chapter 26

Rob felt like an asshole as he approached the cop sitting at the front desk. He leaned in to speak into the voice vent in the glass partition that guarded the officer. He didn't know if he was about to spill his guts or buy movie tickets.

"Can I help you?" The cop had barely looked up from his paperwork to greet him.

"Yeah," Rob began. "You know I don't even know where to start," he began with a nervous laugh. With that he had the officer's attention. His nametag read "Yemane."

"I'm in need of some help. Maybe even protection. Is there an officer here I can talk to for a few minutes. I need to file a report."

"Sure. Let me buzz you in."

"Okay, great."

Rob walked over to the pale yellow metal door with a small glass window at face level that was next to the reception desk. He assumed this was the door Officer Yemane meant. He heard a loud buzz and suddenly Yemane swung it open, almost hitting him in face.

"Sorry," Yemane said, "come on in." He put a hand on Rob's shoulder and gently nudged him ahead. He closed the door behind them and led Rob through a short corridor into an office packed with desks and cubicles. Glass enclosed rooms lined the sides, most of which were empty. One was filled with about five or six officers who looked like they were having dinner. As

Yemane and Rob passed by the room one of them came to the door.

"We have your sandwich in here."

"Yeah, I'll come get it in a second," Yemane answered, waving him off.

"Whatever." The cop closed the door again and went back to join his friends.

Yemane led Rob down an aisle of desks filled with cops, either talking on the phone, filling out paperwork, or talking to each other. Just like in the movies.

He was surprised at how busy the place seemed. Yemane stopped about four desks down and turned to face Rob.

"I think this guy can help you out," he said with a smile. An older officer stood up and nodded at Rob. Rob read his name tag: Grettco.

"Officer Grettco?"

"That's me." They shook hands.

"My name's Robert Martin."

"Have a seat." He held out his hand to offer Rob the chair across from his.

"Thanks, Yemane."

"No problem," Yemane threw over his shoulder as he went to retrieve his sandwich. Rob turned to see Yemane disappear into the dinner room. When he turned back to Officer Grettco, the man was looking him up and down.

"So, how can I help you? 'Robert' you said, right?"

"Yes, Rob. Um…" Rob took a breath and was suddenly aware of all the sets of eyes and ears on him. He looked around and saw that most of the officers were now very aware of his presence and whether they were going to make it obvious or not, they would be listening.

Rob leaned in toward Officer Grettco. "Is there

anywhere we can talk that's a little more private?"

"It's all right, no reason to feel uncomfortable. Just say what you need to say." Grettco had taken out a small notebook and pen and had it poised to start writing as soon as Rob started talking.

"Okay, well," he paused again, this time thanks to a huge wave of exhaustion that hit him like a ton of bricks.

"A couple weeks ago someone chased me through the subways in the city after work, and I think he's after my girlfriend now."

"Okay, first of all what's your last name again, Rob?"

"Martin. It's Robert Martin."

"Okay, and where do you live?"

"Right over here, in the Darren Hayes."

"So you work in the city?"

"Yes, right."

"And did you report it to the NYPD after this happened?"

"No."

Officer Grettco stopped writing at that and frowned. "Well, that wasn't very smart. Why not?"

"Well, he threatened my life, and Maryanne's for that matter."

Rob had to sit back in his chair and take a few deep breaths. He was feeling extremely dizzy, and his skull started to feel like it was closing in on his brain.

"Are you all right?" Grettco asked as he watched Rob's eyes roll around in his head. Rob shook his head and pinched the bridge of his nose.

"Yeah, yeah, I'm fine."

"All right, who's Maryanne? Is that your girlfriend?"

"Yes, Maryanne is my girlfriend."

"And where does she live?"

"She lives in the Darren Hayes, too."

"Where does she work?"

"She works in Westchester."

"Where in Westchester?"

"Uh, it's in Ossining. You know Prerogative magazine?"

"Prerogative magazine, huh?" he said, writing it down. Rob wasn't sure, but he thought he noticed Grettco pressing extra hard through the paper on those words.

Rob narrowed his eyes at him. "Yeah, that's right."

Grettco put his pen down in the binding of his notebook at that point, leaned back, and folded his hands over his belly.

"She's an editor there."

"Well listen, if this happened in New York City, we can't help you. It's not in our jurisdiction."

Rob could tell by the tone in Grettco's voice that this conversation was going nowhere fast. "I can understand that, but I'm here because I believe my girlfriend saw him also. In the cemetery."

Grettco frowned and temporarily picked up his pen again. "So you're saying you believe the same guy who was chasing you, your girlfriend saw in the cemetery? The Sleepy Hollow cemetery on Route 9?" Grettco pointed in the general direction.

"Yes."

"All right, where's your girlfriend, Mr. Martin? I'm going to need to get this statement from her if she's the one who saw him."

"She's not in the country right now. She's in Shanghai, covering a story for a couple of weeks."

Grettco frowned again, this time shaking his head.

He jotted down a final note in his notebook then slammed it shut abruptly, causing Rob to jump back a bit.

"Well, then we can't help you right now."

"Can I at least explain the situation? This man told me that if I valued my life and hers…"

"Mr. Martin," Grettco said, holding up one hand. At this point, a lot of the other officers had turned to see if the conversation was going to end or get more heated. Rob looked around at all of them.

This is exactly what he'd been afraid of. He started to resign himself to the fact that he wasn't going to be getting any help from this venue.

"Your girlfriend is the one who saw him here," Grettco said, tapping his finger on the desk, "in our jurisdiction. So, when she gets back, bring her in and we'll take the statement from her, nobody else. What you need to do is go to the New York City police and file a report of your own."

Rob just glared at Grettco's desk, nodding.

"That's how it works," Grettco said, his mouth set and his arms folded.

"I see." Rob looked around again at all of the officers staring at them.

"To be honest with you though, it doesn't seem like you're of the mind right now to give a statement to anyone."

Rob lifted his eyes to meet Grettco's. "What does that mean?" he asked, indignantly.

"It means you seem very out of it, and I think it would bode well for you to make your exit now."

Rob knew what the man was implying.

"Say no more. Thanks for nothing."

He got up and made his way back up the aisle

Yemane had led him down. He could feel the eyes on the back of his head as he did. No one stopped him and no one called out to him. He reached the large metal door that he'd entered through and pounded on it. Yemane emerged from the small ticket box that sat right next to it.

He was smiling, but his smile faded once he saw the look on Rob's face. "Did you get what you came for?" he asked.

"No."

Rob looked over at him and could tell that Yemane was trying to think of something helpful to say.

"I just want to go home now, man."

Yemane looked at him for another moment and reluctantly buzzed Rob out. As soon as he heard the door open, Rob pushed through it and left. Yemane stared after him through the small, glass window on the metal door when it closed behind him, as Rob went through the front door and down the pathway toward the sidewalk. He made a left as he expected him to, heading toward the Darren Hayes apartments.

Yemane shook his head. He was about to go back to his desk when he realized someone was behind him. He turned to see Grettco standing there, hands in his pockets, also watching Rob as he made his way toward the safety of Beekman Avenue.

"They're initiating again," he said to Yemane, giving him almost an apologetic look.

"So we're just going do nothing about it? Again?"

"That's right!" Grettco said, pointing at him, but making his voice low and stern. "Because he runs this place, and he writes my paycheck and your paycheck. He bought you a handicap-friendly home, or should I say mansion. Oh, and he kept your daughter alive by paying those medical bills that our shitty insurance policy wouldn't cover."

Yemane gulped. The blandness and matter-of-factness with which Grettco said those final words chilled him.

The two men stared at each for another few moments. Then Yemane gave him one simple nod and went back inside the reception box.

He actually liked the nights where his shift called for him to work the front desk. He felt like it was his own private safe house against matters such as these.

Grettco went back to his desk, where he wasn't surprised to see his phone was ringing. He picked it up.

"Is he gone?" the voice on the other end asked without so much as a hello to preface the question.

"Yes," Grettco said. "I think I squashed the matter."

"Good. Let your light so shine before men, Officer Grettco."

"The same to you."

Grettco hung up and went back to the quiet evening he was enjoying before Robert Martin had arrived and threatened to ruin it.

By the time Rob had gone a couple blocks, his embarrassment had quickly morphed into anger. He hoped something did happen to him before Maryanne got back just so he could rub it in Grettco's face.

The man had basically refused to help him. He refused to even so much as listen, and then accused him of being on something while speaking to a cop.

Well, that's the end of that.

He wasn't going to the NYPD. Not after that. He refused to subject himself to this embarrassment again. They would deal with this on their own, at least until they had something a little more concrete to go on.

As he walked up the pathway to Building J, he wondered why the fuck his bag was so heavy. He stopped at the entrance and opened it. When he saw what was causing the offending weight, a glass juice bottle, he grabbed it and without thinking threw it against the brick siding of the building with all his might.

He pushed the door open and walked up the stairs to his apartment with a little more skip in his step. Beth, the old lady who lived on the second floor, who sometimes talked to Maryanne and Lily, peeked her head out her door as he passed it.

"Did you hear that?" she asked in a bit of shaky voice that made Rob feel a little bad for frightening her, but not bad enough.

He shrugged. "Um, yeah, I think it was on the other side of the courtyard."

"Oh, it sounded so close though!"

"Yeah, nothing to worry about," he said, giving her a warm smile. "Goodnight."

He turned and rolled his eyes once he was out of her line of sight. He heard her gently close and lock the door behind her. He pulled out his keys and finally stepped foot into his apartment. Despite the night's festivities, he couldn't have been happier to just be home. No one was home either to have to interface with. God must have decided to give him that single, sweet grace for the evening.

He got to his room and put down his bag next to his computer. After getting changed and splashing some cold water on his face, he picked it back up to remove the Tupperware that had held his lunch. As he fished around in it, his hand fell on an envelope. He pulled it out and realized it was the note Randall had left for him that he'd never gotten to read; probably more than a note as it was pretty thick.

He tossed the bag on the floor and sat on his bed to read it.

He pulled out a letter that was obviously several pages long and had a large post-it stuck to the front of it:

I sent this to our board of directors who ignored it. You can consider it my resignation letter. –Randall

"What?" Rob yelled. He unfolded the letter and started reading:

President Oliver and Esteemed Board Members,

I am writing this letter to make you all aware of the despicable acts I have seen committed here at Shelters for Hope. For all I know, you might even have had a hand in them as well. Please forgive that statement, but you have to understand that my spirit is now dead and my confidence in others completely shot after this year's events. Anyway, I am hoping that you are in fact not aware of what is going on behind the scenes here and will be just as enraged as I have become upon hearing about them. This is a cry for help of sorts for myself, but more importantly, our clients for which we work so hard to obtain a better quality of life.

I came to work for SfH about two years ago, because it was an organization that was a voice of hope for those less fortunate than I, or so I thought. From what I can see, that is just a front to keep minorities right where Norman Racketts wants them, in the sewers and gutters he believes they belong in.

If anyone had bothered to do a background check on this man as I was forced to do in light of recent events, they would have found that he might have been a so-called "champion for minorities" as a defense attorney in upstate New York, but it came at a hefty price for them. He would trick and enslave former clients by having them sign a document so packed with legal jargon that they couldn't understand it. They signed it anyway, entrusting their cases and their lives to him. What they didn't know was that the document basically bound them to him for life, and in exchange for a constant roof over their heads, he would enlist their help in doing his dirty work. If they gave him any trouble, he threatened them with purposely blowing their case and putting them in jail. With no other resources available, they would have no choice but to agree. Magically, not one of them has ever decided to speak up against Mr. Racketts.

Talk to Mr. Michael Sachen, who sends him twenty percent of his paycheck each week, no matter how small it might be from the little construction work he's able to pick up. Or Alexia Brown, who's so desperate to keep her former life of prostitution and drugs a secret from her current husband, she figures sleeping with her CEO boss, a close personal friend of Mr. Racketts, is a better trade-off than having Racketts reveal her past to her husband. He threatens her with it on a regular basis if she doesn't keep his friend happy and satisfied.

Better still, try listening to the story of a former client who signed this deed of servitude unknowingly, and is so hell-bent on not returning to jail ever again, he would rather serve as Racketts mercenary. I'll spare you the horrific details as I swore I would keep his story an anonymous one.

He plays on their lack of self worth and self-esteem to have them believe that this is all that they are worth. That's what one of Mr. Racketts's former clients told me when I asked her why she never reported what he had put her through; she doesn't believe she deserved any better than this treatment.

This is the man you have entrusted to lead this non-profit organization. I wish I was done, but I'm not.

The true reason I have for writing this letter is that Norman Racketts has been stealing government funding on a regular basis for what should be about two years if my calculations are correct. For the past year I have been an accomplice to that. It all started at a desk-side audit, which I facilitated last winter. The auditor questioned me regarding a filing entitled, "psychiatric evaluation services rendered," something I assumed was conducted for a certain client or group of clients. I collected this and two other claims from the auditor and presented them all to Mr. Racketts, who told me he would supply the invoices to me for each item. Upon receipt, I faxed them to our auditor and made extra copies for my own files. Shortly after, Mr. Racketts asked me to return the invoices to him. For some reason, I found it an odd request. He wasn't aware that I'd made extra copies for my own records, which I decided to retrieve and contact the vendors for verification. Two out of the three checked out. The vendor responsible for psychiatric evaluation services rendered, however, I'm sure has never even taken Psychology 101. I'm guessing Mr. Racketts never suspected anyone would dare question him, because he certainly didn't go too far to cover his tracks.

Renaman Psychiatric Services had a New Jersey contact number, which I called first. The voicemail was for a man named Leonard, whom at the end of his message said, if you are calling for Renaman Psychiatric Services, please dial 555–727–8888. So I did. Raymond picked up right away. When I told him I was trying to reach Renaman Psychiatric Services, he told me I'd called the right place and that he was the owner. Upon further questioning, he told me his name was Dr. Leonard Renaman and he had indeed performed testing on three clients at the Bronx residence. I also asked him to verify the address we had on file, which he did: 1333 Rockford Place, Studio 4, Bronx, N.Y., 10452.

It was something in this man's voice that prodded me to go and check out the location. I live in the Bronx, and I didn't recall any sort of commercial building being at Rockford Place. So on my way home from work that evening, I drove over to Rockford, which is about a ten-minute drive from my own home.

Upon arrival, I found that Number 1333 was an apartment building and Studio 4 was Apartment 5 with a piece of yellowing construction paper that read Studio 4 over the number five. I didn't bother knocking.

While I am aware this does not necessarily deem Renaman Psychiatric Services not a legitimate establishment, this does: I decided to leave well enough alone, but the next day, after most people had left the office, Mr. Racketts approached me and asked if I wanted to grab some dinner with him. It was an odd request as he is not a co-worker I am particularly close with, and my boss to boot, but I agreed to it. He also told me to bring my stuff with me. I said I had a lot of work left to do and was planning on staying late tonight, so I would be returning to the office. He again insisted I take my belongings with me in case it got to be a late night. Again, I conceded although it was odd. I picked up my brief case and we stood awkwardly in the elevator, waiting for it to hit the ground floor. I led the way out the door, and I turned and asked Mr. Racketts where he would like to go for a meal. We ended up at Mustang's, where he requested a table away from the happy hour crowd. I was confused as to what exactly was going on, but he cleared that up for me right away. As we ate, he revealed to me that he had someone follow me when I drove over to Rockford Place the other night. When he said this, I knew this situation was a whole other beast all together, that I was not dealing with the person I thought I was dealing with.

"I assume you've figured out by now that Renaman Psychiatric Services is not a legitimate establishment," he said.

I stared at him for quite some time, not knowing how to answer the question. I feared, and rightfully so, that I might be dealing with a dangerous man.

"It crossed my mind, sir, but it's nothing I had put too much effort toward worrying about," I said.

"Well, you should put a lot of effort toward it, Randall. A lot indeed."

It was then he first offered me money to go along with his lies. Racketts went on to tell me that Renaman was one of five fake vendors that he was using to get certain friends the money they needed. He didn't explain the who, what, where, or why, but he told me if I were to agree to help him out with these phony transactions, I would get ten percent of the amount he would expense for each vendor every six months, which could possibly account for an additional $50,000 per year if I played my cards right. I know it was wrong, but I agreed, convincing myself I needed the money, and that Racketts' friends needed this money for good rather than bad. I built it up to be a Robin Hood scenario that I always knew in my heart wasn't true. For the next year I facilitated these transactions, but the guilt and fear was too much for me. I approached him with a check for all the money I'd accrued from this deal. I told him the pressure of all this was weighing too heavily on me and that I couldn't continue. I wanted to give the money to the SfH as a private donation and be done with it. I told him I would keep my mouth shut about what had gone on and what he was doing, I swore to myself to find a new job as soon as possible.

He looked at me, obviously amused. When I was done, he laughed.

"Well, Randall, I'm afraid it's not that simple."

He took my check and ripped it up. He told me I better reconsider, and reconsider hard. I told him my decision was final.

From then on, he has gone out of his way to make my life miserable. I've learned first hand what Mr. Racketts thinks of minorities in this country, and it is not pretty. To him we are no better than the vermin that burrow in the mud and grime of NYC subways. I'm writing this letter as a plea for help. I'm willing to cooperate in any way I can to stop this evil man and everything he stands for.

You know where to find me.

Sincerely,
Randall Hardgrove
Finance Associate

The letter had been typed, but there was a handwritten addition, addressed directly to Rob, at the end of it:

Rob,

I won't go into details, but he has given me no choice but to flee the area. Please, do not try to contact me. I know what I did was wrong, but I am leaving you with all of the information that I believe you will need.

There is another check, the same one I tried to give Racketts, for $58,678 in the back of the top, far right drawer of my desk in a long, white standard envelope. Please take it and return it to the agency.

More importantly, here is a list of the five aforementioned vendors, that I know of, who helped Racketts take money from the government, and in turn, from SfH. Again, please do not try to contact me. Thank you for everything:

—Renaman Psychiatric Services=Dr. Donald Alfonso, Edgewater Medical Center

—Givenchee Consulting = Gene Rockferd, Rockferd Realtors

—Ottomen Fabricators =Albert Deichman, The Law Offices of Leibert, Leibert, and Deichman

—Blackwell Insurance=Christopher Stockton, American Symphony Orchestras

—React Financial Planners = Joseph Goldberg, RWB Publishing

Rob dropped the letter when he read the last line, causing papers to fly everywhere. He eventually bent down to shuffle them all back together. He stood there for a moment with the pile in his hand then headed for the door. He took the stairs three or four at a time and started pounding on Lily and Maryanne's door.

Chapter 27

Lily opened the peephole after about a minute of Rob's banging.

"What the fuck is going on?" she asked as she opened the door, which took Rob down a notch. He frowned at her.

"I'm sorry, were you sleeping?" he asked as he looked at his watch. 7:30 p.m., it read.

"I was taking a nap. I just got home like ten minutes ago," she said, rubbing at her eyes. "Is everything okay?"

"No," he answered immediately, grabbing her forearm, pulling her into the living room, and onto the couch. He took out the last page of the letter and handed it over to her.

"Look at that," he said, pointing at the last line that incriminated Joseph Goldberg, RWB Publishing, as a recipient of government funds from Norman Racketts, SfH non-profit agency.

"What is this?" Lily asked, turning the paper over.

"It's a letter from my Finance Associate, stating that my boss has been stealing money under the guise of needing it for fake vendors which he made up, and then paid out to for god knows what reasons. It's a letter saying that your boss is one of them."

"What?" Lily asked, almost laughing. "Wait, can I read it?" she said, holding out her hand for the rest of the papers. He handed them over.

"Here. What I gave you is the last page. These

should be in order though." Rob got up from the couch and paced as Lily read.

It took her about five minutes to get through it, leaving Rob to wonder if she'd actually read the whole thing.

"So, this guy you work with is saying that your boss was making up phony expense reports to get money from the government to give to certain people, and Joseph is one of them?"

"Exactly," Rob answered.

"How would they even know each other?"

"I don't know! They're both big-time Jews involved in charities and politics. They all, at the least, know of each other."

Lily laughed. "Well, do you believe this guy? What are the chances he's making any of this up?"

"Well, he pretty much admitted to a felony and has now fled the area. So, no, I don't think he's making any of this up."

"I see your point," she said, frowning.

"Well, are you going do anything about this?"

"What do you want *me* to do?" she asked, looking like she knew there had to be something she was not getting and was embarrassed by that fact.

Nevertheless, Rob saw her point. Even if this were true beyond the shadow of a doubt, how would Lily ever be able to go about proving it without Joseph knowing and putting herself in any danger? Still, she might be able to uncover little bits and pieces.

"I don't know, can't you go snooping around his office or something? He's rarely there a full day, right? Maybe you can even sneak me in one night and I could look around?"

"Uh, I don't know about that." Lily was standing up

now.

"Why are you acting like this? I thought you'd be all over it; you guys hate Joseph. Not to mention everything you guys have found out about him as of late. Did you forget about all of that?"

"No, I haven't, but I mean, what does all that really have to do with us directly? Yeah, it doesn't speak well of him, but he gave us all a chance you know?"

"Are you crazy?" Rob asked. "It doesn't concern you that your boss is taking money from someone who is stealing it from the government? Do you understand that if this gets out you could be held accountable, too? Do you realize what it could do to the magazine and its reputation; hell, your reputation, too?"

He saw the expression that came over her face when he said that. It finally hit home.

"Well," she started and paused, putting her hand over her forehead, the way she does whenever she's feeling attacked. She finally let go of a deep breath and said, "Yeah, you're right."

Rob went over to the couch and started to gather up Randall's letter. "I'm going to go tell Maryanne about this. I'll tell her to get in contact with you and maybe you guys can figure this out together as to what is the best way to proceed. You read the letter, Lil. Norman is malicious, and anyone associated with him is probably not too off that mark."

"I know. Yeah, I'll talk to her at some point tomorrow from the office. I can tell her if you want so you don't have to spend the money on the call."

He shook his head for a moment in consideration.

"Well, what are you going to do?" she asked. "You're the one who's closest to the line of fire working directly for him."

"I don't know," Rob said, shaking his head. "I really don't know."

Chapter 28

The next night, Lily was alone at the office, just about ready to throw in the towel. Her mind kept returning to the letter Rob had presented her with last night and she couldn't get any work done. She'd use the ride home to clear her thoughts and finish her work up there. She got up to start shutting everything down. After turning off the heat and lights, all switches for which were at the back of the office, she made her way back to the alcove she and Maryanne shared. She was gathering up her things when she saw an e-mail come in that she'd been waiting for all day. Perfect timing, just when I'm about to leave, she thought.

She sat down to respond to it quickly, surrounded by the darkness of the office, when she heard a voice approaching. She stopped typing, heard the jingle of keys, and then the front door open. It was Joseph.

She got up to go let him know she was there, but his conversation stopped her just before she was about to step out of the door. She backed away from it cautiously instead.

"Yeah, I couldn't talk around Alexandra, but I'm here now," he said. "Well, tell him you need to see it. Who knows what he put in that fucking letter!"

Lily's eyes went wide with the image of the papers that lie before her just the night before fresh in her brain.

Maybe it is true.

"Just tell him as CEO you need to be privy to all correspondence, especially from someone who just left the company. Assert your authority for crying out loud."

Lily silently tucked herself underneath her desk to hide so that she could continue listening. It was too late to reveal herself now. There was silence for a few moments. Then he spoke again with such malice in his voice it made Lily shiver.

"Fuck you, Racketts. If you ever ambush me again like you did at that dinner you'll be sorry. I'll ruin you and you know I can!" he shouted, making Lily jump. She started to feel very hot in the face and light headed.

"The CNN piece? Yes, of course I saw it, of course she's in Shanghai, that's where the fucking office is going to be. Do you think I'm stupid?" He was talking about Casey now, she knew. She was the only one they currently had working on anything in that city.

"I scared her into submission, trust me she'll do the necessary."

Huh?

"What did Patrick say last night? Did you talk to Grettco? Good. Yeah, I think Patrick's time might be up," he said with a snicker. "Of course. What about them?"

Lily clamped a hand over her mouth to keep her breathing as quiet as possible. She heard Joseph put one heel after the other up on his desk, a cocky position they often found him in.

"I don't care how you feel or what any of the others *feel*," he seethed. "This is my magazine. Do you fucking hear me? Mine!" The rage had returned to his voice. "You all will have to kill me first if you think I'm going to just hand it over to anyone. That includes you, the brotherhood that I have maintained single handedly in this area before you came along, thank you very much, and those two little bitches. You think I couldn't have gotten rid of them already if I'd wanted to?"

Lily's mind and heart raced, and she prayed he didn't find her there at this point.

"This is my son's future we're talking about here, you forget. No, uh huh. I'll send them to a place where they can't threaten us anymore. I mean who knows what was in that letter and if he's shared that information with anyone."

Lily wondered who he was talking to, but could only imagine it was Norman, Rob's boss. She'd heard him address the person as Racketts.

"Well, find out and call me back tomorrow."

With that the conversation was over. She heard him mumble a couple things under his breath, gather up a few papers, and then head out.

Lily let her breathing get a little heavier after she heard the door shut. She finally crawled out from underneath her desk and stood up straight. Her sight started to get fuzzy and she felt herself losing her balance. She tried to grab onto the arm of her chair to break her fall as she fell to the ground and passed out.

About an hour passed before Lily woke up that night. She was terrified when she opened her eyes to the pitch black of the closed-down offices, her head pounding with pain from where she'd fallen over and hit it. Her chair was laying on top of her, as it was unsuccessful in helping her gain her balance. She groaned as she tried to sit up. That worked, but standing was a lost cause. She squeezed her eyes shut and put her hand to her forehead. Then the scene that occurred earlier all came rushing back to her, and she was suddenly all too aware of her surroundings.

She cautiously tried again to stand up, and this time

she made it to her feet. She was careful not to make any noise, scared that someone might still be here. She couldn't remember if Joseph had definitely left before she'd passed out.

Once she made it to the doorway of her office she froze. She somehow knew that she wasn't alone. Even through the searing pain her head was delivering, and the darkness, she could see him standing in the corner. A man, judging by his size and girth, was standing with his back to the room, facing the corner, and wearing a red flannel shirt. Lily quickly brought a hand to her mouth to keep from screaming. She took about two seconds to decide whether she should use his stance to her advantage and catch him off guard or simply run out of there as fast as she could. It didn't take her long to decide on the latter. She slid out of her office and tried as hard as she could to press herself against the wall to hide in the shadows in case he did decide to turn around.

Once she hit Josie's desk, she bolted toward the door hoping it had not been locked. She burst through it, barreled down the stairs, and ran out the door where she conveniently remembered her car keys and wallet were still upstairs.

"Fuck!" she yelled out into the night. There were no cars in the line of parking spots in front of the building, except one.

Standing in front of her, as if sent by God, was a running taxi, the driver asleep in the front seat. She walked quickly over to the driver's side and knocked on the window, which startled him awake immediately.

He rolled down the window.

"Hi. Listen, I need to get home, but lost my wallet. Can you drive me back to my apartment in Tarrytown, and I can run upstairs and get you money to pay for the fair?" She hoped he would put his faith in her and allow the request.

"Que?"

"Oh, god, he doesn't speak English."

She simplified this time. "Tarrytown?" she said, pointing south.

He sat up and rubbed his eyes, and looked around as if to make sure nobody was watching. He shook his head "yes" finally and pointed for her to get in. She hopped into the back seat and slammed the door. He pulled out of the space and did an incredibly blatant illegal U-turn in the middle of the intersection. Lily didn't even notice as she had her eyes and attention trained on the front door to see if anyone would exit.

Nobody did.

She made sure she didn't take her eyes off it until it had disappeared into the distance. She turned around once it had to face the front with a "humphf!" and folded her arms across her chest.

"Address?" asked the driver.

"Oh, 95 Beekman, the Darren Hayes apartments."

Lily's heart was starting to settle back into a normal beating pattern again. About ten minutes later, when the cab pulled up to the entrance, she leaned forward and yelled at the driver as if he were a deaf person. "I'm going to run upstairs to get your fair!" She didn't know if the cabbie necessarily understood, but he shook his head at her. "Money upstairs?" she said, pointing up. He shook his head again and threw a hand toward the building. Lily ran out and went straight up to Rob's apartment. Scott was the only one home and was kind enough to loan her the fare. She ran downstairs, paid the cab driver, and then asked the security guard in the courtyard to let her into the apartment. She lied down on the couch and tried to finally regain her composure.

Lily didn't know who the person was she'd seen standing in the corner, or if she'd even seen him at all. She was mostly convinced her mind had simply been playing tricks on her after the stressful situation she'd been in just moments before.

Should they go to the police? she wondered. She picked up her cell phone and found Rob's number in it.

"Hi, Lil," he answered.

"Hi, where are you?"

"Just getting some dinner with Steve. What's up? Did you talk to Maryanne today?"

She took a deep breath. "No. I didn't give that letter much credit to be honest with you, until tonight."

"Uh, what do you mean?"

"Something's happened. Are you coming back?"

"Yeah, we're just up the road, I'll stop by."

"Okay. Good."

About ten minutes later, Rob knocked at the door. "What's going on?" he asked, a look of concern on his face. "Is Maryanne okay?"

"Oh, yeah, she's fine. We were e-mailing for a bit today."

"Well, why didn't you tell her about that letter I got from Randall then?" He was obviously annoyed.

"Just sit down," she said, pointing at the couch. He did as he was told and she rehashed the entire scene. He listened quietly for the most part, until she got to the part where she heard Joseph call the person on the other line "Racketts."

"So they do know each other!" he shouted and hopped up off the couch.

"That is your boss' last name, right? I couldn't remember for absolute sure."

"Yep. Ain't that some shit?" he said, shaking his head.

"Should we go to the cops?" she asked him.

He looked over at her for a moment, debating on telling her he'd already tried that route.

"Let me talk to my boss first about the letter. He'll know exactly how to handle it."

"Your boss?"

"Yeah, Geffin. Geffin Marcus. He can find out if the letter even went to the board or not. For all I know, it did and they are already investigating it."

She shook her head in agreement and then took a breath.

"Yeah, it was all really upsetting and scary, and I ended up passing out."

"Oh, god, are you okay?"

"Yeah, I'm all right. My desk chair broke my fall."

"Wait, you passed out there? He didn't find you, did he?"

"No, no, it was after he left. Unless he came back," she said, trailing off. She started to get a bit nervous as the possibility occurred to her.

She looked back over at Rob. "When I woke up, I saw someone in the office."

Another worried look took over Rob's face. He shrugged and asked, "Who? Who was it?"

"I don't know," Lily said, embarrassed, putting a hand to her forehead. "I don't even know if I really saw anybody or if I was just still out of it and imagining things. That's why I took a cab home. I freaked out and ran out of there without my bag or keys or anything."

"What exactly did you see?"

"I saw a man standing in the corner."

Rob froze. This was starting to sound all too

familiar.

"He had his back to me. It didn't appear as if he was trying to hide or anything, but his back was to me, and he was actually facing the corner. He had on a red flannel, that's all I know."

Rob's jaw dropped slightly, noticeably to Lily.

"What?"

It took a few moments before he could answer her. He took his hat off and lied it down on the couch. "Maryanne never told you about her dream, I guess?"

"No."

"She had a dream about a man in a red flannel. She dreamt that she saw him here in this apartment."

When he said that, Lily jumped up as if she'd just found a bug on her seat.

"She claims it's also why she wandered into the woods the other night at the pumpkin blaze. She saw him at the tree line and got an urge to follow him."

"What? Is she nuts?"

"Yes. Yes, she is," Rob said, sighing. A vision of his own assailant came to mind, and he hoped that he and the man the girls were seeing were not one in the same. He also wondered if they were, in fact, not dealing with a figment of their imaginations, but a real person. He stood up. "I'm going to go try to call her."

"Warn her to be careful, and find out what the hell is going on with Casey! Find out what he meant!"

"I will," he said, heading for the door.

"Should we go to the police tomorrow with everything?" she called after him.

No, he thought to himself. *If you value your life...and hers!* "I'll find out what's going on over there and talk to Geffin first thing in the morning. We'll figure it out from there."

"Okay," he heard her say meekly as the door shut behind him.

Rob watched as Geffin read Randall's letter. He was relieved to see his immediate supervisor's eyes widening farther and farther as he went from page to page.

When Rob had gotten in that morning, he'd checked Randall's desk for the check, and indeed found it in the back of the drawer he'd left it in. It was now sitting next to Geffin's forearm on his desk.

Rob couldn't wait to get Maryanne on the phone to tell her what was going on. He'd tried a few times to reach her over in Shanghai last night, but she hadn't answered the phone in her hotel room.

When Geffin was done, he pushed himself up and out of his seat.

"Shit!" He paced for a few moments. "How could all this have been going on right underneath our noses?" He looked over at Rob and he seemed so lost and confused that Rob almost got up and hugged him. Instead, he shook his head and dropped it.

"I really don't know, Geffin. I feel awful though that he was going through all of this. We need to find out who on the board received it and why they ignored it."

Geffin shook his head and sighed. "Yeah. I mean, I wonder what their story is going to be."

"You know what's weird?"

"What?"

"Right before Iris brought the letter over to me, Norman said something that was pretty fucked up. It almost, like, gave it away. It was the perfect prelude."

"You mean besides his little outburst earlier in the day? That didn't give him away enough for you?"

"Well, yeah, besides that, of course." Rob had a

flashback of the ring he'd seen almost leering at him on Norman's finger that day.

"He came in to apologize to me."

"Really?"

"Yeah, that night. Right before Iris walked in, he told me it's not that he doesn't appreciate what he does, it's just they all have a ghetto side just dying to get out."

"He said that? What does that mean?"

"He was talking about Randall," Rob said, holding Geffin's gaze to drive his point home. Geffin sat back down in his chair with a thud. He looked as if someone had dealt him a hard and fast blow.

"I thought I knew this man," he said, shaking his head.

"No kidding. Now, according to what Lily overheard, he's going to come question me about what was in the letter."

Geffin waved a hand at him. "Tell him it was just an apology letter for him leaving so abruptly, if he does." He paused. "I don't know why I'm only thinking about this now, but did you ever report getting chased that night?"

"What?" The question caught Rob completely off guard.

"That night. Did you ever report it?"

"Well, not exactly."

"Why not?"

"Look, I was so upset and exhausted that night I couldn't even think about trying to find a cop or a station at that time. I just had to get home. So yesterday I went to the cops in town actually, and they were no help whatsoever. They wouldn't even take my statement, Geffin."

"Well, of course they didn't take your fucking

statement, Rob! That was a huge mistake not reporting it that very night!"

"I know, I know!" Rob said. He desperately wanted to get Geffin off this subject, so as to avoid having to go further and explain Maryanne's involvement, her sighting in the cemetery, and how that related. His heart was bursting to tell him why he freaked out the day Norman walked out of the meeting, the real reason why it had taken him so long to go to the cops. He had risked so much already that he didn't want to possibly put Maryanne and himself in any more danger by reaching out for more help.

He could almost feel the pounding of his heart and the weight of exhaustion on his body from that night as he'd sprinted down the alley to safety away from the man in the red parka and wavy, graying hair. Suddenly, he was consumed with anger.

"Geffin, I have to tell you something."

Rob had always thought of Geffin as a mentor, and at the moment, he needed to tell him. He knew Geffin would take part of the weight off his shoulders. He always seemed to know exactly what to do.

Geffin got up and shut the door. "Yes, please fill me in on what the fuck is going on here." He rolled his desk chair out from behind it and planted himself right in front of Rob.

"There's a reason I acted so strangely the day Norman refused to acknowledge Randall, and it's related to why I waited so long to talk to the police about getting chased that night."

"Well, what is it?"

"After I called you that night, I thought I'd lost the guy, but I didn't. He caught up to me, in a really bad neighborhood no less."

"Did he hurt you? I don't remember seeing any bruises or scrapes on you at all," Geffin asked, a highly concerned look on his face.

"No, not really, that's just it. He wasn't after me to hurt me. He wanted to tell me something I think. He dragged me into this alley, and once it was obvious he had the upper hand and I couldn't go anywhere, everything finally calmed down."

"Did he say anything?"

"Yes. I don't remember the exact words, but he told me he had come as a messenger and that: 'You can't escape it.' Meaning me, I can't escape whatever it is. Then, after he said that, he put his left hand over his heart and said, 'They need you.'"

Geffin just stared at him in amazement. He had no idea what to make of Rob's story. Rob was starting to get emotional, mostly because it felt so good to finally be talking to someone about this who actually cared about what he had to say.

"The thing is, I've been having dreams like this. Where people are after me and they keep repeating that phrase: 'They need you.' Or sometimes it's, 'We need you.' I don't know, all I'm sure of is that I'm getting chased down, and it's not for something good."

"Holy shit," Geff mumbled under his breath.

Rob got a hold of himself. "But when he put his hand over his heart, I saw a white gold ring on the middle finger of his left hand, and some of the people I see in my dreams are wearing rings on the same finger."

"Well, what does this have to do with Norman?"

"I saw a ring on his left hand that day. It was the same type I saw on the man who chased me, same finger, and the same ones I'm seeing in my dreams."

Geffin sat back in his chair and exhaled deeply.

"What happened with this guy?"

"I punched him as hard as I could in the stomach and took off in the other direction."

"Good for you." Geffin gave him a firm nod.

"And as I ran down the alley, he had one last thing to say: 'If I value my life and hers,' he said, I'll 'keep my mouth shut.'"

"And hers?"

Rob shook his head. "He had to be talking about Maryanne."

"Are you sure?"

"Yes. I have no reason to be either, but I just know."

"And that's why you didn't report it right away. Because you were afraid."

"Yes. After a few days I realized how crazy that was and that I needed their help, so I just went to the police in town, thinking for sure they'd be able to do something for me. But they told me they wouldn't take my statement. I told them someone chased me through the subways and now I'm afraid he's after my girlfriend who saw him in the cemetery the other night. They said they couldn't help me, particularly because what happened to me was in New York City. What they needed was Maryanne there to tell them about what she saw in the cemetery because that was actually in town and under their radar. So they wouldn't take down what I had to say about it; they would only speak to her. And as you know, she's currently on the other side of the freaking world right now."

"Maryanne saw the same guy that chased you, in the cemetery in Sleepy Hollow?"

Rob exhaled deeply. Maybe he should have kept his mouth shut because now he was being forced to reveal more than he wanted. It was impossible to hand over one piece of the puzzle without the rest.

"Well, I'm not sure. I'm afraid that it might have been. She saw someone watching her from the trees that line the cemetery in town. We were there for this Halloween event."

Geffin was near flabbergasted at this point.

"I don't know. I think I'm severely paranoid now after all this."

"Well, understandably. So you went to the police yesterday? The same day you got this letter from Randall."

"Right."

Geffin got up and ran a hand through his hair, then dug his hands into his pockets, his turn to exhale, and loudly, too.

"I don't like this Rob."

"Yeah, you and me both."

They sat in silence for a while.

"Well, first thing's first," Rob said. "What do we do about this?" he asked, pointing to the letter. "That's the most glaring, concrete thing right now, right?"

Geffin sighed again. "Well, yes, you are right," he said, standing behind his desk again and placing his fingertips on the actual letter. "I just don't know. I don't know what we're dealing with here."

Rob frowned and nodded.

"Well, if everything in this letter is true, we're dealing with a pretty deranged criminal," Geffin said, lowering his voice. "And everything that you just filled me in on doesn't help Norman's case."

Rob looked around nervously, realizing that maybe even Geffin's private office with the door closed wasn't exactly the smartest place to be discussing this.

Geffin continued. "That being said, these are some

hefty claims, and I don't know if we should be accusing him based on one letter from an employee who didn't even stick around to back it up. He might just be looking to get back at Norman for poor treatment; but with everything her roommate overheard last night…"

"Well, exactly. He was so scared he skipped town, Geffin. And I mean the check is right there. What more do we need than that?"

"This is nothing, Rob. This is just a piece of paper, until we can verify it," he said, holding it by his index and thumb, shaking it in the air. "Have you tried contacting him?"

"No."

"All right." Geffin paused for a moment, obviously thinking things through. "Is she sure she heard him say 'Racketts' on the phone last night?"

"Yes."

"And Maryanne's still in China, right? Until when?"

"Um, she gets home in a few days I believe."

"You have to call her and tell her everything, and tell her to make sure she plays it safe. Make sure she doesn't go anywhere by herself and that she's alert and watches her back. The same goes for when she gets home. For both of you. Hell, the three of you! Her roommate, make sure she's careful, too."

Rob shook his head.

"Crazy how they know each other," Geffin said shaking his head, referring to Norman and Joseph. "God, Maryanne must be a wreck after you get chased and she sees some stranger staring at her in the middle of a fucking cemetery."

Rob frowned. "Well, she doesn't exactly know about that," he said sheepishly.

"You never told her?"

"No! I told you what he said to me! I was petrified! I didn't want to get anyone hurt, especially her, Geffin. I swear to God," Rob said, choking up, "if anything happened to her I wouldn't be able to live with myself."

Geffin hung his head and nodded. "All right, listen, don't breathe a word of anything to anyone else around here. Especially Iris. I'm going to talk to Allan to see if he or anyone else on the board did in fact receive the letter, and if so, what the story is on why the hell they ignored it. Then I'm going to have this check investigated."

"How?"

"First, I'll go to the bank and see if I can indeed cash it. Second, I'll see if we can get a listing of where Randall's most recent deposits into his accounts have been."

Rob looked at him as if he were crazy. "They're not going to give you that information."

"I know, that's why I'm going to the *proper* authorities," he said. Rob got up and all but bum rushed Geffin's desk, which did startle his boss.

"Geffin, I don't know if that's a good idea. I mean the more people we tell and get involved, the more dangerous this can become."

Geffin put a hand on Rob's shoulder. "Relax. Roger and I know a private detective; a trusted friend for many, many years. He will keep this completely confidential. Telling him will be like telling your dog."

Rob relaxed a little and almost got excited at the thought of legitimate help. "Really? Well, why the hell didn't you mention that in the first place?" he asked, with a nervous laugh.

"Because I wasn't sure how serious this was, until you explained yourself. We'll have him trace the money and see what he comes up with. In the meantime, please be careful. Call Maryanne at your first opportunity and fill her in on everything, you understand me?"

"Yes."

"All right, now go back to your office. We still have jobs to do around here."

Rob walked out still feeling a bit defeated, but at least now there was some hope of figuring out exactly what was going on.

Finally, somebody was taking him seriously. Now all he had to do was avoid Norman for the rest of the day.

Chapter 29

She opened her eyes and saw the ceiling was covered with small webs and a spider in each one. She gasped, suddenly wide awake. She blinked her eyes, but they were still there. As the seconds ticked by, they all began to dissolve away until all that was there was the cream-colored ceiling, eggshell, to be exact.

Maryanne shook her head and sat up in bed. She built about three pillows up behind her and sat back again, looking around the hotel room. That was the first time that she'd seen that many of them.

Usually it was only one or two. She took it as a sign that things were getting worse. Maryanne hadn't found any sort of relief in Shanghai. In fact, the trip was only proving to leave her more disturbed. The Green Light! schedule was pretty tightly packed, so she hadn't had too much time to spend with Casey, but the time she spent with her had only proven that something was indeed going on with her cousin.

Casey hadn't seemed too excited when Maryanne had called to tell her she was coming to Shanghai. She'd even sensed a twinge of panic, but dismissed it as her simply being paranoid. When she had finally arrived though, she found Casey still acting the same. Maryanne arrived on a Thursday and was in and out of meetings, events, and tours for Green Light! up until Sunday, their one day off on the press tour. So she met up with Casey for a day of sightseeing.

"I saw him again," Maryanne said, as the two

cousins walked along The Bund.

"No, thank you," Casey said quickly and curtly to a street vendor who was approaching to hustle them into buying whatever toy he was pushing. Casey hadn't let him get even a word out. "Wait, saw who again?"

"The man I saw in my dream."

"You had another dream?"

"No, not another dream," Maryanne said, looking over at Casey knowingly.

"Well, what are you talking about?"

"I saw him in the cemetery."

"Wait, what?"

Maryanne was looking straight ahead now, almost trance-like as she spoke. "I saw him in the cemetery," she repeated. Maryanne looked over at her again and saw the confused look on Casey's face. She looked back down at the ground.

"We went to the pumpkin blaze, and they had the cemetery open across from Route 9, so we all went over there. I'm telling you, without even realizing it, we'd gravitated toward Cecily's grave."

"That's the little girl you keep going to see?"

"Yes. I saw this light coming from her gravestone."

"A light?"

"Yeah. There's a glass cross on top of it, and it was, kind of glowing."

"God, Mare, this is getting really strange. Like something you'd see on 'Unsolved Mysteries'."

"Tell me about it. So I went over to her grave and once I'd turned and was facing the front of the tombstone, and could see the woods that line the top of the hill, I saw him standing there." Casey was dumbstruck. "So I followed him."

All the color drained from Casey's face with that.

"Maryanne, are you out of your mind? You followed a man into the woods, from a cemetery, no less, at night?"

"It was like I had no choice! I had to follow him!"

"Oh, come on? You had to?"

"Yes!"

Casey tried to settle herself. "So, what happened?"

"Well, I went after him. I lost sight of him by the time I got into the woods, but I found a shed."

"A shed?" Casey was secretly thinking this was all getting too ridiculous for words. "Let me guess. You went in?"

"Not right then. Rob found me before I could."

"Well, thank God for small favors. Did you tell him why you were in there?"

"Yes."

Casey felt relieved she wasn't the only one Maryanne was entrusting this story with. Plus, she knew Rob would do everything in his power to protect her.

"So, we had agreed that once I got back from this trip, we'd go check it out together."

Casey shook her head. "Well, be careful. You guys make sure you go during the day."

"I already went back."

"When?"

"It was like, the day before I left to come here."

"So, what did you find? Did Rob come, too?"

"No, I didn't tell him I was going to see it."

"What? Maryanne!" Casey stopped and buried her face in her hands. She walked away from Maryanne and over to the railing along the walkway that lines the Huangpu River.

Maryanne followed her. "Casey, I didn't want him involved in all this craziness anymore than he had to be. If anything happened to him, I would never be able to live with myself."

"What are you talking about? It's not like you would have done anything to him on purpose."

"No, but it would be thanks to my connections. My involvement with certain people."

"Well, that's beside the point right now. Let's just pray that nothing happens to any of you guys." After a long pause, Casey couldn't wait anymore. "So, what did you find in there?"

"It was so bizarre, Casey."

"And this was in the woods behind the cemetery? How far in?"

"Not too far, maybe a couple hundred feet. Forget 'Unsolved Mysteries', it was something straight out of a horror movie. It was really tiny and could fit ten people at the most. It was dirty, austere, and spider-ridden, but the creepiest thing of all was what was written on the walls."

"What?" Casey asked.

"I wrote it down." Maryanne fumbled through her purse and pulled out her wallet. She retrieved a folded piece of paper and read from it.

"Let your light so shine before men."

She looked up to meet Casey's eyes. "It was written in huge letters, and the phrase circled the entire room."

While it was frightening, Casey didn't know what all this meant, or where this left her cousin at this point. All she knew was where it left her, more worried than ever. She looked across the river, not really sure what to say.

"Case, are you all right?"

The question caught her so off guard she jumped a bit. "I'm fine, besides how I feel about what you just told me."

Maryanne shook her head. "You're lying to me.

You're not fine," she said, her voice starting to shake.

Casey turned toward her, her eyes almost bloodshot at this point, which left Maryanne even more taken aback. It looked like Casey was struggling to find words, and it made her a bit hopeful that this might be the moment her cousin finally broke down and opened up to her. That hope was quickly squashed.

"Mare, let's just get out of here," Casey said, and without waiting for a reply, she walked past her cousin and around the tea house that was on the other side of the river walk, disappearing from Maryanne's sight. She followed after Casey to find her standing next to a taxi with the door already open.

"I don't need it, Casey, I'll just walk. It's right there," she said, pointing in the direction of her hotel. She was so frustrated she didn't want to spend another awkward second with her cousin and started walking away.

Green Light! had put up the journalists on the trip in the Park Hotel, a property with a lot of history in Shanghai. Joseph hadn't been happy about her taking the trip, but he really had nothing to say as it was all being covered. When he heard where they were staying, he sneered and said, "Well, well maybe they do have more than rocks for brains. Christopher Choa restored that lobby in 2001 I think it was."

"Famous Jewish-American architect…" The girls had simply rolled their eyes at each other.

"Maryanne!" Casey called after her, but she ignored her and kept on walking. She didn't turn around, not even once.

She reached her hotel room, threw her bag down on the bed and flopped down on it, face first. This left her head staring at the phone that was donning a blinking red message light.

She raised her eyebrows and swung an arm over to pick up the receiver, trying not to get too excited. It could just be Casey calling to apologize. She dialed the message center, which said she had two messages.

One was from her mother, just checking in. The second was from Rob, and she kicked herself the second she heard his voice. She had promised to e-mail him with a good time to talk today, but had forgotten.

"Hey, babe. Just call me when you get this." She could hear through his even tone that something was wrong. She panicked even further when she caught a glimpse of the clock. It always escaped her that she was a whopping twelve hours ahead of everyone she cared about, and it was a very strange notion she was literally on the other side of the world from them all. If it was 3 p.m. here, that meant it was 3 a.m. there, and the message had been received just a half hour ago, according to the phone. Her heart beat faster as she sat on the bed next to the receiver and dialed Rob's cell, which he'd set up to receive and make international calls on for this trip, so they would have no problem keeping in contact. He didn't usually do that whenever Maryanne was away, but considering everything that had gone on as of late, he changed his mind. Rob picked up pretty quickly considering it was one of the longest distance phone calls one could possibly make.

"Hello?" He sounded wide awake for it being the middle of the night.

"Hi, Chilly."

"Hi. Ugh, babe, we got a lot to talk about," he said with a nervous laugh.

"What is it? What's going on? What time is it over there? Isn't it like 3 a.m.?"

“Yes, I’ve been trying you forever. I didn’t want to leave a message and freak you out.”

“I’m sorry, it’s been a really jam-packed sched—”

“He’s back,” he blurted out. “Lily saw him, too. The man in flannel.”

Maryanne’s eyebrows shot up to her hairline. “Where did she see him?” she breathed, slowly lowering herself down onto the bed.

“She was at the office.”

“What?” Maryanne squeaked.

“You need to go check your e-mail.”

“What? Why? No, wait, explain to me what happened.”

“I’m trying to do that, you need to go read the e-mail I just sent you,” he said, irritated. “And you have to concentrate and stay calm because a lot has happened that you need to know about in order to stay safe. You and Case both.”

That was all she needed to hear. “Okay.”

She sprang into action and went over to her computer. Rob had scanned a copy of Randall’s letter earlier in the day and e-mailed it to himself and Maryanne when he’d gotten home.

“Read the attachment, and read it all the way through,” he instructed, and waited. He heard her gasp and utter profanities as she read through the letter.

"Babe, what is this? It's from Randall?”

"Yes."

"And he says Norman was, well is, paying Joseph for something?"

"Listen to me. We think you and Casey are in danger. You need to get home immediately."

"How do you know?"

"Because Lily saw him after overhearing Joseph on

the phone the other night talking about this letter."

"So it's true?" Upon her first read Maryanne didn't think it held much weight. Everything Rob had ever said about Randall hadn't exactly made him out to be the sharpest tool in the shed, so her first reaction to all this was that she didn't think him even capable of it all.

"Yes, it's true. I found the check he mentions at the end right where he said it would be."

"All of it I mean, about Joseph. What Ramsey told me, that guy Andy in Vegas…"

"Oh, well, yeah, probably. More importantly, she overheard him make some threats against you and Lil, about 'getting rid of you guys' or something, and he mentioned Casey and having scared her."

Maryanne's nostrils flared. Who the fuck did Joseph think he was? Not to mention Casey was her other trigger besides Rob, and she'd do anything she could to protect her.

"I knew something was wrong, she's been acting completely bizarre. We actually just got into a fight about it."

"Really?" Rob said, his voice rising. Maryanne was almost relieved to finally hear a little bit of inflection in his voice.

"Yeah."

"It's him, I know it. Grab her and make sure she comes home with you."

"Oh, don't worry, I will. My God, I can't believe Lily saw that man, too! So she's seen this letter? What does she think of it?"

Rob sighed. "Listen, there's more to this."

"What are you talking about?" Maryanne's skin started to crawl and she turned from her desk chair to glance around the room to make sure she had no unexpected visitors.

He sighed again. Obviously, what he was about to say was serious and she steeled herself to get ready for it. "A while ago, somebody chased me through the subway."

"What?" she practically shrieked.

“It’s why I acted so strangely after you wandered into the cemetery. I was afraid you’d seen the same man who chased me.”

“When exactly did this happen?”

“It was while you were in Vegas.”

“That was a while ago! How could you not have told me this? What happened?”

“Maryanne, you were away, and I didn’t want to call and upset you while you were on the other side of the country.”

“So you do it when I’m on the other side of the world instead?”

“I know, babe, it’s just that even more has happened. I don’t want you to be all the way over there unaware of all of this stuff; it’s better that you know as soon as possible, right?”

She scoffed. “Well, yeah!”

“You promised you wouldn’t get upset at me. I’m telling you now.”

She paused for a moment to compose herself. She had kept things from him, too, and she knew his motives were the same as hers, they were just trying to protect each other.

“You’re right. I’m sorry. Tell me everything,” she said with a gulp. “I’m listening.”

Rob went on to re-hash the entire sordid tale. From his own dreams, to the scene in the office with Norman, where he saw the same ring on his finger as the man from the subway, to his frustrating attempt to enlist police help.

"I just can't believe you kept all this from me. I mean, I told you about how I've been sneaking off to the cemetery for Christ's sake!"

"I know, babe, I just didn't want to put you in any danger, and before this it was only these crazy dreams."

"But what if something had happened to you? Nobody would have known anything about this and would have had no clue where to start."

"I know, you're right, but I didn't care. You're all that matters."

Maryanne felt a huge lump start to grow in her throat. She wiped silent tears off her cheeks. She didn't want him to hear her cry anymore.

"You're all I've got," he said quietly.

She dropped her head and a few tears fell into her lap before she could wipe them away.

"So they know each other," she said quietly. "Norman and Joseph."

"You know, I almost forgot about this, but I remember Norman seeing that picture of us from Atlantic City on my desk one day. He asked about you. It was strange."

"I'm really getting freaked out now." She started to pace. "I mean, you remember what Ramsey told me about the political cartel in town right?"

"I know, but why would Norman be a part of that? He lives in the city."

"So, that doesn't mean this doesn't reach out further, or cover more ground for that matter."

"What do you mean?"

"Well, maybe it's not just for political power, as Randall's letter suggests."

"Right, but definitely control in general."

"Exactly." She paused for a moment. "I went back to the shed."

"You went back by yourself when you swore to me you'd wait and we'd go back together?"

"Yeah, well you've kept quite a few things from me too, at this point, so don't throw stones."

"Yeah, but I didn't lie directly to your face! That's a little different!"

"I know." She sat down and buried her face in her free hand, rubbing the heaviness out of her eyes with her fingertips. "I just…I had to find out for myself."

"Bullshit! Why did you do that? God damn it, babe, you can't keep being so fucking reckless."

She stood back up and puffed out her chest. "I was trying to protect you, too."

“Ugh!” he sighed, incredibly frustrated with her careless behavior.

"I told Geffin."

"You did? What did he say?"

"I had to show him Randall's letter. He said he knows a private investigator; a really close friend of his and Roger's that can look into all of this for us. I told him how the cops were no help. He swore to me this guy will remain invisible and not rile anyone up any further."

"Well, what is the investigator going to do exactly?"

"He’s going to start by checking out Randall's claims, I'd assume. Then, if those are true and we have physical evidence to show against Norman, we'll use that to get the help we need to look into everything else. In the meantime, Geffin will contact the board of directors and see if they did get that letter from Randall and ignore it like he said."

"Is he going to try to see if someone is following us?

They should look into everything going on in town, too. If we can nail Norman, then that nails Joseph and then…"

"Babe!" Rob stopped her. She was going a mile a minute. "I'm going to leave this to Geffin for now. We'll see what he comes up with initially, then go from there, okay?"

"Okay."

"So, how 's everything there? Nothing strange going on, right?"

"No. Besides Casey's behavior, everything's fine, really."

"Well, be very careful. Talk to her and find out what the story is and just get yourselves out of there as soon as possible. Keep your eyes out for anyone suspicious looking, all right? That's why I told you about all of this. I didn't want you to not have the information."

"I know. I'll be careful, I promise. I'll let you know when we're on our way back."

"Good. And can we make each other a promise right now, please? Let's never keep anything from each other ever again."

"You got it."

"We're never going to be able to protect each other if we keep things a secret."

"You're right." She laughed a little. Such an obvious statement that she had no idea how they could have lost sight of it. "I'm going to get Casey now."

"Good. I love you, babe."

"I know. I love you, too, Chilly."

Maryanne got up quickly, grabbed her bag, and left the room, not wanting to lose any momentum. She dug out the business card for Casey's hotel and showed it to the bellhop at the door, who hailed her a cab and told the driver where she needed to go.

The Lapis Casa was a good twenty minutes away, even more thanks to the masses of traffic that plagued the streets on any given day, which didn't help her nerves. By the time the cab pulled up, she barely remembered to pay him before bolting out the door and into the main lobby.

The Lapis Casa was a unique space in the city. Filled with antiques, all hand picked by the owner, none of which related to each other, but somehow managed to work. It reminded her of an old Spanish church, with stained glass everywhere, dark wooden pieces and millwork, and softly flickering candles everywhere. She went to the front desk and simply said, “Casey Guardino.”

Westerners could feel a little more comfortable there, as the receptionists were on the younger side and spoke fairly good English. She didn't need to spell out the name ten times only to have to write it out on paper. They called Casey, who came downstairs to get her. She looked very weary, but definitely relieved to see her cousin. They hugged immediately.

"I'm sorry I left you," Maryanne said.

"It's okay."

"Let's go upstairs. I just got off the phone with Rob and we need to book you a plane ticket home. You’re coming back with me on Tuesday."

Casey stopped dead in her tracks on the stairs they were ascending and whipped her head around to face Maryanne. "What? What do you mean? I can't just leave, I'm not done!"

"Oh, you're done, honey," Maryanne said, taking her by the shoulders, turning her around, and pushing her in the right direction.

They got to Casey's room without any more protests from her. Maryanne shut the door and locked it behind her. "You need to sit down."

Casey looked around awkwardly. "Where?" she asked, shrugging her shoulders.

"I don't know, Case, wherever, just sit down," Maryanne answered, frustrated.

Casey sat down on the bed, her eyes darting all over the floor. She looked like a scared animal, just waiting to be struck by its owner.

Maryanne resisted the urge to grab her by the shoulders and shake her until she started acting normal again.

"Look, Rob got a really disturbing letter from one of his coworkers. It basically said their boss has been stealing government money and giving it to fake vendors. Meaning, he'd make believe these people had done the agency where they work some sort of service, but in reality, they were just some friends of his that he was giving the money to for free."

"That's awful, but why do I need to go home because of that?"

"Because one of these friends is our boss."

"Joseph?"

"That's right."

"So, Rob's boss has been giving money to Joseph? Why?"

"Who knows? It's extortion. They pretended he was a law firm, or something I think it said, that the agency needed to use for whatever reason, but that wasn't the case."

"How did the guy who wrote the letter know that?"

"Because he was the one paying out the money to the real people."

"So why do I need to go home?"

Maryanne's eyes went wide. It was time to get serious with Casey.

"Because obviously things are not okay here as it is. Something is wrong with you. Something you can't even tell me! So, add on top of that the fact that we are working for a really shady motherfucker, and I am officially not comfortable with you being all the way over here by yourself on assignment from him! Lily also overheard him on the phone talking about this letter, and he made a mention of you that he'd 'scared' you or something. Now you tell me right now what he's talking about."

Casey looked down at the floor for a moment, then her upper body caved in as a sob came through. Maryanne rushed over to her cousin.

"Casey!" She sat next to her and held her as tight as she could so as to stop the shudders running through her body. She held her head tight to her chest and started to feel it soak from Casey's tears. She was almost to the point where she was getting short of breath.

"Please, Casey," she whispered, "please, tell me what is wrong. Please." She was pleading with her at this point.

After a few moments, Casey started to get a hold of herself. Her sobs softened and her breathing was even again. She lifted her head from Maryanne's chest. Her face was beet red from crying so hard, and the veins in her eyes bulged out from the whites of them. She reminded Maryanne of a zombie. She had to get this out of her cousin right now. Casey didn't make it difficult this time.

"So, I get over here, and when I got into my hotel room he was here."

"What? In this hotel room?" she asked, looking around. He was waiting in here when you got here?"

"Yes!"

Maryanne tried to think back and recall Joseph's schedule from the past few months, but she couldn't remember him making a trip over here. Obviously, he had lied about it. "What was he doing when you got here?"

"He was sitting at the desk writing something."

Maryanne just kept listening.

"So, anyway, I got kinda scared ya know?"

"Of course!"

"I was just trying to be real nonchalant and find an excuse to get out of here and go ask the main desk how long he'd been up there, and why the hell they'd let some man into my room!"

"Right."

"So, I told him I was going to go back downstairs to see if I'd left my other bag there. He got up, shut the door behind me, and was like, 'No, you're not going anywhere.'"

Maryanne's heart started to race. She had no idea what it was her cousin was about to tell her next.

"His entire demeanor had changed. He wasn't the person I'd met, that I had signed up with. He told me to sit down at the desk and I just kept thinking, 'Is this really him?'"

Maryanne shook her head and tried to stay calm and listen to Casey's story.

"I sit down and he points to the piece of paper in front of me. There's a name and a phone number on it. He tells me the previous schedule he'd given me no longer applied and there would be a new order of events now. He says the next day I was to call this guy whose name and number he'd written down and that they would both be meeting me here. He said we'd discuss a few things in the restaurant downstairs. Then he tells me what I was really here for. He said he and a lot of other people had a lot to lose if Green Light! was able to make a success out of the new office they were going to open over here. He said he was going to bury them in order to make sure that never happened. He told me I was going to write the expose that would do it, and that he had people here watching me. He said if I didn't comply, they'd hurt me, and get the message back to him that I wasn't cooperating. If that happened, he'd make sure you and Lily got punished for my actions as well."

Maryanne was shaking her head in disbelief. "We have to go back to the police."

"Go back?"

"Yes. Rob went already, but they told him I had to be there to tell them what I saw in the cemetery in order to take a statement." She looked Casey dead in the eye. "Did he explain to you what he was so afraid of happening with GreenLight!?" She recalled that he seemed upset when they told him about the trip, but not too upset. Perhaps it was just good acting on his part. He hadn't refused to let her go and cover the story though.

"I don't know. When I tried to get him to explain anything he would never answer."

"Okay, so what's been happening these past few weeks?"

"Well, I was petrified to say anything to anybody. I would try to get bits and pieces of info that would paint them in the negative light he wanted, but it was never enough for Joseph. I was just awful at lying, getting anybody and everybody to talk to me about GreenLight!, and I could tell he paid them to say what he wanted."

"What were they saying?"

"That the organization was a scam; they steal donors' money and don't put it toward environmental efforts, they put it toward fancy cars and million dollar homes for members. Stuff like that."

"Really?"

"Yeah, but you could tell they were lying. They had absolutely nothing to back up what they were saying; no one was willing to be quoted directly. It was bullshit."

"God, Casey, why didn't you try to let anyone know what was going on?" Maryanne was crying now, too. She felt so responsible for everything Casey had been through.

"Because he told me he'd hurt you if I told you, or anyone else for that matter. Just to prove to me how serious he was, he showed me some pictures." A sob ran through her, and she had to stop for a second. "They were pictures of you and this guy leaving a coffee shop."

Maryanne's eyes went wide.

"He said he has people and eyes watching everywhere, so not to think I'm safe all the way over here. He said to me that 'your cousin has been talking to someone who shouldn't be talking,' and that this was what happens to people who shouldn't be talking. Then he showed me a picture of a guy beaten up and in a hospital bed."

"Oh, my god," Maryanne breathed. She was starting to feel dizzy and felt a heaviness in her chest starting to develop.

"Who was the guy?" Casey asked.

"He's…he's a businessman in town. He was telling me some information I needed to know."

"Well, like what?"

"More about Joseph."

Casey shook her head. She knew she probably should know whatever it was that Maryanne learned from this man, but didn't have the stomach for it right now. Again, she started to cry. "Mar, I can't come home! He'll know! He'll see!" She buried her face in Maryanne's chest again.

Maryanne nodded and tried her best to console her.

She shook her head and racked her brain to try to think of a way to get Casey home. "Do you have records with any sort of correspondence you had with him?"

"I kept e-mails."

"All right." Maryanne got up and walked over to the phone.

"Who are you calling?"

Maryanne didn't answer.

Rob didn't answer his phone. She wanted to let him know they needed this private investigator of Geffin's to help get Casey home. She assumed he was probably out cold, which was good. He needed the rest. She would just have to talk to him tomorrow. She hung up the phone and turned around to face Casey once again.

"He's not answering. Hopefully, he's finally fallen asleep, but Rob has someone who might be able to help us get you out of here."

"Who?"

"Don't worry about it right now. I'll keep trying to get in touch with him before I leave, but there's a good chance I might have to leave you behind. Are you going to be okay if you have to stay here?"

"What if they saw or heard us?" her voice grew into a whisper and she clamped her hand over her mouth.

Maryanne felt her nerves spike for a moment, and she even started to look around the room herself. She wouldn't put bugging a room, or anything else for that matter, past Joseph at this point, but tried to convince herself they were both being a little overly dramatic. Suddenly, a picture of Ramsey's bloody and bruised face, with an overly swollen eye, popped into her mind. She shook her head to snap herself out of it. If they had just been recorded there was nothing they could do about it now.

"You'll come stay with me until I leave."

"Okay."

"Pack a bag."

Casey got up quickly and started throwing a few things into an overnight bag. Maryanne began helping her. "By the way, he wants this story done in a month," Casey said.

"A month? What do you need to find out by then?"

"I just have to compile all of the lies and bullshit I've collected into a story. He wants it done…," she paused as Maryanne shook her head and threw more clothes and toiletries into her bag, "…and my name has to go on it."

Maryanne stopped and looked at Casey knowingly. She knew she had to get her cousin out of here before that happened.

Chapter 3Ø

He picked at his tuna roll. For a sushi restaurant in China, it sucked. Where does he have to go for the real deal? Japan, he supposed.

He listened to them pack up Casey's things through the inner earpiece he was wearing. She wasn't trying to leave the city, and that was all that mattered.

She'd come clean to Maryanne, and the boyfriend (he refused to give him a name) had filled them in on the deal between Joseph and Norman.

Not a big deal on either front. At least that's what Joseph had told him.

"Babe" this and "Babe" that, and, "Oh, I love you so much" and "Oh, babe, if anything ever happened to you I don't know what…" Arrrrgh!

He threw his chopsticks to the floor and grabbed feverishly at his hair. Those seated around him stared, genuinely frightened by the angry Westerner.

He held on tight to the fistfuls of wavy gray hair he was massaging through his fingers. His eyes were closed and his head hung low over his plate.

"Sir?"

He looked up quickly to find his waiter standing over him, looking genuinely concerned. For a few seconds, he actually felt bad that he'd worried the man.

"I'm fine." He got up, threw some money down on the table, and left the restaurant. A couple of seconds later, he walked out the main entrance to the Lapis Casa hotel.

Chapter 31

M.J. felt nauseous and tears had started to well up in his eyes. The last time he could remember actually crying was when he was eight years old and his cousin Thomas had beaten him at a video game that he'd spent hours and hours playing.

He sat on the couch and looked up at Kayla, who was standing over him, her right hand on her hip and her right foot cocked slightly inward, a stance he would have once giggled at, but the woman he was looking at was someone he barely even knew anymore, and that realization was what was making him sick.

He continued to try and reason with her. "I know you want a baby more than anything, but there are other ways, Kayla! Hell, we wouldn't even be able to afford it with the timeline you're proposing!"

"Exactly!" she fired back. "We will never be able to afford it! No one is going to give a baby to two struggling lower incomers." Then that glazed look overtook her face again. He'd seen it all too often in the past few months. "If only they knew how much love we could give to it." She turned and started to walk away from him. She landed in front of one of the windows that overlooked the Darren Hayes courtyard.

He stared at her back and found himself wishing he could find Joseph Goldberg and beat the living piss out of him. He'd had enough of the lies and bullshit he'd been spoon-feeding his fiancée.

M.J. got up and walked up behind her, putting his

arms around her waist and his chin on her shoulder. "We will be able to afford it eventually. It's just going to take time," he said gently.

She pulled away fiercely and whipped around to face him. "I won’t wait that long," she said so coldly, so matter-of-factly, that M.J. didn't even recognize her voice. She stomped her way into the bedroom and slammed the door behind her.

All the wind had been knocked out of him. He was starting to feel like there was going to be no resolving this.

Chapter 32

Joseph walked slowly through the rows of tombstones. He was nowhere near Cecily's grave, and thank God for that. He'd never admit it to anyone, but seeing it always gave him the creeps. He hated admitting that, even to himself. It was the cross on top that really did it. It seemed to have a mind of its own, like it could actually see you.

He'd reached the baseline of the woods and entered cautiously. He still took his time reaching the shed. Norman was there, he knew, maybe even Patrick by now, and he wanted to give him plenty of time to sit there in the austerity, dirt, and cobwebs. He knew Norman would find such a place beneath him and their purpose for that matter, and he found himself smiling at what was surely Norman's discomfort.

Joseph on the other hand, found the shed to be a perfect representation of what they stood for. It was gritty and hard. No more than ten of them met there at one time, so as not to draw too much attention.

It was home base and kept them close to those who went before them, always keeping them focused on their goals. It housed the words that needed to be kept in the forefront of their minds at all times:

"Let your light so shine before men." ~Matthew 5:16

It certainly wasn't his idea to make this their motto, but even though the phrase belonged to a book he didn't believe in, it didn't mean he couldn't appreciate its meaning. Let your light and your purpose line the path for all to follow, whether they like it or not.

He came upon the shed and opened the door slowly, trying not to make much noise. It was kept unlocked on purpose. The wooden planks made long creaking noises every time he took a step, and his knee flared each time as well. He saw Norman jump to his feet when he heard Joseph coming.

"I've been sitting in this fucking hole in the ground for two hours!" he yelled at him.

"Keep your voice down!" Joseph snapped back. The intense pain his knee was serving up was kind of ruining the buzz he was enjoying over Norman's discomfort, and it was putting him in a pissy mood.

He sat down and took a few deep breaths until it subsided. The light from the candles that surrounded the room flickered in the reflection of his glasses.

"Where is he?"

"Patrick?"

"No, the boogieman. Yes, Patrick. Who the fuck do you think?"

Norman stared at him wide-eyed. He couldn't believe how blatantly antagonistic Joseph had the nerve to be when he was skating on such thin ice. He wasn't delivering on his end of the deal, and he'd be damned if he was going to walk away after all this with nothing but a dead nigger on his hands.

They both jumped when Patrick burst through the door, dragging Randall in by the neck. He was petrified and sweating, as was Patrick. His graying curls looked darker somehow when wet.

"Oh, God," Randall said upon seeing Norman. Norman was still too worried about Joseph to enjoy Randall's horror.

"Sit him down," he barked at Patrick, pointing at one

of the wooden benches that lined the shed. Patrick pushed Randall up against that wall. Randall subconsciously placed his hands up in surrender, pressing them and his body to the windows behind him.

"Please, don't do anything to me," he said, his voice quivering, face turned away, and eyes squeezed shut. "My wife knows. She'll know if something happens." His whole body was shaking.

"Well, that was stupid move, Number 500," Joseph snarled at him. Then he started to laugh and shake his head. "My God, you really have a death wish don't you?" he asked, genuinely amazed. The kid had balls, he had to give him that. He guessed he really never thought it would come to this. Now they'd have to go shake down the wife as well. Sometimes the body count really got under his skin.

Norman got in front of Randall, grabbed him by the back of the head, and forced him to face him. "Who else knows? he asked.

Randall started to cry and shook his head like a baby. The tears managed to escape from beneath the lids that were closed so tightly they were nothing but wrinkles. Norman proceeded to smack him across the face, which made him jump back farther than necessary and start crying much harder.

The men laughed, but became stone-faced again very quickly.

"What did you put in that letter?"

"What letter?" Randall asked, trying desperately to feign ignorance, but his fear revealed the knowing behind his eyes.

"I was there when she gave it to him, you stupid fuck. Did you think you could just drop it and run?"

He was clenching and unclenching his fists, and

Patrick was watching the glint off the commitment band on Norman's left hand, from the light of the candles.

Norman turned on him and saw him standing there, glazed over and staring at him. It made him even angrier than he was at Randall at the moment. He walked up to him and backhanded him with the same hand Patrick had been staring at like a damn fool. "Wake up!"

Patrick staggered back and rubbed at his jaw.

Joseph giggled. "Handing out a lot of bitch slaps tonight, huh, Norman?"

Norman spun to face him. "You think this is funny? This is the moron whose hands you have this in?" he said, pointing at Patrick, who was still pathetically nursing his jaw.

Norman walked up to Joseph. He was a good six inches shorter, but it didn't phase him. "I'll take back every red cent, Joseph. You know I can, too."

The two men stared at each other for a few moments, seething.

Norman shook his head and took Joseph by the arm. "Take care of *him*," he threw over his shoulder to Patrick, referring to Randall.

"Well, what does that mean?" Patrick asked.

"I guess that's up to you now, isn't it," Joseph said.

Patrick frowned and looked over at Randall, whose breath quickened.

"Come on," Norman said, leading Joseph by the arm. Joseph went along, but limped his way out the door. Norman slowed and looked him up and down.

"What's the matter?"

"Nothing, it's just my knee," Joseph said, looking around to see if there was a tree stump or something he could sit down on. The woods were barren, but open and clean, which made him happy. He liked to think it was because their gathering point was there, and the earth knew their mission was right and true.

"You listen to me," Norman said, his finger suddenly in Joseph's face. "You get him in line. I'm serious. I want some God damn results by next week."

"Look, this works both ways," Joseph started, shrugging. "I'm sticking my neck out, too, with this kid being over in Shanghai, I mean she could…"

"I'm the one shelling out the money!" Norman screamed in his face. "I run this!" he yelled feverishly, smashing a fist against his own chest. "No one else!"

Again, a stare down.

Norman took a deep breath and let it out slowly. He'd been in worse situations than this. He wasn't going to let it get the best of him. He took out his handkerchief and dabbed the sweat beads off his forehead. Then he placed his left hand over his heart. It was dark, but Joseph could see the moonlight pick up the shine on his commitment band. After a few seconds, Joseph placed his own over his heart. They slowly placed their arms back down at their sides.

"Follow me," Joseph told Norman. The two suited men walked over to the shed where two shovels leaned up against the siding. They each took one and walked over to the trees.

They began digging, covering a wide area. Eventually, they got on their hands and knees and focused on a more acute spot, using their bare hands. Joseph glanced over at Norman as they worked, their hands becoming caked with dirt and their fingernails running over with mud, as they dug deeper and deeper. For a moment, he considered telling Norman everything Patrick had told him today about Shanghai, but quickly thought better of it. Neither of them so much as paused when Randall's screams began.

Chapter 34

Maryanne looked over at Rob, who was in a deep sleep. She could tell because of how heavy and long his breaths were. She was glad that he was though, and not tossing and turning like she'd been for the past few hours. She was also glad her tossing and turning had managed not to disturb him.

She'd known it was going to be a nightmare trying to get back on New York time, no matter what the surrounding circumstances had been. So it's not like she wasn't expecting this. It still made her uneasy to be the only one awake. Even Lily was fast asleep, and it was only midnight. Lily was notorious for keeping ridiculously odd hours.

She got up as quietly as possible, so as not to wake Rob. She threw on a sweater and pulled on her sweatpants, tripping over them in the dark. She shuffled out into the living room where Ronald immediately jumped off the couch and submitted a request for food.

"Are you crazy?" she whispered to just a pair of glowing eyes, although she was beginning to make out the white parts of his fur at that point. "You've got a few hours to go before you can eat, buddy."

She tauntingly opened the refrigerator door and did feel a slight bit of guilt when she saw the glimmer of hope in his eyes. She pulled out the orange juice, and then gave a sigh of acquiescence. She grabbed the bag of cat treats off the counter and shook a few of them out into his food bowl.

She walked back into the living room, her slippers making a scuffing noise as she all but dragged them across the hardwood floors. She looked at the TV, but decided against it. Instead, she plopped herself down on the tuffet that John usually sat on to have a smoke out of the window. She propped her knee up on the couch end next to it and put her elbow on it, resting her chin in her hand. She glanced quickly into the hallway wondering if he was sleeping over and would eventually get up to reclaim his spot. She saw the window was open a crack, which meant he probably already had.

She actually lifted the windowpane a little more, even though they had recently dove into much colder temperatures. It felt good on her face and skin, and it started to do the trick of clearing her mind a bit, but it didn't stop the image of Ramsey's beaten-up face popping into her brain.

When she'd gotten home, she'd tried to contact him, but he hadn't responded to any voicemail messages yet. She'd wait a couple days more before asking around to see where he was, so as not to unsettle the dust. In her mind, this pretty much proved he'd been harmed for talking to her.

She wasn't able to dwell on it because she'd been worried sick about Casey. She could hardly bare the thought of leaving her cousin in Shanghai, but she knew it was necessary in order to keep her as safe as possible, although it was really just the lesser of two evils.

Casey, on the other hand, had seemed oddly back to her old self, probably due to the fact she no longer felt alone in her situation.

One month. That's how long they had to actually fix all of this. When she'd gotten home and filled Rob and Lily in, they were hardly surprised at this point. Rob immediately called Geffin to let him know how it all extended to Casey and what the deadline was. Apparently, his friend, the detective, was already hard at work, but Maryanne wasn't putting too much faith in that. Nevertheless, Geffin added this to his list of things to do.

She and Rob had considered going to the police in town again now that she was home, but Geffin told them to hold off until the PI reported back to him on some initial findings. Rob said while she was gone, Geffin had gotten in touch with the president of SfH's board of directors and asked him if they had indeed received this letter from Randall. He'd told Geffin no, and Geffin said it could be that he's just paranoid at this point, but it seemed like he was faking it.

Who knows, she thought to herself. Shaking her head, she looked up at the moon. The same moon Casey had seen just a few hours ago.

She and Casey had left it that Case would continue with business as usual. If it got down to the wire, or Casey felt things intensifying over there, they'd do whatever they needed to do to help her if Geffin's private investigator couldn't. They'd go to the FBI, hell, even go over there themselves to help her. On a less important note, Maryanne and Lily would just refuse to run the Green Light! story, or coyly switch it out with something else. Then his anger would hopefully be directed at them rather than Casey. She'd be home by then anyway, and it would be easier to protect her.

One way or another, that story could not be published. There were no two ways about it. Green Light!, or even just the individuals involved, would certainly sue for slander, or worse, and bury her, and Joseph would simply point the finger at Casey and wash his hands of it. The sources he connected her with would certainly run, or deny their words, or say they were misquoted.

It wouldn't matter, the seed of doubt against Green Light! would have been planted, and Joseph would have accomplished his goal. The rest of the media would run with it and the damage would undoubtedly be done.

She could feel herself getting really upset and knew she had to calm down if she wanted a chance in hell of getting some sleep that night. She looked down into the courtyard and her eye was drawn to the light coming from the entryway to each building. K, L, M, N… Her eyes went from one to another, and then another, each letter sat next to the doorway of each building. "No 'I'," she mumbled to herself, remembering they never did find out why.

She glanced over her shoulder into the dark hallway. She turned back to the window, stood, pushed it shut, and shuffled back to her room. She looked to her right into the kitchen as she passed and saw Ronald still sitting at his food dish, munching on the few treats she'd given him a few minutes ago. He looked over his shoulder at her as she passed by.

She went back into her room, but failed to shut the door, not sure if she was in for the night yet. She sat down at her desk and turned on her computer. She looked over her shoulder and frowned, hoping all her moving about wasn't waking Rob up.

Her laptop powered up and she opened an internet browser. She typed in "Darren Hayes apartments + Sleepy Hollow" into Google.

A few links to sites for apartment searches came up on the first page, but nothing of interest. The building didn't even have its own Website, actually. She went back up to the search bar and deleted the original one. This time, she typed in "Darren Hayes I building + Sleepy Hollow, NY." A few articles popped up regarding the complex itself, including one from when it was first built in 1930 by John Rockefeller, architect Andrew J. Thomas, and real estate advisor Charles O. Heydt, for the employees of the old General Motors plant just down the road by the river. She clicked on the second page and her eyes scrolled from top to bottom; still, nothing of interest. Once she hit the third page, the fourth article down caught her eye immediately. Fire Claims Life, Takes Out Building in Sleepy Hollow Complex

"Oh, my God, that must be it!" she said, slowly, but audibly. She immediately clamped her hand over her mouth and turned to look over her shoulder at Rob. He hadn't moved a muscle. She rolled her eyes and turned to face the laptop again.

"Somebody died?" she whispered softly.

She clicked on the article, published by *The Journal News*, dated June 2, 1996.

Sleepy Hollow—A fire burned down the I building of the Darren Hayes apartments on Beekman, taking the life of the intruder who set it. The complex is comprised of 26 buildings, one for each letter of the alphabet, which circle an entire block. The I building sat on the Pocantico Street side.

Police are not sure what the man's intentions were in the building, but say he was probably looking to rob apartments. Luckily, all other occupants were able to evacuate the building as a smoke alarm was immediately sounded.

“The surrounding buildings had minimal damages

and will be repaired shortly," says Darren Hayes owner, Joseph Goldberg.

Maryanne's jaw dropped. She just sat there, staring at his name on the screen for a good two to three minutes.

Joseph owns these apartments? How could they not have known this?, she screamed at herself. She suddenly felt very self-conscious, like she was being watched from every angle. She wrapped her sweater tighter around her body and crossed her arms. Her breathing quickened and her heart sped up.

He could have this entire place bugged.

She looked back up to the screen to finish reading the article.

The intruder's name will be released after dental records reveal his identity.

"What?" she whispered in the darkness. She brought her hand up to her face. Her mind was blown at this point. Joseph owns the apartments they're living in. She considered waking Lily for a second, but decided to let her enjoy her sleep.

She couldn't believe all the frightening information that was beginning to pile up against their boss.

Suddenly, the heat started to clang, startling her. It banged so loudly against the pipes in the Darren Hayes it sounded like a body builder was hitting them with a sledgehammer. She turned again to look at Rob, who was still breathing deeply and steadily. She could see his bare chest rising up and down in the small amount of light coming from her laptop and whatever moonlight had made its way to the bed from the window. It would puff up, and then cave back in. Up and down. Up and down. Up . . . down . . . up . . . down . . .

Her breathing fell in line with Rob's, although she was awake; conscious, however, was a different story.

They came from the cracks where the walls met the ceiling first, then from the radiator in the corner. She remained fixated on Rob's chest. Up . . . down . . . up . . . down . . .

They pushed their way through the hairline cracks between the planks on the hardwood floors.

Spiders.

Coming toward her.

Their breathing was perfectly in sync now. As they crawled along the floor, all shapes and sizes, she stood. Keeping her eyes on Rob, she backed up toward the door of her bedroom, and then turned.

She walked out and turned into the hallway, spiders close behind. They surrounded her feet as she neared the front door. They stayed with her all the way to the cemetery.

When Maryanne woke, Rob was gone. She just vaguely remembered him kissing her goodbye, which was odd because she was usually a very light sleeper.

She rolled over to her nightstand to pick up her cell phone and see what time it was. 9:30 a.m.

Ugh. Whatever, she thought. She still had a few days of using jetlag as an excuse coming to her. She'd be sure to milk it for all it's worth.

She had to take a shower, so that would set her back even further. She kicked off the covers and swung her legs out and onto the floor. As she went to push herself up into the standing position, she glanced down at her feet and gasped.

"What the hell is that?" she muttered. She checked the bottoms of her socks and they were even worse, caked in dirt.

"How the fuck did this happen?" she said out loud. She got up and went over to her door. When she opened it and peeked her head out, she was pretty sure no one was home. The deadness in the air gave it away, as did Lily's open door. She walked further down the hall to see the room more clearly and found, in fact, no one was in there. Her sheets were in a tangle in the middle of her bed. She turned to walk back into her room and leaned down to take each sock off and examine them further as she made her way back into her room. She went to her bed and sat down. She rubbed the muddied fabric of one of them between her thumb and forefinger, leaving them wet and dirty.

She took a deep breath and let it out slowly, trying desperately not to cry. She put her face in her hands and then tried to rub the sleep out of her eyes with her fists. She tried to remember last night, if she had stepped out of the building for whatever reason. Although she knew how ridiculous that was, as it was pretty cold out at this point.

That's when the memory of the article hit her. She got up, tossed the socks into her hamper, and walked over to the computer. She turned it on and found the article again. This time she printed it out.

She threw on some clothes and grabbed her keys. She stopped for a second as she wondered how they were still in the same place as she left them last night, so how would she have gotten back into the apartment if she'd left? How could she not remember doing this?

She shook her head and marched out the door, keys and article in hand. There was one person she knew for sure would have some answers, and she wasn't going to waste any time in reaching out for her help.

A couple of seconds later, she was knocking on Beth's door. She could hear her shuffling around in the kitchen, and some plates clinked against each other before the door lock started to come off. Beth slowly opened the door and smiled when she saw who it was.

"Oh, hi, hon. I just finished making coffee." She glanced down at the papers in Maryanne's hand, and back up at her troubled face. "Come in, there's a full pot."

Maryanne walked in and stood awkwardly in the hallway for a few seconds. Beth's little white Maltese, Fritz, did a few laps around her legs, barking incessantly, which didn't help her nerves. "Fritzy! Stop it!" Beth said, shaking her finger at the little dog. She looked up, and became visibly shaken by Maryanne's stare.

"Why did you act so strangely the other day?" Maryanne asked.

"What?" Beth asked. Her hands, which held too very hot cups of coffee, were quivering.

"The other day. When I told you I had a dream about a man in a flannel shirt, you couldn't get away from me fast enough," she answered, in as even and calm of a voice as she could manage.

They stared at each other for a couple of moments, Maryanne's eyes pleading, and Beth's looking as if they were about to burst into tears.

"What do you know about this?" Maryanne asked, slowly lifting the papers out to her. Beth leaned over to see them and read the headline. She frowned, lifted her chin, and then her eyebrows.

"Come on," she said, walking past Maryanne with

the coffees. "Let's go sit down."

Maryanne followed her into the dining room. She looked around and found it funny that, although they basically had the same apartment, Beth's was more of a home than the girls could ever dream Apartment 322 could be. She could feel the cushion of the carpeting underneath her feet. They sat down at the dining room table and she tried to settle herself. She had no reason to be angry with Beth and kept reminding herself of that.

"This has gotten further than I expected," Beth said, placing the cups down, and then turning to head back in the kitchen for milk and sugar.

"Yeah, I'll say. I saw him, Beth."

"Saw whom, my dear?" she asked, her eyes wide. She stood there with her arm in mid-air, holding the milk.

"The man in flannel. I saw him in the cemetery again. Lily saw him, too!"

She watched as all the color drained from Beth's face. Her arm with the milk went limp and she dropped it. Maryanne got up, picked it up off the floor, and helped Beth back to her seat at the table. She settled the old woman into it, and then reclaimed her own.

"Tell me what you know. Please, Beth." Her voice was so full of despair and a dire need for answers.

"I hadn't heard of anyone seeing him for a while."

"So other people have seen him?" Maryanne instantly felt a wave of relief come over her, but she kept it in check until she knew exactly what Beth meant. Maybe she wasn't going crazy after all.

"Yes," Beth answered, starting to regain her composure. She took a few deep breaths and was then back to her old stoic self. She picked up the article and read it. Maryanne waited patiently for her to finish.

Beth used the table to push herself up, and then went over to her china closet on the other side of the room. She fumbled around in the couple of drawers that sat underneath the glass encasement. Maryanne watched her pick out a certain photo, lift it up to see it better, and then nod. She brought it back over to the table and placed it in front of Maryanne. "Is that him?"

Maryanne looked down at it and saw the man in flannel sitting on a couch with a darker-haired, middle-aged man. He wasn't wearing a flannel this time, instead he was wearing a crisp, white button-down shirt and held a beer in one hand. He was watching something off to the right-hand side of the photo, what she assumed to be a television, and the dark-haired man was looking directly at the camera, smiling broadly; but it was him, she was sure of it, which made her heart start to speed up.

"That was taken in there," Beth said, pointing at the living room. Maryanne looked over her shoulder, then back to Beth, shocked.

"Here? You knew him?" She had to get up and walk over to the living room and hold up the photo to compare. Everything was still arranged almost exactly the same. "Was this recent?" she asked, almost shrieking as she rushed back into the dining room.

"No. Years ago."

"Oh," Maryanne said, hoping, despite everything, she hadn't insulted Beth's tastes with her question. She tried to get a hold of herself and rubbed at her weary eyes with her fists. She sat back down before speaking again. She took a deep breath. "I don't understand. Who is he?"

"He was a friend of my husband's," she said, looking down at her coffee as she swirled it with a spoon. "He died in that fire." She nodded with her eyes staring at the article sitting on the table.

"What?" Maryanne grabbed the papers and scanned the article once again. She looked up, eyes wide, and realized what this must mean. "He was the intruder?"

"No."

"But it doesn't say anyone else died."

"It doesn't say a lot of things, hon," Beth said, looking at her disapprovingly, as if to say Maryanne should have known that.

Maryanne stared at the woman, unable to believe there was so much going on at once that she didn't know, and that it was this difficult to drag it out of Beth.

"What is it leaving out?" she asked slowly, and as politely as she could manage.

"A number of people died in that fire."

"What? Well, why wasn't it reported? Was it reported anywhere?"

"It was on the news, mentioned briefly, but it wasn't a network, that much I remember. It was local, News 12, I believe, but nothing in print. It was very strange. Jim, my husband, even looked into it."

"What do you mean?"

"Well, he called The Journal when we saw this to see why it didn't do more extensive coverage, and more importantly, to ask why they didn't report it truthfully. A number of people died!"

"How many? Who?" She could barely find her words and an image of Cecily's grave was embedding itself in her brain.

"Was there a little girl? Did a little girl die in that fire, Beth?"

Beth furrowed her brow and looked at her a bit confused, as she thought. She finally shook her head.

"No. I don't remember there being any children. My goodness, no, trust me, I would have remembered that. That would have been even more tragic, if that were possible. Anyway, Jim even went to the police. He was a retired officer, did you know that?"

"No, I didn't."

"He wanted to know why these people's lives weren't being honored. Why there was, what seemed like, a cover-up going on."

"Maybe some sort of foul play was at work with that fire."

"There had to have been. Jim and I both came to that conclusion. Something was not right about this."

They sat in silence for a couple of moments, Maryanne letting this new information sink in.

"He was a strange man, in my opinion. Just kept to himself. Sometimes I think Jim only spoke to him because he felt sorry for him. He would often come and sit by himself on the benches out here. Jim would go out and talk to him so he had someone to enjoy the warm summer air with. Sometimes they would go out for a drink once they were home from work, but typically they just hung around the courtyard, and when it got too cold, they'd come here. Never to his apartment."

"Why not?"

Beth shook her head and shrugged her shoulders. "We didn't know. Whenever Jim suggested it, he always said no, he preferred to come here." She smiled. "Jim always said it was because he liked looking at my rear end." She snickered and sipped her coffee. Maryanne did the same.

"Maybe he did," she said, smiling warmly.

"Oh, stop!" Beth said, waving a hand at her.

They both giggled.

"So, what happened? This was when?" She took the papers and checked the date again. "1996. How long had Jim known him at that point?"

"Maybe two years."

"My god. Did the guy have any family?"

Beth paused to swallow, but shook her head "no" at the same time. "We don't think so, but he was *very* secretive," she said, shaking her head disapprovingly again.

"Well, how could you not know if he had a family?"

"Jim never got near that apartment, but we did see him going in and out of that building a bunch of times, so we're pretty sure he did live there. Plus, Jim asked him once and he gave him a strange answer."

Maryanne waited. It was like a game of cat and mouse, talking to Beth.

"He said he had a family once. So Jim left it alone, not knowing what that meant really, if he was talking metaphorically or if they'd passed away. We didn't know, and we didn't want to ask any further."

"That's strange."

"Yes, it was, but Jim felt he was doing a good thing by being a friend to this man."

Maryanne nodded. "What was his name?"

"Ray. Raymond. I can't remember his last name, though." She paused as she tried to remember. "Now that's going to haunt me."

Maryanne gave her a tiny smile and shook her head. "It's okay. So," she said, taking the article and skimming it again, "Jim never got anywhere with the cops?"

"No. It was very strange. They kept giving him these ridiculous excuses. That revealing the names and the number of people who died might compromise their investigation or something."

"So they did do an investigation?"

"Well, yes, they had to find out how it was started. If it was, in fact, this man, the intruder."

"And?"

"We don't know. They never released any more information. Jim tried, but they said he wasn't privy to that information anymore. A number of people he considered close friends began to alienate themselves from him. It was very strange. Very strange," she said, shaking her head and stirring her coffee.

Maryanne frowned. "You said I'm not the only one who's seen him?"

Beth shook her head no. "Jim saw him a couple of times after that fire, both sightings a couple of years apart, but he was wearing the same thing you saw him in, a red flannel. There have been others, too. I've heard it around town. It's turned into an urban legend of sorts. For a while, people questioned if he did, in fact, die in the fire."

Maryanne frowned and looked down at her lap. Both ladies sipped their coffee for a few moments.

Beth leaned in, resting her arms on the table. She looked lovingly at Maryanne.

“You know,” she started, “there are always spirits surrounding us. They’re everywhere,” she said, pointing around the room.

Maryanne looked up with tears threatening to fall from her eyes.

“They all have their own reasons for being here, some good, some bad. Because I don’t believe when we pass it’s a one-way ticket. Sometimes, we need to come back to help those we left behind.”

“But I never knew this man,” Maryanne said.

Beth shrugged. “And sometimes that doesn’t matter.

If God thinks the message is important enough, he'll make sure the two of you connect. It's our job, though, to always be paying attention, and to remember that it works both ways."

"What do you mean?"

"Well, just as the Lord above has messenger angels, so does the Lord below," she said, nodding.

Maryanne gulped. "Did they ever release the identity of the intruder?" she asked, trying to change the subject.

"Nope. Never did an update on that either. We thought of filing under the Freedom of Information Act, but we knew they would just state again it was classified police information and that revealing it would jeopardize the integrity of the case." She paused. "Jim couldn't believe it. He couldn't believe how corrupt the station had gotten since he'd left. It wasn't like that when he was there."

Maryanne thought of how Rob had said the police were so uncooperative with him. "Well, it hasn't gotten any better since."

"What do you mean, hon?"

"Rob went there to get some help a while ago, and they were not very responsive."

"Really." She didn't pry, but looked at her intently.

Maryanne sighed. "Did you know my boss owns these buildings now?"

"You're kidding! What's the name?"

"Joseph Goldberg."

"Ah, yes. He's very active in this town. Does a lot of charity work, no?"

Maryanne scoffed. "Yeah. Charity work."

"Well, that doesn't surprise me that he owns it. It probably changes hands more times than we'll ever know." She paused, then looked directly at Maryanne. "I would think that's why you girls moved in here. He never mentioned it?"

"Nope. Not even once."

"That is strange."

Maryanne stared at the table for a few moments, and then glanced over at her now cold cup of coffee. Suddenly, a rush of adrenaline went through her.

"I have to go," she said, jumping up.

Beth looked taken aback. "You haven't finished your coffee!"

Maryanne stopped, looked at it, and frowned. "I know, I'm sorry," she said as she hugged Beth quickly and tightly. She grabbed the article off the table. "Thank you for telling me all of this. Seriously. It's been a huge help to my peace of mind."

She looked down as she choked back some tears. She looked up to see Beth's expression, desperate to help, but not knowing how. There was nothing Maryanne could do. There was too much left she didn't know herself.

She grabbed Beth's hand and squeezed it. "I'll be okay." Beth shrugged and shook her head in surrender.

"Well, let me walk you out."

As they approached the doorway, Beth grabbed her wrist.

Maryanne looked down at her hand, then up to meet Beth's eyes.

"Just be careful, honey. Don't do anything reckless, but more importantly, don't be afraid of him."

Maryanne could only hope she meant Raymond.

Chapter 35

Patrick watched Maryanne leave Beth's apartment from the peephole of the apartment next door. His face fell. He was rapidly losing control of everything and he knew it.

Sandra's face popped into his head. He'd failed her.

He heard the woman whimper behind him and turned around to face her, sitting in the chair he'd tied her up in, tears still streaming down her face and looking terrified. Her two-year-old child was still asleep on the couch.

Everything he'd done flashed before his eyes: Randall's screams; all the corners he'd skulked in as he watched and hunted; the feeling of Rob's neck in his arm as he dragged him backward into an alley. None of it had been enough.

He deserved what he had in store and welcomed it. He would do it for Sandra.

Chapter 36

About fifteen minutes later, Maryanne was in her car, racing to work. The second she hit Route 9, she dialed Rob. He picked up as she passed the Old Dutch Church that stood next to the cemetery gates.

"Hello?"

"Babe?"

"Yeah."

"Where are you?"

"I'm at work, where do you think I am?"

"Do you remember anything from last night?"

"Like what?"

"Like me not lying next to you for most of it?"

"No, babe, I was exhausted and dead to the world. Probably able to sleep that way because I thought you were there."

"Well, I woke up and it looked like I had been walking around in the dirt."

"What are you talking about?" he asked. She also heard him mumble something to someone else. He was obviously in the middle of something, but this conversation couldn't wait.

"I said, I woke up and my socks were covered in dirt and kind of wet, so much so, that they could only have gotten that way if I'd gone outside with no shoes on."

"Babe, uh, I have no idea. Do you remember anything?"

"No. That's another thing. The last thing I remember

is reading an article online that you need to hear about. After I woke up this morning, I took it down to Beth's to show her and she told me something even more interesting. Apparently, this guy I keep seeing died in the Darren Hayes!"

"What? Again, what are you talking about? You're throwing way too much information at me at once right now."

Maryanne paused a moment and looked around to make sure there were no cops nearby. She took a deep breath.

"You know how there's a building for every letter of the alphabet except 'I'?"

"Right."

"Well, I couldn't sleep last night and I decided to Google it to see if there was anything online that explained why. An article came up from The Journal News saying that it burned down in '96. Some guy was in there to rob a bunch of people and ended up setting the place on fire."

"Wow, really?" Another few mumbles. "Wait, so how do you know the guy you saw in the cemetery died that way?"

"Beth knew him! He was a friend of her husband!"

"What was his name?"

"Raymond."

"Raymond," Rob said under his breath. "Well, where's the article? Can you e-mail it to me?"

"Yeah, I'll find it again when I get to work. I printed out a copy of it though."

"All right, well, I can just see it when I get home then."

"Why are you not more freaked out by this?"

"I don't know, babe," he said, starting to get pissed.

"I'm supposed to believe some old lady who lives downstairs? How does she even know this is the same guy?"

"Because she had a picture of him!"

"Oh, wow, really? Did you keep it?"

"No." For a moment she realized maybe she should have.

"Well, why not, so I could see it?"

"I don't know. Her dead husband was in it. I guess she wanted to keep it."

"Maybe we can go ask her to take a look at it later."

"Maybe, but anyway, I'm not finished. This article said nothing about any other deaths. It said the intruder died, and they were going to release his identity once they were able to decipher the dental records. She said they never even did that. I mean, I've got to do more research, but she said they didn't, and her husband, he was a retired cop, went after them to see why not and why the names of the others who died weren't released, and it was this huge cover up, and…"

"Babe! Slow down!"

"Joseph owns the apartments!"

"The Darren Hayes?"

"Yes!"

She took a deep breath and sat back with a "humph" in the driver's seat. She was almost at work at this point.

A million things were running through Rob's head. Everything was getting a little too close for comfort. "God, I've got to tell Geffin this."

"Yeah, definitely!"

"Ugh, God, babe, stop screaming!"

"Sorry, I'm riled up." She was about to pull into a parking spot.

"He had an update for me this morning."

She slammed on the brakes a little too quickly. "He did?"

"Yeah. He heard from his, uh, friend."

She took that to mean the private investigator. "And, what did he say? Is he going to help us get Casey home?"

"He's working on it, babe. He is. Geffin said they're really trying to keep tabs on Joseph so they can get her home whenever he's looking the other way."

"Well, he better be looking the other way soon, because, babe, I don't think we should even bother going to the cops because I don't think we're going to get anywhere."

"Why not?"

"Didn't you hear what I said? What Beth told me? Her husband was an ex-cop and even he couldn't get through."

"Well, we shouldn't put all of our eggs in one basket with this PI either. That was years ago that he tried."

Maryanne sighed. She looked around to make sure no one was close enough to the car to hear her talking. "I know. I mean, can he offer any protection for Casey over there?"

"I don't know, babe, this all costs money you know. We're not getting this help for free, which is why I think we need to make another plea to the actual police in town." He lowered his voice before he continued. "He's been looking into the letter. He's finding out some really scary stuff. I feel like I'm in the Twilight Zone right now. It's crazy."

"Like what?" Maryanne breathed.

"I'll tell you everything tonight."

"Okay," she said, which killed her because she was dying to know what was going on, but she knew he couldn't talk about it at the office.

"All right. I'll see you when we get home. Try to tell Geffin everything I just told you."

"I'll try."

"Okay, bye. Have a good day, if you can at this point. Love you."

"Love you, too."

Maryanne looked up through her driver's side window at the window of her and Lily's office. She let out a deep breath, grabbed her bags, and heaved them over her shoulder. When she got upstairs and walked in, Lily and Joseph were both hovering over a newspaper, he standing, she sitting at her computer.

"Hi," Maryanne said, breezing past them to get seated as quickly as possible. Neither of them answered. After her computer booted up, she turned to see what was going on. They were both still hanging their heads to finish reading an article, she assumed. She shrugged and turned back to her computer.

Eventually Lily spoke first, timidly and cautiously.

"You're right. They make solid arguments."

"That's what I'm saying!" Joseph said, an octave too high for casual conversation and holding his arms out at his sides. "Just talk to him. That's all I'm asking," he said, then turned and sauntered out of the room.

Maryanne turned slowly to look over her shoulder at Lily, whose back was still to her. She turned back toward her computer. After a few moments passed, she asked quietly, "Whom does he want you to talk to?"

"I'll e-mail you," Lily said.

Maryanne frowned, but the e-mail came through immediately. She opened it and found a link to an article and a one-line note at the top:

He wants us to tell the other side of this…

Maryanne clicked on the link, which led her to CNN.com.

(CNN)—Two men were arrested yesterday outside of the Helena Civic Center, in Helena, Montana, for attempting to assassinate senator Donald Speedman. Speedman was set to give a talk to a group of electrical engineers about the benefits of alternative energy, but he was quickly escorted out and away from the building once his safety was deemed in jeopardy.

William Korkel and Eugene Asten (a.k.a. Alexander Lane) barricaded themselves in their car in the center's parking lot, surrounding it with homemade bombs hooked up to a remote detonator, which the men held with them inside the car. They threatened to blow them up if police didn't let them leave the scene. Law enforcement was able to overtake the men shortly after they were allowed to flee. They are now being held at Clark County Jail awaiting arraignment. Korkel and Asten told investigators they planned to fire fourteen rounds into Speedman at close range, as he spoke underneath and in between the four circles of the University of Montana's presidential board, sponsors of the room he was set to speak in at the Civic Center. Placed together, the four circles make up the number eighty-eight. Both fourteen and eighty-eight are symbolic in the white supremacy movement, of which Asten and Korkel claimed to be starting a new breed. They said they needed to "prove their loyalty," to the dogma and lore that had gone before them, while showing that the next generation is not afraid to take truly drastic measures to achieve their goals.

Korkel and Asten said they planned to sneak the

weapons in a single backpack into the Civic Center, a venue known for its lackadaisical security measures. Arraignment dates have yet to be set.

Maryanne recognized the name "Lane", but couldn't place it just yet. She didn't have time to rack her brain either to recall where she'd heard it. She turned her seat so she was almost facing Lily dead on.

"What's the 'other side' to this?" she asked, a definite edge to her tone.

"He wants to write something for us from jail," Lily threw over her shoulder.

"Who does?" Maryanne asked sharply.

"One of those guys. I think it's Asten."

Huh? Maryanne thought. She turned back to the article and scanned it for their names. Oh, right. The one that caught her attention also went by the name Eugene Asten. *Now why the hell do I know that name?*

It's beside the point. She swiveled her chair around again to talk to Lily's back. "You're going to let some lunatic write a story for us?" she hissed.

"Well, that's what we're about, isn't it? Giving everyone a voice no matter what? Like I have a choice!" Lily said, obviously very frightened.

"But this guy? He tried to kill someone because of the color of his skin. Someone that you respect!" she whispered furiously. She knew Lily was scared, but come on!

Maryanne whipped her head around to face her computer again. She brought up Google and searched the name "Alexander Lane." The Wikipedia entry for him popped up immediately as the first link. She clicked on it, and the first line told her all she needed to know: Alexander Lane (December 19, 1990) is the youngest son of infamous American white nationalist leader, David Lane.

This man who wanted to use their magazine to preach his hate was the son of one of the founders of white supremacy. She went back to her Google search and a few links down was the article that had been tiptoeing around her memory. It's where she had first heard Alexander Lane's name.

The piece had first appeared in a small local paper in Memphis and was then picked up by the wires shortly after. Lane was a renegade of sorts, as even his father had decided to lead his party away from more violent methods of pushing and living their ideals. He felt that, while deserved, causing physical harm from the groups they targeted, only kept them from affectively infiltrating their societies.

Alexander had decided to ignore his father's new path and stick to the party's roots: stopping at nothing to make sure they stay true to their God and beliefs. "We must secure the existence of our people and a future for white children," was their motto, by any means necessary.

Old and New Guard Face-Off

Memphis, Tenn.—Police arrested 25 people today as two warring factions of the white nationalist group, The Order, sparred off in a small community center off of Route 78 that many of them had considered a sanctuary, and haven of sorts, in the tiny neighborhood of Walsh. They had used it as a meeting spot, a hangout, and even a safe house at times, but for some that will no longer be the case.

It remains unclear as to what the showdown

was about. Officials are still questioning those involved as to why weapons were drawn and shots fired. No one was injured in the confrontation.

Various members of the community speculate that it's what they see to be a rift growing between two branches of The Order. One leaning toward more "traditional" ways of life, others looking to integrate newer "alliances" and "ways of thinking." Residents wouldn't elaborate any further than these vague terms.

The article had stuck in her head mostly because it gave no answers. She'd checked back almost daily for follow-up articles, but had found none.

Frustrated, she pushed her chair back and walked out of the office. Lily looked up, startled, as Maryanne's chair had smacked into her own.

Maryanne walked down the hallway to the kitchen where she found a full pot of coffee. It made her take a breath and smile for the first time that day. As she poured herself a cup, her mind became surprisingly clear. She strode back down to the office and took a seat in front of her computer. She got herself a little better organized for the day, surfed around on the Internet for a few minutes, and then went in for the kill.

"Joseph?" she said loudly and suddenly, very much disturbing the near-silent office.

"Huh?" he yelled over the wall, obviously startled.

She chuckled slightly and shook her head. Then went on.

"So, when was it that you bought the Darren Hayes?"

Silence.

Maryanne could feel Sarah's deer-in-headlights eyes

staring at her from the cubicle across the aisle that separated them.

A few moments passed and she heard him get up from his seat and saunter over to the doorway of their office. When she turned to face him, he was wearing a look that asked who, exactly, did she think she was.

"What did you ask me?"

"I said, when did you buy the Darren Hayes? I mean, we've been living there for how long and it never occurred to you to tell us you own it?"

"Well, I don't think it's any of your business."

"Oh, really?"

"No."

"Okay," she said, nonchalantly. He had an edge to his voice that sounded like a two-year-old boy getting ready to throw a tantrum.

"Why would I tell you that?"

"We only live there. You'd think if more than half your company lives in the same building, you'd alert them to the fact that you actually own it."

"Well, now you know," he said and walked back over to his office. Once he was gone, Maryanne turned to look at the back of Lily's head.

Lily looked to her left and saw that he was gone, then immediately whipped around to face Maryanne, wearing an incredulous look on her face.

“Where’d you hear that?” she mouthed.

She shook her head and waved her hand in the air, glancing at the door, insinuating they’d talk about it when it was safe.

The rest of the day was a surprisingly quiet and productive one. Maryanne needed time to process everything that had happened that day, and she was able to by focusing on work for the time being. She was able to bang out a number of tasks she hadn't been able to wrap her head around previously with everything going on, but today she'd tackled them, and then revisited everything she'd learned. Once Joseph left, she'd been able to fill Lily in on her conversation with Beth earlier. By the time she got home to Rob at the end of the day, she'd formulated a plan.

When Rob opened the door to let her in, she breezed right passed him and barely even said hello before launching into it.

"Listen, I think the private investigator needs to maybe hint to Joseph that he's on to him and investigating him, and then I think that would really scare him, and then…"

"He quit, babe."

That stopped her dead in her tracks in the middle of Rob's living room. She finally looked him straight in the face for the first time since she'd gotten there. His hair was oily, he was pale as a ghost, and he had bags under his eyes so big they could have carried groceries. A film of sweat covered his face and neck. He looked so awful it took her breath away.

"Oh, babe." She walked up to him, kissed him softly, and wrapped her arms around his neck. She'd been so worried about Casey that she'd barely taken the time to consider how this was all affecting him.

She pulled back, looked at his face again, and then hugged him hard around his waist.

They held each other for a few moments, and then Rob took her arm and sat her down on the couch.

"What happened?" she asked, unable to ignore the terrible sinking feeling in her stomach. This was leaving them with no recourse.

"Geffin doesn't know, but he did find out some

stuff."

"Like what?"

"First of all, Randall is missing."

"Well, we knew that."

"No, apparently, he hadn't gone anywhere yet. The idiot was still home. He got a hold of his wife, who said that she came home one day and he was gone."

"Well, did she go to the police?"

"No. Apparently, he told her if he ever disappeared one day, it had meant they'd gotten to him and to just let it go. If she pursued it, they'd just kill her, too."

"So, her husband disappears and she's just going to do nothing about it?"

"Pretty much. They were very, very religious. The PI said his wife just sat there and kept saying over and over, 'It's in God's hands, it's in God's hands.'"

"Oh, God. Anything else?"

"Our board president did get the letter. Well, it was definitely delivered to his office. Whether he actually saw it or not, I guess we can never really know for sure."

"That's it? Did Geffin confront the guy?"

"No."

"Why not?"

"He told him not to."

"Who, the PI?"

"Yeah."

"Why?"

"He said something like, 'You have no idea what you're dealing with.' He told him to just let it be and move on."

"Let it be? Someone's missing!"

"I know."

"What kind of a private investigator is he? I hope he has a day job!" She got up and threw her hands in the air. She needed to move around the room.

"He was doing Geffin a favor. No promises, no strings. He doesn't feel safe anymore, so he's got to take himself out of it."

"I guess," she said, absent-mindedly shuffling the boys' mail around on the small card table behind their couch. Internally, she was starting to panic. How were they going to get Casey out of China safely? Suddenly, Rob's hands were on her shoulders.

"What are we going to do?"

"We're going to have to go back to the cops," he said softly into her ear. He kissed her lightly on the cheek, and then took her chin and turned her face toward him.

He kissed her deeply, and she right back, all of their frustrations, stress, and fear being released on each other. The next thing she knew her head hit the pile of pillows on Rob's bed. She pulled his t-shirt up and off his head. He stopped kissing her for a moment to let it happen, and then went back to it. He was pressing so hard it almost hurt her mouth, but she didn't care and lost herself in it. She ran her fingernails up and down his back.

She could feel all of the tension releasing from her muscles; all of the fear and anxiety that had taken over her body and mind as of late was washing away. She kept her eyes shut tightly to make sure the feeling didn't stop.

She felt one leg touch the back of her left hand that was clinging to Rob's lower back. Then, before she knew it, there were eight legs crawling up her forearm. She felt the weight of it and that burst the bubble they were both enjoying all too quickly.

She sucked half the air out of the room, gasping. Rob jumped up and off of her.

"What? What's wrong?"

"A spider! On my arm!" she started to sob uncontrollably. She wrapped her arms around herself and started to rock back and forth. Rob stood there for a moment staring at her, too scared to move. He turned to see Steve and Scott standing in the doorway. He hadn't even noticed them come in. Her screams must have sprung them into action. They just stood there, looking back and forth between Maryanne and Rob, confusion and worry written all over their faces. He waved them away and went to sit next to Maryanne. He held her as tightly as possible to stop her from rocking and sobbing.

"It's okay. Everything's going to be okay," he began whispering.

Despite it all, she continued to cry uncontrollably as Steve backed out of the room and shut the door behind him.

Chapter 37

The next day, Maryanne heard her phone ring as she walked to her car after work, still feeling a little numb. She dug around in her purse for it.

"Come on," she mumbled to herself. Finally, she fished it out and couldn't recognize the number looking back at her on the face of the phone.

"Hello?" she asked, confusion obvious in her voice.

"Hey, Maryanne, it's Stacy."

Maryanne paused as she tried to recall if she knew a Stacy.

"From Westchester Today."

"Oh, right! Hey, Stacy!" she said with a laugh. "Sorry, it just took me a minute there, I was like 'Stacy who?'"

Stacy laughed. "No problem. It's not like we talk all the time."

"True. So what's up?"

She opened her car door and sat down in the driver's seat, wondering what Stacy had for her.

"Well, I have some bad news."

Maryanne sighed. "God, Stacy, I don't know how much more bad news I can take."

"Oh," Stacy said, sounding perplexed. "I'm sorry, what's happening?"

"Well, there's a lot more to what we were discussing at that event that we're trying to deal with here."

"Yeah, you're tellin' me."

"What do you mean?"

"Ramsay's in the hospital."

Maryanne paused for a second, perplexed. Then she was transported back to the day in Casey's hotel room in Shanghai when her cousin told her Joseph had used a picture of a man beaten up as a scare tactic, insinuating this was the same man that her cousin had spoken to in the coffee shop. She'd never pursued trying to contact him other than a few phone calls and voicemails. She gasped.

"Hello? You okay?" Stacy asked.

"Yes. Uh, yes. What happened? Is he okay?" She was trying to sound like this was the first she was hearing of this.

"No," Stacy said, scoffing. "No, he is not okay."

"What happened, Stacy?"

"He had the crap beat out of him, in a nutshell."

Maryanne's breath caught in her throat. That was the affirmation that made it all very real.

"And he's asking for you."

Her heart stopped. "Why?" Maryanne breathed.

"He won't say exactly, but he called the paper and asked to be connected to me, and when he got through he asked if I had any connections to you. I told him I did, and he asked me to get the message to you without calling your job. So, good thing you gave me your cell number the other night. Otherwise, I would have had to ask Kayla, and we know how strange she's been acting."

"Yeah."

"Well, he wants to see you. He's actually at Hackensack Medical Center."

"Jersey? Why all the way over there?"

"Well, he was at Westchester Medical, moved to Columbia Presbyterian, and then moved to

Hackensack."

"Why all the transfers?"

"I have no idea."

Maryanne shook her head and jotted down the hospital address and his room number as Stacy fed it to her. He's running from something.

"All right, thanks, Stacy."

As she hung up the phone, she could hear Stacy trying to catch her before she did, but she didn't want to hear it. She didn't have the patience, the time, or the energy. She sped off, Casey on her mind as she headed to New Jersey.

Chapter 38

She looked down at her paper as she entered the hospital to remind herself of what room he was in. Her heart began to pound as she got a visitor’s badge and made her way to the elevators. She approached the room slowly and cautiously. She made a right into the doorway and found Ramsey lying in his bed, staring at a blank TV screen. He was alone, and didn't even notice that someone was standing at the foot of his bed.

"Hi," she said quietly.

He turned to face her, and she had to wince and look away. She hadn't been able to see it at first because his head was turned slightly to face the television. Ramsey's right eye was completely swollen shut and an ugly shade of raw meat. It was so swollen, in fact, it looked like someone had sewn a baseball into his face, over his eye. A large piece of gauze was taped directly above it, covering who knows what. She could see his arms were also riddled with scratches and bruises.

"What the fuck happened to you?"

"You know what happened to me."

"But why?"

"Because I talked to you, and I challenged him publicly."

"Joseph? At the dinner?"

"Yes."

"I don't know what to do here, Ramsey. He's got my cousin practically held hostage in China."

"Well, I made Stacy get you in here because I needed you to see what happens when you even come close to blowing their cover."

"Well, what am I supposed to do? I can't just let him do what he wants with her!"

"You're going to have to do this on your own. Figure the puzzle out. I'll tell you what I can, but…"

She dropped her head as a huge lump formed in her throat. She knew he was right and still couldn't believe they were in this situation.

"Rob tried going to the cops, and…"

"He what?" he said interrupting her. He was now trying to prop himself up on his elbow. "Come here." He motioned to her and then the seat next to his bed. "Sit down."

She listened now, worried that they'd put themselves into even more serious danger than they'd originally thought. She sat herself down gently and winced as she was only that much closer to the god-awful swelling happening on his face.

"You guys are in trouble. Judging by the look on your face you know that already, don't you?" She broke down and started to weep.

"They have a monopoly on absolutely everything, including the police."

She nodded her head that she understood.

"What did he tell them? The police I mean. More importantly, who else have you been talking to about this?"

"A lot of people. Stacy and my neighbor."

"Your neighbor?"

"Yes, her name is Beth Gallagher. Her husband Jim Gallagher was a retired cop."

A knowing look came over his face. "They're on

their list. Let me ask you something, do you know how her husband died?"

“Beth told us once he died of a heart attack.”

"It certainly wasn't of *natural causes*," he said, using air quotes for emphasis. “That’s what she’s been told to say.”

"Then what do I do?" she asked in desperation, holding her hands out, palms up, as if he could place simple, neatly wrapped answers into them. "What do I do, Ramsey? They have Casey held hostage in fucking China!"

"I'm going to help you," he said, "but you have to stop talking to anyone about this from this moment on!"

"No, no way. Helping me got you in here in the first place. I wouldn't be able to live with myself if the next place I had to come visit you was in a funeral home."

"It's okay, I have a plan this time," he said, his jaw set firmly.

She raised her eyebrows at him, prompting him to explain himself.

"I have friends, too," he said, leaning back to rest his head on his pillow. He stared fiercely at the ceiling. "Loyalty from the outside might be iron-clad, but let me tell you, it's flimsy at best amongst themselves. They'd backstab one another in a second. We just have to use that to our advantage."

Maryanne's heart was racing. She wanted out of the Twilight Zone and knew it'd still be a long way until they were out of Dodge. First thing was to start weeding through the ridiculous piles of crap.

"What does that mean?" she asked, using a no-nonsense tone to her voice that woke Ramsey right up. He whipped his head toward her, glared for a moment, and then smiled. With his swollen, bruised face, it was a ghastly one.

"We're going to use his own flesh and blood."

"You mean David, Joseph's son?"

He nodded, holding her eyes.

Maryanne was skeptical. David could be dumb as rocks at times, quite frankly, and didn't seem to care that passionately about anything. She didn't think he'd have enough hatred inside of him to go up against his own father, but she was interested to hear what Ramsey had in mind. So she sat and listened for the next two hours.

She left the hospital with her mind spinning even more than it had been before her visit to Ramsey.

By the time she pulled into the parking lot, it was around 10 p.m., and for some reason, she had a strong urge to connect with Kayla. She texted her on her walk back to the building and she responded right away that, yes, she was up. Maryanne popped in on Rob, who was practically out cold, to kiss him goodnight, then she headed up one flight to Kayla's.

It took her a while to come to the door and Maryanne was pulling out her phone to call her again just as it opened and Kayla peeked out.

"Oh, hey, did I wake you? You said you were still up."

"No, no, come in."

Maryanne walked past her into the apartment and wasn't so sure if she believed her friend. She noticed Kayla's eyes were pretty blood shot, and she looked peaked.

As she walked over to the couch to put down her purse, she realized the apartment had a very weird vibe to it.

"Is M.J. here?" she asked.

"Oh, yeah, he's asleep," Kayla said, motioning toward their bedroom.

Maryanne glanced in that direction. The door was open and she saw an empty, unmade bed. She sat down on the couch feeling uncomfortable and confused.

Kayla came over and sat on the opposite couch. She looked like she was on high alert and her eyes kept darting around the room like a nervous bird.

"Are you okay?"

"Yeah, I'm fine, why?"

Maryanne studied her friend for another moment or two. "Why do you think?"

Kayla rolled her eyes. "Oh, he was just pissing me off that day. It's no big deal."

"M.J. is always pissing you off, yet I've never seen you act like that. Ever."

"Maryanne, it's none of your business."

"I just don't want to see you push him away or ruin anything for yourself."

"If he was going to get pushed away, don't you think it would have happened by now?"

A smirk came over Maryanne's face and they both started giggling. Kayla was right. She was a heck of a lot to deal with, and the fact that she always admitted to that made her that much more likable. The moment warmed Maryanne's heart to see a glimmer of her old friend again, but the giggles faded away and Maryanne's face dropped.

"I keep seeing him, Kayla. The man. The man from my dreams."

When she looked up, Kayla was staring back at her, looking like she wasn't sure what to expect next, like she didn't want to make any sudden movements.

"I'm sure it's just a re-occurring dream. I have them

all the time."

Maryanne shook her head. "Beth knew him. He used to live here," she said, pointing to the floor of the apartment. She studied her friend closely, then watched all the color drain from Kayla's face.

"How do you know this?" Kayla asked without moving a muscle in her seat.

"I told her I was having strange dreams and she showed me a picture of him and her husband."

Kayla was silent.

"He died in a fire here."

That seemed to wake Kayla up out of her trance. "Oh, that's ridiculous. There was never a fire here."

"Yes, there was, but you'd never know it based on the coverage. I'll show you the article. It barely says anything, let alone that someone died."

"So, how do you know he died in this fire, because Beth told you?"

"I never said she told me that."

"Well, she told you everything else about him."

Maryanne looked away and for a few moments neither of them said anything.

"He died here, and someone tried to make sure nobody asked any questions. Someone tried to make people forget as quickly as possible."

Kayla started to shake her head. "There's no evidence of any sort of fire here," she insisted.

"Exactly!"

Kayla's jaw jutted out the way it does whenever she gets really, really angry, and her eyes narrowed. "You shouldn't be talking about things you know nothing about."

"Excuse me?"

"You heard me."

Maryanne leaned forward. Kayla did not back down.

"Well, what I do know is I'm having dreams about a dead man that I never knew about before and I'm going to find out why."

She got up and made her way to the door. She heard Kayla get up and follow her down the hallway.

As Maryanne opened the door, she paused for a moment and turned to face Kayla.

"I have a question. Did Westchester Today ever cover Joseph's purchase of the Darren Hayes?"

"No," she answered too quickly.

"Why not? That's definitely something they would have reported. Are you sure?"

"Yes, I'm sure," Kayla answered, as calmly as she could muster. Maryanne could tell she was seething under the surface.

Maryanne's heart sunk. She nodded and walked out the door, and it shut behind her just a little too loudly.

She wasn't sure how Kayla knew that Joseph owned the Darren Hayes, but as Ramsey had so astutely pointed out earlier that day, if she did it was a bad sign.

When she got back to her apartment, she called Ramsey at his hospital room.

Chapter 39

Patrick turned away from the shed and walked deeper into the shadows. He looked down at the knife, which was reflecting moonlight into his eyes.

He looked directly up at it, and his tears fell freely. He saw that a light snow was also beginning to fall.

He'd failed. He'd failed everyone, but worst of all, he'd failed Joseph. A man who'd saved so many lives, including those of his own family. He'd made his bed, and now he'd have to lie in it…forever.

Without realizing it, he'd come to the spot, and the last thing he saw was their sacred line; the line that he couldn't live up to, carved into the tree ahead of him: "Let your light so shine before men…"

Chapter 40

The next night, Maryanne's teeth chattered as she sat on the steps of Building J, waiting for Rob and Steve to finish their cigarettes. It was annoying enough that it's something they never did, but even more so because they'd decided it needed to be done now, when the colder temperatures were finally upon them.

Rob seemed more relaxed and happy than she'd seen him in a long time, just hanging out with his roommate, that she really didn't want to pull him away. It made her smile despite the chill.

"Hey, guys!"

It was Scott's voice and it'd come from directly above them. Steve and Rob looked up, and Maryanne got up off the stoop to look up as well. He was shouting to them out of Rob's bedroom window.

"Get up here, they found somebody dead in the woods."

Maryanne's heart dropped. Rob and Steve put out their cigarettes and they all hurried back upstairs. When they walked into the boys' apartment, Scott was standing in front of the TV with the remote in his hand.

"Behind the cemetery," Scott said, pointing at the TV with the remote.

Maryanne was the last to walk in and she looked up at Rob as she caught up to his side. She watched the color drain from his face and his eyes bug out of his head.

"What?" she turned to the TV and saw wavy and graying's face staring back at them. She gasped. It was the man who'd started talking to her in the park.

Steve and Scott turned and looked at them with concerned faces.

"You knew him?" Steve asked, confused.

Maryanne and Rob stood there with their jaws on the floor. Maryanne was the first to snap out of it. She looked back at Rob who was still staring at the television.

"Uh, I've seen him around," she said, shrugging, trying to sound nonchalant, but she didn't know why Rob had such a strong reaction. She was scared to find out.

He finally looked over at her. "Yeah, yeah, I did. I saw him around a lot." He turned and went into the kitchen. Maryanne looked back over at Steve and Scott and saw how they were looking at each other.

She decided to try to bring their focus back to the TV.

"Crazy, huh?" she said, directing it mainly at Steve, the more excitable of the two.

"The body is believed to be that of Patrick McWolden of Tarrytown. No further information is known about the victim at this time," said the news anchor. "In high school sports," she said, moving on so easily.

"Shit. Is this on again at 11 p.m.?" Maryanne asked.

"Uh, yeah. Should be," Scott answered.

"Okay, thanks."

"Babe, I'm going to go lay down," Rob said, standing in his bedroom doorway. "You sleeping over?"

"Yeah, just let me go change."

She went downstairs and got ready for bed as

quickly as she could so she could get back upstairs and find out what was going on.

When she opened the door to Rob's bedroom, the lights were on full blast, and he was perched at the edge of his bed, glued to the 11 p.m. rerun of the news.

"What's the matter with you?" she asked.

"He's the one," he said to her immediately. "He's the one who chased me."

"What?"

"That is the guy who chased me through the subways!"

She came around to face the television. A picture of wavy and graying, or Patrick McWolden, was on the screen.

"I've seen him, too," she said, staring numbly at the TV.

Rob looked up at her, confused.

"He started talking to me one day in Patriot's Park."

"Here? You saw him here? In town?" he asked, pointing adamantly at the floor.

"Yes," she answered, trembling.

She could not wrap her brain around what could possibly be going on.

"We have to go back to the police now," Rob said.

"We can't!" Maryanne screamed.

"Shhhh!" Rob said, jumping up and putting a hand over her mouth, only panicking her more. She threw his hand off.

"Don't do that!" she said and started to cry out of frustration.

"Look," he said, feverishly grabbing her shoulders and pulling her in close. "We have no choice at this point," he said, talking low and fast.

"But Ramsey said…"

"I don't care what he said!" he answered, shaking her. "This is insane at this point. Do you realize that if we don't go to them, we'll be withholding possible evidence in a murder investigation?"

"What you don't realize is they don't care!" she said, bringing her face even closer to his. He let go of her and stepped back, deflated. He plopped down at the edge of the bed again, knowing she was right.

"Who knows if he was murdered," she said. "You have no idea what happened to that man and why, and you never will because whatever gets reported will probably be a lie."

"You're right. He wasn't murdered."

She turned from the TV to look at him.

"He killed himself. Just like they had to in my dream."

"How do you know this?"

He shrugged, staring down at the floor. "I feel it," he said, shaking his head. "I think Norman sent that guy after me, and when he didn't come back with what he'd sent him for, they forced him into it."

Maryanne stared at him in shock.

"It all makes sense now," he said, hanging his face in his hands, and then rubbing his eyes with the heels of his palms. "The cops and how they wouldn't listen to me…"

He looked up at her with tears in his eyes. He felt such despair at this point, and for the first time, really couldn't tell if everything was going to turn out okay or not. "The rings they wear," he said, his voice choking. "Just like the one he wore and the one I saw on Norman," he said pointing at the TV.

She rubbed his back. "You let me feel like I'm the crazy one, and all this time I'm scared you'd think I'd lost it, and meanwhile, you're going through it, too. We could have helped each other, babe."

"I know, I know," Rob said, shaking his head. "He cut his throat," he said, his voice barely above a whisper, remembering his dream. "He cut his throat right in front of us because he'd failed them."

Maryanne stared at him, truly shaken to her core at this point. Unable to turn to the authorities, all she could do was pray that they all had the strength to take this on together, and that Ramsey knew what he was doing.

Chapter 41

"I want to know how they know," Joseph, seethed. He was trying to figure out how the girls knew he owned the Darren Hayes apartment complex.

"Maybe there was some piece of evidence of it you missed," Sandra said, beside herself with mourning, a feeling she was way too familiar with.

"Shut up!" Joseph roared, turning and pointing his finger in her face.

Sandra was so numb at this point she barely flinched.

"I'm not perfect. At my level of responsibility something was bound to slip." Joseph stood staring out Sandra's kitchen window.

"Never in our history have things gotten so sloppy and it's in large part thanks to your new husband," he said, shaking his head.

"You mean my dead husband!" she screeched. "My second dead husband! Because of you!" she stood, flinging her arms out at Joseph.

He moved toward her in one fluid motion and grabbed her wrists.

"I just want my life back," she cried, sobbing uncontrollably.

"You will, Sandra. You'll get everything you were promised."

"I don't believe you anymore."

"Well, you have no choice," he growled into her

face. "Because without me, and without that 'belief', you've got nothing, need I remind you? All you have now are these two vile brats for kids, brats you never even wanted, and the little girl you've been waiting for so long to see again, will stay a distant, distant memory," he seethed.

Sandra was glaring into his eyes with, what Joseph knew, to be an extreme hatred.

"Say it to me," he said.

She was silent.

"Say it!" he screamed.

"Let our light so shine before men," she said in a lifeless, monotone voice.

"Louder!"

"Let our light so shine before men," she said with more, yet feigned, gumption.

"That's right, and what does it mean?"

"That just as the sun's rays creep through cracks and crevices, our ways will seep through society, undetected."

"And how do you project your beliefs?"

"By serving you, our leader, our prophet, our friend," she wept.

He just stared at her, as she hung her head. "Continue to do so, Sandra. Continue to do so, and you will get everything you've been promised."

He gently sat her back down and she seemed to have settled a bit. He sat across from her, his hands still holding hers.

"Now I need you to do one more thing for me before she can be revealed to you."

Sandra bit her lower lip and looked up at the ceiling trying to find the last bit of strength left inside her.

"Okay," she said, nodding. "Anything." And she

meant it.

"You have to help me trap him."

Sandra gasped. "No," she barely whispered.

Joseph shrugged, and then dropped her arms. "Up to you. If not, I'll just make sure I get in touch with Child Protective Services and let them know exactly how and why your child died. They'll be here by morning I'm sure to take the two you have left away from you." Now his back was turned to her and he was leaning up against her kitchen door that led to the back yard, peering out it into the night.

She couldn't help but feel a sense of pride that he'd asked her to help. The brainwashing still hadn't worn off yet. The guilt rushed in for how she'd behaved earlier, and she hung her head in shame as she started to weep once more.

He came back over to her and brought her face back up to meet his. "No more tears," he said, caressing her cheek. He was keeping one eye on the clock, hoping the histrionics would stop soon. It amazed him that she was completely oblivious to the fact that this was, of course, a set up.

After all, he wouldn't be in this position if it weren't for her husband, Patrick. If he'd just done his job and been able to successfully recruit Rob over to them, he would have been able to bring Maryanne over, too, at the least, and he'd have the control he needed over all of this again. But he'd failed and was forced to suffer the fate of all failures. So now it was Sandra's turn to help them get a hold of Rob, and once they had him, he'd have the proper attention of both his editors as well.

They needed an excuse to get rid of Sandra anyway. Once Maryanne and Lily got to her, which he knew they inevitably would, he'd put the blame on Sandra and call for her immediate termination.

"Okay," she answered, managing a proud smile for him.

"Good." He kissed her on both cheeks before standing. "I'll be back soon to let you know the next move."

She looked confused when he turned to leave. He took out his phone as he walked out of Sandra's home and closed the door behind him.

"Hello?" Norman answered, sounding flustered.

"I'm just leaving now."

"Listen, there's fucking movement in China, Joseph, did you know that?"

"What? How, who?"

"I don't know, but that's what I'm told. Joseph, if that story doesn't publish, it's going to be your head!" With that, he hung up.

Joseph's heart started to race.

I'll bury that girl, too, if she even tries to leave that country.

Chapter 42

"So Ramsey told you Andy's father gave him a large sum of money?" Lily asked Maryanne as they sat parked 'cop style,' as they'd dubbed it. One would be parked front wheels to the curb, the other with back wheels to the curb, so their driver's side windows faced each other. The meaning of life was often discussed in the cop-style position, and often evoked the most profound of revelations.

"Yeah," Maryanne answered as she chomped away on her Wendy's.

"And you don't know for what?"

She shook her head "no."

"Does Ramsey?"

"I don't know if he knows and just won't say or if he doesn't know period."

Lily nodded looking away for a moment.

"Maybe it was for the Darren Hayes."

Maryanne stopped dead in her chewing tracks. "It's possible. I mean, I guess we could figure out if it makes sense or not, time wise. Would a purchase like that be public knowledge? Is that considered a public building? No, I guess not, well, what we could try first…"

A buzz of her new phone put the brakes on her ramble. "Oh," she rifled through her bag for it. "Can't believe I agreed to this thing," she mumbled under her breath. It was an e-mail from Joseph that'd just come through.

Lily watched her face drop as she read it. "What is it?"

Maryanne gulped. "He's sending me upstate."

"Upstate? Where?"

"Some town called Gloversville?"

"For what?"

She read Joseph's words to Lily from the e-mail:

We need to start covering these once thriving industrial towns whose industries have now moved overseas. This would be a great one to profile. Meet up with police chief Greg Horning Thursday morning and start there, how crime has been affected by dying businesses and economy.

She dropped her phone into her lap and looked up at Lily, who had her "I'm panicking inside, but if I sit here really, really calmly, and don't make any sudden movements, it will all go away" face.

"Ugh, I don't want to go up there by myself!"

"Yeah, I don't think that's a good idea."

Wednesday night, Rob and Maryanne hit the New York State Thruway and took it all the way up past Albany to Exit 26 where they met a very cold, bitter, and barren upstate town that had already seen its fair share of snow in November.

As they got out of the car, Maryanne admired the snow drifts that sparkled under dry, cracking branches. The rustle as the icy winds whipped through them brought her back and she looked up to see Rob looking at her in expectation.

"Come on."

She followed him up to the door of the small bed

and breakfast they'd be staying in for the next few nights.

"Maureen was the name?" he turned to her and asked.

"Yeah," she answered as she took his arm and held on tight.

Rob rang the doorbell and a tall, thin older woman with short, white hair and a raspy voice answered the door. Maryanne heard only a muffled version of the transaction, as she was lost in her own head. She checked back in when all of the bags had been brought upstairs and the door safely locked behind them.

Rob sighed. "There's only like three rooms in this place. I didn't know that qualifies as a bed and breakfast."

It wasn't easy getting the time off from Norman, as Rob suspected he knew exactly why he needed it, but Rob didn't care. No way was he letting her go up here by herself after all that had happened.

Maryanne shrugged. She was staring out of the large bay window in the small living room they had, Casey weighing heavily on her mind. She just hoped Ramsey's plan was in motion, and more importantly, working.

Rob came up behind her and wrapped his arms around her waist. He rested his chin on her head. "Let's go to bed. You have a long day ahead of you."

"Yeah, I know."

He turned and started to unpack a few things. Maryanne took one last, hard look at the dead winter outside wondering whom, if anyone, might be lurking and leering back.

Maryanne and Rob spent the next day wandering around town, interviewing business owners, the few and far between pedestrians they came across, and some key officials in town, including the police chief Joseph had set her up with, the mayor, director of the Chamber of Commerce, and the district attorney. Maryanne left that office wishing she could have asked her a thing or two.

They were both wiped by the time they sat down for dinner at the tiniest, kitschiest little diner Maryanne had ever seen. She had a soft spot for places like this and couldn't wipe the goofy grin off her face.

Rob giggled at her as he munched on his French fries. "You're such a nerd."

"I know," she said. "It's sad, this place."

"It certainly is," Rob said, looking around.

"No, I mean, the whole town in general. It obviously had such a charm and life to it that's really died out, and they're probably never going to get it back."

"I want to live in one of these towns. Well, obviously, one that has more to offer, but somewhere like this, where everyone is so nice. They all seem so genuinely happy and honored that we were even here."

"I know, and did you see..." Maryanne was interrupted by her phone ringing.

Rob gave his usual "ugh!" while she dug around in her purse for it. It was Lily.

"Hello?"

"You have to get back here," Lily said, sounding out of breath.

"Why, what's going on?"

"I just saw the craziest fucking thing!"

"What? What is it?"

"I was downstairs throwing out the garbage, and I heard the door shut behind me, but I was separating the recycling, so I didn't bother to turn around and look at whoever it was. When I finally did, I saw Kayla go into that fenced-off room all the way at the other end of the basement and disappear."

"Are you sure it was her?"

"Well, I was pretty sure, but called out to her anyway and got no response. So I walked over there and peered inside and you can't really notice it at first, but in the back right corner is a door."

"Oh, my God, Lily, you're creeping me out."

"Well, this is the least of it so hunker down! So anyway, at first I didn't see it, but then realized a few of those decrepit bikes were leaned up against a doorknob."

"But wouldn't that just lead to the street?"

"That's what I thought, but, no! So I pick up this random piece of wood I find on the floor as a weapon just in case, and go to open it."

Maryanne couldn't help but giggle. Even Lily had a bit of a laugh in her voice. She felt like she was describing a scene out of a movie.

"So, and I swear I'm not even kidding you, I start walking through this tunnel. The further I go, the louder the voices in my head start screaming to turn around, but I just can't. So I keep going and going, and it's getting darker and murky, and just as I'm about to turn around, I see a staircase."

"How long were you walking for?"

"Oh, at least ten minutes."

"Ten minutes? Are you nuts?"

"I know, I know, but I couldn't stop! Anyway, I see this staircase, and once I'm at the bottom of it, I start to hear voices. So I creep up it really slowly and open the door at the top. Then I'm in a really tiny hallway, with some shelving and stuff, and on the other end is another door with a small window. I can see the backs of a bunch of people who are listening to some guy talking. I can see they are all holding candles and then I realize where I am. It was that little shed in the woods behind the cemetery that you saw that night."

"Holy shit."

"I know! So I'm trying to hear what's being said, but it's all very muffled, and then I realize one of them is Kayla."

"So it was her?"

"Yeah. She turned to her left quickly, and when I recognized her, I got so startled I gasped and stepped back and ended up hitting the back of my head on the door frame. I freaked out that one of them might have heard or saw me, so I shut the door and ran down the stairs and back through the tunnel."

"What the fuck was that? What was she doing?"

"I have no idea, but it doesn't look good."

"We're coming home now."

"I think that's a good idea."

Maryanne hung up the phone.

"What's going on now?" Rob asked.

She simply gave him a stern look, turned toward the counter, and yelled, "Check, please!"

Chapter 43

"It must run directly under Broadway and under the cemetery if she said it took her a little over ten minutes to get there. That's about how long it would take," Rob said as they pulled into their spot in the lot down the block from the Darren Hayes.

"I know," but Maryanne was barely listening. Her stomach was in knots, and she'd been trying the entire drive home to think of what she could say to pull Kayla out of the fog she'd been in. What the hell had she gotten herself into? She had a million questions, and this time she wasn't going to hold any of them back.

They parked and she took off for the apartment building, for once walking faster than Rob.

"What's the rush?" he teased.

She shot him a dirty look over her shoulder and he grinned back.

When they finally reached her apartment door, they could hear someone sobbing inside. They looked at each other, confused. Maryanne hurriedly got her keys out and let herself in. When they cleared the hallway and got to the living room, they found M.J. sitting on the couch, crying with his head in his hands, surrounded by a grim-faced Lily, who'd obviously been crying as well, and Steve and Scott.

"What happened," Maryanne asked, her voice catching in her throat.

M.J. looked up at her, startled. "She's dead! She's fucking dead!" he yelled, starting to sob again.

Maryanne felt a numbness come over her entire body. She looked over at Lily, who was sitting with her hand on M.J.'s back. Lily gave her a little nod to confirm it was true: Kayla was gone. Maryanne turned to Rob and planted her face in his chest, as her own sobs started to wash over her.

Chapter 44

They all moved upstairs to M.J.'s apartment and sat around the TV to watch the 11 p.m. news.

M.J. had gone back to the police station for another round of questioning. They all warned him to exercise caution when dealing with them, as they had no idea of the cops' motives at this point.

"A second death in two weeks, of the exact same conditions, has police on high alert this evening in Sleepy Hollow as they still have not determined if the first was a murder or a suicide," said the anchor. They then cut to a wide-angle shot of the cemetery.

"The body of Kayla Jared was found by a jogger a few short hours ago in the woods behind this famous cemetery in the village where many celebrities and philanthropists have been laid to rest. Including the story's very own Washington Irving. Both victims, the other being Patrick McWolden, found just ten days ago, had their throats slit and bled to death, in the exact same location. While each had a knife in their hands when discovered, police are still skeptical to label these as suicides."

The report then switched to Officer Grettco, who'd given Rob such a difficult time when he'd gone to the station for help. "This fuck," Rob said in disgust.

"There's no way for us to make the call until the weapons have been properly tested for foreign prints and DNA, and we get those results back from the lab,"

Grettco said.

"I just want everyone in town to be on alert and be safe and smart, especially if you're out and alone at night. Residents can rest assured we'll have extra squad cars out and more police on foot patrol, and really just ramping up security in general to keep everyone safe. I don't want anyone jumping to any conclusions though, until we know for sure the nature of these deaths." The report then returned to the news desk.

"Officer Grettco also would like citizens to know that if, in fact, these deaths are ruled suicides, police will be working to figure out a connection, if any, between them."

The group was just starting to turn to each other when the anchor started up again unexpectedly. "And now here to discuss these horrifying events as of late, Joseph Goldberg, known to many throughout Westchester as a highly proactive member of society as he has belonged to the Westchester Hometown Society for thirty years now, and of course, as the very well-respected publisher of Prerogative magazine."

"Thanks Alex, good to be here," Joseph said, a used-car salesman smile on his face.

"Oh, my God," Maryanne said under her breath. Everyone else was too disgusted to speak.

"What's your reaction to these two strange deaths, which are, for the most part, very out of character for this area?"

"It's deeply disturbing, Alex, but as I have done in the past, I will be working tirelessly to help get to the bottom of this and keep our area safe."

"Ugh!" most of them grumbled.

"This is ridiculous! How incredibly self-serving. What, is he running for mayor?" Lily said.

"Why is he even on here?" Rob asked nobody in particular.

"He's binding everyone to him," Maryanne said. Everyone turned to look at her.

"He's painting himself into the great savior, again."

"What do you mean?" Steve asked.

She frowned over at him. He and Scott really shouldn't be involved in this conversation, but she leaned forward and went on anyway.

"Ramsey told me that after the fire that burned down the I building, he…"

"No way! That's why there's no I building?" Steve blurted out.

Rob gave him a dirty look.

"He tried to kind of rally everyone around him, holding press conferences and other ridiculous displays, saying he'd lead the charge to find out who did this. That he wouldn't let the police get away with sloppy work, blah blah blah."

"But why?" Lily asked. "I mean, who the hell was he? Didn't anybody ever ask themselves that?"

Maryanne shrugged. "Well, he had the Westchester Hometown Society connection, and Ramsey described it as this weird monopoly he and this certain group have over the town. This strange hold they have over everything. There's even this lineage of people the mayoral position continues to get handed down to."

"He might have a lot more power than we thought," Rob said.

"Well, the more important issue right now is, I think Kayla was somehow involved with Joseph."

"What?" Lily asked. "What are you talking about?"

"She was acting incredibly weird, and you all saw it. That wasn't her. There was something going on, I know it."

"That could have been anything, though," Rob said.

"No. She always acted very evasive and strange whenever I brought Joseph up. Did you know she knew he owned this place?" she asked, turning to Lily. "There's no other way she could have known that."

"I think you're overreacting," Rob said.

"I'm not! We'll talk to M.J. and you'll see. Besides, Ramsey told me he thinks he was trying to bring her in."

"What does that even mean?" Rob said, practically shouting at this point. "And why are you still talking to him? I don't know if we should be trusting him at this point to tell you the…"

They all turned toward the door as it opened and in walked M.J. The second Maryanne saw him she was yanked back into reality and started to weep. She couldn't believe she'd never be able to hear Kayla's laugh again, or be able to call her whenever something great, or even not so great, happened.

She'd lost a great friend who had been bubbly and full of life. They all had. She was the first to get up and hold M.J., who looked like he'd lost about ten pounds in one night. Everyone took turns hugging him.

M.J. took a seat on the couch next to Maryanne, where Rob had gotten up for him. "What was going on M.J.? Something was not right. I know it. Talk to us."

"Babe, maybe…" Rob started, not sure if right now was the best time to get into all of this given M.J.'s physical and mental state. As well as everyone else's for that matter.

"No!" Maryanne insisted, holding up a hand. She'd had enough. She'd lost one of her best friends and that was the last straw. She wasn't going to let this go one step further without learning more.

"I don't even know," M.J. started to everyone's surprise. All eyes were suddenly on him. "She barely told me anything. Said it would all be explained in the end."

"What do you mean?"

M.J. took a few moments and one big deep breath out before he began.

"Months ago, Kayla came home from a doctor's appointment devastated, but it was worse because she wasn't even crying or anything. She just seemed like, literally, all the life and spirit had been sucked out of her." He took another deep breath, and continued.

"They'd told her she couldn't have children and that's when everything changed."

Maryanne's heart sank. She'd just jumped to the conclusion that Kayla had been involved with something underhanded, never considering her friend might have just been breaking down inside thanks to some awful news.

"I told her it didn't matter to me, that miracles do happen. Maybe one day we would have enough saved up for an adoption, but she freaking freaks out on me, screaming that neither of us will ever make enough money for that." He stopped and hung his head. "She could be so hurtful sometimes," he said, starting to cry softly.

"It wasn't her talking, M.J."

"I know," he said, nodding. "Anyway, that's when she started telling me she knew a way we could get or have a baby, and wanted me to come meet the people who wanted to help us."

"What people?"

"'He', sorry, she kept saying 'he', not 'people', so much as she kept referring to just some guy, which of course, for me was not okay either. That she was getting involved with some man who was telling her he could get her a child somehow."

Maryanne's eyes narrowed as she shook her head. This all pretty much confirmed her suspicions, and it was making her sick to her stomach.

"So, obviously, I kept refusing to get involved and told her if we were to move forward, she better untangle herself from this group, or this man, or whatever this was."

"Did she ever tell you any details about 'him' or 'them' or whomever?" Lily asked.

"No," M.J. said, shaking his head. "She kept saying everything would be explained if I'd just agree to meet them and get involved. Whatever that meant. Anyway, it obviously drove a huge wedge between us, as I wanted nothing to do with this, but she kept on pushing. She told me I didn't care about her or our future together. It got so bad I could barely talk to her without her exploding."

"Did you tell the police any of this?" Maryanne asked.

"Not really," M.J. said. "Not after what you guys just told me. I said we'd been fighting, but that basically it was just a simple case of two people growing apart."

He choked on the last few words. "I said it was a case of two people falling out of love." He started to cry once again and this time almost all of them joined him.

"But it wasn't. I never stopped loving her. I didn't want this. None of it."

Maryanne hugged him, and Rob put a hand on his shoulder. It was all too much for Lily to take, and she got up to cry alone in the bathroom.

As Maryanne tried to console M.J., she made a

solemn vow that her friend would not have died in vain. If nothing else, she had to find out what happened to Kayla and why. And, of course, get Casey home safe and sound.

Chapter 45

"I love old paper; the look and feel of it. The sound it makes when you turn the page," Lily said.

Maryanne looked over at her and frowned. "Would you focus, please?"

"Sorry."

The girls were in the Ossining library looking through old newspapers, which the datatician had offered to them either on file, microfilm, or PDFs. At Lily's urging, they decided to look through the actual files, huge overstuffed binders filled with back issues of The Journal News.

"Look what you got us into," Maryanne said, on edge. They were sitting at a table with huge piles of the binders laid out in front of them, when they could have just been sitting in front of a computer where they could zoom in easier.

"Sorry. I'm telling you, I would have gotten a massive headache looking through them either way after only five minutes."

Maryanne shook her head. "I know, I'm sorry."

"It's all right," Lily said, rubbing her forearm. "We'll find something useful, I know it."

They were scouring the back issues trying to find any information they could on Joseph, the Darren Hayes, the fire, the Westchester Hometown Society, election results, and police corruption. Anything that might lead them to some answers about what Joseph is involved in and what he tried to lure Kayla into with the promise of a baby for her and M.J.

"All right, let's go through that week one more time."

"Which one?" Lily asked.

"The week that had the article in it I'd found online that night about the fire. I think it was June 7–14, 1996."

"Oh, right," Lily said, lifting up one of the massive binders that had been sitting to her right and plopping it down between them with a huge thud. Lily had placed a small post-it on the page with the infamous article on it.

"Wait a minute," Maryanne said, pointing to the article's byline.

"William Massen," she mumbled. "There was no byline on the version I saw online!"

"Really? Let's look him up," Lily said. To their surprise, phone books still existed and they magically found only one William Massen in Westchester County.

"Okay. Let's get out of here," Maryanne said after she'd jotted down the address. As they started to gather up their stuff, Cecily's tombstone flashed in her head.

"Wait a minute." She sat back down. "God, why didn't I think of this before?" She opened the same binder with the article in it. She checked the obits for a couple days after the fire and gasped, slapping a finger down on Cecily's.

"What?" Lily asked. "Is that the little girl?"

"Yes! Oh, my God, it gives no details on her death." Maryanne gave a quick scan of the room, and quickly and quietly ripped Cecily's obituary out.

"Let's go find this William Massen," she said, getting up and breezing past Lily, leaving her friend scrambling to grab the rest of her stuff and catch up.

Lily and Maryanne pulled up to a quaint, little home in nearby Philipsburg Manor, just half an hour after leaving the library.

They carefully approached the bright-red front door and gave each other a worried glance before Maryanne rang the doorbell. A middle-aged man, with such light blue eyes they almost looked like liquid, opened the door.

"Hi, are you William Massen?" Maryanne asked, looking down at the paper she'd jotted his name down on to make sure she had gotten it right.

He cocked the wide-brimmed safari hat down over one eye as he winked it. "At your service," he said.

Lily and Maryanne looked at each other again, Lily obviously trying hard not to laugh. "We needed to ask you a few things."

"Well, you're obviously with the FBI," Massen said with a smirk, leaning up against the doorway.

"It's about this article," Maryanne said, handing him a printout of the vague article about the fire. He took the article and the moment he looked at it, it was obvious the girls wouldn't have to worry about any future sarcasm on his part.

He looked back up, eyeing them both for a moment. "How did you know I wrote this?"

"We just came from the library," Maryanne answered.

He frowned and looked back down at the article. "Come in," he finally said, and ushered them both through the doorway.

William slowly took off his hat, never taking his eyes off of the article in his hand. He then shut the door, locking all three locks, Maryanne noticed.

"I don't write for The Journal News anymore."

"Okay," Lily said. "Why not?"

He motioned for them to join him in his living room,

which resembled an overpriced knickknack shop.

"Well, this is one of the main reasons," he said, shaking the paper in the air. "You think this is all I wrote? This story…this tragedy, I should say, was going to really rip this town apart, and they wouldn't have it."

"Does this have anything to do with it?" Maryanne asked, handing him Cecily's obit.

He read it quickly and looked up. "What do you know about Cecily Reynolds?" He looked like he was preparing to take a bullet as he waited for their answer.

"Pretty much nothing besides the fact that she's dead. Did she die in that fire?"

"Yes."

"Why wasn't that reported?"

"I tried, of course! This is not my original story. I still have it. Kept it all these years in case I ever needed it to, uh, clear myself."

"I submitted it, and when the paper came out in the morning, this is how it'd been edited. I fought them, of course, tried to report them to everyone I could think of, as this wasn't the first time I'd seen them withhold vital information like that. But nothing ever came of it."

"So you're telling us The Journal News would regularly alter your stories?" Lily asked.

"Not just my stories," he answered. He looked at them for a moment, and then scoffed. "Big brother is very much alive and well, ladies; very much alive and well, indeed. Anyway, I got so disillusioned with the whole industry I left to start my own thing. You ever heard of a little site called Patch?"

"You started Patch?" Maryanne asked.

"I knew his name sounded familiar," Lily mumbled under her breath.

"So, have you posted any articles about how the

powers that be are keeping things from Sleepy Hollow citizens?" Maryanne chastised.

"Of course, I have, but they keep mysteriously disappearing off of our site and our administrators cannot figure out why."

They all paused to take that in.

"But it doesn't matter what gets written or not. He's got the public believing exactly what he wants them to believe."

"Who's 'he'?" Lily asked.

William narrowed his eyes at them for a moment, and they watched as a wave of realization came over him.

"I couldn't place you all this time, but now I recognize you. You don't recognize me?"

The girls looked at each other and shook their heads "no."

He shrugged. "We've covered some of the same local events together. Not many though." He got up and poured himself a glass of water. "I'm talking about your boss."

Lily and Maryanne looked at each other again. What they were bracing themselves for, they didn't know.

"When that little girl died, he had, and still has for that matter, everyone believing the intruder who started the fire, allegedly, was what killed her."

That made Maryanne feel nauseous.

"So he's telling people she was murdered by the intruder?"

"Not just murdered," William said. He stared at them for a moment, letting the insinuation sink in.

"Oh, God," Maryanne said under her breath. She looked back up at him. "And what do you think?"

He raised his eyebrows, questioningly, and then

shook his head. "The man was unlike you or I. Joseph Goldberg took that and ran with it to keep fear high and dissentions low."

With that, he got up and disappeared into another room where they heard him scavenging around for something. He returned with what looked like a mug shot of a middle-aged black man. Maryanne took it from him, looked up, and frowned.

"Could we stop beating around the bush? What are you saying?"

"I'm saying that your boss has never been shy about expressing his opinions about minorities. He used this tragedy as an opportunity to push them even further!" William's voice made his home feel like it was rumbling.

"See! I told you all!" he said waving his arms in the air. "You let these undesirables into our community and this is what happens. Listen to me from now on and you'll never have to experience such a thing again!"

"He said that?" Lily asked.

"Well, that was the general message," William said, plopping himself down on his chair again.

"Do you know anything about the little girl? Her family?" Maryanne asked him.

"No. It was a private funeral, and…"

Maryanne's cell phone started ringing. "Excuse me." She fished it out of her bag and saw it was Rob calling.

"Hi," she answered.

"Hey, where are you?"

"Uh…" she got up and started to leave the room, but didn't want to go too far. She was in a stranger's house. She wandered a few steps down a dark hallway.

"I'll explain later. What's up?"

"Geffin and I just came across a check made out

from Norman to Joseph."

"Really? Where did you find that?"

"It was in a pile of checks he gave us to sign off on for the agency. It's a personal check, he must have lumped it in there by accident."

"How much is it for?"

Rob scoffed. "A lot of fuckin' money!"

"Well, how much?" she insisted, trying not to raise her voice.

"Fifty thousand dollars."

"What? Wow, so I guess that confirms that Randall wasn't lying."

"Exactly."

"I should tell Ramsey."

"If you must," Rob said, sighing.

"When will you be home?"

"Not late, that's for sure. It gives me the creeps being around this guy and he'll be here the rest of the afternoon."

"All right, well, just let me know, I'll pick you up at the train."

"Okay, love you."

"Love you."

Maryanne closed her phone, and went back into the living room where she completely interrupted a conversation going on.

"We need to get going Lil."

Lily looked up at her, confused. "Uh, well…"

"William, can we contact you again if we need to?"

"Sure, what do you ladies plan to do? You know I'd really love to stick it to that guy. I have connections you know. Anything you need!"

As he was talking, Maryanne had grabbed Lily's hand and dragged her out the door, which slammed shut behind them. The only response she'd given him was a curt smile just before their grand exit.

Chapter 46

Maryanne's head was throbbing and she felt so dazed and confused she'd have thought she'd been drugged if she didn't know any better. They were all walking behind Kayla's casket as the procession made its way to her grave in the Sleepy Hollow cemetery.

Now it was all too real. Before, she had successfully convinced herself this hadn't happened. That the old Kayla she knew and loved would come bouncing into her apartment, bubbly as ever, and all would be right with the world again, but that wasn't going to happen.

She was gone for good. Somehow, someway she'd been convinced to take her own precious life, and now they were all left to pick up the pieces and make them whole again, so they could figure out how to get some answers. Or more importantly, help, and provide justice for the grave wrongs that have been committed by all of this brainwashing.

Rob had been trying to support her throughout the day, as at times it seemed like she couldn't hold her own, but for some reason she didn't want it today. She had felt like she didn't deserve it, so she continued to shrug him, and everyone else, off and was walking alone.

She tried to lift her chin just a little bit, and as she did, she glanced to her left at the tree line and saw an all-too-familiar patch of red up against the trees.

There he was again, the man in flannel, staring at her just as he did the day in October when she followed him into the woods and found the shack for the first time.

Without even thinking, she stumbled off the path, and up toward the wood, her black heels not sinking too far into the now mostly hardened soil.

Rob shuffled his feet along the ground, kicking at rocks as he walked in the procession, his hands dug deep into his pockets. He felt completely drained and useless. All of this was to protect her, and now she wouldn't even let him be there for her. He glanced up to make sure he could still see her up ahead.

Where the hell did she go?

He strained over people's heads and in between them, but couldn't pick out the back of Maryanne's head.

He happened to glance to his left up at the woods and didn't even think. He took off running. He could hear Lily screaming his name, but he didn't falter for a second.

When he broke through the tree line, he thought he could see someone up ahead and he yelled out to her. Was that her? He thought he saw glimpses of red, but suddenly, they disappeared. He sped up, not wanting to lose whom, or whatever, it was.

Eventually, he couldn't go anymore and was forced to slow down and catch his breath. He started screaming for Maryanne as loud as he could. As he kept walking, he thought he could see between the trees up ahead to what looked like a small house.

What the hell is that?

He started walking faster and broke out into a light run once again. As he got closer, he realized it was the small shed he was coming upon.

Creepy.

He stood there studying it for a few moments, when he noticed on the ground around the corner was a hand and an arm.

He ran over to it, and when he turned the corner he found Maryanne, lying on her side, passed out.

"Babe!"

He dropped to his knees and grabbed her by the shoulders.

"Babe! Wake up, please!"

"Rob?" he heard Lily yelling his name.

He got up and ran around from behind the house so he was visible. He waved his arms over his head.

"Here, I'm over here!"

He could see her and the others up ahead. They broke out in a run once they spotted him.

Rob turned and ran back around the side of the shed and tried to pick Maryanne up to a sitting position.

The second he touched her again she woke up with a gasp, eyes wide.

"She's his daughter!" she started screaming. "She's his daughter!"

Chapter 47

Soon they were all crowded around Maryanne.

"She's his daughter! Cecily! She's the man in flannel's daughter!"

"How do you know that?" Lily asked her. Steve and Scott just looked at each other, confused.

"I saw him. While we were walking I saw him again, just where I saw him the night of the pumpkin blaze. I followed him here, and once I got to the shed, I must have passed out because that's all I remember."

Lily frowned, recalling her own experience when she saw him in the corner of the office and passed out herself.

"Then I started dreaming, I guess. It was daylight, and I was walking through the cemetery with no shoes on. When I came upon her, she was playing right on her grave," Maryanne described as she started to cry.

Rob rubbed her back, trying to calm her.

She continued once she caught her breath. "I was just admiring her. She was so adorable! I realized the cross on her headstone was glowing pink and I could feel someone was behind me. When I turned around I saw him, and he said to me, 'The spiders are spinning their web.' Just as he said that, Cecily yells out, 'Daddy!' When I turn again she's looking at him, smiling. So I turn back toward him, shocked, and he says to me, 'The last thing he said to me was flies are born to be eaten by spiders.' She screams for him again, but this time it was different. When I turned, she was gone, but the cross was now up in flames."

Everyone stared for a few minutes, then Rob helped her to her feet.

"Whom was he talking about?" Lily asked.

"Who?" asked Maryanne.

"Flannel. He said to you, 'The last thing *he* said to me…' Who is *he*?"

"I can take a good guess."

"Joseph?"

Maryanne nodded. "I know it. I've got to get Ramsey on the phone, right now."

Chapter 48

Well, it wasn’t "right now", but the next morning Maryanne got off the phone with a recovering Ramsey, who was now at least licking his wounds at home, rather than at a hospital.

"Sandra McWolden," she turned and said to Lily, who'd been standing behind her the whole time. "Okay. Where does she live?"

"In town," Maryanne answered as she grabbed her coat and headed for the door. Lily followed closely. As they drove to the address Ramsey had given her, Maryanne filled Lily in on what she'd learned.

Sandra was Patrick McWolden's widow, the man who was found dead just a few weeks before Kayla, in the exact same spot, both killed the same way. He was also known as the man who chased Rob through the subways and started up a conversation with Maryanne in the park. Ramsey said he knows she's been in contact with Joseph, for how long or how extensively he didn't know. He couldn’t confirm anything on Cecily and a father or father figure. His best guess on Norman, the check they'd found, and corresponding letter, was he was also a part of this elitist network.

"Is it that small of a world?" Maryanne had asked Ramsey when they were on the phone.

"You have no idea," he'd answered.

The two pulled up to a dingy house buried far up in the Tarrytown hills. They looked at each other for a moment, and then started up the driveway.

The girls peeked in the living room window and saw a home that looked like someone walked out three years ago and never returned; very tidy, but with a layer of dust over everything that made all the furniture and fabrics look ten times older than they probably were.

"Can I help you?" asked a jumpy woman who'd snuck quietly out the front door and up behind them. She was unkempt, but beautiful nonetheless. Both girls jumped and yelped.

"Oh, sorry!" Maryanne said with a laugh. "I'm Maryanne and this is Lily. We're with Child Protective Services." She was using the intro that Ramsey had advised her to use. He didn't tell her why and she didn't ask.

They watched as all of the color drained from Sandra's face. She didn't say anything for a few moments. "Did he send you?" she asked, barely above a whisper.

Got her, Maryanne thought.

"I think we'd better step inside," Maryanne told her.

She led the two of them into the house, and as they moved further in, they started to hear the sounds of children playing. They reached a kitchen area with large, sliding glass doors that led out to a small yard.

Outside they saw a little boy and girl running back and forth. Maryanne recognized them as the two children with wavy and graying, Patrick McWolden, at the park the day she met him. Sandra turned to face them.

"What do you know about him, huh? No matter what he told you about me, his crimes are far worse, I promise you that!"

Her voice was starting to get shrill, and she was shaking her fists at her sides. Maryanne did not want the kids to hear any of this, so she needed to calm the woman down if she was going to get what she needed out of her.

"Let's just sit down at the table here," she said, gently putting her hand on Sandra's shoulder. Sandra dropped her head into her hands and started sobbing as soon as she sat down.

Geez, doesn't take much to get these people to sing.

"I…I…my husband thought she was holding onto him."

Lily and Maryanne looked at each other.

"He told her to hold onto the back of his shirt and not let go, no matter what."

"Why didn't he carry her?" Maryanne asked. She still wasn't sure exactly what the woman was talking about, but it seemed like a logical question to ask.

"He felt like he'd need his hands. It was bad by the time they'd woken up. He could barely see anything the smoke was so thick," Sandra said.

"And why weren't you home that night?"

"He knows why!" she clenched her fists and stood up. "I can't take this anymore!" she shrieked and threw a coffee mug that'd been sitting on the table at the kitchen wall.

Lily and Maryanne froze.

Sandra pounded her fists against her forehead, and then turned and slammed them down on the kitchen table.

"Where is she?" she screeched into their faces.

The girls turned to each other scared, and more confused than ever at this point.

"Where's who?" Lily asked.

"Cecily!"

Maryanne froze. She could feel Lily do the same

next to her.

"Cecily," Sandra whispered this time. They watched all the energy and anger drain right out of her body. Her shoulders slumped and she plopped back down into her seat. "My daughter."

"Cecily Reynolds?"

Sandra shook her head yes. They watched as her tears dripped into her lap. "He promised me."

Lily cleared her throat. "M'am, you're going to have to explain yourself a little better here, we don't have all day," she said, trying to sound as authoritative as possible.

Her head shot up, and she gave Lily a look of death.

"He promised me my child back," she said, slowly and icily. She smirked at both girls. "Bet he didn't tell you that, huh? That he has her?"

"But your daughter is dead m'am. Are you telling us that's not the case? Cecily never died in the I building fire at the Darren Hayes?"

"That's exactly what I'm telling you. I cannot go on with this charade anymore."

"Well, the floor is yours," Maryanne said.

Sandra swallowed, and then turned to face them.

"After Cecily and my first husband died, or I thought Cecily had died, Joseph was immediately at my side. I'd never met him before, but had heard his name around town. I was confused as to why he was being so helpful and supportive. I just believed his story that he was outraged over what happened, and that he wanted me to help him make sure that any 'outsiders' were never allowed into our community ever again," Sandra explained.

"Did he ever tell you why the whole story about the fire was never reported?" Maryanne asked.

Sandra shrugged. "Didn't need to be. Everyone knew. He rallied people in droves to town meetings and Westchester Hometown Society gatherings to talk about what happened and how we can prevent it from happening again. He brainwashed everyone. Including me."

"What exactly happened?" Maryanne asked with an edge of desperation to her voice.

Sandra glared at her. "I'm not going over this again with you people."

"Well, you better m'am," Lily interjected. "If you expect to keep the two kids you have left."

Maryanne could have sworn she saw Sandra's eyes flash red, but the woman swallowed and went on.

"I was with someone else that night," she said, looking at both of them defiantly, daring them to judge her. "The night of the fire. I was with someone other than my husband. That's where I was the night my little girl and my husband were burning alive. Is that in my file?"

"Just keep going, m'am, enough with the histrionics," Lily said. "We don't care if you were sleeping with the Pope that night."

"He told us all that a black man raped my daughter and set the building on fire. That the police, the lazy pathetic officers who hadn't responded in time, allowed this to happen; the police who are also on his payroll, by the way. He said we couldn't trust them to keep us safe anymore. That we had to rely on him and his 'friends.' And everyone did. Everyone just…believed him."

"Who are his 'friends'?"

Sandra shrugged. "Other high profile people. Members of that Westchester Hometown Society group, which is really just a front for them, by the way," she hissed. "And I get the feeling it extends much further than this shitty town."

Maryanne pulled out the picture of Beth's husband and the man in flannel that Beth had given her.

"Sandra, is this Cecily's father?"

As soon as Sandra looked at it, she began to sob. She shook her head and dropped it into her hands. "Now I'm left with two dead husbands, not just one."

The girls let her compose herself, and she eventually continued.

"He came to me when things had started to die down. Tried to tell me Cecily never died in the fire. That he had to pretend she did in order to get everyone's attention before the town became over run with blacks and immigrants, he'd said. That I'd get her back if I acted as a recruiter for him. He promised me if I could get Patrick to pledge himself to him, I'd get her back. That obviously never happened. Then when Patrick couldn't get his own pledge to commit, he was forced into killing himself."

"He did take his own life, then? It wasn't a murder?" Lily asked.

"It might as well have been!" she screamed back at her.

"Wait a minute, wait a minute," Maryanne said, holding up her hand.

"Who was Patrick's pledge?"

"I don't know exactly. I believe it was a young man. The only person who can know exactly who it is, is Joseph and the recruiter."

Her terminology was thoroughly creeping both of them out, especially because Rob's face popped immediately into Maryanne's head. Patrick had indeed been after him.

"I've finally come to the realization that I'll never see her again." She shook her head. "What a fucking idiot I am for ever believing him in the first place." She turned to the girls, wide-eyed. "Please, please don't take my children from me," she sobbed with her hands interlocked toward them, begging.

"We need more answers before we can promise that," Maryanne said. "What is a pledge and what is a recruiter? Is this some skull and bones organization he's running or something?"

"Skull and bones has nothing on his people, let me tell you," Sandra said. She was starting to look like a caged animal, eyes darting around, searching for a way out. Maryanne sensed that was the most they were going to get out of her for now.

"Are you still involved with him, Ms. Denny?"

The tears began to flow again. "I have no choice," she sobbed. The girls looked at each other, and then stood up.

"We'll be in touch," Lily said. They turned to leave, but before they reached the door, Maryanne paused for a moment. She turned back to face Sandra who was still sitting in her chair, looking very confused by their sudden exit.

"Sandra, do spiders mean anything to you…and the family you lost?"

"Spiders?" She looked around for a moment, obviously searching her memory. They saw the light bulb come on and as her eyes widened, they even saw a glimmer of a smile. "Yes. Cecily was terrified of them. The only one who could calm her when she saw one was her father. He promised he'd always protect her from them."

Maryanne nodded and the girls left.

Chapter 49

"That's why I've been having all these dreams of spiders!" Maryanne was talking high and fast, overly excited by what just happened. "They were trying to warn me!"

"Against what?" Lily asked.

Maryanne looked at her confused, and sort of laughed at the ridiculous nature of the question. "Against Joseph!"

Lily was working a deep frown. "I don't know," she said, twirling a piece of her red locks. "I feel like there's more to this. I mean, isn't something missing here?"

"Like what?"

"I think him wanting to keep minorities out of town under the guise of trying to protect people is even too altruistic."

"Well, what are you saying?"

"I think he caused that fire."

"Why? He owns the place."

"Exactly. I mean that would explain why he never wanted us to know he owned the place. It's probably no coincidence either that we all ended up living there."

Maryanne's eyes widened and her stomach dropped, as she wondered if Joseph had some horrible fate in store for all of them, too. Maybe Lily was right. Maybe he did cause the fire.

"Well, if that's all true, we'll leverage that information to get Casey home," she said as they pulled into the parking lot.

The two got to their building and climbed the three flights to their apartment.

"Rob should be here," she told Lily. "I gave him a key because he said Scott and Steve were having some people over tonight from high school he didn't really want to see."

Lily scoffed. "Who would? Yeah, that's no problem."

They entered the apartment and shuffled to each of their rooms where Maryanne expected to see Rob lounging on her bed, watching a movie or something, but all she found was Ronald staring blankly back at her, leaning up against her pillows. She frowned.

That's weird.

"Huh?"

"Not there?" Lily called from her room.

"Nope." She took out her phone and called him. It didn't even ring once, and his voicemail came up immediately.

She tried to calm the nerves that were starting to bubble up inside her, as were the visions of Kayla and Patrick McWolden lying in pools of their own blood on the forest floor.

"I'm going to go upstairs to see if he's up there," she told Lily.

"Okay."

She went up to the fourth floor and knocked on the boys' door. Steve answered it.

"Hey…" he trailed off as his eyes widened with concern. Even though she was desperately trying to hide it, Maryanne had panic written all over her face.

"Hey, did Rob come home tonight?"

"Uh, no, I don't think so."

He partially shut the door so he could back in and

pop his head into Scott's room. "Hey, have you seen Rob?" she heard him ask.

"Nope."

"What time did you guys get home?" she asked, pushing the door in, startling Steve. She didn't care. Steve backed up and Scott came out of his room, frowning.

"Since like 6 p.m."

"Yeah, me, too," Steve said. "I got out early."

She nodded, and then turned to run back down the stairs.

"Hey, uh, is everything…" Steve trailed off as he and Scott watched her leave, their heads peeking out the door.

She dialed Rob's number again, and his voicemail came up before she'd even gotten all the way through her own doorway.

"Lil, something's wrong."

"What do you mean?" she asked.

She was lying down on her bed, coat still on, her laptop balanced on her perfectly flat stomach.

"I feel it. He took him."

Lily sat straight up.

"I know it," Maryanne said, tears streaming down her face. Lily stood up.

"Where do we look?"

"I don't know. Oh, god," she sobbed.

Lily stood frozen, not knowing what to do next. Maryanne took a deep breath and pulled herself together. She pushed the hair out of her face. "Let's go."

She turned on her heels, and Lily was forced to break into an easy run to catch up. She was lucky to still have her jacket on.

"Where are we going?" she squeaked as they

shuffled down the stairs so fast they were starting to blur together.

"The tunnels," Maryanne said just as they hit the basement.

"But why? Would he even know where to find them?"

"They took him through here, I know it," Maryanne answered with absolute certainty, not losing her concentration for even a moment. She was rifling through the piles of bicycles all the way against the back wall until she found the hidden door she was looking for.

She pushed over a huge row of them that were leaning up against the wall, and they crashed to the ground almost landing on Lily's foot.

"Oh!" she yelped. "Wait a minute, slow down! Why are we doing this?"

"Because!" Maryanne finally stopped and turned to face her. "Lily, I know they took him here. I'm being led here just like I was led to Cecily's grave, all those times."

They stared at each other for another few moments, and then they both turned and ducked into the tunnel.

Chapter 5Ø

The tunnels were in much worse shape than Lily remembered. It was as if they were reflecting the signs of the times.

It was hot, damp, leaking, and muddy. The ceiling was also much lower than she'd remembered and getting darker the deeper they went.

"Something's weird here, it's taking too long," Lily said. "I got there much faster the last time."

Maryanne stopped and turned around. Lily saw that her hair was very damp and almost all wet. She lifted a hand up to her own and felt it was the same.

"What should we do? Turn around?"

"No," Lily said. "Keep going. We'll get there, maybe I'm just disoriented."

She was now fully hunched over as they continued to make their way. She gasped when she thought she felt something brush up against her.

"What?" Maryanne asked, stopping and turning.

"Nothing!" Lily said too quickly. She was certain she was just imagining things at this point. They finally came to a staircase.

"Is this it?" Maryanne asked, obviously panicked at this point. Lily thought she could see tears streaming down her face as well.

"Ugh, I don't know. It doesn't look like the same one, but let's take it. I'm getting claustrophobic."

Maryanne turned and ran up the stairs, almost smacking her face into the single hanging light bulb over them. They reached two cellar doors at the top, which took both their strength to finally heave open.

When the fresh air hit their faces, Lily couldn't help but smile. The sense of relief though was fleeting. When they emerged, they found themselves in the oldest section of the cemetery, with the tombstones of revolutionary war vets from the 1700s surrounding them.

They turned to realize the doors they'd just emerged from were up against the tiny church that stood near the entrance to the entire cemetery.

“Well, this definitely wasn’t the same tunnel,” Lily said.

She glanced at Maryanne and watched her eyes grow wide as she stared through the window of the church. Lily looked in and could see Joseph's profile lit up by a few stray candles. There were others, but the face she focused on was Rob's, duct tape over his mouth and over his forehead, gluing it to the back of the chair he was in, his arms out to his sides and each one tied to marble statues on the church’s altar.

She'd never seen someone she knew in a position like that, and the sight was almost nauseating. Her knee-jerk reaction was to bang her elbow in fury up against the window. It caused everyone to turn and Rob to start screaming through the tape.

Maryanne turned to her, shocked. The two of them took off running through the piles of leaves and light snow toward the entrance to the church, which of course was locked.

Maryanne looked around and found a brick lying to the left of it. She picked it up and started pounding away on the lock. When it finally pinged off the door and onto the floor, the two burst through the doors.

"Grettco!"

"David, get them!"

David, Joseph's son, came over and grabbed Maryanne's arm. He was sobbing.

"Get off me!" she yelled and punched him dead in the face.

Two men in police uniforms came out of nowhere and grabbed Lily by the arms. She started to struggle and that's when David started screaming.

"What the fuck, Dad?"

"Sit down, you fucking faggot!" Joseph roared.

Rob was screaming through the duct tape and trying desperately to move his head and wedge it loose somehow. Maryanne looked up and realized a cross was hanging upside down over his head.

Joseph put an end to that when he turned and punched him upside the chin, knocking him out cold.

"No!" Maryanne screamed and flew at him, but before she could get very far, Sandra stood up from her seat in one of the front pews, turned around, and pointed a gun straight at her forehead. Maryanne stopped and put up her hands in surrender. She hadn't even realized there was anyone sitting there, let alone Sandra.

"Sandra, what are you doing?" It seemed to Maryanne she barely knew where she was, let alone what she was doing.

"Sandra? Sandra do you remember us?" she asked, turning to point at Lily who was still being held by the two officers.

"Of course, she remembers you. You're the scum who reminded her of her little girl's tragic death. Thanks to the same people I tried to save her from," Joseph hissed.

Maryanne furrowed her brow. She didn't know what

crap Joseph was spewing now, as he'd been telling Sandra her daughter was still alive all this time.

"You killed her! You set that fire, didn't you?"

"If I hadn't done it, it would have happened eventually. At least it was controlled with me. Do you know how little it took to get that filthy nigger to go in there and do it? One hit off a crack pipe. That was all," he said, shrugging.

Everyone stood still for a few moments, afraid to move. Joseph started to laugh and breathe a little steadier now.

"You think you guys got hired by chance? Any of you?" he asked, pointing around to all of them. "You were all carefully selected," Joseph said, motioning with his thumb and pointer squeezed together. "And you all made the biggest mistakes of your lives by denying us!" he roared.

"He has Patrick McWolden's blood on his hands!" he yelled, pointing at Rob. "He killed him!"

"What are you talking about?" Maryanne shouted.

"He was Patrick's pledge. Patrick tried to show him the way to a better life and he was too blind to see, so Patrick was forced to take his own life." Joseph paused and smiled. "Just like Kayla."

Maryanne felt the rage and anger boil up inside her. Without thinking, she went after him, but a much less comatose Sandra moved even closer and pressed the gun directly against Maryanne's temple this time.

"I hope that pathetic excuse for a fiancé she has lives in agony for the rest of his life for what he did to her!"

"What?" Maryanne couldn't tell if this was all still an act or if Joseph truly felt he had no culpability in any of this.

"You did all this! You brainwashed these people!

You took their biggest weaknesses in life and used them so you could play them like your own personal little puppets!"

"Did you set the fire, Joseph?" Lily interrupted. "Yes or no?"

"Don't you challenge me, young lady!"

"Did you or not?" Lily screamed. At that, one of the cops holding her hit her in the head with the butt of his gun, knocking her to the floor.

Maryanne was starting to panic. She was left with practically no one at this point, with Rob passed out and Lily stunned.

Joseph walked toward her until he was just about a foot away from her face.

"Do you see that? That's the type of power I have over this town…and others for that matter. I sent him in there to start the fire as I stood to gain some insurance money from it, and the fact that the idiot I hired got so high and passed out after he set it, killing himself and others was just a bonus. It tightened my grip on this place even more. That Raymond died, too? Fucking Christmas. You see, he and that stupid old bat Beth's husband were nothing but a constant obstacle for us with the police, so the fact that he was out of the picture now was beautiful. Thank God for small favors, huh? The kid, eh, took me a while to get over that, but she was a casualty of war, unfortunately. The upside of that is no one gets over the death of a child. No one, and it paid for itself ten times over when all was said and done, considering how many times I was able to use it as collateral, and how many more followers I was able to collect. Especially with these buffoons," he said, nodding at the cops hovering over Lily. "I used it not only to paint myself as the savior this town needed to whip these lazy assholes who let it happen into shape, but also it worked like a charm to bind the entire police force to me. My bidding is their number one priority."

"So there was no rape? No murder?" she asked, tears in her eyes. She was starting to doubt they'd all make it out of this alive.

"For all I know there could have been."

"What?" Sandra interrupted, dropping the gun to her side. It seemed that whatever Joseph had given her to calm her down had officially worn off.

Joseph's eyes widened as Sandra stepped toward him. He had forgotten the gun against Maryanne's head was being held by her.

"Cecily wasn't raped? She really is dead? You lied to me? You don't have her?"

"Sandra, I, of course…" Joseph started, searching to cover his tracks. This just might have been his biggest slip-up yet.

"Where am I?" she asked, looking around.

Joseph didn't waste the two second window he'd been given. He grabbed the gun out of her hand and shot Sandra in the face.

Maryanne started screaming and violently shaking. She was now covered in Sandra's blood, with the woman's remains splattered all over the pews she'd been standing next to.

"You stay with her. You, get up here and get him," he barked at Grettco and the cops, still with Lily.

He grabbed Maryanne by the arm and kept the gun trained on her. When she started to struggle, he tightened his grip and placed the barrel back at her temple.

"Don't even think about it. Let's go, and calm yourself down!" he said to her.

Maryanne could hear Rob moaning behind her as they all started to head for the door.

"Hurry up," he said as they burst through the doors and into the cold. Maryanne's eyes darted around like a bird, searching for an escape, but even if she'd spied one, no way was she leaving Lily, who was being dragged in front of her, and Rob behind her, alone in this situation.

They took them over to the cellar doors on the side of the church that Lily and Maryanne had come out of. As they shoved them all back down into the tunnels, Maryanne's thoughts went to Casey.

She'd hoped to have her home by now. The last time they'd spoken to her cousin she didn't sound any better than when she'd left her. Joseph was still threatening her life if she didn't get this story done, which would basically damn her name and career forever.

"Whatever you do to us, please, just promise me one thing," she said to Joseph. "Let Casey come home."

Joseph scoffed. "I don't think so. That little girl is stuck there until she does what she's told. There's too much money riding on that story."

"So is that what Norman is paying you for?"

He threw her up against the wall of the tunnel, her head hitting it with a smack. This one was much less damp and muddy than the tunnel she and Lily had just walked through. Joseph pushed the barrel of the gun directly between her eyes.

"If you don't keep quiet, I'll splatter your brains all over these walls, just like Sandra, you understand me?"

"Yes," she squeaked. He grabbed her arm and pushed her forward to get her moving again. They'd all stopped and she noticed before they'd started walking again that Rob's eyes were still barely open. All the cops, Grettco in front holding Rob, and another in back holding Lily, had a flashlight and the thin beams were bouncing on and off the walls and the darkness up ahead. As they kept walking, all of them became extremely disoriented from the lights and all the twists and turns.

Lily didn't recognize this set of tunnels either and was starting to wonder if there was actually a whole network of them underneath the city.

Eventually, they came upon what seemed to be a dead end of sorts, with one hanging light bulb. *Where the hell is the electricity coming from,* Maryanne thought. Funny the things that come to mind when your life is in jeopardy.

"Sit down up against the wall, the three of you."

Lily and Maryanne did as they were told, but Rob had to be placed, not very gently, on the ground. Maryanne couldn't believe she wasn't in hysterics yet, as what was coming was painfully obvious at this point. She'd rather die with two people she loved though than beg Joseph for anything, even if it was her own life.

Joseph and the three cops stood in front of them. "Get someone over to the church to clean that mess up," he said to one of them. The cop turned and picked up his radio. As he walked back into the tunnel to radio what she could only assume was the station, she strained to hear what he was saying. Her concentration quickly went from what he was saying to what he was doing. After he put his walkie-talkie away, he took out what looked like an old rag that had been shoved into the inside pocket of his jacket, and a small bottle. He soaked the rag with whatever was in the bottle and walked back over to the group.

Maryanne pressed her back up against the wall as he

got closer. He stood back in line and just as he did, all three men put their left hands over their hearts, each of which had a ring on the middle finger.

She heard Rob, who was now slightly awake, suck in a gulp of air next to her. They were just like the ring he'd seen on Norman, in his dreams, and on Patrick McWolden after he chased him through the New York City subways.

The three recited all in unison:

“You fled from the battle
On cowards' wings
Now that the winds have settled
Face what the Lord brings.”

After that they formed a circle facing each other, left hands still over their hearts, and said at exactly the same time: "Let your light so shine before men."

"What is that?" Lily yelled, fully awake now. It was the same thing she'd heard them chanting the night she came up on Kayla in the gathering at the shed in the woods. She tried to get up to run, but slipped and fell back down.

"Light it," Joseph said, low and quick to the cop with the soaked cloth.

The cop took a lighter out of his pocket and took it to the rag, which immediately erupted in flames. He tossed it over by Rob, who tried to get to his feet until three guns were trained on them all. The four men backed slowly out of the small alcove, then turned and ran, just as the flames began to spread. The floor had caught on fire and now it began to crawl up the wall.

"Get up, get up!" Maryanne yelled, trying to get the other two to their feet.

They both complied, and just as they were about to follow them out of the tunnel, they saw another light up ahead, which seemed to be coming at them. Rob, Lily, and Maryanne were mesmerized for a few moments, trying to figure out what it was they were looking at.

"Oh, my God," Maryanne breathed.

She turned to face Rob and Lily who were both pretty beat up.

"They lit the tunnel on fire on that end, too. We're trapped."

She'd always wondered how she would react in a dire or horrific situation. She only hoped through her fear she'd be able to exemplify some sort of bravery and not succumb to any cowardly acts. She was surprising herself at the solemnity that was washing over her as she watched the flames climb up the wall behind them.

"No. No!" Rob roared. "This is not going to happen!" He grabbed the two girls by their forearms and started to hurry them through the tunnel toward the fire.

"Babe? Baby! Stop!" Maryanne finally managed to yank her arm away and grabbed his. "We're headed straight for it!"

Before they knew it, a cloud of smoke had reached them, stinging their eyes and invading their throats. Maryanne squeezed her eyes shut and started to cough.

"Rob! Lil!"

She reached out in the direction where Rob had been standing, but there was nothing there. She could hear them both coughing though.

"This way," she heard someone whisper in her ear.

"What?" she yelled. She tried to open her eyes, but it was useless. Every time she tried they were burned so badly by the smoke she had to squeeze them shut again immediately.

"Rob?"

"Hurry." She heard it again.

It definitely wasn't Rob, she could tell this time.

"I'm not leaving without them!" she yelled.

"What are you saying?" Lily yelled between coughs.

"Hold onto my shirt," she heard the man's voice again. "This time, don't let go."

She felt whomever it was place her hand on the edge of his shirt. It was warm, and soft, like flannel.

Oh, my God.

"Find me! Rob! Lil! Follow my voice! Find me and grab hold of me! You can't be far!"

She continued to fumble around for them, yelling at the same time. Finally, she made contact with someone's wrist. A few seconds later, she felt a hand latch on to her ankle.

"Let's go," the voice whispered in her ear, and they started to crawl, slowly, but surely. Maryanne still couldn't open her eyes, so all she could do was trust that whomever she was holding onto was leading them to safety, and make sure that both Rob and Lily were still holding onto her.

"Where are we going?" Rob yelled. They could all hear the flames getting closer. At one point, it seemed like they were crawling toward them, as they were getting increasingly more disoriented.

"I don't know! Just don't let go!"

Eventually, the noise of the flames raging started to fade, as did the heat, and finally, they were able to open their eyes.

She grabbed Rob's face when she saw it and kissed it all over.

Lily propped herself up against the wall of the tunnel. "What just happened?" she asked, trying to catch her breath.

Maryanne looked over at her. "I was following…"

her voice trailed off as she looked down at her hand and realized she wasn't holding on to anything anymore. She had no idea when it was exactly she'd let go.

"He saved us," she said, looking up at Lily. "The man in flannel, Cecily's father, Raymond."

Rob and Lily looked at each other. Rob frowned, and then hobbled to his feet. "We have to get out of here."

They'd somehow been led into an offshoot of the tunnel that'd been set on fire. They could see the flames running through it though behind them and knew it was only a matter of time before they started to chase them again.

They took off down the hallway. This arm of the tunnel was made of concrete and even through their panic they relished in the cool air wafting off the walls.

"This is it, I think. Yes! This is it!" Lily yelled. "This is where I was." She recognized the tunnel they'd been led to and sure enough, they soon came upon the same staircase that had led her up to the shack the night she saw Kayla in there with the group.

"There it is! Let's go, that will lead us out of here!" Lily said.

They reached the ladder and were almost laughing with relief as they climbed it. They popped through the latched covering at the top and through the doors that led into the shack.

Rob was the last to come through. Maryanne was the first, and just as she got her bearings, she heard something whiz through the air and heard Rob make an awful, guttural sound. She turned around in time to see him hit the floor.

She gasped, as his assailant stepped out of the shadowy corner he'd been hiding in. She studied his face as she racked her brain to try to remember who he was.

She finally recognized him as Norman, Rob's boss.

"What are you doing here?" she asked, baffled.

"I told you, you weren't all hired by accident," said Joseph, who was standing behind them, another gun trained on her and Lily.

They jumped at his voice and turned to face him.

"How did you three get out of there?" he growled.

Maryanne could see he was sweating and breathing low and short, grinding his teeth.

"Never mind that," Norman interrupted. "You better tell us where the fuck your cousin is."

"What?"

"You heard me!" he shrieked, forcing them both to jump once again.

"Where is she?"

"She's in China! Where you have her trapped!" she yelled, pointing at Joseph, who shook his head.

"We've been trying to get in touch with her for several days and have heard nothing, so we sent an associate over there to put an end to the job."

Maryanne's heart sank.

"But when he got there, she was nowhere to be found."

Just like that, a spark of excitement she hadn't felt in a long time was reignited in her. Maybe she's found a way to get out undetected!

Joseph must have seen the look of happiness wash over her face because he jumped on the opportunity to squash it immediately.

"Don't get your hopes up. We will find her, and when we do it'll be lights out for her. You can thank her big mouth for that, but before that, we'll have a little fun getting out of her exactly whom and what she told about her assignment," he said with a disgusting smile.

"Do you realize how much money that little cunt cost me?" Norman seethed, stepping closer to Maryanne with the shovel still poised over his shoulder.

"What are you talking about?"

"Norman was paying a type of money to get that Green Light! story done that you couldn't even dream of," Joseph said.

"What?" Lily yelled.

"Is that why Rob found a check made out to you from him?" Maryanne asked Joseph, wanting to know once and for all what that money had been for. She tried to kneel next to Rob, but Norman came at her with the shovel, causing her to stumble back.

"Let's go, you two," Joseph said, keeping the gun trained on them as he opened the door to the dingy, dank little shack.

Lily and Maryanne looked at each other, and then Maryanne looked down at Rob. Norman lunged at them with the shovel forcing them both out the door quickly.

"This way," Joseph said, motioning to the right with the gun. The girls walked carefully in that direction, led by Joseph, followed by Norman.

Up ahead, Maryanne could see a large mound of dirt illuminated by the moonlight peeking through the trees.

"What is that?"

When no one answered, she started to back up, but it was Lily who pushed her forward this time. "Just keep going," she said under her breath. Maryanne looked over at her in shock. They couldn't just give up!

They moved closer and closer to the mound until they were finally upon it and saw it was a huge ditch. The two girls looked over the side and both realized there was something at the bottom of it.

"What is that?" Maryanne shrieked.

Norman and Joseph smiled at each other, and then Norman took a flashlight out from his back pocket and shined it down toward the bottom of the ditch.

Maryanne started screaming, wrapped her arms around her waist, and hunched over in a ball. Right before she shut her eyes, she saw the mutilated body of Randall, Rob's co-worker who'd gone missing.

"That's what is going to happen to your stupid fucking cousin!" Norman yelled.

Joseph yanked Lily's hair, pulling her head to his mouth. "This is what happens to people who cause trouble for us," he spit into her ear, and then pushed her into the ditch.

"No!" Maryanne screamed as Lily fell.

Lily hit the dirt feet first with a thud. Maryanne reached in to grab her hand.

"Shoot them!" Norman screamed. "Shoot th—" he wasn't able to finish the word.

Maryanne watched as Norman fell into the ditch as well, his head hitting Randall's stomach. It was Lily who started screaming this time. Confused and shocked, Maryanne looked up and saw Rob swinging to hit Joseph as well with the shovel Norman had left behind after they'd exited the shack.

Joseph took a shot at him. Thankfully it missed Rob, who did make contact, but was only able to stun Joseph.

Rob dropped the shovel and reached in to help lift Lily out. She grabbed onto each of their hands and the two were able to lift her out.

"Let's go!" Rob said, and the three of them took off into the woods.

Joseph's gunshots whizzed by them.

The three broke through the tree line and into the cemetery, unscathed.

In the distance, amongst the sea of headstones, the cross that sat above Cecily's pulsed a red glow through the darkness.

Chapter 51

Rob and Maryanne were having breakfast on the deck of their tiny townhouse overlooking the ocean. It was a lazy Saturday morning, with no plans for the rest of the day. No errands. No one to see. No one to run from. Nothing to fear. The two of them couldn't be happier. Maryanne never saw a spider again after they moved to North Carolina that spring. Once she, Lily, and Rob had escaped from the woods that night this past winter, they were a mess, badly beaten and covered in blood. They weren't sure where to go first. The Sleepy Hollow police station was obviously out of the question.

They decided the emergency room was a must. Lily and Rob were both treated for concussions and Maryanne was treated for some scrapes and cuts. All of them were treated for smoke inhalation.

They knew they needed to tell their story to someone. Thankfully, Geffin’s PI friend actually came through this time after hearing what happened and connected them with the FBI.

He put them in touch with two agents who told them they'd been watching Joseph and his clan for quite some time. They'd had great difficulty proving anything over the years, as they always had very little cooperation from the police, who would clean up after Joseph and his henchmen all too well, and of course those he and his group had put the fear of God into. The agents had confirmed that as Joseph said, his network was much greater than just the small town of Sleepy Hollow. It reached across state lines and possibly even oceans. Rob had, of course, handed over the letter outlining where some of Norman's income and outgoing funds were and their alias', but they were never able to prove any of it as a lot of money and transfers were dealt with in underground banks, run by people who could make anything and everything disappear without a trace at a second's notice if need be. They also brought them back to where they'd found Randall's body, but it was of course, never found, and neither was any trace of the ground ever having been dug up in that area.

While the FBI couldn't offer them answers or justice, they were able to offer them protection and help in tracking down Casey, but they ended up not needing it.

Just a few days after their near death experience, Casey showed up on Maryanne's doorstep. She was a little worse for the wear, but in one piece, which was all that mattered. The two embraced and sobbed as if finding each other again for the first time in years.

Joseph had somehow built up an amazingly genuine, honest group of ad sales representatives for Prerogative all over the world, who were keen to his underhanded ways in life and in business. Casey had managed to get herself to India under the guise of further research and interviews for her story, where she met up with Arjuna Bhathagar. She told Arj her story, and thankfully, he believed her and agreed to help. He knew how to avoid Joseph's watchmen, and more importantly, who they most likely were.

He was able to get her to Turkey, to Defne Aydintasbas, who then transferred her to Dirk Bolachec in Brussels, Belgium, who finally got her safely on a plane home.

Casey stared at her cousin in shock as Maryanne told her of that horrific night when Joseph almost ended their lives as well.

"It was the man in flannel, Cecily's father, who saved you," she said.

Maryanne shook her head "yes" as tears fell down her cheeks.

"I never saw him. The smoke was too much for us to open our eyes at all, but it was him, I know it was.

It was true that Raymond, the man in flannel, had died trying to save his daughter Cecily, both of whom had been asleep when the drug addict Joseph had hired to set fire to the I building did his job.

It probably was no coincidence that Joseph chose the I building, Raymond's home, to set on fire, as he and Jim, Beth's husband, had been on to Joseph and his crew for quite some time; particularly Jim, who'd made things difficult for him since back when he was a cop. Once he retired and befriended Raymond, he continued to do so, bringing Raymond into his campaign to bring Joseph down. He'd had a number of confrontations with both of them, and although painfully quiet, there was something about Raymond that shook Joseph to his core. He seemed to have a spirit that could never truly die. He was a simple man who loved his family at all costs, something Joseph didn't understand, and therefore, feared.

It turned out that the large sum of money Joseph had borrowed from Andy's father, as Ramsey had reported, was indeed to purchase the Darren Hayes and build the tunnels that led from there to the cemetery, the church, and the woods. Andy knew Raymond and Jim back in the day. He'd known Cecily, too.

Their deaths were the last straw for him, and Joseph

didn't need to do anything to get rid of him, as he made it easy when he and his wife moved to Las Vegas.

Ramsey's status and place in town was mainly solidified thanks to his lineage. Although the powers that be would always be waiting in the wings to give him a "slap on the wrist" when necessary, but he really sealed his case shut by successfully parlaying Joseph's greatest asset, and greatest weakness, against him, his son David.

David had been instrumental in helping guide Casey back home. Ramsey worked with Arj, Defne, and Dirk to get her from one country to the next, using Casey as a bargaining tool. David had always been head over heels for Casey, and Ramsey promised he'd get them together if he helped distract Joseph when needed.

Joseph eventually caught on to what was happening, which prompted him to kidnap Rob.

As she'd promised, it was Sandra who'd trapped him. Pretending to be wounded and hurt in a tiny side street off of Beckett, the road Rob walked on from the train every day, she called out to him. Once he reached her, Grettco and the other cops nabbed him, threw him in a waiting police car, and got him to the Old Dutch Church at the cemetery.

Sandra went with them and he saw them force something down her throat, undoubtedly the source of her disorientation to start. Who knows what it could have been, but all everyone did know is the woman had met the same fate that many involved with Joseph and Norman's cult had met, an ugly death.

Raymond had been Sandra's first husband, and she'd been with Patrick, her then lover, the night of the fire; the fire that killed the one thing she loved the most in this world, her little girl. Joseph had successfully used that guilt and shame to bind her to him, and eventually, was able to brainwash her into thinking that Cecily was still alive. That was just the opposite though, as both she and her father were trying to guide them all to safety from beyond.

As for the rings they wore that plagued Rob's dreams, they were symbols of the cult's absolute loyalty to each other and the god they served. The fact that Rob's dreams proved to be a premonition of Patrick and Kayla's deaths shook everyone left behind to their core. Because they couldn't successfully bring their recruits, M.J. for Kayla and Rob for Patrick, in, they were brainwashed into believing they didn't deserve to live.

Maryanne and Rob exchanged similar rings, but ones with a much different meaning to them at their beachside wedding that took place just a few feet away from where they sat right now. In the vows they wrote themselves, they promised never to keep anything from each other ever again. How things might have been different if they'd just been open with each other from the start of this entire mess.

"Here you go," Rob said, as he handed Maryanne the half and half for her coffee.

"Thank you," she said, lifting her face up to his for a kiss. Rob sat down, but she didn't lower her head. She let the warm sun shine down onto her face. She looked out at the ocean and then over at her now husband and smiled.

Life was good and she had a new found appreciation for it that she wouldn't trade for anything. Except to have Kayla back.

M.J. and the rest of the crew, including Lily, had remained in Sleepy Hollow at the Darren Hayes. Joseph was still there as well, and still running Prerogative. Lily was currently working on a new publication, funded by none other than Ralph Ramsey.

What Lily needed to be afraid of at this point, was the day Joseph finds out about the new publication, if he didn't already know. They were getting ready to debut it in just a few months.

Maryanne suddenly realized Lily's final letter from the editor had run in the most recent issue of Prerogative. She went inside to grab it then came back out onto the deck. She settled back in her seat and started reading:

There's a storm brewing and it's going to be an ugly one.

As the editor of Prerogative, I need to keep my finger on the pulse of our society, that means socially, mentally, financially, and beyond. In pursuit of that, I always have the privilege of meeting people from all walks of life. From those who own four homes, to those who are coming to realize they'll probably never be able to even afford a home of their own.

So I can tell you from experience that the numbers are growing at astoundingly disproportionate rates on one side, and they are angry.

Angry that the American dream they were promised has been ripped out from under them as they slept. As they dotted their Is and crossed their Ts, because that's what they were told would take them there. Told that's what would award them with everything their parents had achieved: a house, a good job with benefits, and the ability to raise a family.

The youth of America's future is a bleak one, where their college educations are worthless, attached to loans, and they can't find any jobs (let alone one their degree might apply to) to start trying to pay them off.

They watch the news and see Wall Street taking what was promised to them, with yearly bonuses totaling more than what many of them could even hope to make in a four-year period. Their anger grows, being fed by it like a caged beast just dying, salivating to get loose. Once they do, once they've had it up to here, they're going to unleash a reign of terror on those that have taken what is theirs. This war will not be one that plays out on a battlefield, or a senate floor, or even a boardroom. It will be waged in the streets, so it will inevitably be a dirty one.

And they will shout:

You cannot steal from us.

You cannot quiet us.

You cannot stop us.

And we will take back what is rightfully ours as citizens of this country.

Beware. We will fight and we will fight dirty.

—Lily Deckmeyer

Rob laughed as he watched her eyes get wider and wider by the second, and eventually, her jaw drop.

"What?" he asked.

"Here, read that."

Rob took the issue, opened to the letter page, and read it.

"Whoa. She basically just gave him the finger with that."

"I know," she said, feeling uneasy and nervous now for Lily.

He reached over and took her hand.

"They're working on it, babe. There's no way he

covered all his tracks and erased every last detail. They'll find something concrete, and soon. I'm sure of it."

He leaned back in his chair and lifted his own face up toward the sun.

"Every criminal has a secret desire to get caught, especially one as sick as he is, and then he'll rot in jail forever, or Hell."

Maryanne had her laptop next to her and noticed a story had popped up under her Yahoo local news ticker, which she still had set to Sleepy Hollow and the surrounding areas, with a dateline of Sleepy Hollow, NY.

She also noticed the word "blaze."

She clicked on it, and a new window led her to the Tarrytown Patch.

She gasped as she started to read.

"What now?" Rob asked. He got up to look over her shoulder and read it, too.

"Damn sun," he mumbled, putting his hand over the top of the screen to try to shield it.

The story went on to reveal that two nights ago both Joseph and Norman's Westchester homes had inexplicably burned to the ground. While Norman wasn't home at the time, Joseph was, but wasn't hurt as he and his wife made it out in plenty of time.

"Firefighters were baffled, because despite all their efforts, flames continued to rage until both homes were cindered into literally nothing more than piles of dust. They were, however, able to keep the fire contained to just those two sites."

"It was him," Maryanne said quietly.

Rob squeezed her shoulder and kissed her cheek.

"Come on. Let's go inside and get ready to go to the

beach."

She nodded and got up, following him into their home. Rob slid the deck door shut behind them.

Chapter 52

That night Maryanne had the last dream that would ever take her back to her old life in Sleepy Hollow.

In front of her was a beautiful home, on fire, in the middle of a heavily wooded area. In front of it, with his back to her, stood the man in flannel.

He watched it burn until there was nothing left.

About the Author

After a strange set of dreams and many walks through the village cemetery, AnnMarie developed the plot for her upcoming novel The Hollow, a paranormal thriller set in the legendary Sleepy Hollow, New York. She's traveled the world over the past 10 years as a reporter and editor and also drew from those experiences to craft this haunting story.

www.downwarden.com/blackbedsheet

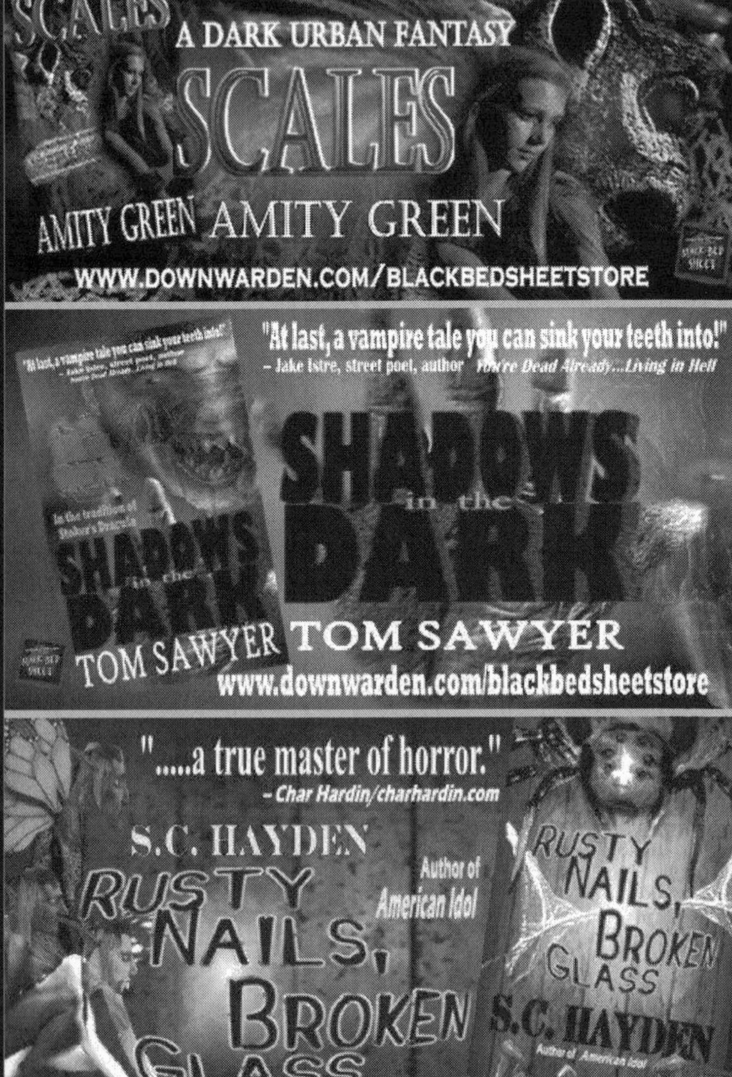

www.downwarden.com/blackbedsheet

"A terrifying psychological thriller."
- Mark Edward Hall,
author of The Holocaust Opera
BLOOD RELATED
WILLIAM COOK
978-0-9858820-4-5
www.downwarden.com/blackbedsheet
FRED WIEHE
"Dangerously entertaining!"
--Jonathan Maberry,
NY Times bestselling author,
DEAD OF NIGHT
ALERIC: MONSTER HUNTER
978-0-9886590-7-0
www.downwarden.com/blackbedsheetstore
"A bullet train tale..of killer creativity
and a thrill worth reading ten times more!"
--S.D. Hintz
Blood Orchard
JASON GEHLERT
-with- Joe Rutigliano
JEREMIAH BLACK
978-0-9858829-9-0
www.downwarden.com/blackbedsheet

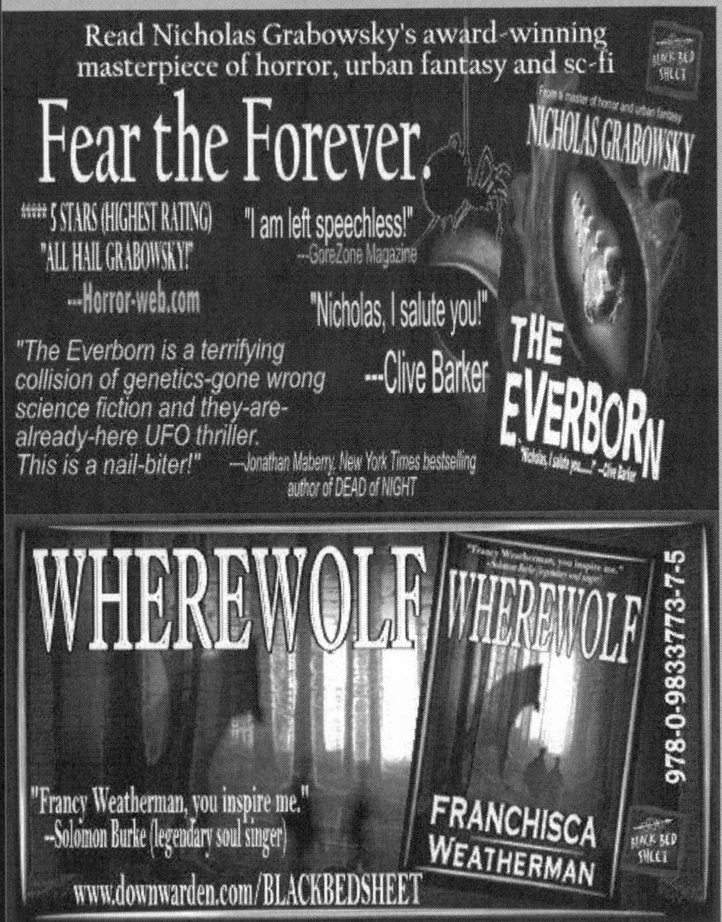

Wherewolf by Franchisca Weatherman.

978-0-9833773-7-5

When a pack of werewolves hits a small southern town, the local Sheriff realizes this is one case he can not solve alone. He calls in the F.B.I. to help him take down the killers that are taking the lives of the local teens. When the wolves abandon the town for the streets of New Orleans during Mardi-Gras celebrations, the hunters become the hunted in an all-out war where no one may survive....

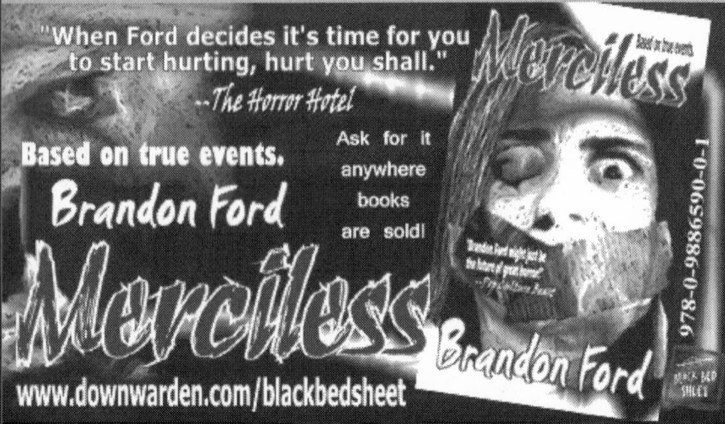
"When Ford decides it's time for you to start hurting, hurt you shall."
--The Horror Hotel
Based on true events.
Brandon Ford
Ask for it anywhere books are sold!
Merciless
www.downwarden.com/blackbedsheet
Merciless
Based on true events.
978-0-9886590-0-1
Brandon Ford

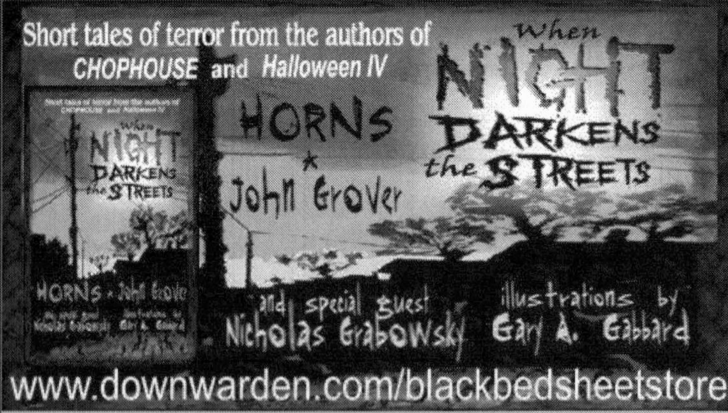
Short tales of terror from the authors of
CHOPHOUSE and Halloween IV
When NIGHT DARKENS the STREETS
HORNS
John Grover
and special guest
Nicholas Grabowsky
illustrations by
Gary A. Gabbard
www.downwarden.com/blackbedsheetstore

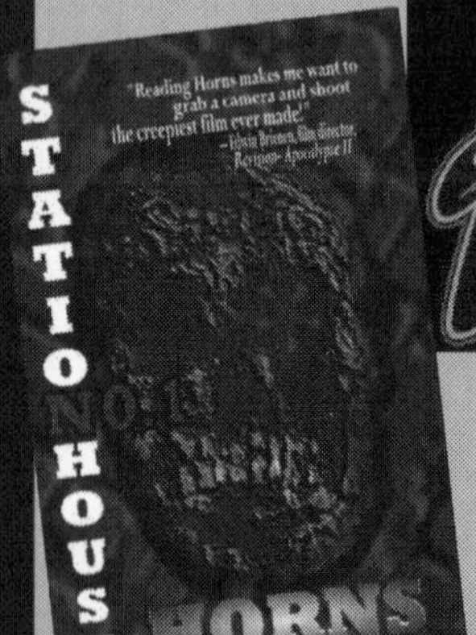
STATION HOUSE
"Reading Horns makes me want to grab a camera and shoot the creepiest film ever made!"
HORNS
author of Chophouse

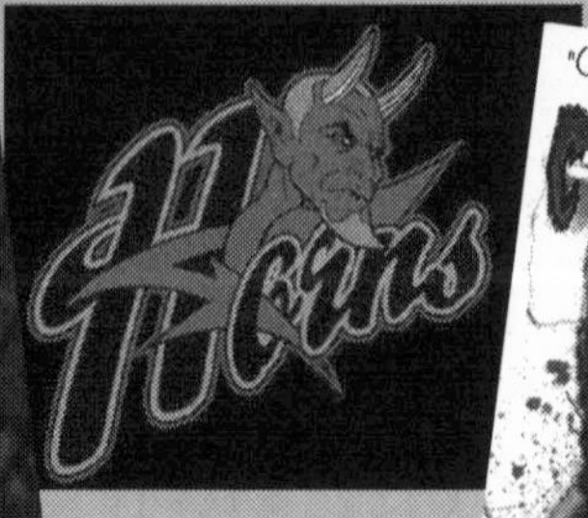
Horns

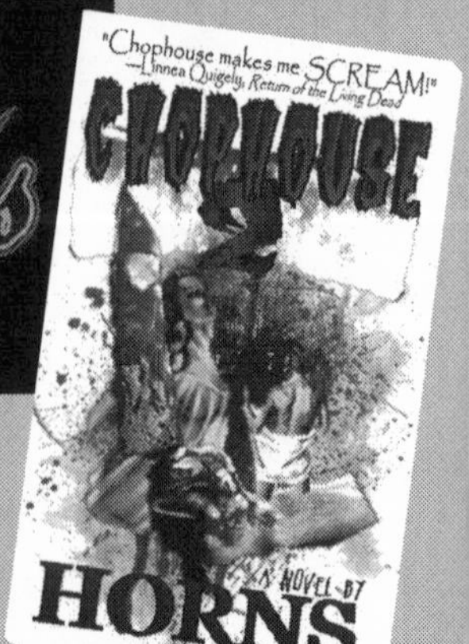
"Chophouse makes me SCREAM!"
—Linnea Quigely, Return of the Living Dead
CHOPHOUSE
A NOVEL BY
HORNS

www.downwarden.com/blackbedsheet

HACKER'S
SOURCE

www.downwarden.com/blackbedsheet

www.downwarden.com/blackbedsheet

Satan's Holiday Welcome to Your Nightmare

THRILLING ANTHOLOGIES

Courtesy Yvonne Mason & dressingyourbook.com

DISLOCATED THOUGHTS

"Reyna Young
is a
staple in the horror community!"
-- geektyrant.com

dark poetry by

REYNA YOUNG

celebrated horror host Miss Misery

www.downwarden.com/blackbedsheet

We employ and recommend:

Foreign Translations

Cinta García de la Rosa

(Spanish Translation)

Writer, Editor, Proofreader, Translator

cintagarciadelarosa@gmail.com

http://www.cintagarciadelarosa.com

http://cintascorner.com

Bianca Johnson

(Italian Translation)

Writer, Editor, Proofreader, Translator

http://facebook.com/bianca.cicciarelli

EDITOR STAFF

Felicia Aman

http://www.abttoday.com

http://facebook.com/felicia.aman

Kelly J. Koch

http://dressingyourbook.com

Tyson Mauermann

http://speculativebookreview.blogspot.com

Kareema S. Griest

http://facebook.com/kareema.griest

Mary Genevieve Fortier

https://www.facebook.com/MaryGenevieveFortierWriter

http://www.stayingscared.com/Nighty%20Nightmare.html

Shawna Platt

www.angelshadowauthor.webs.com/

Adrienne Dellwo

http://facebook.com/adriennedellwo

http://chronicfatigue.about.com/

William Cook

http://lnkd.in/bnC-yMd

http://www.amazon.com/Blood-Related

and HORNS

32017847R00273

Made in the USA
Charleston, SC
05 August 2014